THETA OMNIBUS

THETA AND THETA BEGINNINGS MINISERIES

LIZZY FORD

CAPTURED PRESS

ONE

ALESSANDRA

TWO MONTHS later

IF I WERE STILL ENOUGH, and concentrated hard, I could feel the cool forest breeze tickle the back of my neck and breathe in the scent of trees and wet earth after a summer storm. Patches of sunlight warmed my skin, while the vibrant green canopy of leaves overhead prevented the full heat of the sun from reaching me. Nature possessed a rhythm, a gentle pulse of energy, I first experienced when I left the boundaries of my forest home. The gentle ebb and flow of the world rocked through me, teasing my own internal rhythm, until we were synced and swaying together in a peaceful, timeless dance.

The magic of the natural world reached me here, in the heart of Washington DC. It surpassed the towering walls and thick barricades established by the military, penetrated kilometers of cement and manmade structures, and traveled unnoticed by and through millions of people to join me underground in a dance only the two of us could share.

This peace, this dance ... it was wrong. I didn't deserve its attempt to comfort me, not after I'd twisted the gentle thrum inside me into a weapon of incredible power that had claimed the innocent lives of thousands.

You're becoming so much stronger. A female voice said into my mind.

My eyes opened. Seated cross-legged in the dark cavern belonging to the Oracle of Delphi, I was swaying from side to side with the rhythm of the world. The scent of sulfur and other exotic spices transformed my mind into an open state less burdened by the life I lived outside this cavern.

"That's not a good thing," I whispered in response, studying Cecelia, the current Oracle of Delphi.

My passing is inevitable. You will need your strength to harness absolute power, but you must subdue the full emergence of your power a little longer, until you can handle it. The mark on your arm is a warning to you and me.

I touched the birthmark self-consciously. It resembled a double omega, and those around me believed it represented my ability to annihilate the world. "Nothing like absolute power when I can't control my own mind," I said sarcastically. "I'm trying *not* to become stronger until Cleon is out of my head."

You are so much stronger than I was when I experienced my first vision. If you haven't glimpsed the future yet, then we are on the right path to keep your power in check. We cannot unleash the waters behind the dam all at once, or you will finish off what the gods started five years ago. Be patient and cautious.

"You sound like Herakles," I replied. "If I don't find a way to get rid of the parasite in my head, my destiny won't matter. Cleon is standing between where I am and where I should be."

You assume he's not supposed to be there.

"Why would he ... ah. Because life sucks and is hard."

Something like that. He is in your life for a reason. Sometimes we don't know why some events occur until long after they happen. Perhaps his presence forces you to restrain power that might otherwise be too much to control. Cecelia's amusement was transmitted telepathically and through the brightening of the lights around her enclosure.

"Maybe," I said, not liking the idea. "Have you figured out how I get him out of my life, or what happens if I don't detach him before my power fully manifests?" For now, we were protected from the inevitable, because I didn't complete the third trial required for an Oracle to assume her full power. The Silent Queen had challenged me to murder the Oracle. I wasn't about to murder the person who had the key to helping me not accidentally end the world!

If only I had my full power again. I might be able to pinpoint the correct sequence. The Oracle grew serious again. *If I die soon, you will have the power you need, without the control to use it. If the parasite dies first, part of you may be lost as well, and you will not have the power you need to survive.*

"Then you can't die until we know the right sequence," I told her firmly. If a woman who saw the future didn't know what to do, how was I supposed to figure it out?

I swallowed hard and touched the scar at the back of my head. Whatever the Supreme Magistrate did to my brain connected us on a level that could destroy us both if severed carelessly. Without me, humanity would never be safe. No one else could send the gods back to their domain – permanently.

Over the past few weeks, the Oracle had warned me repeatedly against outright killing Cleon and helped me learn to control my power so it didn't grow until we had a feasible option for expelling him from my mind.

This was not the first time I had heard the truth, but it was never easier to acknowledge how bad my situation really was. Did Cleon understand what he was doing, when he connected our minds? How did I fight someone in my head?

"The good news is he can't kill me either," I said with some vindication.

There is no good news for those born into our position.

It didn't take a dismembered woman trapped in a bubble to remind me of the curse it was to be born with the power of a goddess.

"There has to be a way," I said, unwilling to admit defeat. "I'm not giving up yet. We will find the best sequence of events, or maybe, I'll wake up with my full power before he knows it's there and snap this connection. I'm not going down without doing what I was born to! I will crush the gods for what they did to us."

I applaud your eagerness, but tread carefully. You have three thousand, two hundred and ninety four reasons not to use your power. The more you use it, the greater it grows, and the more danger you pose to humanity.

Her harsh reminder snuffed the fire behind my anger immediately. I slumped. I didn't intend to add to my body count. I had been diligently following her lessons on how to restrain my power, in case Cleon tried to force me to use it again. If I played dumb, and acted as if my power wasn't cooperating, I would hopefully continue to prevent him from hurting others. I didn't want anyone else's death on my conscious.

Although, at this point, I often thought it was too late to save my soul. Was there a limit to how many people someone could kill, before redemption was no longer an option? Had I crossed that line already?

What exactly was redemption? Forgiveness from those I had hurt or from the outside world? Or was it my own acceptance of my actions and self-forgiveness? Or was it dedication to committing more good than bad in the world? And if so, how was that remotely possible, given what I'd already done?

These were the kinds of questions I used to discuss with Herakles, my longtime guardian and protector, the man who murdered my family, kidnapped me, and hid me from men like Cleon for twelve years. He was the very incarnation of a man who strove for redemption.

I forgave him, because he didn't know what he was doing when he hurt my parents. His mind had been controlled and erased by the very man who was using my power to destroy. If I were capable of loving Herakles despite what he did, would everyone else one day decide the good I'd committed in the world weighed heavier on the scales of justice than the bad?

How much good would it take to make up for ending so many lives? Did the possibility of redemption even matter, when I would never forgive myself or the man who forced my hand?

As much as I wanted to find a happy ending in Herakles' life story, I was also reminded of his scars whenever I thought of him. He had purposely burned and slashed his face until it was unrecognizable. He did it out of shame for becoming a monster and a tool of the Supreme Magistrate. I loved him despite his involvement in the deaths of my parents, and he had raised me with gentleness and fairness.

But he was a tortured soul and would probably be one until his death. Was that the fate of everyone who craved redemption?

This topic, and the subject of what good could possibly come from my purpose and my life, left me thoroughly confused. Herakles was gone from my world, and so was his earthy logic. I was left alone to grapple with the knowledge of what I had become and to stumble through the maze the Fates had created for me.

On days such as this, revenge seemed a more fitting use of my power and frustrated anger. I could destroy Cleon, even if that meant I died with him, and left the fate of the world in the hands of Cecelia. Except ... she wasn't strong enough to stop the gods from finishing off humanity.

Alessandra, I don't know if I can outlast Cleon's influence on you, or if I could survive long enough to make a difference, if you did take down Cleon now, Cecelia said, reading my thoughts. Her desperation crossed our telepathic link.

Fear trickled through me. "You have to. You've been protecting DC from the gods and helping me learn about my powers. Without you, no one will survive the gods' wrath."

DC will need a new protector when I'm gone. You can't become this protector with Cleon working against you.

"That settles it. You can't die."

There might be a way to help me. Would you consider it, if so?

"Anything," I breathed.

It's a transfer of power, similar to a blood transfusion, but performed telepathically. You'll need to touch me, though, so we can connect. I would siphon off enough of your power to help me survive long enough for us to understand what needs to happen.

I was on my feet before she finished and went to the control panel at the side of her bubble. "Okay. How do I lower your glass bubble shield thing?"

It's simple. You -

"You've been ignoring me," interjected a soft, male voice.

I tensed. Even the effects of the Oracle catnip – the scents of the chamber – were unable to soften my anger towards the individual intruding upon my quiet time with Cecelia. "Then why don't you take the hint and leave me alone?" I snapped. My eyes went to the Oracle. "Why do you let him in here?"

"I move through shadows. She has no dominion over me there," Lantos, the Supreme Priest and member of the Sacred Triumvirate, replied with amusement. He was a man of great persistence and power, the gods' representative to humanity, and universally distrusted after he betrayed the two people closest to him. "It's one of the very few benefits of being the son of a Titan."

I hated Cleon – the Supreme Magistrate – for what he forced me to do. But with Lantos, my anger burned brighter, not because of his actions towards me, but because he callously betrayed someone I cared about to the depths of my soul. It hurt worse that I noticed the absence of Mismatch-Adonis every time I saw Lantos.

"I'm in the middle of something," I told him and returned to the screen before me. This wasn't the first time Lantos had interrupted an important discussion with Cecelia, and I suspected it wouldn't be the last, unless I did whatever it was he wanted me to.

"You need an ally like me, Alessandra," said Lantos. "I have powerful friends who have been trying to talk to you."

"By *friends*, you mean enemies you tricked into trusting you. The gods are my enemies, too, Lantos, except I don't try to pretend to be something I'm not!"

"Does it matter where I stand, when you have no one else offering to help you? You can't survive this world alone, Alessandra. You know this."

It sounded too trite, too much like a lecture from someone who thought he was doing me a favor, for me to ignore. Twisting in place, I glared at him. He was smart enough to keep his distance. As the head of SISA, the religious police, Lantos controlled a security force the size of an army. But right now, not one of his men stood between us to protect him, if I decided I was through with him.

"I don't want you as an ally," I replied with calmness I didn't feel. "You've already proven you suck at it."

He was too much of a politician to read. His smile appeared genuine, but how could it be? He drew nearer, green eyes bright in his handsome face. He appeared refreshed and upbeat, as if he never spent one second of his day questioning his decisions, no matter whom he hurt.

I resented him – and was also envious. I could think of nothing else but whether or not I could ever balance my own scales, and here he stood – cheerfully oblivious to the pain he inflicted upon those around him.

My anger was powerful enough for tears to prick my eyes. He wasn't worth crying over. I turned away, preferring the vision of Cecelia in pieces to Lantos.

"I might have a way to convince you to reconsider," Lantos said.

"There's nothing you can say that would make me give you the time of day!" I retorted.

"I received a letter from Adonis. It's for you."

Just like that, my inner world shifted from bubbling rage to soaring hope.

"Do you want to read it?" Lantos asked, as if he didn't know Adonis was tethered to me in a way no human or god could break.

Your name is seared into my soul. I will always return to you. I replayed Adonis' parting words in my mind at least ten times a day, and a dozen more times every night when I awoke from the nightmares of the monster I was becoming. My reaction to Adonis was as wildly uncontrollable as my reaction to Lantos – except on the exact opposite end of the scale.

My task at the screen of the control panel was trumped by the possibility of learning something about my Mismatch after two months of nothing. I approached Lantos, searching his face for some sign he was toying with me.

He held out a letter with another of his smiles.

I reached for it.

He snatched it back.

The hair on the back of my neck rose as my power coalesced in the space around me, reacting to my emotions.

So much stronger, Cecelia said.

"Yeah, she is," Lantos agreed. "But not advancing. I wonder why."

I shrugged off the magic and held out my hand. "Give it to me, Lantos."

"One condition."

I snapped my mouth closed and ground my teeth.

"You hear me out and remain open to what I say."

If I were learning anything in DC, it was how to lie. "Fine."

"Tonight, seven o'clock. Drinks at my place. I'll arrange it with your escort."

Nodding instead of hitting him was as politically correct of an act as I was capable of.

He handed me the letter.

I snatched it and started to turn away when I noticed something about the envelope. "You opened it," I said, glaring at him.

"Of course I did."

"It's dated six weeks ago."

"You wouldn't see me," Lantos said with a shrug. "I wasn't going to lose my leverage by sliding it under your door. I may have something else of interest for you, if you meet me tonight."

"What is it?" I replied suspiciously.

"The file on your parents you've been trying to find since you got to the compound."

"You have it?"

"I do. It's yours, if you meet with me."

"Why now?" I challenged. "You've been bugging me for weeks. Why offer up something you know I want now?"

He was looking at Cecelia. "Let's just say I had a moment of clarity recently."

What an asshole. He would never reveal his true agenda. Taking the letter farther from Lantos, so I had some semblance of privacy, I opened it with eager hands.

If ever there were something about Adonis that irritated me – aside from his penchant for mass murder – it was his brevity. Even when he admitted to having my named carved into his soul, he had not felt the need to expand on what exactly that meant, and I was too afraid of being wrong, or revealing too much of what I felt, to assume or ask.

ALESSANDRA,

I hope this letter finds you well.

I have arrived to the land I once ruled. The beaches are as I remember them, four thousand years ago, and the waters are just as clear. I intend to leave here as quickly as possible, but I must first complete the mission Artemis gave me.

Yours,

Adonis

I WAS MOMENTARILY STUCK between frustration he chose to write at all, when he said nothing of value, and awe he'd signed it *yours*. As in, he was really mine, and he experienced the same feelings towards me as I did him?

Or was it simply the closing he had chosen out of the dozen customary closings available?

At eighteen, lacking all experience with the opposite sex, I had no idea how to interpret the short note, except it made my stomach twist and heart flutter knowing I was holding something Adonis had touched.

"That's it?" I growled at the letter.

"With men, it's more about the action than the words. He values you enough to send you a letter. His lack of poetry or substance is somewhat appalling, but it's also a sign he chose to write despite not knowing what to say," Lantos explained. "He cares for you. But you know that."

Wrong person, right message. It disgusted me that Lantos used my connection with Adonis to manipulate us both. No part of me believed the timing of Adonis' departure was coincidence. Did he just happen to leave on the same day Lantos betrayed him?

No, Lantos would never risk Adonis being around when he yanked the rug out from under my feet and served me up to Cleon on a silver platter.

Re-reading the short note, my anger fizzled. I had never been as confused or as wildly euphoric about anyone or anything as I was about Adonis. I didn't know how deep this connection ran, or what to say or think around him, but I never felt like my world was spinning out of control when the grotesque prince was close. How was it possible to yearn for someone I barely knew, who had probably murdered more people than Cleon and Lantos combined?

What right did I have to judge him, when I had over three thousand lives on my soul? My thoughts about him were as complicated as his personality.

Come home, Adonis, I willed him without any hope he could hear me, thanks also to Lantos, who had blocked the bond I shared with the grotesque prince.

I tucked the letter into my pocket and gazed at Cecelia for a moment, deep in thought.

Lantos was right. I needed allies, and the two men I trusted most in the world were lost to me at the moment. I had wandered onto a reality board game and was competing against people who had not only mastered the rules, but also spent years positioning their pieces. And I was supposed to ... what? Win, when I didn't understand what game I was playing? The kind of person who could help me was the kind of person I innately knew better than to trust, because he had been in this game for far too long.

I did need help. During moments like this, someone like Lantos made sense, and that spooked me even more. Life would be easier if people with unsavory intentions wore black masks instead of parading around disguised as normal people.

Cleon's grip on me was growing tighter, and I was no closer to harnessing my magic. As much as I adored Cecelia, she preached restraint rather than understanding. I didn't think I needed to fear my power to control it. Maybe I did need to meet with Lantos in private and discuss a few things, as much as I didn't want to.

And ... if he had another letter from Adonis ... was I justifying sitting down with one of my enemies, because I hoped Adonis said more in his second letter than his first?

Pain shot through my temple, and I gasped.

Come. Now. Cleon's voice in my head was louder than Cecelia's. He prefaced anything he had to say with a flash of pain, applied through the mind control device he'd had fused to my brain. It linked us mentally, a combination of technology and the magic of the god, Dolos, who blessed the chip in my brain.

"I have to go," I said reluctantly. "I'm keeping the letter."

Lantos didn't protest.

I went to the elevator on the other side of the chamber and rode it to the surface. Dread filled me as it did each time I dealt with Cleon.

I couldn't predict what he wanted until I showed up and heard the latest installment of his crazy plan to use my magic to keep the political elite of the world in line. The soothing scents of the chamber beneath ground dissipated by the time the elevator door opened to reveal the armed escort Cleon had assigned me at all times.

Joining them, I was led out of the tiny building guarding the underground chamber and into a warm, balmy day. It had rained last night, and the puddles in the mall and sidewalk reflected the blue sky.

Whenever Cleon summoned me, I was only ever taken to one place. Familiar with the path, I allowed my focus to shift to the ribbons hovering above everything and everyone around me. My power as an Oracle – once I was able to access it fully – was the ability to manipulate ... well, everything. Matter, time, the fabric of the universe. It was too much for me to understand, too beyond my imagination and everything I'd ever learned about myself and my life.

Until the current Oracle was dead, I could only access a fraction of the magic belonging to the gods. But I, too, felt the swell of power growing. It had started as a trickle I could only feel when I was absolutely still and quiet. Now, it flowed through me and around me, connecting me with the natural magic of my world.

To add to my impossible situation, whatever I did with my power, Cleon felt. I was in a lose-lose situation. I needed my power to get rid of the man whose consciousness was tethered to mine, but he felt when I tried to manipulate our connection and either sent his lackey to tranquilize me or pushed the pain button until I passed out.

Aside from Cecelia, who was too weak to help, I had no real allies. At least, none who were powerful enough to help me leave this place, though I had begun to believe it was going to take a god or goddess to fix what had been done to me.

Or maybe Adonis. The grotesque prince had a mind for strategy and manipulation I never would, and he was bound to me, too. Combined, we would either become the world's most effective mass murdering team, or we would barely survive Cleon. I didn't know which would emerge from our partnership, but I wanted the chance to witness it.

I was led into the House, the building reserved for the Supreme Magistrate. My escort didn't turn down the hall I expected them to, and I pulled myself from my thoughts warily. We went to the second floor lined with private offices rather than the public spaces on the first floor.

Two guards stood outside one closed door. My escorts stopped and stood aside for me to approach. I didn't bother knocking. I'd been summoned, and I did my best to ignore any sense of social protocol I thought might please Cleon. It was one of my limited methods of rebelling against his absolute control over my life.

The politician sat at a large desk of dark woods in front of a window. The drapes and carpets were heavy and darkly hued while the walls of the office glowed a pale yellow.

"You rang?" I asked, striding into the room.

"I would appreciate it if you knocked," he replied without looking up from the papers on his desk.

"I know."

He glanced up at me then back. Lowering the papers, he leaned into the plush leather back of his chair. "There's no need to be unpleasant, Alessandra," Cleon lectured me. "Why not make the best of your situation?"

"My situation. You mean being enslaved by someone who melded my mind to his against my will?"

Cleon released a controlled sigh. "And behaving like a child makes it better somehow?"

I had been warned by many people not to push him too far, but none of them were dropped to their knees in pain a few times a day by the man before me. If I were reckless, it was because I was afraid of someone who knew no limitations on how far he would go, and because I didn't know how else to react when my life and my mind were no longer exclusively mine.

"We're getting stronger," he said at my silence. "We'll soon be at full strength, I believe."

"Nowhere close, according to Cecilia," I replied. I hated how he used *we* when he was a leech piggybacking off my power. "She says I have a long ways to go."

"Maybe you should try harder."

Did he know I purposely didn't push myself? It was hard to guess what knowledge Cleon possessed and what he hid. "What's the rush?" I replied. "You already have control of the protected zone and the armies."

"Neither of those things seem capable of quelling the insurgency growing beneath our noses," he replied. "The sooner I can stop fighting them, the sooner I can execute my plan."

I had never asked what exactly his plan entailed after learning he was interested in world domination. Cleon was driven by power and control, to a point he didn't seem to care if he murdered everyone in the process of ascending to the unchallenged position of emperor of the worlds.

Fortunately, for the time being, the insurgency was safe. As long as the Silent Queen and Theodocia stayed a step ahead of Cleon – and consequently safe from my ability to destroy – I wouldn't worry about Theodocia being dragged into one of the chambers downstairs and subjected to whatever torture Cleon ordered.

"The insurgency is my problem," Cleon continued. "I summoned you here for another reason. Tonight, we're meeting with the Ambassador to Greece."

"I'll wear my best dress," I snapped.

"I've already instructed your servants what you'll wear."

"Great. Is that it?"

"I intend for there to be a demonstration tonight. Something different."

I waited, uncertain what exactly that meant. Normally, he had me destroy something or bring inanimate objects to life and then destroy them as a means of showing his important guests that he controlled me, and I had the powers of a goddess.

He was gazing at something on his desk. Assuming he was done with me, I started to turn, then froze. A sensation like a subtle nudge shifted the pulsing magic inside me enough for me to notice.

The stapler on his desk hopped. My eyes went to it, and I frowned. The one ribbon that was distinctly mine – a green one – had joined the other two ribbons possessed by inanimate objects. My magic brought it to life, but *I* hadn't ordered it alive.

"I'm growing stronger alongside you," Cleon said, pleased.

"You did that?" I asked, startled.

"I did. And I can do this, too." He held out his hand and made a fist. Another tug of my power, and the stapler crumpled in on itself, crushed.

How is this possible? My heart began to beat faster. Power in my hands was relatively safe, since I feared using it and hurting someone. Unlimited power in Cleon's hands?

"I'll be able to wield enough of your power soon to repair the protected zone and extend its reach. You'd be surprised what world leaders and the wealthy will pay for the privilege of owning a private protected zone," Cleon said and lowered his hand.

"Don't you have enough money?"

"Money is a side benefit. I want to make the world a safer place, and plan to use your power to do so."

Cleon's vision was never what he claimed it was. He wanted to rule, and he wanted absolute power. He hid these motivations behind pretty words I no longer believed.

"Now you may go."

I stayed where I was, staring at the stapler, seeking some visible sign he had manipulated it before I arrived. The green ribbon remained, and I automatically reached out for it, not wanting the stapler to be in pain, since it was technically alive the moment my magic touched it.

Absorbing the green ribbon, I turned away.

My concern deepened at the newfound question circling my thoughts. How could he access *my* magic? To my knowledge, not even Adonis had been able to do this.

Cecelia might know how this was possible and the extent of Cleon's ability. Closing the door to Cleon's office behind me, I began walking, when one of my escorts spoke.

"Time for your two o'clock."

"Not today," I replied.

"The Supreme Magistrate's orders."

I stiffened and bit back my retort, instead deciding I'd rather attend my afternoon session with Niko than be tranquilized and locked in my bedroom until it was time for the event this evening.

Armed escorts led me from the House and into the bright sunlight. I released a breath, my mind racing with wild speculations about what Cleon intended to do this evening during his demonstration. Crushing office supplies in front of the elite seemed beneath him, but I didn't understand the depths of his capabilities anymore than I did mine.

Maybe that's the problem, I thought. Maybe by denying my power, I was setting myself back in the hope I could prevent what was coming, while Cleon was spending hours a day devoted to trying to use my power. But didn't growing my abilities mean he, too, potentially had access to more weapons to use against innocent people?

Pensive, I barely noticed the long walk across the compound at the heart of DC until we reached the gym where Niko and I trained daily.

My escorts left me at the door to the gym, and I walked in alone. The sight of the muscular, tattooed mercenary-turned-army commander left me in a less pleasant mood. He stood in the center of a boxing ring where we sparred daily. Since Cleon dictated my daily exercise, I naturally resisted. But the truth was more complicated. I liked physical activity. I needed the release after my angst-filled days, even if I were forced to deal with Niko, who selectively didn't pull his punches, instead of my sweet Herakles.

Not that I would ever give Cleon the credit for forcing me to do something I enjoyed.

"Drop the attitude," Niko snapped. "You know I make it worse for you when you walk in here with one."

He did. Always. If there was one thing about Niko I could always depend upon, it was his uncanny ability to read people – especially me. I hadn't even looked at him yet, and he knew I was pissy.

"I'm not having a good day," I told him.

"I don't care."

I rolled my eyes and sighed. After my brief interactions with Lantos and Cleon, I didn't feel up to having my ass kicked, but maybe that was what I needed to help calm my mind. I stripped down to my sports bra then tugged off my shoes and socks and pulled my hair up into a bun.

Climbing into the ring, I studied him. The solid man was bare-chested and already sweating, a sign he'd been lifting weights up until my appointed arrival at two. Normally, I looked forward to sparring with him, even if he was much rougher than Adonis and Herakles. Niko was easier to understand than Cleon, Lantos, and everyone else currently parked in my life. The former mercenary possessed absolutely no sense of honor. He cheated when we sparred. If he had to choose between saving my life and his, he'd probably put a bullet in me to save himself the trouble of deciding.

Knowing what he was, and where I stood with him, somehow made him easier to tolerate. He was at least predictable with no hidden agenda.

"You know I'm the most powerful person in the world, right?" I asked.

"I know you're *supposed* to be," he replied with a snort.

"And you still won't help me escape from Cleon."

"Kid, *when* you're the most powerful person in the world, I'll do whatever you want me to. Until then, I'll side with the man who's in charge."

"You think I'd keep you around at that point, if you refuse to help me get there?"

"Hands up."

I lifted them and lowered my stance. We began circling one another.

"You know what I can and will do for you, and you know my price," he replied.

The reminder we were both here for reasons beyond ourselves put me on even footing with the one person I should probably never, ever, ever, trust, because he would sell me out for a penny more than I offered him in a heartbeat. Except I knew his secret. He wasn't operating out of an interest in money and hadn't been in quite a while. Tommy, Niko's son with Theodocia, was the reason he obeyed Cleon without question. I couldn't offer to protect Tommy, which was how the person who was supposed to be the most powerful woman in the world became completely worthless to Niko.

He lashed out at me first. I blocked. His second strike went through my defenses and sent me sprawling on my back. I lay still, the breath knocked out of me. Several seconds later, I sucked in air then coughed and sat.

"You should've caught that one," Niko said, unconcerned. "You're distracted."

I was. Around anyone else, I didn't have to worry. But the farther away my mind was, the harder I could expect Niko to hit. He'd broken ribs once and left me bruised and in tears of pain on more than one occasion.

He was grinning, which pissed me off more.

Rolling my shoulders back, I settled my gaze on him. "I'm ready."

"Fighting isn't supposed to be pretty or easy," he reminded me. "You don't have Herakles' size or Adonis' speed."

"They're both more disciplined than you are."

"True, but I fight dirty, and that's what you need to learn if you're going to take on men like us." This time, when he attacked, he pierced my defenses and smacked me across the cheek hard enough to jar me out of my senses.

Catching myself against the ropes, I spun, anger flaring to life inside me. My cheek burned from the strike.

"There we go. That's what we need," Niko said. "Now you're ready." He waved me forward, inviting me to attack.

I didn't know why he pushed me the way he did, but I didn't care.

I attacked him with everything I had.

We sparred for over an hour, until I was panting too hard to move, and Niko was satisfied with what he called progress, which was the name he gave to undoing the training I'd already been taught. Herakles had done everything with honor, even fighting, whereas Niko did nothing with honor, especially *not* fighting. His philosophy was to win at any cost.

"You're probably not going to survive Cleon, but at least you'll be a little harder to take down," Niko said.

Asshole. Doubled over, I struggled to catch my breath.

"And the answer is no about meeting Lantos," he added. "I'm not even going to tell Cleon the request came in."

Niko threw me a towel then draped one over his neck.

I straightened. On the surface, Cleon was in control of my life. But Niko was the one managing me day-to-day and reporting my activities to Cleon. I didn't want to meet with Lantos, but I didn't want anyone else telling me what to do with every minute of my life either.

"Lantos already knows I don't want to see him," I said when I'd caught my breath.

"He'll be out of your hair soon enough."

"What do you mean?"

"The Queen is gone. There's only one man capable of competing with Cleon for power left in DC."

"You think Cleon will expel him?" I asked, genuinely curious at the insight.

"If he's smart, he'll take a more permanent approach and not let

Lantos escape like he did the Queen," Niko answered. "We've almost completed consolidating SISA into my army, and the gods aren't doing shit for us now. There won't be a need for a Supreme Priest, once Cleon is satisfied."

Niko was not normally this talkative. If he had a purpose in revealing this information to me, what was it?

The army commander said nothing more and left the gym floor for the locker rooms. I wiped sweat from my brow and hopped down from the boxing ring, my legs wobbly. I snatched my clothes off the floor as I crossed to the door. My escorts were waiting.

We all trekked back to the villa that was mine, and I entered alone, passing the other guards stationed just inside my doorway. As I reached my bedroom, I caught sight of Leandra, my servant and long-time classmate from the forest where we'd both been raised.

Was Niko warning me about Lantos' fate, because he thought I'd tell Lantos? Was it a warning for me to behave?

Or ... did Niko give me false information because he suspected what Leandra was – the head of a spy network created by the priests who knew my fate? Leandra was my connection to Theodocia, the leader of the insurgency. If Niko or Cleon ever found that out, I'd be on the wall where Cecelia was now, and Leandra would probably be dead.

The beautiful blonde girl my age was nibbling on the afternoon snacks she had placed on the table near the bay window in my room. If anyone would know what Niko was up to, it was Leandra, who was trained in human intelligence.

My eyes went from her to the tall, wide wall opposite the door. Despair unfurled within me, along with a sense of being completely overwhelmed. On the wall, I'd handwritten the names of everyone I murdered the night Cleon ordered me to destroy a five block radius in DC. The area was completely filled with writing, and I'd started adding the names to the adjacent wall as well.

It was a reminder of what I could be, of my power, of those who suffered the moment I stopped trying to fight the fate Cleon wanted for me. The names were the first things I saw in the morning and the last before I fell asleep. They watched me slumber each night, and I imagined the spirits of those I'd killed hovering around me.

I had nightmares every night, and it was rare when I didn't fall asleep crying.

My power had so much potential to do good – and evil. The memorial had become my motivation to resist Cleon's directives and subdue the depths of my magic, so I never unleashed the flood that could finish off what the gods started when the Holy Wars began five years ago.

Dropping my gaze to the floor, I swallowed hard and refocused on what I needed to talk to my only remaining friend about. "Hey, Leandra. Something weird ..."

Dizziness washed over me. My feet grew hot, and the air around me sizzled with the scents of charred metal and burning flesh. The brilliant white daylight pouring into my room melted away, replaced by the dark night sky. I was somewhere else completely. The ground beneath my feet was stone and resembled the area atop the walls I'd seen once before.

Heat rolled over me and stung the inside of my nose. I covered my nose and mouth and blinked ash out of my eyelashes, unable to understand what was happening. Turning to face the source of heat and light, I shielded my eyes and stepped forward.

DC was on fire. Every last bit of it burned, and gaping holes punctuated the cityscape where there was no fire. The walls on which I stood were black, with much of them crumbled. I took in the destruction, awed by its scope, and began searching the ribbons for signs of life.

There were none. The fire gave off three ribbons and everything else two, as if the entirety of the population had been destroyed, along with the buildings.

This can't be real. I turned away, towards the darkness stretching outside the walls of DC as far as I could see. Smoke gagged me, and I moved towards the outer edge of the wall. My attention followed the twisting smoke towards the sky.

No moon.

No stars.

The skies were filled with nothingness I'd seen once before in my life, in a vision of my past.

"What's happening?" I asked aloud, praying someone would answer.

No one was left alive to respond. I turned all the way around again, and then I froze when I saw someone else before me.

Adonis. His form was ghostly, faint and varying shades of black, white and gray. He stood a meter from me, not moving, watching with sadness in his gaze.

Brilliant light spread across the distant horizon, bright enough to draw my gaze. Orange flames arced into the sky from the earth and began to spread, devouring everything in their paths as they raced towards the city. Behind it, nothingness swallowed the ashes, chasing the flames and consuming everything.

"Mismatch!" I cried, facing him again.

His ghostly form was gone. I was completely alone.

DC burned behind me, and ahead of me, the rest of the world was exploding into fire.

TWO

"COME BACK, LYSSA."

The words were soft, and unfamiliar energy tugged at the swaying magic in my blood. Too horrified by what was ahead of me, I barely registered hearing the voice and definitely wasn't going to take my eyes off what was coming.

"Lyssa. Come. Back."

The tug became stronger, and I was dragged away from the fire, into an in between place where I felt I was part of neither world, before I was then yanked out of the dream completely.

My vision cleared to reveal the ceiling of my room.

Bewildered by the idea I was right back where I had been, lying on the floor with Leandra's worried face hovering over me, I had the sense I was floating, not fully released from the world of fire and darkness.

I snapped into a seated position and grabbed her hands, needing to ground myself with physical sensation. Her hands were soft and warm. The marble flooring beneath me was cool and solid, and no trace of flames or nothingness remained. I became aware of panting, and the sweat that coated my body. I shook from the intensity of the premonition – my first, which I'd been waiting for since learning I was supposed to have them.

"Gods, are you okay?" Leandra, who had bullied and tormented me in school, was concerned. She took my face in her hands and forced me to focus on her. "Lyssa. Are you okay?"

I blinked rapidly until the final wisps of the heat were gone, and only the cool air conditioning grazed my skin. Leandra's pretty blue eyes were glowing eerily, and a strange tingle of electricity flew through her fingers into me. Just as quickly, both were gone, but I felt more grounded, as I did sitting with the Oracle in our cavern.

Leandra's shoulders dropped, and she released me as she relaxed.

I touched my cheeks, where her fingertips had been. The lingering vision playing on a loop in my head captured and held my attention.

"I have to go." I climbed to my feet and darted towards the door.

"Lyssa! Wait!" she cried.

Ignoring her, I raced by my assigned guards before any of them could react. While I would never be faster than Adonis, I was lighter on my feet and more agile than anyone else I'd ever meet.

I ran, trusting my instincts to guide me to where I needed to go. Vaguely aware of those chasing me, I bolted across the mall, through puddles and mud, and back to the tiny shack situated on top of the Oracle's cavern.

One of the two guards moved forward to challenge me. They were under orders not to harm me, but even if they weren't, I was too possessed by fear and horror to care. I punched him and maneuvered away from the second. Darting into the building, I whirled and slammed the door closed with my magic then used my power to bring a table and chair to life and ordered them to corner the startled guard.

I rode the elevator to the caverns.

The powerful scent stopped me in my tracks and yanked me out of the crazy state I was in. I breathed them in, becoming self-aware once more. I trembled, and sucked in air as if I'd been underwater for two minutes.

"Cecelia!" I hurried across the caverns to her. "My gods ... something ... something terrible is going to happen! I had my first vision, and it ..." I trailed off, gazing at her, waiting for her response.

Unlike usual, her eyes were closed. The machines and computers keeping her alive were all functioning, and her life signs read as normal.

I sensed, more than saw, something was different.

Leaning across the railing separating her bubble from the rest of the chamber, I pressed a hand to it.

"Cecelia. I need you right now," I whispered. "I don't understand what's happening."

She didn't respond.

Was she non-responsive, because I didn't share my power with her? Was this my fault? My panic started to form again. The vision was crisp in my mind, too vivid for a dream. It had been as real as I was standing before Cecelia, waiting for her to wake up and help me interpret what I saw.

Five minutes passed. She didn't move. I lowered my hand, struck by the sudden sense of being utterly alone with power I couldn't control to prevent the fate I had glimpsed.

"You're well?" Lantos asked from somewhere in the room behind me.

"Leave me alone," I replied.

"Niko's on his way. If he has to break the door down, he's going to take it out on you."

Unable to steady myself fully, I didn't exactly want another ass beating by Niko or to be sentenced to my room for the rest of my life.

"If you're lucky, he won't mention this incident to Cleon." Lantos joined me at the railing. One of his unique powers was the ability to turn into a shadow and travel unseen through the world. He'd made it down here when no one else could, because of this ability.

His handsome profile was relaxed, despite the words. There were no real consequences for him to be here, or anywhere, when he could easily disappear. It seemed fitting that he stood with me in this very spot. The charming politician had been the person who introduced me to Cecelia, and my fate, months ago. Of all the reasons I despised him, foremost in my mind was the fact he alone was probably the only person on the compound who could help me understand what I was going through, and I didn't want him to.

"Her mind is quiet," he said, lifting his chin to indicate Cecelia.

My gaze returned to her. "I don't know what that means."

"She's in what I'd call a coma. She's barely alive. I can read secrets and shadows in one's mind, but hers has neither."

I gripped the railing, my heartbeat soaring. "She can't die," I whispered, stricken.

"Not that I mind seeing Cleon upset, but what happened that caused you to set off the alarms?"

Any other time, when I wasn't terrified I'd just seen the end of the world, I would have ignored his question. But I couldn't stop shaking, couldn't dismiss the vision in my head.

"I saw something," I replied.

"Saw something *how*?"

"A ... vision. My first."

"What was it of?"

I shook my head. Even considering voicing it left my throat too tight to speak and my mouth suddenly dry.

"That bad, huh?" he asked, looking at me for the first time. "Oracles have visions. It has always been this way. Is it the vision itself that alarms you or the experience?"

"The vision. Do they always come true?"

"No. That machine there," he pointed to one of the many panels of lights behind Cecelia, "is a quantum computer. It helps Cecelia interpret visions and how they might, or might not, come to pass."

"But she doesn't always know the answer."

"We have free will, and even a quantum computer can't calculate what billions of people will choose to do every second of their days. Either that, or she doesn't share what she knows. Cecelia holds much more power than anyone knows," he said. The dark note in his tone drew my gaze.

"You don't mean what I think you do, do you?" I ventured. "You think she's hiding things from us? From *me*?"

"You're learning to read between the lines. If you pay enough attention, you, too, may experience an illuminating moment when you realize all you knew was wrong," he replied with one of his dazzling smiles. "Soon you'll be able to keep your own head above water instead of relying on the little spy in your household."

I flushed, irritated the master of secrets had discovered Leandra. If I knew anything about Lantos, he would keep that knowledge safe and quiet, until he needed a favor from me.

"So you foresaw something terrible and came here." His focus returned to Cecelia. "I don't think she can help you, Alessandra. If she could, I don't think she would choose to, either."

"She'll always help me," I countered. "She just has to wake up."

"I don't see that happening."

"You don't know that!" Nothing scared me more than the idea I was alone to prevent an apocalypse and had no insight into how it came about. "What am I supposed to do?" I asked in general, not expecting Lantos to know the answer.

"Interpret what you saw from every perspective you can. From my experience with Oracles, every vision has multiple meanings and just as many subtle clues hidden within it as to what might lead to its occurrence as foreseen."

I listened, torn between gratitude and anger that, of everyone who might help, Lantos was the one to step up.

"Niko's coming," Lantos moved away from the railing. "It wouldn't be wise for me to be caught here." He shifted towards the shadows edging the room.

Now was not the time for my pride to win this battle, and I quelled the indignation in favor of accepting his limited assistance. He began to fade. "Because you helped me, I feel like I should help you," I said grudgingly. "Niko thinks Cleon's going to get rid of you soon."

"Yeah. I know. He'll try." Lantos winked.

"I think we should talk."

"I'm always open to a dialogue. Come by tonight."

Too distressed to say more, I returned to Cecelia. Silence filled the space behind me, indicating Lantos was probably gone. Seconds later, the elevator door dinged and slid open. I tensed, sensing Niko before he exited the elevator car.

"Five seconds before I tranq you just for shits and giggles," he called.

"Something's wrong with Cecelia," I replied quickly. I waited, shoulders hunched, for his reaction. Sometimes, Niko didn't care what my reasoning was. My first two weeks on the compound alone, he had shot me with a tranquilizer gun ten times.

After a moment, he approached and paused beside me at the railing. The tranquilizer gun was in one hand, in case I decided to use my magic in a way that was not approved by Cleon, or in the common circumstance where I became too uncooperative. Niko and I both knew he could beat me into submission, and I wouldn't use my power against him out of a damning sense of honor. I was pretty sure he *liked* shooting people, especially me.

Niko went to the screen on the wall nearest him and tapped through the commands, paused to read, then placed the tranq gun in its holster at his thigh. He was dressed in his urban fatigues featuring his appointed rank of a four star general, armed to the teeth, and smelling lightly of soap.

"I'll let Cleon know," Niko said. "You have somewhere to be soon."

I didn't want to leave, in case Cecelia suddenly woke up.

The sinking feeling in my stomach, however, led me to believe that wasn't going to happen. My worst fears were all happening at once. Cleon could use my magic, and I was alone to prevent the apocalypse.

Niko glanced at me, and I stepped back from the railing. The Oracle catnip of the chamber was calming me, giving my world a surreal feeling, though nothing was ever going to scrub the vision in my mind away.

After two months here as a semi-prisoner, I was accustomed to feeling as if the ground beneath me would collapse at any time. The new sensations tearing through me were so much worse than being unsteady, for one reason only.

I was powerful enough to stop anything that came my way. So ... in the future I foresaw, why hadn't future-me prevented what I witnessed firsthand in the vision? And how did I ensure this particular future never happened?

Shouldn't I, potentially the most powerful person on the planet, know what to do?

"Whatever happened, fix yourself before dinner," Niko said firmly. "You look like you ran into a drunk and horny Zeus in a dark alley. If you don't want Cleon suspecting anything, fix this shit." He studied me.

I didn't like his too intent gaze. He suspected something. Niko was an enigma, someone who saw far more than he let on, and who was smarter than his roughened edges indicated. If one person here could force me to talk, it would probably be Niko. Not because I trusted him, but because he spoke to me in a language I understood: that which Herakles had taught me. Fighting, survival, physical strength over mental agility.

Maybe that was the real reason I asked Niko every day if he had reconsidered helping me. There were parts of him that reminded me of Herakles. Niko suppressed a lot of my acting out; this much I knew. He dealt with me on his terms, but he didn't tell Cleon when I was disobeying the Supreme Magistrate's direct orders, or I'd spend more time locked up.

A small part of Niko was looking out for me. Or perhaps, since he was so selfish, he was hedging his bets and keeping the door opened in case I did become the person I was supposed be.

Either way, I enjoyed a level of leniency I wouldn't, if someone other than Niko were overseeing every second of my day. It was this that convinced me to do what he wanted when I would have preferred to challenge him.

Turning away, I went to the elevator. Someone had disabled the office furniture I ordered to contain the guard, and I plucked the green ribbons from the objects to render them inanimate again. The door to the building had been smashed through, probably by Niko.

No one challenged me as I left. My escort was waiting, along with Leandra, whose eyes were large. She breathed an audible sigh of relief when I joined her. As my personal servant, she couldn't speak to me openly in public, but she fell into step behind me as I hurried back to my chalet.

Only when we were alone in my room did she break the silence. Far from the obedient, docile type, Leandra smacked me on the back of my head.

"What in Hades was that about?" she demanded, rounding on me.

At my look, she softened. I felt like crying, and she sensed it.

"Chocolate makes you feel better." She brought me the tray of snacks and sat down on my bed. "Come on. Talk to me."

I went. I gazed past her briefly at the names scrawled in purple marker lining the wall.

I'm going to need more space, if the vision is true, I thought and then shuddered. I nibbled on a chocolate croissant, trying to wrap my head around how to explain what I'd seen. Leandra waited patiently.

"I had my first vision," I said finally. "It was of the world ending."

Leandra stared at me.

"You all knew what I was long before anyone told me," I continued. "What am I supposed to do? Did the priests tell you guys anything about my powers at all?"

She didn't speak for a full two minutes. At last, she shook her head. "We knew what you were, but we assumed you would know what that entailed when the time came," she said. "What exactly did you see?"

I shared the vision with her in as few words as possible and then mentioned Cecelia's coma.

"Cecelia has been helping me suppress my abilities, because of Cleon," I continued, distraught. "But now, Cecelia's in a coma, and I have no one to help me understand what I'm capable of."

"You have to learn. You have to figure it out," Leandra said urgently. "Damn Cleon. You have to become as strong as you can, so you can stop this from happening!"

"But that's the opposite of what Cecelia says. She says my power has to stay contained, or I'll wipe out everyone. And this is proof." I pulled up my sleeve to reveal the double omega tattoo.

"I may not know much about what you're supposed to do, but I do know you have to fight a battle. Maybe more than one," Leandra said. "How can you do that, if you're suppressing your power?"

From anyone else on the compound, I would've ignored the advice that ran counter to what the only other Oracle in existence claimed to be best for me. Leandra's rationale was nearly identical to what Herakles would say. If I weren't as strong as I could be, how could I *win*? I sometimes wondered if I shouldn't at least experiment with my magic, to see what I could do, and wasn't there some benefit in foreseeing the future? Wouldn't that give me an advantage?

Since arriving to this compound, I'd been in a state of profound confusion. I knew Cecelia was angry; her emotion reached me often during our lessons. Was her judgment clouded, or did she advise me to suppress myself because she foresaw what happened if I *didn't*?

With her out of the picture, I had no one else to help me navigate what I was, aside from Leandra.

"You're the strongest since the first," Leandra added. "What if Cecelia is trying to help you but doesn't really know how, when you're destined for something only one other Oracle in ten thousand years has done?"

Leandra made sense. "What about Cleon? He can manipulate

some of my power now," I said, torn. "What if he's the reason the apocalypse happens, because I became stronger and he uses my power to destroy the world?"

"Alternately, what if you being weak is what allows him to act?" she challenged.

I sighed. I was paralyzed by the morality of wielding the power I possessed.

Leandra appeared pensive, chewing on her lower lip, before she stood and paced. "We weren't prepared for this," she admitted. "Give me a couple of days to see what I can learn. I'll talk to Theodocia, too. I can't tell you how to handle your own power, except to say I think you need to be as strong as possible to withstand what might have to be done to Cleon."

Her words sent a chill through me. If there was one name I wanted on my wall, it was Cleon's, but not if it meant all of existence ceased as well.

"Come one. We need to get you ready for tonight. When you're at the dinner, I'll send word to Theodocia," Leandra said with a glance at the clock on my nightstand.

Talking to her helped me feel far less alone handling the fate of all of humanity. As I showered, I forced myself to review the vision in my head. Lantos claimed there were clues or information in the visions I should be able to interpret.

I was drawing a complete blank, though. I'd been so upset, so stunned, I saw no details, only a ghostly Adonis, the flames and noth-ingness. How often would I have visions? Would I have a second shot to try to interpret this one, or had I condemned us all already because I was too overwhelmed to notice hints that could help me change the future?

Tears rose as hot water washed away the sweat from my workout. I hated being helpless. Herakles had trained me to be strong, and Adonis believed in me. Swallowing hard, I decided I was going to have to make a choice without Cecelia. I could no longer dwell in the gray area of whether or not I'd enable Cleon by becoming stronger. I certainly would never be able to stop the annihilation of everything, if I were weak.

It was terrifying to know, with complete certainty, at least one of the paths open to me led to the annihilation of everything, and I had no idea which one this was.

"Artemis, if you're there, I need some guidance," I said. I held my breath and listened for her voice. She had spoken to me on top of the walls, when I destroyed the five-block radius around her principal temple in DC.

If she heard me, she didn't respond.

I finished up my shower. Leandra helped me into the formal dress Cleon had ordered me to wear this night. I stood in front of a floor length mirror, staring at myself while she went through the various jewels belonging to the treasury of the Oracles of Delphi.

I was pale, and my eyes were haunted. I didn't look well at all. Physically, I was tense and my muscles sore from sparring. Mentally, I was a mess. If I'd had a choice, I'd have skipped the event tonight.

Leandra draped a pendant with a thumb-sized, teardrop diamond around my neck. I slid my feet into my favorite wedges and then strapped a knife to my thigh, beneath the dress.

Leandra either didn't notice or didn't care. She was normally more concerned about how others would see me than whether or not I could defend myself. This evening, her features were taut, and she was quieter than usual.

"No comment about my fat feet or wild hair?" I asked. I was worried – but it was my responsibility, not hers, to spend sleepless nights terrorized by the thoughts of what I'd done and what I would do. After all, I was the only person who could prevent the apocalypse.

She lifted her gaze from the two scarves she'd laid out on the dressers at the center of my two-story, walk-in closet.

"I can't stop thinking about your vision," she said.

"That makes two of us."

"Yes, but I have faith you can stop it. My concern is detaching that parasite from your powers."

I forced a smile and smoothed out the pale yellow dress. I wanted to be the person she believed in.

One of my mandatory escorts knocked thirty minutes before I was scheduled to be at the House. I went to the door of my bedroom reluctantly and joined the single guard sent to fetch me. Trailing him through the beautiful villa, I couldn't help wondering how I was going to sleep tonight. Not only were the names of those I'd murdered looking down upon me, but the vision of the world ending was replaying through my head.

As much as I didn't want to, I kept thinking about Lantos and how he was likely the only person on the compound who might be able to help me. He did nothing for free, however, and I had nothing to offer. He ranked second only to Cleon on my list of people I despised.

I walked with my escort across the compound to the House. Guests were already arriving, wearing designer clothing and adorned with larger diamonds than the one I wore. The crowd was larger than usual. Cleon hosted ambassadors and politicians several times a week, and rarely was a Tuesday soiree attended by more than ten people.

By the line forming to enter the House, this gathering consisted of a hundred people, if not more. Now that I knew what his alleged plan was – selling safe zones – I was no longer surprised this many people wanted to meet him.

The moment I was noticed, the movers and shakers of the world parted. Most fell quiet, while some whispered. Everyone looked. Despite the warm summer evening, I shivered, as I always did when put on display.

I bypassed the security checkpoint and followed my escort through the bottom floor to the entertaining wing. The ball-room was bright and filled with a small army of serving staff circulating through the room with snacks and alcohol. A full bar was in one corner, and a string quartet playing softly in another.

How could anyone pretend life was normal? How did the elite attend swanky parties, knowing the world outside the walls was in chaos, and they were in the presence of someone who had destroyed a large part of the city?

I would never fit into this world.

Cleon, however, was in his element. He stood in the center of the room, on a raised dais, speaking to a man in a well-tailored suit who was flanked by two assistants. Cleon rarely introduced me to anyone. I assumed my usual position behind him, off the dais, a trophy with the power of a goddess obediently standing behind her master.

It made me despise him more.

The people trickled into the room slowly. I never understood how they could even *appear* pleased to be here. Either everyone in the ballroom was bored enough to find a stuffy event like this enjoyable, or they were damned good actors. Cleon stayed on his dais, the center of attention. Most people paid homage by stepping up for a moment to meet him and speak a few words before descending to the main floor with the rest of us.

My skin always crawled at these things, because so many people were watching me. Most appeared curious, some leery, and still others troubled, as if they weren't pleased to see me there.

One man in particular was staring at me from across the room. He clutched a flute of champagne too tightly to be natural, and his suit was baggy and untailored, which didn't happen with this crowd. If not for the high level of security at the event, I would've been suspicious. But everyone in attendance passed through a body scanner that took x-rays to ensure no weapons were hidden anywhere. Still, I'd been trained by Herakles to pay attention to my instincts. They were warning me about this strange man with his glare.

"Are you prepared for our demonstration?" Cleon asked, stepping down from the dais to speak to me.

"Sure," I replied, uninterested.

"I want to wait until everyone is present."

I glanced up at him. On the surface, he wore a smile, and his eyes held genuine warmth. I never understood how he could look at me as if we were friends, when I was his prisoner. Of everyone I'd met since leaving the safety of my forest, Cleon was the one man I couldn't figure out. That he loved power of any kind was clear, but that was all I knew with certainty. His true agenda was hidden beneath many layers and an unhealthy obsession with world domination.

Niko appeared at the entrance briefly and scanned the partygoers before ducking out again.

I wasn't the only one who noticed when he left.

The strange man shifted away from the side of the room and headed towards the dais.

I reached for the knife at my thigh.

A crowd of partygoers came between us, and I lost track of the man. When the people cleared, he had vanished. I searched the faces around us then lowered my hand.

"It's time." Cleon ascended the dais with the confidence of a member of royalty.

I turned to face him, morbidly curious about what he planned for his demonstration. I needed to gauge just how much of my power he could tap into, and tonight would answer that question.

"First, I would like to give my heartfelt gratitude to those of you in attendance today. This is a very special occasion, one I chose to share with my closest friends and colleagues."

I rolled my eyes and tuned out, fed up with his speeches after hearing them several times a week. I didn't believe one word he said, but the people around me were smiling. Cleon could be charismatic when he wanted to be.

" ... especially, the Ambassador to Greece, who is rumored to manage the accounts of Her Majesty, the Silent Queen, who has inexplicably disappeared ..." Cleon was saying.

The man he addressed was tall with thick, dark hair and eyes. He smiled when Cleon motioned to him, and the crowd clapped politely.

Cleon stepped down from the dais, speaking of the Ambassador's many wonderful traits and deeds, none of which were of interest to me.

Instead, I kept an eye out for the stranger who tripped the warning bells of my instincts. I thought I glimpsed him once through the crowd and lifted up on my tiptoes to see better. Disappointed not to spot him again, and unable to leave my assigned place without drawing Cleon's ire, I continued searching the audience visually. I had once heard Cleon talk about someone for thirty minutes, non-stop, pouring compliments all over this person without pausing for breath. If this was another of those nights, I was going to explode from the wired energy zinging through me, leftover from my vision and fear.

Turning to peer at the area behind me, I scoured the audience in the hopes of spotting the man who gave me the creeps. Twice more I thought I glimpsed him and made an attempt to discreetly reposition where I stood.

Ignoring Cleon, I didn't notice he had stopped talking, but I did see the looks of surprise crossing the faces of the crowd. What random inanimate object had he decided to bring to life then crush?

To my surprise, Cleon stood over the Ambassador, twisting the ribbons only we could see above the man's head. The Ambassador's features were contorting, his face red to the point of purple, as if the life were being squeezed out of him.

I reacted fast, or tried to. Cleon could use my power, but his handle on it appeared clumsy. He kept shifting and repositioning his hands. I started to shove his hand aside by manipulating my magic, so I could fix the ribbons he was slowly tearing.

Someone grabbed my arm from behind. At the sensation of cold metal of a weapon at the center of my back, I froze.

"I lost my entire family when you smashed my apartment build-ing," someone whispered.

Guilt settled into my stomach.

"I will put this knife through your spine, if you breathe wrong."

"And I will take off your head, if you try it," Niko responded.

A stir of alarm went up from those around us, and people hurried away. I was temporarily caught by the memory in my head of the night when I'd become a mass murderer. How many other people hated me enough to track me down and try to kill me?

Could I blame them?

"Don't take all day, Lyssa," Niko growled.

Unable to see what was going on behind me, I gauged the situation. The point of a knife pricked my back, giving me the man's placement behind me and the angle at which he was holding the weapon.

I ducked and whirled, whipping out one leg to knock the man's feet from beneath him and tearing the silk of my dress in the process. He dropped hard, and I straightened, knife in hand, but didn't pounce. He had every right to be angry, and to try to attack me. I only hoped he wouldn't end up thrown in the dungeon beneath the House for his actions. He'd suffered enough.

Niko stood, gun in hand, behind where the man was. He smashed the man's wrist holding the knife then reached down to flip the attacker onto his stomach. He cuffed and hauled the man up.

Troubled by the sneak attack, I waited for the mercenary leader of the army to say something. He didn't, and Niko shoved the attacker towards the two guards behind him.

"Don't hurt him," I said quickly for Niko's ears only. "Please."

The army commander glanced at me without responding.

More murmuring erupted around me, while strange silence came from behind me. I turned to stop Cleon from murdering a man.

Knocking his hand out of the way, I snatched the ribbons and quickly began to repair them.

Cleon didn't even look at me before he hit the pain button.

At once, agony shot through my head, blinding me and dropping me to my knees. Unable to see or help the Ambassador further, I gripped my head and waited for it to pass.

The pain stopped. I remained on my knees, shaking, weakened by the torture.

"Ladies and gentlemen. I am thrilled to have given you two demonstrations tonight!" Cleon announced.

The crowd was silent.

I lifted my head. He was messing with the Ambassador's ribbons again.

I reached out to undo what he was doing. If anyone died because of my power, even if Cleon committed the murder, it was my fault.

Feeling me yank the power away from him, Cleon glanced at Niko. I braced myself, aware of what was coming.

"It's not your day, kid," Niko said and then shot me with the tranq gun.

Pain smashed into my shoulder. The effects of the tranquilizers were instant. My body became heavy and slipped out of my control. I groaned, slumping. Before I was completely unconscious, I felt Niko pick me up and walk through the crowd.

"I'll make sure that guy is sent to the north side of the protected zone and not downstairs," Niko said quietly.

I was too numb to respond. By the time we were at the front door of the House, I was sliding into unconsciousness.

And that's when the second vision erupted into my mind.

THREE
SILENT QUEEN

MY HANDS TREMBLED, and I lowered the bloodied knife. I stood over the corpse of a man I hadn't wanted to kill. Eventually, the logical side of my mind would accept that, not only did my survival depend upon me killing anyone standing in the path of my goals – with my own two hands, if necessary – but it likewise meant I was going to commit other acts I'd regret, probably forever.

Death is a political necessity. I had learned this before my seventh birthday, when the curse of the Bloodline was revealed to me. Whether one called it murder, assassination, or collateral damage was irrelevant. Death was a tool to be wielded discreetly with the same dispassionate state of mind as trade treaties or any other resolution needed to settle a diplomatic matter between two entities in disagreement about an outcome.

My position as a member of the Sacred Triumvirate was complemented by an indisputably royal title, wealth built up by my family over the course of ten thousand years, and the favor of the gods. When I needed someone dead for any reason, my principal High Priestess, Theodocia, had coordinated it using whatever elements of my power she needed. Or, she chose to execute someone herself.

Blessed by Artemis and Thanatos – the God of Death – Theodocia held rare, special favor from two deities. My will was always done.

My entire life, death had also been *easy*.

A month after leaving the pampered safety of my former life, I understood death with clarity I did not before. The first time I took a life, I spent ten days trying to scrub the feeling of his warm blood off my hands.

The man at my feet was my tenth kill since then. He was destined to die at my hands this evening, no matter how difficult it was for me to kill him or what I might one day feel regarding my actions. Out here, in the chaos of the world abandoned by the gods, there was no room for guilt or remorse or hesitation. Beyond the walls of DC, where all of humanity had been stripped of its dignity and civility, these emotions were a death sentence. Whoever flinched first, or showed mercy, died.

You should not have been there the night a god took your body, I told the corpse silently. *But you were, and this is how it must end for everyone in your position. I can promise you, I will murder those responsible for your suffering, your lost soul and your death.*

I wiped my palms on the cloak I wore and replaced my weapons. The scent of rotting flesh was in the air, and my nose wrinkled.

My new protector, a scarred, massive ginger named Herakles, rounded the corner into the narrow passage between two buildings. He was sweating, and his weapons were covered with blood. He hadn't touched the handgun at his hip; neither of us did, not when ammunition was scarce and valuable. He killed with his hands. I used knives.

"You okay?" Herakles asked, eyes searching my face.

Some of my revulsion at killing melted. Herakles always asked about me first, always tended to my wounds before addressing the matter at hand. His approach to doing business was the opposite of mine. I preferred to deal decisively with what was before me and then handle the fallout and consequences – physical and emotional – after the loose ends were tied.

On days like this, when some distant part of me that I refused to acknowledge felt the full impact of murdering a man, I appreciated Herakles' more humanitarian approach.

I nodded.

"Are you hurt?" he pressed.

I shook my head.

"I told you that was a lucky knife," he said with a faint smile, eyes on the bloodied hilt of the weapon I'd sheathed.

Lucky was not the word I would use to describe the weapon I'd used to kill four men this week.

But ... in truth, the men I slayed were already dead.

Herakles knelt beside the dead man. "This one is maybe three days old." He flipped open the man's vest, searching for weapons. "Did you get his name?"

I wrote the answer in the dirt beside the body.

Herakles gazed at it then shrugged. "This is your domain, not mine. His name means nothing to me."

My protector was very different than me in this respect, too. He could barely read and hardly knew any of the deities. If he ever had a formal education, it stopped too early for him to understand many of the complex religious, scientific, cultural and mathematical concepts with which I was familiar.

At first, our differences had left me feeling alone in a crowd. It was not until I began to appreciate and admire the talents where Herakles was superior to every other person on the planet – even the gods – that I understood how two puzzles pieces like us could work together.

I wrote three more words in the dirt.

"God of Roads. Hmm." By his expression, Herakles was not impressed. "Any lead on Zeus or the others?"

I shook my head.

"Well, let's keep going." Herakles stood and walked away from the dead man.

It was harder for me. Not because I didn't think my choice was the right one – it always was – but because I didn't like the idea of leaving behind a person who had been abandoned first by the gods. I wasn't like them, and I wouldn't behave like them.

When I didn't move, Herakles sighed and stopped walking. "All right. We'll burn him, so no one else can use the body. Let me grab the others."

Thank you, I responded telepathically. He couldn't hear me. No one out here could.

My eyes fell to the corpse again. The cowardly gods had stooped to a new low at some point within the past five years, since the Holy Wars began. While on Earth, the gods and goddesses existed in energetic forms humans could not see. To communicate with normal people, the deities would possess the body of a human messenger – usually one of the priests or priestesses dedicated to them, or another human with the dormant gift of telepathy – in order to pass on a message. The interactions lasted several minutes, never more, because the deities respected the human's life. When they possessed the body of a volunteer, the gods pushed out the soul of the human temporarily and caused the host's body to start to die.

Somewhere along the line, the deities had begun doing more than passing on messages. They possessed bodies – and stayed, until the human forms rotted out from beneath them. They leapt into another body at that point, and the process repeated itself over and over. None of the gods and goddesses we'd found would share with us the reason they chose to possess humans instead of remaining in their energy forms. Herakles and I had concluded their existences had been in danger, or it would not have become a widespread necessity.

I knew none of this when I'd lived inside the walls of DC.

Then again, most of the horrors I'd experienced since leaving had been suppressed by the media and politicians. No one could render the gods-forsaken war zone outside of DC pleasant, but they had definitely managed to keep our focus inside the protected area and edited out the harsh reality the majority of survivors in the world lived in. According to the media lie I'd believed, SISA and the military were purportedly using martial law to help those outside the walls establish colonies capable of sustaining themselves and ruling themselves with order.

The truth was the opposite.

People slaughtered one another for food and unpolluted water sources.

SISA and the military raided settlements and colonies for food to help feed those in the protected zone.

Deities slaughtered humans for hosts.

The world outside DC was a horrifying battle for survival.

Herakles returned a moment later and deposited two more dead bodies beside the man I'd killed.

Stepping aside, I watched the people's champion and former Olympian tear wood off the side of a building and bring an armful to the corpses. He arranged the wood with military efficiency and expertise then stood and sprayed the makeshift pyre with petrol.

The only good thing to come of the deities possessing people: when they were in the bodies of their hosts, they were vulnerable. They could be killed permanently in a way the gods and goddesses couldn't be when in their other forms on Earth.

"Three total. Were there any others you noticed?" Herakles asked.

I shook my head.

"No one will talk," he growled. "How can these parasites discard a human life like trash?"

Knowing another human lost his life to a selfish god tore me apart, too.

Knowing we'd removed three more deities, even minor ones, from Earth this night filled me with triumph.

I had sworn to rid the planet of the foul supernatural beings. I never expected it to occur in this fashion, just as I never expected to become one of the only people outside the wall capable of tracking the deities who had taken human form.

A priest or priestess would be able to do it as well. However, those with even the smallest telepathic gift who had managed to survive the bloody onset of the Holy Wars outside the walls were the first possessed by the deities.

I moved to stand beside Herakles. A lighter was in his hand.

"I have yet to learn a proper prayer for people like you," Herakles murmured to the dead. "But even if I knew one, I don't think I'd waste my time appealing to the very gods who did this to you. After what I've seen, I believe in only two gods: Thanatos and Hades. They alone never fail in their service to anyone. For what it's worth, I hope Hades finds your souls, wherever they have gone, and takes them to safety."

If you can hear me, Hades, please destroy the souls of the gods who did this. Thanatos, please protect the men who lost their spirits to a parasite and guide them home, I added silently. Unlike the rest of the gods, I held far less anger towards those of the underworld, who seemed to largely stay out of the political and Holy Wars mess making up my world. Even gods and goddesses could die, and their souls had to go somewhere. The gods of the underworld didn't discriminate and were the most neutral entities in existence.

We watched the fire start to burn the boards before it leapt to devour the clothing the men wore. Only when the corpses' skin began to melt did we turn away.

Glancing up at Herakles I made a familiar sign in the air, that of a Z.

"Yeah," he agreed grimly. "None of our hunters can find anything out about Zeus' whereabouts. But he has to be here. Somewhere."

I nodded. Zeus was my primary benefactor, and he was the ruler of the deities. The list of reasons behind why I wanted to find him was long and increased daily.

Herakles and I walked away from the alley where the bodies burned. He was always on guard, and his eyes sought out any sort of danger. I trusted the three-time Olympian, who towered above everyone else I'd ever met, with my life. He was tough on the outside and soft on the inside, a combination I had never really experienced before. Everyone I knew was hard on the inside, capable of measured concern and affection, but never selfless love. Even Theodocia had turned hard inside, when she was touched by Thanatos five years ago.

Though he could tear a man apart with his bare hands, Herakles was selfless. He was *good,* and his heart was so very sweet. His existence was a reminder of why I had to fight on days when my anger at the gods was not enough to motivate me.

Our convoy of seven vehicles waited for us in the parking lot of an abandoned mega-store less than a block away. Ammunition was rare, but petrol was everywhere, a relic of a bygone era that had ended suddenly five years ago. Clothing, land, tools, and some other products were in large supply across the country. When the Holy Wars began, it was estimated eighty percent of humanity was destroyed overnight, leaving a surplus of resources where there had been a hearty dearth before.

In the moonlight, the gray asphalt glowed. The warm air smelled of summer rain and the first traces of what promised to be the most humid week yet.

Herakles and I climbed into the command vehicle, an armored Jeep, and headed back to camp. My fleet of vehicles was over five hundred strong, thanks to the members of Mama's army with mechanical skills. On our compound, we lived in a world of selective modern conveniences. Solar and wind power provided electricity. Running water was in place, and the engineers in the army had expanded the existing sewer system to accommodate the number of men and women in the army. They were also responsible for the entrenchments and other defenses around the mall we'd taken over upon being expelled from DC.

That was where the modern conveniences ended. Our communications were limited to radios. About forty percent of my army on any given day was absorbed in the logistics of feeding us. They hunted, tended farm animals, skirmished with SISA and military forces, and traded precious ammunition for fruits and vegetables. I hadn't had the time to establish a farm, but it was on my list to start next spring, assuming I wasn't able to take DC before then.

Which isn't looking likely, I admitted as I gazed out the window at the dark, quiet forests surrounding the small town in northern Virginia where we'd sought temporary refuge. The staggering count of personnel required to meet the needs of daily survival had caught me off balance when we first arrived here. It hindered my ability to plan for a large-scale insurgency against the Supreme Magistrate's forces. My army was decent sized, but his was larger and better supplied. I didn't plan to lose when I attacked. I had to be better prepared and fight smarter than they would.

But my people also had to eat and needed clean water sources. Our focus since setting up camp was basic survival.

This was the main reason we began searching for a few select gods and goddesses with gifts we could exploit to maintain the army and advance our cause faster. At the top of my list were two deities whose powers we could use to our advantage: Zeus and Ares.

We arrived back to the compound and waited for the drawbridge to lower across the trench. On the other side was a wall built from cement taken from disassembled roads around the former shopping center.

Five minutes later, we halted in the well-lit motor pool.

Two men with *M* patches on their arms awaited us. One bore an additional patch with an image of a scroll, while the second wore a patch with a crown, which represented my elite command corps. I left the vehicle and approached them.

They both glanced from me to Herakles, who trailed me. I wanted to think they waited because he was my mouthpiece, but sometimes, I sensed the army was a little uncertain of the tiny Queen leading it and more comforted by the presence of Herakles, who was beloved by every last soldier in my forces if not for his unmatched fighting prowess, than because he genuinely cared for the welfare of everyone he spoke to.

"We caught SISA scouts near the south side of the city," the commander reported when Herakles was standing beside me.

I tapped my throat, which by now, everyone understood was the issuing of a death sentence.

"Make sure the bodies are taken farther away this time," Herakles added. "They were left within five clicks of the town last time. It's too close."

"Of course," the commander replied. "It's not like SISA to send so many scouts after us. The military, I can understand, since our presence outside the walls is a military concern. If we interrogated them, perhaps we would know what the religious police seek." His eyes went from Herakles to me.

I tapped my throat again.

"There you have it," Herakles said with a smile. "The official word is no."

"We will obey the command at once," the commander said and nodded his head in deference.

I didn't need them talking to the SISA scouts. I knew why the religious police were snooping around: because their leader, Lantos – my former lover, who had betrayed me – was looking for me. I wasn't going to give him the satisfaction of using his spy network to find me. When the time came, I would confront him myself with my lucky knife in hand.

"We also received word from Theodocia," the messenger with a scroll patch said. He held out an envelope to me.

Though I wanted to tear it out of his hand and devour it, I accepted it with the grace and composure befitting my royal title. Theodocia's letters came semi-monthly, and I incessantly worried about her in the period of time stretching before the arrival of a new one.

"We also have a prisoner," the commander said and cleared his throat.

I looked up from the envelope to meet his gaze, raising an eyebrow in quizzical inquiry.

"He found one of our scouting teams," the commander continued. "He said he has a message for you from someone you seek."

Tucking the envelope into the pocket of my cargo pants, I motioned for him to lead us to this mysterious prisoner.

"Are you not under orders to kill deities posing as humans?" Herakles asked. He fell in behind me, and we followed the commander.

"He gave us reason to consider him useful."

I glanced over my shoulder at Herakles. At my expressive look, he spoke again.

"Her Majesty wants to know what you mean by this."

"He healed all the wounded and sick in the infirmary," was the quiet response.

There were several gods and goddesses with the ability to heal. Until I met this one, I wouldn't know which it was.

"Including my son and wife, who were stricken with dysentery from the initial source of polluted water we tried to use," the Commander added. "And he's not fully possessed."

I didn't think it possible for someone to be halfway possessed. Either a god had forced its way into a human body, or it hadn't.

"That is a useful ability," Herakles said with a considering glance at me. "Dysentery's killed sixty so far."

My jaw clenched. Aside from dysentery, we'd lost another fifteen lives during negotiations with other towns for food, or at the hands of either marauders who lived in the forest or by the townspeople themselves. Another twenty-four were dead from hunting deities. I'd been to visit each family of someone who died, and we'd created a separate pyre for each man and woman. Every night, we held a new wake. The names and faces of those who had died were a blur in my exhausted mind, which was a source of embarrassment to me. If these men and women sacrificed their lives for my cause, should I not remember their names?

Between managing an army, visiting grieving families, and hunting for deities, I barely slept. When I did doze, I had nightmares.

I understood too well how useful a healing deity could be.

But I much preferred a dead deity.

We passed through the main shopping mall, whose stores had been converted into barracks where the soldiers lived with the other members of their units. Of the three anchor stores, only one had survived the gods' wrath. It was transformed into our headquarters, which contained barracks for all the command personnel and common areas consisting of public baths, showers and restrooms, a dining hall, and a massive refrigerated storage area where we kept every last tiny piece of food that was brought in by hunting parties or left over from the nightly wakes. Soldiers slept in other abandoned stores throughout the mall. Outdoor kitchens prevented the buildings from becoming too hot and freed up living space. Most of the design aspects of our compound had been based off of Herakles' ideas. He had a knack for the basic building blocks of surviving anywhere, with any kind of resources.

We exited the headquarters. Many members of the army had brought families or close friends with them from DC. Those who were not official soldiers or support staff lived in the adjacent buildings of a strip mall across the street but still well within our protected compound. The lights were out in the other buildings, and it was quiet this time of night.

I had no place designated for prisoners of war, since I never planned to take any, and was curious to see where the soldiers kept the imprisoned deity. I sensed the god before I saw where we were headed.

Fitting, I thought, amused for the first time in weeks.

They'd placed him in the livestock barn, which was constructed out of material left over from one of the destroyed anchor stores. Safe inside the defenses, we didn't guard the livestock except to place young men and women in charge of making sure the animals were well. Four guards stood in front of the barn doors, confirming my suspicion the god was inside.

The guards opened the doors when we reached them, and all four of us entered.

The barn smelled of horses, cows, pigs, sheep and hay, and light glowed from the lamps ensconced along one wall.

In front of the bales of hay and straw, a man in his twenties sat bound to a chair. He appeared the worse for wear, as if my men had beaten him before he managed to talk his way out of the fate I declared for every deity. His clothing was ripped and bloody and his dark hair mussed – but he bore no bruises or signs of injury. He was relaxed and dozing.

"Is it one of them?" Herakles asked me quietly.

I nodded.

"Give her room," he instructed the others and waved them back, towards the door.

Ever my protector, he stayed close to me when I stepped forward.

Who are you? I demanded of the god.

He jerked awake and lifted his face to see me. His skin was dark caramel – but his eyes were brilliant blue.

"Your Majesty," he said and dipped his head. "I wasn't expecting you."

I repeated my question.

"Paeon."

My eyebrows lifted.

"Who?" Herakles asked.

The god appeared surprised briefly before he responded. "I am ... I *was* the personal physician to the gods and goddesses," he replied.

"A god doctor. I didn't know they needed such a thing."

Paeon didn't seem to know how to respond. I waved Herakles back a step, impatient to interrogate the prisoner before I put him to death for stealing a human body.

"But I didn't steal it."

I blinked. For several weeks, no one around me had been able to hear my thoughts. I was becoming lazy in guarding them.

"He was dying. I offered to heal him, if he volunteered to host me," Paeon explained.

Volunteered? I repeated skeptically. *Your kind has been usurping the rightful spirits and forms that belong to the humans!*

Paeon blinked – and his eyes turned from brilliant blue to dark brown.

"He's telling the truth." His voice became deeper, softer, and the sense of being near a god … changed. Became fainter. "My name is Kyros. I was beaten and left for dead by thieves after my food."

Was it possible for someone to be half-possessed?

Has he hurt you? Tried to eject you from your body? I asked warily.

"No. Never. We take turns, and he keeps my body healed and healthy, no matter what."

I studied him critically. The sickly sweet scent of rotting flesh was not present, and there was a healthy glow to this man's features. I had never heard of a god possessing a body and allowing the human soul to remain.

So you share? I asked.

"Yes. We both needed help."

I perked in interest. *Why would a god need help?*

Kyros shook his head. "He says I shouldn't have said that." He smiled, a strangely unguarded display. "We don't always agree. It's been a learning experience, having someone else in my head." He blinked – and his eyes turned blue. His expression became more guarded, and he sat up straighter.

I had never considered the possibility that a god could co-exist with a human soul inside one body. It left me even angrier with those deities I'd murdered. They didn't give the humans a chance to share but stole the bodies.

Why is your kind doing this? I demanded.

"I'm not here to discuss this," Paeon said firmly. "That is not for you to know."

Startled by his words, I stared at him. If my men doubted me, they at least kept their feelings quiet and obeyed my orders. Not even Herakles would challenge me. How had I forgotten the natural arrogance of a god? Perhaps because those I crossed paths with now were desperate and more likely to beg than allow their substantial egos to speak on their behalves.

"I have a message for you from someone you seek," Paeon said.

I waited.

"He says to stop seeking him. He says, you must focus on what is happening inside the city, because we are all in danger. He sent me as an olive branch. I am to serve you and help your soldiers heal from battle and sickness and any other malady that might befall them. When you are ready, I am authorized to broker a peace with you and work with you to defeat our common enemy."

I ignored his nonsense about a common enemy. I had one real enemy: the gods. Cleon was a very annoying obstacle standing between me and the military forces I needed to defeat the gods.

Zeus sent you? I asked.

"Yes. I'm here to help you."

"Or to spy on us," Herakles said. "There will be no truce after all your kind has done. Not ever."

"I see neither of you trust deities. It does not surprise me that you do not, strong one, but I am surprised by you, Your Majesty." Paeon studied me. "Have you forgotten your special bond with us? Have you forgotten how blessed your family is? Have you forgotten Zeus, the king over all the gods, *chose* to become your patron?"

His self-assurance, along with the light accusation I heard in his questions, blinded me with fury as few things in this world were capable of. I crossed to him and slapped him hard, hating the words flowing out of his mouth. He was so confident, so certain what his people did to my family was a *blessing* when we lived under a curse that enslaved us for all time in stone – an inescapable, living death meant to last for eternity! My soul, and the souls of everyone who came before me in the Bloodline, would never go to Hades, never find peace, because of this *blessing*!

Too angry to deal with this creature anymore, I whirled and left the barn. Herakles followed me. I walked blindly for several minutes before realizing where I was, at the edge of the forest.

Releasing a breath, I shook out my upper body without freeing up my chest, which felt like it was being squeezed by an angry god. My breathing was ragged and shallow. Tears of anger stung my eyes. My emotions had been bubbling just beneath the surface since we left DC.

Herakles was a silent presence behind me. He said nothing as I struggled to regain my composure. Gradually, as the humid night breeze swept by me, I was able to pull away from the hate and rage that filled me whenever I thought about my destiny and the fates of everyone in my Bloodline.

I had long ago decided the curse of the Bloodline would end with me. I would not perpetuate the curse the gods had placed upon my family, and I didn't intend to allow it to befall me, either.

I had to find Zeus. I didn't care what message Paeon carried from my patron god. I owed neither of them any loyalty.

Facing Herakles, I was about to motion to the notebook he kept at his waist when he held it out to me. I gave him a tight smile and wrote my latest orders in as few words as possible, aware of his literacy challenge.

Find Zeus. Do whatever it takes.

Handing it back, I watched him read it slowly. He nodded.

"If I may ask ..." His gaze dropped to the envelope sticking out of my waistband.

My anger softened. I missed my mother figure, Theodocia, and Herakles ached for the girl he had adopted, the next Oracle of Delphi, Alessandra. She had been taken prisoner by the Supreme Magistrate before he attempted to destroy my army and drove me out of the city. Theodocia stayed behind, coining the moniker DC Mama, as she led the insurgencies inside the city. My code name was NOVA Mama, referring to the local parlance for Northern Virginia.

Herakles and I were both suffering from not knowing the fates of our loved ones trapped in the city. Tugging the letter free, I scanned through it briefly. Theodocia rarely said much, in case the letters were intercepted before they reached me.

Our insurgency was not going well. She gave no specifics. At least, not to the naked eye. Because we both possessed the ability to speak to the gods, and were touched by the magic of more than one deity, we were able to communicate in code only a god could understand.

The message I alone was able to see was encoded in a drop of blood at the bottom of the letter. I touched it, and Theodocia's recorded message whispered into my mind.

I hope you are well, Phoibe. Know that I am safe, and so is Tommy, she said, referring to her son, the little boy who had become like a brother to me. *SISA is getting close to our location, and the military closing in on yours. Cleon's control of the Oracle grows. Artemis believes Alessandra is in great danger. Keep Herakles focused out there. I think it's time we start discussing a coordinated attack. If we wait until winter, we're going to face the additional challenge of snow and ice. If you can meet, when and where?*

The blood message ended. I shivered involuntarily. The eerie sound of her voice in my head, when she was so far away, left me momentarily distracted by my feelings. I missed her more than I ever thought I would. We'd been together for twelve years.

Shaking my head, I handed the bland letter to Herakles.

"She says Lyssa is doing good," Herakles said, relief crossing his features.

Theodocia's lie was safe with me. Herakles was unable to read the encoded message. I needed him here, as my trusted advisor, or I would reveal Alessandra's difficulties to him. Theodocia had been reporting that there was something wrong with the Oracle for the past few weeks without specifying what exactly the problem was. Either she didn't fully know, or it was of a nature she did not feel comfortable sharing, even through our encoded messages.

I wrote another short message for Herakles and handed the notebook to him.

"Safe place to meet near DC?" he asked. "Your Majesty, I don't think there is such a thing right now."

I lifted my chin.

He smiled. "But I'll find one. You want to meet with DC Mama?"

I nodded.

"Then I will make it happen." He returned the letter to me. "I know and agree with your position on deities stealing human bodies. But I feel we can use Paeon, and I grow weary of the nightly wakes. If you will agree to let him care for our sick and injured, I will ensure he stays bound and guarded at all times."

I studied Herakles. He was never arrogant or forceful. He was always honest, another trait we did not share. At times, I needed his perspective, when my own was frustrated. My instinct was to murder Paeon this night, but Herakles' gentle argument held a ring of truth I wasn't able to ignore. If we continued to lose soldiers to bad water and on missions to find food, we would have no one left to attack the protected zone and take the city.

I nodded once to give my permission, in spite of my reservations. I would keep an eye on Paeon, too, and ensure he wasn't masking his real intention in being here.

"You need rest," Herakles advised.

I raised both eyebrows, unaccustomed to being told what to do, even if he often said those very words.

"Queen or Oracle, I know that look." The skin around his eyes crinkled with warmth. "You may not like to hear it, but it is true. I am not sending you to bed without your dinner. I am advising you that you have not slept in two days, and you are as mortal as I am. Take it how you will." He ended his speech with a deferential bow of his head.

My temperament was less befitting my position than normal. I'd reached out of anger to Paeon when normally I was capable of calmness in any situation.

Nodding in reluctant acquiescence, I turned away from my trusted advisor and returned to the headquarters building. My quarters consisted of a private manager's office converted into a small bedroom with simple necessities: a bed, box of clothing, a chair and desk, and my own private bathroom with a shower installed by the engineers in my army.

Stepping into the quiet room, the tension in my shoulders and neck began to release. My accommodations were plain but comfortable.

Leery of what nightmares awaited me if I dared sleep, I opted for a shower to scrub the blood off my skin. Hot water trickled over me, and I sighed deeply. My mind was on Theodocia's hidden message, and I closed my eyes.

There was another reason I approved of her idea of attacking by winter, another reason for hating Lantos. Another reason my temper was short, and I was afraid to sleep, in case I missed the opportunity to locate Zeus before it was too late.

I allowed the water to wash away all my worries, to cleanse my skin and soothe my mind. Recent developments of a personal nature led me to believe I was not likely to live long past the start of the New Year, several months away.

FOUR

GROTESQUE PRINCE

A FEW SECONDS before the fire of transformation flew through my body, I dropped to the ground from my perch in a branch in the massive olive tree overlooking a beach. The first rays of dawn crested the horizon as I changed from monster into man.

"I'm still waiting," I whispered.

With my challenge of turning into a monster at night, I'd had to select my transportation across the ocean carefully, choosing the kind of companions who didn't ask questions once enough money was exchanged. My trip in total took two weeks to reach this point, and I'd spent the rest of my time searching every beach within kilometers.

The nearest village to this part of the coast was surrounded by a handmade moat. While peaceful, the towns and cities I had encountered thus far on my journey rarely welcomed strangers. I could think of dozens of reasons, ranging from limited food stores to the fear of possession, a reality I had initially chalked up to paranoia, until I met the first god in human form. I passed civilization by without stopping. I traveled half by night, half by day, hunted for food at night in my monster form and feared neither man nor god.

My progress was slower than I liked, though generally unimpeded by anyone. But, after weeks of searching, I had lost any real hope of finding the plaque Artemis had tasked me to recover or of running into any god who might assist me.

"Please. Just let me go," came a wan voice from the base of the tree where I'd spent the night.

I glanced at the rotting body of the teenage boy without a drop of pity. The god possessing the youth had identified himself as Cyamites, a minor terra god, and had made the lethal mistake of crossing my path in search of a new host several days ago.

"When you pass my message to the goddess I seek, I might consider it," I replied. "I know you all can communicate tele-pathically."

"I've told you every day since you found me. She will not answer me."

"Then you will not live."

"I have never harmed a human before I was forced to. Look at all I've done for this world," the god pleaded. "You can't let me die here, like this!"

"The world will survive without the god of beans," I replied, amused.

Cyamites sighed. His body had disintegrated to the point he could barely move, which left me free to explore without worrying about the god wandering off to seize someone else's body.

I strode from the orchard, neglected and weedy, across a narrow, dirt road to the beach. It had seemed much larger when I was young, four thousand years ago. The stretch of sand ran for a kilometer along the brilliant, blue green Aegean Sea and was capped on either side by jagged rocks. Over the past few weeks, since arriving, I had used my human brain and my beast strength to alternately inspect and then tear up every inch of beach in the hopes of finding the elusive plaque Artemis had sent me around the world to find.

The sea breeze ruffled my hair, and I stood, listening to the sounds of the waves rushing up the beach. I was at a loss as to what to do next. Every day I remained here, I placed the woman I cared about in more danger by leaving her alone to face the political madhouse that was DC. I had faith Alessandra could handle herself, especially when she possessed the powers of a goddess, and my most trusted friend, Lantos, was there to shield her from others if needed. It was more of an instinct that had been needling me. I kept seeing her face in my thoughts and dreams, and she was distraught every time.

I hadn't been able to shake the sense something was wrong. Alessandra hadn't used our connection to summon me. Even so, I should have been able to *feel* her presence in my soul, as I had since we became reacquainted several weeks ago.

"I have to be missing something," I murmured and began to pace along the beach. I was not the kind of person who overlooked any detail. Ever. But the idea that I sought wasn't here, and I'd been sent away out of some unknown motivation by a fickle goddess, left me furious with myself as well as with her.

Half an hour passed. The sun perched on the horizon, and I grew impatient. Returning to the olive tree I had adopted as my temporary home, I sat on a boulder nearby, upwind, so I didn't have to smell the rotting god seated at the tree's base.

"If you'd tell me what we're doing here, maybe I could help," Cyamites said, not for the first time.

"Unless you were on this beach four thousand years ago, there's nothing you can do to help me."

"Well that's simple. This beach didn't exist four thousand years ago. No one was here."

I glanced at the god and then back. "I was here."

"I planted these olive trees ten thousand years ago. They stretched for another two hundred meters at that time. The sea has swallowed the beach that used to be here."

My eyes went to the sea. I hadn't considered this possibility. "You're saying the beach I remember is underwater?" I stood. "You couldn't tell me this several days ago?"

Cyamites was quiet.

I looked at the god. Cyamites' eyes were open and blank, and his body was limp.

Had he even revealed this information to me, or had someone else?

For a moment, the timing struck me as odd. Artemis was known to work in mysterious ways. Had she planted Cyamites here to guide me? If so, why hadn't the god of beans told me this information earlier?

Because gods never stop playing their games, even on their deathbeds.

I would never know the truth, and obsessing over what exactly just happened wouldn't help me.

I left the corpse and strode onto the beach, stopping only when my feet hit the water. I gazed two hundred meters out and judged the water to be somewhere around ten meters deep. As a human, I was stronger than most and faster than everyone. But as a beast, I had ten times the strength of the strongest human. I could pierce the water and reach the sand at its depths with little effort in my monster form.

Restless to find the plaque, and also aware of how much easier it would be in my secondary form, I relented and sat higher up on the beach, prepared to watch the waves all day until the sun set.

The morning became warm quickly. Fortunately, the cool sea breeze prevented me from needing to leave my spot for shade. I'd created a routine since arriving and understood when the hottest points of the day were, when the tides intruded upon my ability to search the beaches, and the rhythm of Hesperides and Aurora.

As I sat, I thought about the last time I had been to this part of the world, when I ruled a vast kingdom and spent most of my waking days on battlefields. Crowned the head of the armies at the age of fourteen, I had left my comfortable palace near the sea the day following my coronation and never returned. The curse of the Bloodline befell me at the age of seventeen, and I had been frozen in stone as a temple guardian for four thousand years, until Alessandra awoke me.

Alessandra wasn't the only person occupying my thoughts. I had left DC reluctantly, on the orders of a goddess I had sworn my life to on this very beach. I left behind the temple guardians – thousands of members of the sacred, royal Greek Bloodline waiting for me to rescue them, and the sole living heiress to the Bloodline, the Silent Queen. The first and only grotesque to be re-animated, it was my responsibility to save the others. They were my family, my predecessors and successors, and I would rescue them from the hell they all endured as immortal stone, sentient statues.

At least I saved one of my descendants, I thought, mind on Phoibe. The Silent Queen had followed the instructions I gave her when she was six. As long as she never spoke the invocation, and never reproduced, she would not fall prey to the Bloodline's curse.

Alessandra was the key. If she had saved me, she could save everyone else.

Deep in thought, my beast senses picked up on the man and animals approaching long before I acknowledged them with a direct look. I didn't feel the presence of a god, indicating the elderly man walking with a cane was human. With him were three large dogs.

The moment the canines caught wind of me, all three raced down the beach towards him. As the alpha of all predators, I was accustomed to other hunter species reacting with excitement and prey fleeing at the sight of me.

"Calm down," I told the dogs as they neared. They obeyed, to an extent. I was soon surrounded by canines with wagging tales. They licked and rubbed up against me, and I reached out to pat the head of the dog burrowing under my leg.

Their master took more time to reach me. Sizing him up through my peripheral, I waited for the old man to come within earshot.

"It's not safe for you out here," I said in flawless Greek. "Shouldn't you be in hiding with the others?"

"I might ask you the same," the old man said and paused, leaning heavily on his cane.

"I am far scarier than anything I might run into," I said with a smile. "You should take that into account."

"My dogs favor you. They are good judges of character."

The truth was much more difficult to explain to a stranger. The man lowered himself carefully to the beach and sat with a sigh. One of his dogs joined him and licked his face. With close-cropped white hair, large, dark brown eyes, and leathery olive skin, the elderly man was handsome despite his age.

"What brings you here?" he asked.

"I'm not sure I know," I answered. "It wouldn't make sense to you anyway."

"I've seen a lot in my time. Try me."

You haven't seen four thousand years. I'm the old man here, I responded silently.

When I didn't speak, my visitor seemed to take the hint. "I'll be on my way," said the elderly man. "Do you need a place to stay or are you passing through?"

"I don't know that either," I replied.

The old man climbed to his feet with effort and steadied himself with his cane. "Well, I live around the bend." He pointed past the rocks on the north side of the beach. "If night falls, and you need shelter, we will welcome you."

"Thank you." I didn't take my eyes off the sea. It wasn't likely a mere human could help me, and I was grateful for the solitude while I waited. Giving the dog sprawled on the ground a final pat, I draped my arms over my knees.

The old man whistled, and his dogs raced after him. Aware of their progress with my beast senses, I didn't have to watch them to track their movements.

Before they reached the road, I sensed something was wrong. Twisting, I saw the man sprawled on the ground. His dogs were standing over him, one whining and another licking the back of his neck.

One person's life wasn't much of a concern to me, when I

already had too many people to save as it was. The butcher I'd been as the head of SISA, before I rediscovered my memories, wouldn't have cared for the fate of a million humans, let alone someone who was far beyond his prime. Likewise, the prince I had been four thousand years ago would have viewed the old man's visit as an inconvenience.

But I wasn't either of those people anymore. I wasn't a monster. I wasn't a prince. I was something in between, or perhaps, someone new, and I didn't really know what that was.

After a pause, I stood. I didn't fully understand what drew me to consider helping, when kindness had never been a trait of mine in any of my lifetimes. Unable to explain my reaction, I nonetheless never hesitated to act once I made a decision, and trotted across the sand to the old man struggling to stand.

I shooed the dogs away and knelt. "Are you well?" I asked.

"I am old," was the response. Pain was in the old man's voice. "Sometimes the sand upsets my joints."

I helped him sit then took his arm to help him stand. The old man leaned heavily against me as he climbed to his feet.

"Thank you," he murmured. He took a step – and collapsed, or would have, if I didn't catch him.

"Walking doesn't suit you today," I said. Without waiting for an invitation to help, I bent and swept the old man up into my arms. The elderly gentleman was light. His baggy clothing hid his frailness well. "Around the bend, you say?"

"Yes." The old man pointed. "I'll have you know my pride does not agree with being carried." He laughed hoarsely.

I had no response, because I couldn't understand my willingness to help anymore than I could unravel the mystery of what I was doing halfway around the world when I needed to be in DC.

"What is your name?" the old man peered up at me.

Had I thought his eyes dark brown? In the direct sunlight, they were closer to the hue of whiskey.

"Adonis."

"Ah. Your parents named you well. Very fitting to be named after the god of beauty."

"It's just a name," I replied, aware of how false my words rang when I'd traveled around the world for the sake of a name. "And you are?"

"Menelaus."

"I hope you had better luck in your life with women than the king you were named after."

Menelaus chuckled. "Unfortunately, I did not."

"I'm sorry to hear it. But maybe you're better off without a woman in your life."

"You've known the pain of loving a woman, I take it?" Menelaus was grinning, revealing the gaps in his teeth.

"I don't know," I replied, unsettled by the question but more so by my quickening pulse whenever I thought of Alessandra. What I wanted, and what I sometimes felt, had no place in a world as dangerous as mine. I was a monster posing as a human, a danger to everyone around me.

"What *do* you know, boy?" Menelaus challenged.

"Only that I'm lost."

"There's something to be said for knowing when you don't know anything, I suppose."

I ignored him. As I walked along the road, carrying the man easily, I began to doubt his mind. I had been up and down the coast multiple times in man and beast form, and never noticed this cottage of which he spoke.

The dogs ran around us, at times bounding quite a distance ahead and at times darting behind us to pursue rodents.

We rounded the bend, and I spotted the small cottage overlooking the sea. My step slowed. How had I missed this place?

Had I missed it?

"You're far from the village," I observed. "Aren't you afraid of the thieves, wild animals, and gods?"

"I've lived my life. If one of them comes for me, so be it,"

Menelaus replied. "This is my home. I have no desire to leave. Besides, this place is said to be enchanted. A temple of Apollo once stood here. I am safe."

His explanation did little to quell my curiosity. I approached the front door and shifted the man so I could open it. The door wasn't locked, and I withheld my rebuke. It was one thing to risk the dangers prevalent in the world and quite another to *dare* them to enter. Enchanted or not, he needed to use some common sense.

I nudged the door open and examined the three-room cottage quickly. Menelaus owned few possessions. The cottage contained minimal furniture, fit for one occupant, few decorations and no pictures anywhere. It was neat and clean despite the three dogs who circled the living space and promptly piled onto the couch acting as the only sitting space, aside from a rocking chair.

I went to the bedroom off the main room and carefully set Menelaus down. I straightened and debated leaving. He shifted with a pain-filled grimace. With nothing left to do this day, except wait on the beach, I sat on the edge of the bed. His eyes were dark again in the relative shadows of the house. I noted the change without understanding why it occurred.

"What hurts?" I asked.

"My knee." Menelaus bent to pull up the leg of his pants. "Doesn't look too bad."

I frowned and reached out to straighten the man's leg. The kneecap was off to one side, and the bony man's knee was swollen thicker than his thigh.

"It's bad," I said.

"You a doctor?" Menelaus squinted at me.

"Not exactly." As the head of the SISA interrogation program, I knew as much about anatomy as most doctors for the purpose of learning how to manipulate or otherwise cause pain to the human body. I also recognized the extent of damage done, in order to gauge how much more the person could stand or how much more pressure was necessary for the desired results.

Menelaus didn't need to know anything other than I was aware of how badly he was hurt.

I rose. "I'll get some ice," I said.

"I wouldn't want to keep you from the beach."

I said nothing. I crossed to the tiny kitchen and the fridge that came up only to my shoulder. I wrapped ice in a towel from the sink and returned to Menelaus.

"I have pain pills in the bathroom," the old man said and accepted the ice.

I retrieved the bottle and a glass of water. The knee looked bad enough for a trip to the hospital, which wasn't an option since the Holy Wars destroyed most medical centers.

One of the dogs scratched at the front door. I opened it to let him out then stepped into the late morning. I could understand why Menelaus wasn't interested in giving up his home. From this perch on the rocks, the sea stretched out in three directions. In the far distance was the smudge of land on the horizon. The rocking of waves against the base of the slope below was peaceful, and the sea air was cool.

I stood at the top of the shallow cliff running ten meters down to the sea and breathed in deeply. I had come too far to return without finding what I sought. Isolated here across the world, I had no access to the internet or television to learn what was happening in DC. Restless, I tried to recall some details of my past that might aid me in finding the plaque Artemis sent me to find.

I circled the cottage to discover a small vegetable, herb, and fruit garden on the other side. The dog trotted back inside, and I followed.

"Menelaus, I'm going back to ..." I trailed off as I reached the door to the old man's bedroom.

Menelaus was sound asleep. One of his dogs had leapt onto the bed and knocked the ice pack off.

I straightened it and lingered. How had someone this old, and in this shape, survived out here on his own for five years? My guardian instincts stirred. As the warden of a kingdom, and a protector for the gods' temples, I had spent most of my life in the role of protector. If ever anyone needed a guardian, it was the feeble old man snoring peacefully in his bed.

I closed the door to the bedroom and went to the living area. It was too cramped for my preference, so I propped the front door open and went to sit on the cliff overlooking the ocean. Hours stretched between now and when dusk fell and I could dive beneath the surface of the sea to search for the ruins of a four thousand year old kingdom.

One of Menelaus' dogs joined me, and I sat in silence, brooding and still, guarding the sleeping stranger as I had the temple of Artemis long ago.

"Anytime, Artemis," I whispered. "We both know what's at stake if I don't return soon."

The sounds of waves crashing into the cliff were my only response. When I became too drowsy to remain seated much longer, I stretched out onto my back to sleep.

I slept until it was almost dusk, at which time I rose and went into the house. Menelaus slumbered deeply. I turned on the lights for the old man, in case he awoke later, then left the house. Peeling off my clothing, I shivered as the chilly evening breeze grazed my skin.

I closed my eyes and let the fire of transformation take me, contorting my body into that of a grotesque. My senses came to life with the night, and I unfurled my long wings to stretch them before I leapt into the air. Powerful strokes sent me skyward and warmed the muscles of my shoulder and back. I circled Menelaus' cottage several times, checking the area for anyone or anything that posed a threat to the incapacitated old man, before I turned in the direction of the nearby beach.

I soared over the beach and outward. Folding my wings, I dived downward, beneath the surface of the sea. My beast eyes were able to see in the dark water, and my senses far better attuned to my surroundings, even underwater, than they were as a human. Unaffected by the cold water, I dived downward. My tail and powerful legs propelled me to the bottom of the sea in seconds, and I caught myself against the soft sand with my hands.

I began to search with all my sense for anomalies in the sand that might be ruins of the kingdom I once ruled. The sandy floor of the sea was bare, aside from a few clumps of corals and rocks. I swam from object to object, surfacing every few minutes for a new breath of air.

I searched until hunger seized control of my beast body. Only then did I leave the water to hunt for dinner.

By dawn, I'd fed and spent another two hours searching the sea floor.

No remnants of any human settlement, ancient or modern, remained beneath the sea.

Disappointed, I returned to Menelaus' cottage and transformed into my human form again. Dressing, I watched the sunrise, let the dogs out, and settled onto my belly for a nap. My thoughts fluttered between the world I'd left behind and the frustration of being no closer to finding the great secret Artemis sent me here to uncover.

The sound of breaking glass caused me to snap awake when the warm sun was directly overhead, and I sat up, body tense and senses alert.

"Menelaus?" I called into the cottage as I pushed the door open.

The old man was on the ground of the doorway to his bathroom, as if he'd made an attempt to walk out of the restroom and crashed to the ground. One of his hands was bloodied from the tumbler he'd been carrying, and shards of glass glittered on the floor around him.

I hurried to him and picked him up. I dusted off the glass from his body before replacing him on the bed.

"I thought you'd be gone," Menelaus said with a smile. "Or do you not know where to go, either?"

I wrapped the dishtowel that had contained the ice the night before around Menelaus' hand to stop the bleeding. For reasons I could not explain, Menelaus' words troubled me.

"I'm looking for something that may not exist," I said.

"And you think it's here?"

"Yes."

"I've lived here my whole life. What is it you seek?" Menelaus asked.

I hesitated. "A relic of a bygone era."

"Are you a treasure hunter?"

"No. This thing is of no value to anyone but me."

Menelaus was quiet. I glanced at him.

"Could I trouble you for fruit?" Menelaus asked. "And water. I don't trust my leg to carry me to the kitchen."

I went to the kitchen and lopped off a chunk of bread, slathered it with honey, then sliced up figs and apples for the old man.

"Do you cook your own bread?" I asked, noting the items in the kitchen that seemed out of place.

"One of the residents of the village takes pity on me and brings me cured meat for the dogs and bread for me once a week," Menelaus answered. "I trade him for herbs and vegetables from my garden."

I brought the breakfast and a glass of water to the old man before I returned to the kitchen to feed the expectant dogs. I then began to sweep up the glass sparkling on the floor.

"If it is not treasure you seek, what is it?" Menelaus asked between mouthfuls.

"An engraved stone containing an epithet of an ancient prince. I think it's buried beneath the sand offshore a short distance."

"Then it's gone."

I paused in my cleaning and looked at the old man.

"Typhoons," Menelaus explained. "Several natural disasters swept everything off the sea floor and sent what was there either deep into the ocean or somewhere far from the coast. Before the world ended five years ago, college professors tried to find ruins and relics off the coast and concluded nothing remained."

I absorbed the words as I might a blow. For a long moment, I couldn't speak. Why had Artemis sent me here, if what I sought didn't exist? How was I ever to understand why my name was important enough that it was the one detail of my past I was unable to remember?

"With everything that's happened in the world today, how can you be searching for a museum piece?" Menelaus asked, brow furrowed. "It is worth nothing, if you try to sell it. The world does not value its past as it once did."

I don't know. I returned to my task of sweeping up the broken glass.

"Why is this relic so important to you that you came so far?"

"How do you know how far I've come?" I asked.

"You stand out. You aren't from around here." There was warmth in Menelaus' voice.

"It doesn't matter anymore."

"Does it have anything to do with why you sprout wings and fly?"

I looked up sharply. His eyes were whiskey-hued once more. The subtle change wasn't caused by light, because he was seated facing away from the sunlight spilling through the windows.

"My bladder is old, too. I woke up and saw you transform into a ... thing," Menelaus said. "I've seen a lot in my years. That was one of the most intriguing. You are strangely beautiful, for such an ugly thing."

I studied him, uncertain how anyone could witness my transformation firsthand and react this calmly. "You are not afraid?" I asked.

"I am too old to fear anything anymore," Menelaus said. "If you wanted to eat me, you would have already, wouldn't you?"

The corner of my lips lifted in a half smile. "Yeah."

"I've grown wise." Menelaus tapped his temple. "I have always had an affinity for animals and hunting. Are you a man who transforms into a beast, or a beast who becomes a man?"

"I'm not sure there's a difference." I returned to my cleaning and finished checking the floor for any shards of glass I missed. "I am both at all times, no matter what I appear to be."

Menelaus was quiet, eating his breakfast. I straightened the kitchen, frustrated further by the information about the ruins offshore. I began to think Artemis had forced me away from DC for nefarious reasons. She had called in the oath I gave as a prince, but perhaps, I should not have honored it.

I didn't understand who I was, and what role I played, in the bigger scheme of things. Alessandra's birth was prophecy, and every other player in the ring with her had a part to play. I was a wild card, more so after I regained my memories and began to realize I didn't belong in this time or this place at all. I had hoped the discovery of my name would shed light on my purpose or at least, complete the puzzle of who I had been in my past in the hopes I might learn who I could become.

"Will you leave, now that you know your search is over?" Menelaus asked when he finished eating.

"I should," I replied.

"If you stay until I can care for myself, I will send you away with my infamous dried fish."

No reward will make up for the latest slight by a deity. I preferred raw meat anyway. I glanced at the old man's exposed knee. The swelling was half what it had been. "I can stay a couple of days but no more. It's a long journey to where I must go."

"I will be grateful for the company, and so will the boys." The skin around Menelaus' eyes – which were dark brown once more – crinkled when he glanced towards his pets.

I didn't sense a god, as I had when I met Cyamites, but something about Menelaus was ... different. I couldn't pinpoint what.

"What's it like to fly?"

"Pure freedom," I said without hesitation.

Menelaus sighed. "I hope your bones never give out on you, and you can fly forever."

"So do I," I answered. *But I'm almost certain the world will end before I have a chance to grow old.*

"Since you are here to help, can you bring in the basket of fruit in the garden?" Menelaus asked.

I replaced the broom and left for the garden. The brilliant blue-green sea caught my attention again, and I sought to feel my connection to Alessandra.

It wasn't there. Something had to be wrong.

I couldn't remain here much longer, whether or not I found what I sought.

FIVE

ALESSANDRA

"COME BACK, LYSSA."

With those three words, the vision shattered. The ground felt like it dropped out from beneath my feet. The scenes playing out before me broke and fizzled away, out of existence. The answers had been here. All of them. Everything I needed to know had been right in front of me.

Unlike the first, this premonition was more fragile than a dream. I tried to force my mind to remember one tiny fragment of everything I'd seen. Colors, faces, and places – they slid through my hands and thoughts like fine sand and poured into the void far below me.

No, no, no! I was screaming and helpless as I fell out of the vision, grasping at whispers. I had to remember something ... anything ...

Adonis. His face flashed before he, too, disappeared into the abyss.

My eyes flew open, and I sat up before I registered where I was. Voices swirled in my thoughts, the same ones I'd been hearing since Lantos gave the deities the ability to speak to me. It was rare when I could actually understand them, but for a moment, I had been addressing them. I had looked into the past, present, future – and I'd understood *everything*. Everything that ever had been. Everything that ever was. Everything that ever would be.

And now, everything was gone, except for the lingering image of Adonis.

I uttered the foulest curse Herakles had ever taught me and flung off my bedding. My head throbbed, and I flinched when the bottoms of my feet touched the cold marble floor. My eyes went up automatically to the wall with purple names scrawled across it.

At once, my mind quieted. No matter what I felt or thought upon entering my room, the memorial wall distilled it all, grounded me, and turned my focus towards solid resolve.

Two emotions settled into me as I gazed at the names on the wall. The first, regret, was mine. The second, satisfaction, emanated from the burr that was Cleon in my mind.

I whirled, expecting to find him in my room.

He was nowhere to be seen – but Leandra and Niko were standing beside the seated Dr. Khan, Cleon's personal physician who patched me up from time to time. The three of them displayed different expressions, but their silence and stillness was enough to tell me all of them were surprised.

"How are you feeling?" Dr. Khan was the first to speak. The slender woman of Middle Eastern background stood and approached me, a stethoscope draped around her neck.

"Fine, I guess," I replied and glanced down. My body moved well, and I experienced no pain, which made the physician's presence unwarranted. My stomach growled, and I patted it. "Why? What happened?"

"The Supreme Magistrate's monkey used too much tranquilizer on you," Leandra replied icily with a sharp look at Niko.

"I used the same amount as usual. This *episode* was something entirely different," Niko replied calmly. "Something to do with her powers."

"Don't be ridiculous," Leandra snapped and trailed Dr. Khan towards me.

"So what's going on?" I asked, puzzled. "Niko tranqs me all the time. I never had a welcome home party waiting for me when I woke up."

"Niko's use of animal tranquilizers on a young woman is another matter entirely." Dr. Khan gave the former mercenary a look of disapproval before her concerned gaze returned to me. "Whatever happened, you've been asleep for three days."

"That explains being hungry," I murmured. I thought back to the last thing I remembered and frowned.

Cleon had been murdering the Ambassador of Greece when Niko tranquilized me. A sense of euphoria – distinctly not mine – floated through me as I recalled the man's swollen face. I instinctively reached to the scar at the back of my head, where the chip was implanted into my brain.

Before, I'd been aware of Cleon being in my head without really feeling him. I didn't like the idea of experiencing his emotions in response to *my* memories any more than I wanted him using my power.

"I need to do a quick exam," Dr. Khan said. "Would you like to sit down?"

With a shrug, I went to the chaise in the bay window, across the room from my audience. The physician took my pulse then checked my pupils, heart, reflexes and lungs.

"I'm not seeing anything of concern," she said.

"I don't feel right," I said. "But it has nothing to do with my body or the tranquilizers."

"Thank you," Niko growled.

"What doesn't feel right?" Dr. Khan asked.

"My involuntary brain surgery." I rubbed the spot again. "Something is different."

"I'd like to get you in for a CAT scan."

"No," Niko responded.

She pursed her lips before twisting to face him. "If the chip has moved, or is damaging her spinal cord or other parts of her brain, we need to know."

"No."

I wasn't the only one resenting Niko in that moment. Dr. Khan made no more objections. She stood. "I'm done here," she said. "Whatever happened, I can't explain it, but she seems fine. I would advise – again – very strongly against using tranquilizers on her, Niko. They were designed to bring down a rhino or elephant, never to be used on humans."

Elephant?

Cleon's emotion was one of amusement.

Agitated to hear Niko had been using such powerful sedatives on me, I wasn't surprised when he pointed to the door in response to Dr. Khan's concern.

The physician left, and Niko studied me. No part of me was about to tell him I had begun having visions. If I was truly asleep for three days, and I couldn't recall anything, it would sound foolish to admit it anyway.

"I'll let Cleon know you're well enough to return to your duties," Niko said. He walked slowly to the door.

"He already knows," I replied. "Whatever you all did to me, it's getting worse."

He said nothing and left.

No sooner had the door closed than Leandra was at my side, features tight. "What did you see?" she asked and sank onto the chaise beside me.

Cleon's interest piqued as well.

"Nothing. Everything." I wiped my face, frustrated. "I forgot it all as I was waking up."

"You forgot three days worth of visions?"

"Yeah."

She released a breath.

"I can feel Cleon in my head," I told her. "And he's aware of everything I'm doing and going through."

Surprise crossed her pretty features. "Everything?"

"I think so. I can feel his emotions."

"Then you should be careful of discussing anything you don't want him to find out," Leandra advised. Her surprise turned to alarm, and the meaning behind her words shot through us both.

We couldn't talk as we used to – about Theodocia or the insurgency or even the visions, if I didn't want him to find out. If I'd struggled before, how was I going to deal with him now, when he had insight into everything I did or said?

"I'll bring you some lunch," Leandra said and rose. She strode to the door and left, leaving me alone with my scary thoughts.

Surely there had to be something I could do that Cleon wouldn't see. Could he read my mind?

I sensed he didn't yet have this capability, or his emotions responding to what I thought of him and my situation would probably be much more apparent. He had no problems seeing what I did, to include the images of memories that popped up in my head. Could I assume he was aware of only pictures, not thoughts?

I didn't like this development at all.

My eyes fell to the names on the wall again. His positive emotion about the event that cemented his position at the top – and left over three thousand people dead – repulsed me.

At the familiar sound of shuffling, I looked around for the animated teddy bear from my past that Adonis had left with me.

"Mrs. Nettles?" I called softly.

The rustling came from beneath the chaise. I dropped to my knees and plucked the animal – a cross between a teddy bear and a cat I had created when I was five – from beneath the chaise.

Awake, she observed.

"I am," I replied. "Were you hiding?"

She nodded, tugging at one of her oversized ears with her stubby arms. She purred like a cat and had the appearance of a stuffed koala bear. Whenever I saw her, I smiled, recalling when I'd brought her to life. Adonis had protected and cared for her for twelve years before she found her way back to me.

As a child, I'd understood more about how to use my power than I did now. Or maybe ... I played with it, without the fear of unleashing the apocalypse.

"When I was little, I used to do amazing things, didn't I?" I asked her.

She nodded again.

Cleon was intrigued.

I didn't like the idea of him knowing what I was doing and being aware of how strong I became. But I didn't see much of a choice, either. Whenever I started to back away from what I was supposed to be, the memorial wall reminded me of what happened if Cleon or I unleashed my power. The image of the world ending in flame and darkness challenged my desire to obey Cecelia and repress my power. I tried that approach for weeks, and it clearly didn't work. Cleon was growing stronger, and I had to stay ahead somehow.

With unlimited power at my fingertips, I could also stop the apocalypse, if I understood better how to manage my power. Repressing it wasn't going to give me that edge.

I set Mrs. Nettles down on the chaise and gazed around me at the ribbons hovering above and around the objects in my room. Mnemosyne, the goddess of memory, had explained to me in a vision of my past that I was able to create and destroy and manipulate the fabric of reality. I didn't understand what that meant exactly, or how I could use my power without the kind of mass destruction I'd already exacted upon the city. Leandra and I had discovered I could animate objects better when I wasn't thinking about them too hard, when my mind was either distracted or under the influence of alcohol.

Cecelia had instructed me about how to pay attention to the signs my magic was about to fly free of me, so I could stop from unintentional creation. The more I used it, the more it grew, which was bad, if I wanted to protect those around me.

As I stood in my room, contemplating how to stop the fate I'd seen, I began to think I suffered not from a lack of power, but a lack of imagination. I didn't know what I was supposed to do or how I should try to do it. Herakles had taught me to be part of my world, to be aware of my physical self and capabilities at all times. He valued practicality over imagination, and I'd adapted his way of thinking.

What if I had to supplement what I'd been taught to believe about the world my whole life with something less tangible?

You aren't ready yet to handle what comes. You MUST use your power in order to grow it. The voice originated from Mrs. Nettles. I had heard it once before, so I knew it didn't belong to my animated stuffed animal but to the goddess temporarily possessing her. *Do not view what's before you as parts in a puzzle, but as a whole.*

I glanced towards the teddy bear sitting on the chaise, watching me. I didn't want to say her name aloud, in case Cleon caught on.

"I don't understand," I replied, heart quickening at the thought of speaking directly to this goddess, one of the two deities I was raised to respect and worship.

You would handle a piece of pie differently than you would a whole pie, wouldn't you?

In my very limited interactions with gods and those touched by them, I'd discovered the divine to have a very unusual speech pattern. They didn't seem to understand how to say something directly and spoke in circles. Even Adonis shared this trait most of the times, leaving me floundering in the space between what was spoken and what he intended.

When you destroyed the temple and the buildings, you didn't manipulate them one by one, did you? She tried again.

"No," I said aloud. I had grabbed the ribbons of everything for a five-block radius then crushed them.

See the whole, not the parts.

"But ... I don't want to use my power. What if I hurt someone?"

Your power can do only what you will it to. If you use it for good, then it will hurt no one.

"That's kind of the opposite of what Cecelia says," I hedged. "I've hurt enough people."

Do you trust me? Artemis asked.

My pulse raced.

I have protected you your entire life. I stood beside your mother when she gave birth to you, and I will be with you when you defeat your enemies.

My face felt hot. Even the priests who raised me – and Herakles – had always assured me Artemis was the one goddess we all could trust, because she wanted what was best for humanity.

"Yes," I said. "I trust you. I'll do as you ask." Even if it scared me. "How do I see the whole? I'm standing in the middle of the pie."

Shift outside of it.

I was about to ask how in Hades it was possible to shift outside of *reality* when the door opened. Leandra carried a tray loaded with food, and I glanced at Mrs. Nettles then back. The stuffed animal was shuffling towards one of the pillows on the chaise. She was obsessed with bright and soft things, and I sensed the goddess who spoke through her was gone.

"Most of your faves are here," Leandra said and set the food on the table..

I ignored her, distracted by the idea of how I was supposed to see the whole when I was in the middle of it. I closed my eyes and formed a picture of the room in my head, to include seeing Leandra and me. The scent of mac-n-cheese distracted me temporarily, and I breathed it in deeply, imagining a tub of it appearing in the middle of my room.

"I could eat a vat of that right about now," I murmured. Torn between my empty stomach and understanding the lesson Artemis was trying to teach me, I chose food.

"Really?" Leandra asked, hands on her hips. "You have the powers of a goddess, and you use it for *that*?"

Opening my eyes, I spotted the meter-tall tub of steaming mac-n-cheese in the middle of my room, where I'd seen it in my mind.

I started to laugh then stopped, uncertain what this meant. It was another unintentional creation. I had to get better about purposely using my abilities.

"You don't need that much pasta," Leandra lectured me. "You won't fit into your clothes if you eat it. Can you send it away?"

I'm not sure where it came from, I admitted silently. I tried to form the picture of my room in my head without closing my eyes and found it impossible while Leandra was moving around. So I closed my eyes again and imagined the room without the tub of pasta.

"Much better," Leandra said. "Now, come eat."

I had sent it away without knowing how. As with my first vision, I was too immersed to notice the details. But I swore I'd try it again later and pay attention to how exactly I could manifest anything seemingly out of thin air then send it back to wherever it came from.

"Does my power bother you?" I asked her and sat at the table.

"No."

"It bothers me. How can you be so calm?"

Leandra met my gaze briefly and then shrugged. I sensed she had a response but feared giving it when my mind was violated by Cleon. If I couldn't talk to my only confidante, life was going to become more difficult, very fast.

I ate in silence.

She left me alone, and I sat down on the chaise and closed my eyes.

This time, when I tried to zoom out on my room, I noticed how grainy everything appeared. It wasn't the crystal clear, high-density screen of a television but more like I was viewing the world through a thin veil or watching shows on a super old television in black and white. I was present yet apart. Uncertain how this would work, I pulled back into the corner farthest from my bed, until I could see my seated form and the names on the wall. The ribbons floating around everything were still visible despite the sense of being separated from the physical world.

Instead of mac-n-cheese, I decided I needed a chocolate fountain in the middle of my room. I caught the movements – subtle yet speedy. Ribbons from around the room sent fibers to the center of the room, where they coalesced and twisted into new ribbons to form a new object.

My power was to rearrange matter, not necessarily create it. On instinct, I stretched out with a ghostly, translucent hand and gathered up the ribbons over the fountain. Crushing them, the fountain disappeared, but the ribbons remained. Usually, I absorbed them, and this circumstance was no different.

Glancing down, I almost screamed when I saw myself. Translucent, my body was made of millions – billions? – of fibers in every shade of gray, white and black in existence. When I patted my thigh, the ribbons I had crushed disappeared into the myriad of fibers inside of me.

The reason I sensed and felt the rhythm of the world became clear. I was part of it, and it was part of me – literally. Creating and destroying were simple rearrangements of matter and energy. Which meant, in theory, if I could perform those tasks, I could also alter my world in any way I could dream of.

Scared by the thought of losing control, I reminded myself that Artemis had encouraged me. It was going to take me a while to trust myself, after the fear Cecelia had drilled into me about what went wrong, if I unleashed my magic.

"Artemis said it's okay," I said aloud.

I was about to think of what I wanted to try, when I became aware of the strange sense of not being alone. My instincts had been right about the stranger at the soiree the other night. I wasn't about to ignore my gut now, even when my rational side said it wasn't possible for someone to be here with me now.

I turned away from the room. The wall was behind me ... and not. The harder I stared at it, the more transparent it became, until I was able to see through it into the neighboring room. The guest bedroom was empty, but the presence remained.

I strode through the wall with fascination, walked through the neighboring bedroom, then through a small study in this wing before I passed through its walls, too, and paused in the grand foyer of the villa.

Cleon was present – twice. It took me a moment to realize what I was looking at. His solid form in black-and-white sat on a chair in the formal waiting area, while his in-color spirit stood nearby, gazing around in consternation. We were both the only things in color here. Unlike me, he was not made up of the fibers. He appeared more like a rock in the middle of a stream – solid whereas the magic of the world moved through and around me.

"What have you done?" he asked when he spotted me.

"I don't really know," I replied, frustrated he found me here, too.

"But you are doing this?"

"I believe so."

"We are both spirits," he observed. "How is it possible for you to displace us? Can we return to ourselves?"

"I imagine so," I replied. "I've never done this before."

Not again. Come. Back. Lyssa.

I was yanked from the foyer, through the study and guest bedroom, and back into my room fast enough to knock the air out of my lungs. Shaking off the sense of being pulled away, I focused on my surroundings until the veil was thin enough for me to see through.

Leandra was crouched beside me. Her fingertips were on my cheeks, and her hands glowed with magic of her own, a collection of blue fibers that swirled around her as she called me back again.

"Lyssa," she said.

My eyes snapped open, and I once again joined my reality. "I just had the weirdest experience," I breathed.

Relief that was not mine trickled through me, a sign Cleon had returned to his body as well. For a moment, I was seated in the foyer, gazing at the pillars flanking the grand space. Blinking, the image was replaced by Leandra's concerned face.

Was it just me, or did my connection to Cleon become stronger, the more I used my magic?

I opened my mouth to tell her everything, when she spoke first.

"Is it something you can discuss with your loyal, faithful servant?" Leandra asked pointedly.

"Cleon's here at the villa," I said.

"He is," she replied, eyebrows lifting. "He came to drop off your schedule of events for the next week."

"Because the most powerful man in the world just happens to drop by when he could send a servant."

"I'm sure he came to check up on you after your three day nap." Leandra stood. "I'll set out your clothing for your two o'clock."

I was curious about the abilities I was discovering yet leery as well. Cleon knew what I did, which was going to make it hard to plot how I was going to escape DC and find Herakles again. How did I defeat a man inside my head, let alone the apocalypse?

My headache remained. Leandra set out my clothing then took away the tray of leftover food. I changed, and thirty minutes later, I was in the gym with Niko. I settled into our sparring round without speaking. It was hard for me to believe I'd been out for three days, until I realized how rested my body was. I fought better than usual, probably because no part of me was achy or bruised from a previous session with Niko.

When we'd finished, I went to my corner to down water, breathing hard and tired.

"You going to tell me what's got you spooked?" the former mercenary with the keen eye asked.

Damn you, Niko.

"I'm not spooked," I retorted. "I'm not afraid of anything."

"Hmm."

Rolling my eyes at him, I ducked between the ropes and started away, not about to be cornered or tranquilized again.

"Someone wants to talk to you," he called after me.

I paused. "Who?"

"Come on."

He leapt down from the elevated ring and strode across the room, towards the men's locker rooms. The gym was ours this time of day, and I didn't hesitate to follow him in. Uncertain what to expect from someone as unpredictable as Niko, I was on guard when I stepped into the wide-open space.

A boy around the age of eleven or twelve sat on one of the benches, cell phone in hand. He glanced up with a smile as he caught sight of Niko.

"Tommy, this is Alessandra," Niko said in a clipped tone and then folded his arms across his chest. "My son has a unique ability."

I started to smile. "Theodocia's son," I said, recalling how shocked I'd been to learn the two of them procreated when we all first met. The mercenary cared for nothing in this world, except for the boy sitting in front of me. Suspecting it took a great deal for him to introduce anyone to Tommy, and that today was somehow special, I didn't say what I wanted to and sat by the boy instead.

"Hi Tommy," I said cheerfully.

"Hi." His eyes were identical to Niko's – bright green – while his caramel coloring was unmistakably Theodocia's. "I have a message for you."

"From ..."

"Thanatos."

I blinked, not certain I heard him correctly.

"He gets his ability to talk to gods from his mother," Niko said with a scowl, none too pleased.

"Wow. Okay." I studied Tommy. "Can you tell me in my head what the God of Death wants me to know?" I was not yet certain if Cleon could hear when someone spoke in my head and not about to risk getting the boy in front of me in trouble, if Cleon picked up on something he said aloud.

Anger trickled through me. Cleon wasn't happy with the request, which I was taking as a win for me.

Tommy tilted his head to the side. *Thanatos says to be careful when you tread into the realm of Hades.*

My mouth dropped open.

He says to stay on the other side of the curtain.

"Holy Zeus. I had no idea," I replied. *Is Hades angry?* I asked him telepathically.

Tommy shook his head. *He knows things aren't right. But Thanatos says he's moody, and if he decides he doesn't want you there, he will take you away.*

By the boy's smile, he either didn't understand what that meant, or he was as amused by death as his father was. I didn't know him well enough to figure it out. I had witnessed firsthand how lethal his mother and father were. That the God of Death spoke through their child seemed very fitting, given what I knew of the former couple.

"That's all," Tommy said.

The short message was intense. So Thanatos and Hades had their eyes on me. I was as willing to disappoint either of them as I was Adonis, and I didn't think the gods would take anything I did as well as the butcher who used to be in charge of SISA.

"Can I ask him one question?" I pressed.

Tommy nodded.

Why can I hear the deities in my head but not communicate with them?

Tommy tilted his head once more, as if listening, before he blinked and smiled. "He says because you aren't listening."

I rolled my eyes. "Sometimes they're so stubborn."

Tommy nodded, as if accustomed to the strangeness of gods. At his age, I was learning to track rabbits and other small prey in the forest, not talking to gods, though I wondered if I should have been doing the latter instead. Whenever I started to regret my upbringing, I thought of Herakles. My protector had done his best, and what he'd taught me had already kept me alive. I wasn't able to resent him, of all people, for being the only one who tried to prepare me for a life none of us were able to imagine.

Why are they even in my head? I asked.

"He says because they want to help you."

My eyebrows went up. The voices had claimed similar on the

night I destroyed part of DC, as well as asserting that I had been deceived about who my real enemies were.

Why were they lying to me, when the evidence of what they had done to humanity was so visible outside of the protected zone? Troubled, and feeling as if I were once again caught in a blind maze, I fell quiet.

At times, I sensed something else was going on without being able to identify what. How did I decipher what my instincts couldn't make out, either?

"Time's up," Niko said, clearly uncomfortable with me talking to his son. Was it *me* or his son's unusual knack for communicating with a god? The head of Cleon's armies, and my security detail, was not the spiritual type.

"Thank you, Tommy," I said and stood.

Niko led me out of the locker room and back into the gym. He gripped my arm as I passed him and turned me to face him. With the tension in his frame, and the tightness of his hand around my upper arm, I didn't need to hear his words to understand he wasn't pleased.

"Leave my son out of this," he told me. The protective edge in his voice was new, and I sensed it was present only where his son was concerned.

"I'm not placing him in any sort of danger," I replied. "But you have to know by now my life and my power are both out of my control. I can't cause him any harm, but I can't keep him safe either."

"Keeping him safe is my job."

"Niko, you can't fight what's coming. Only I can, and only if I have my mind as my own. Tommy's dead otherwise." The brazen, but true, statement was spoken out of frustration and out before I could censor myself. Then again, I was never really good at censoring myself in the first place. I didn't want Niko angry with me, but he also needed to know the truth.

Niko's jaw clenched, and fire flashed in his gaze.

Cleon was displeased to the point of angry again, and I had the brief satisfaction of knowing how angry he would be from here on out when he heard and saw everything I was doing.

I started to pull away, but Niko yanked me closer.

"If you threaten my son again, I don't care who you are or what magic powers you possess. I will strip your skin from your body and melt your organs while you're still alive. Do you understand?"

Herakles would tell me never to provoke someone whom I had no chance of winning against. Niko was one of those men. At least, when we were on his territory, he was.

I nodded without speaking. It didn't matter that he misunderstood me. When he was calmer, he might view our conversation differently. Convincing him the world was going to end if I didn't get Cleon out of my head wasn't my most immediate concern. Niko wasn't ready to make a move against his boss, because I had nothing better to offer him. I hadn't proven myself the most powerful Oracle in existence yet.

He released me, pushed me away then whirled and strode back to the locker room.

My arm was bruising already. I was accustomed to rough treatment from him, but his intensity still scared me. Even when he was beating my ass in the ring, or tranquilizing me, he was in command of himself. What that man would do, if someone tried to hurt his son ...

I had no intention of ever finding out. I would have to remember to phrase my warning better next time.

Cleon was openly amused.

"Get out," I said through clenched teeth and squeezed my temples.

There had to be a way. Maybe, I could lose him on the wrong side of the curtain, and Hades would snatch up Cleon and carry him away.

Cecelia's warning returned to my thoughts. Cleon couldn't die before we were disconnected, or I risked losing part of my power and mind. Or both. Or neither. The most frustrating part: no one knew with any certainty what would happen, least of all me, the greatest and mightiest Oracle in ten thousand years.

Filled with self-loathing, I left the gym. Trailed by my security detail, I returned to my villa and went to my room. No events were scheduled for tonight, and I had a date with my mind, hopefully on the right side of the curtain this time.

"Sorry about that," I said, uncertain if the two gods were watching me or not. "But I don't really know what I'm doing, so if I end up on the wrong side, please be patient while I learn."

Mrs. Nettles was napping on my bed, purring in her sleep. I stood over her, tempted to wake her and hope Artemis was paying attention.

When she didn't stir, I stretched out beside her and closed my eyes. With a great deal of excitement, and just a little anxiety, I entered the meditative state that allowed me to step outside myself.

My body relaxed, and the picture of my room formed in my mind's eye. It was gray and hazy again. Puzzled as to how I was supposed to know how to do this without guidance, and without stepping on the toes of any deities who didn't want their realms disturbed, I lingered in my room for a moment.

If there were a door, I didn't see it. I pushed my hands forward to see if this curtain of which Thanatos spoke were something I could pierce. I couldn't see it, and my hands didn't slide through a veil into the real world.

"I'm not trying to trespass," I whispered. "But I don't know how to leave your side of the curtain, Hades."

No sooner had the words left my mouth, when I felt the hot breath of someone breathing down the back of my neck.

I tensed and whirled, expecting to see the wall behind my bed.

Someone – rather, some*thing* – else was there instead.

SIX

"HOLY ZEUS," I said and stumbled away. I craned my neck back until I could see the top of the creature before me. The three-headed guardian of the underworld was growling from all its muzzles, its teeth exposed and red eyes glowing. The monster stood twenty feet tall at least, with legs that were thicker than my torso.

Behind him, instead of the wall to my bedroom, a black cavern yawned open. I didn't have to guess where it went, or why the monster was here. Thanatos had warned me about trespassing again.

"Nice puppies ... uh, puppy ... whatever," I murmured and stepped back. "I'm sorry, Hades. I wasn't trying to –"

Cerberus lowered one head and smashed into my body with its muzzle. I flew backward, across the room – and heard the strange sound of fabric ripping. The world erupted into color. Unlike the black-white-gray world of Hades, and the normal color of my world, this version of reality was my world on steroids. The colors were vibrant enough to cause me to squint.

Landing on my backside, I scrambled to my feet. Cerberus remained where he was, behind a thin veil that rendered him and everything else behind it gray.

The monster turned and walked away, retreating toward the dark hole leading to the underworld behind it.

Relieved, I released a breath. "Thanks," I called.

The creature ignored me and disappeared into the hole, which also vanished once the beast had passed through. It was replaced by something more solid than a veil. A mirror reflected my world and me, except everything was in black, white and gray. The lack of color distinguished the two realms. Where I belonged, there was color. Where I did not, it was gray.

I blinked until the loud hues of this world no longer hurt my eyes. Studying my reflection in the black and white world, I couldn't imagine how I was supposed to learn how not to pop up in Hades' territory without help from someone. Would Cerberus be this helpful next time around?

My thoughts turned to Cecelia, and I began to wonder if she was trapped in a place like this. With my body safely lying on a bed beside a slumbering Mrs. Nettles, I floated through the walls of my villa and out the front door. Tensing when I passed by the guards stationed at my front door, I reminded myself every few steps no one could possibly see me when I was outside my body.

The sun was brighter outside, and the grass so much greener than normal. The colors were dazzling, a little overwhelming, but beautiful nonetheless. Ribbons were even more vibrant and expressive in this place. They danced subtly, like tendrils of smoke twisting and shifting in a light breeze.

I felt *real*. The ground was solid beneath my feet and the sun warm. But I moved faster. It didn't take me thirty minutes to cross the mall and arrive at the Oracle's cavern. Barely a minute passed by my count, and I was suddenly there, passing more guards into the security station. I didn't wait for the elevator but sank through the floor to arrive in her chamber.

The smells of the Oracle's cavern were stronger, too. They ensnared me, filled my senses and sent me tumbling into euphoria. I floated in the state of joy for a moment, forgetting why I had come, before I recalled my purpose in visiting. I shook my head and focused on the Oracle.

Her body was still, her eyes closed, though the machines connected to her assured me she was alive. She, too, was made up of billions of tiny fibers in so many colors, it would take me a lifetime to name and count them all.

I didn't know what to expect, but I'd hoped to find her here, in this strange one-off dimension, maybe seated beside her body, where we could talk. She wasn't present, and I glanced towards the mirror demarking the separation of this world from Hades'. Nothing was unusual or different at all about the caverns in the reflection, and I began to wonder where the Oracle was, if she weren't in the human realm, this one or Hades' territory.

Disappointed, I sat down before her, awed by the bright green rainbow above her head. I couldn't see what was above mine. All of the ribbons of the world were visible to me, except for those belonging to me. I searched through all of hers to identify if any of them were broken or jagged or otherwise showing me why she had fallen into a coma. I couldn't identify any difference between what was in front of me and what had been there before her coma. I had tried unsuccessfully several times to fix the tears caused by her dismemberment.

Everything was as I assumed it was supposed to be, which left me more deeply concerned. How could I, with the power of a goddess, not help Cecelia or even understand what was wrong to start off with? What was I missing? Why had she fallen into this strange sleep, where not even Lantos could see her mind?

I sat and gazed at her sadly, wishing she could tell me what I was supposed to do. This world was very quiet to the point of complete silence. I didn't care to be so alone with my thoughts or to be reminded of how alone I really was.

Dropping my eyes to my hands, I willed there to be ice cream. Fibers from the ribbons around the room peeled off from their original objects and formed a half-gallon of ice cream in my hands. I then sent it away, and the fibers of the world rearranged themselves. I did it again with a pair of shoes I saw in my head then sent them away, too. With the comforting scents of the chamber, I immersed myself in experimenting with my power on a small scale. Eager to create inanimate objects, I considered creating a living creature – perhaps a cat – but decided not to. Were there rules to what I could and should do? I had been raised strictly by priests and Herakles. Even when I bucked their rules, the world wouldn't end because I didn't play along.

Except for the first time I stepped over the boundary of my forest. I lowered my hands to my thighs, recalling the rule I'd broken that sent my world spinning out of control. To this day, I could not believe how one small step had brought me here and changed my life in countless ways.

Was acting against Cecelia's advice going to condemn the world?

Of everything I missed about the forest, I yearned to see Herakles again. I loved the trees and nature, but it was the man who had been my anchor for most of my life that made my throat tight and my eyes well with tears whenever I thought about how much I'd changed from the sheltered girl he raised. The knowledge I possessed now about the world was far from anything I had ever imagined.

After my twentieth cycle of creating and un-creating, I felt the drain. It was mild, a sense of needing a catnap before I tackled the rest of my day. Was it using my power that drained me, or lingering in this world?

Frustrated again that I had no one to guide me, I stood and turned away from the Oracle. I willed myself up, through the floor, and walked out of the guard shack above the caverns.

It was dark out. I had passed the day in the caverns. The flash of first responder lights in front of the House caught my attention. No outward sign of an emergency was visible at the House. I crossed to my villa, anxious to be back in the real world so I could find out what was going on. I hated that I had to care about Cleon, not because he meant anything to me, but because we were connected, and his danger was my danger.

The half-full moon overhead lit my way, and I hurried across the green lawns of the compound.

As I neared my villa, a flash of movement crossed my peripheral. I turned and saw a tall brunette walking through the grass, away from me, towards the darkness that filled the space where the Silent Queen's secondary palace used to stand, before it exploded the same night I destroyed Artemis' main temple downtown.

I had turned away and ascended the stairs to the door of my villa, when the uniqueness of the woman's presence struck me. The guards and people I'd crossed – and ignored – in the mall area appeared differently than this woman. They were faded in a world where everything else was noticeably brighter.

But the woman in white ... she was in rich color, fully present, like I was.

Twisting, I glimpsed her just as she disappeared into the darkness around the Silent Queen's destroyed palace. I started after her when a faint voice called to me.

"Lyssa!"

Someone was tugging me inside.

Resisting, I raced across the mall, following the path of the woman in white. When I reached the hole in the ground remaining from the explosion that decimated the Silent Queen's palace, I paused and strained to catch a glimpse of the mysterious woman.

A flash of white came from the thatch of forest on one end of the immense compound housing the political elite of the world. I ran after her, not stopping to question whether or not I should. I raced through the Queen's scorched gardens and across the open area between her space and the forest.

Pausing at the edge of the trees, I waited for another glimpse and spotted the woman not far ahead of me. I pursued her, slowing when I neared.

"Hey!" I called.

She turned, and my stomach sank. This woman wasn't Cecelia.

Her features were too heavy to be beautiful, her eyes too far apart. Her skin was dark olive and her eyebrows thick and black. Despite her lack of physical beauty, she carried herself with the same dignity and rigid posture as the Silent Queen. The dress she wore glowed and shifted in an invisible breeze, as if she were not fully part of any world.

I sensed I was in the presence of someone important without understanding who she could be.

"Um, hi," I started awkwardly. "You're the only person I've seen here."

She waited, expressionless. Her features were partially lit by the moonbeams that pierced the forest canopy overhead. The directness and intensity of her gaze left me unsettled.

"I was wondering if I could ask you a question or two," I said at her silence.

She did not speak.

"Lyssa." The voice was calling to me again, trying to pull me back to my body. For the first time in a long time, I felt like I was close to someone who knew an answer I needed.

Blinking, I realized I'd been dragged to the edge of the forest, leaving the woman in white at its center. I hurried forward with frustration, sensing my time here was dwindling.

"Please. I just need to ask ..."

"*Lyssa!*"

Abruptly, I was sailing away from the woman. I was yanked across the compound and through the villa so fast, my surroundings turned into a whirling kaleidoscope of brilliant colors. Off balance and sick to my stomach, I didn't stabilize until I stood in the middle of my bedroom. Leandra was at my side, worry on her features.

But it wasn't her that caught my attention.

The woman in white wasn't the only other person in this dimension. Cleon stood over my bed, peering down at me pensively.

"What are you doing here?" I demanded, alarmed to find him spying on me.

"You pulled me into this place," he replied and faced me. "We have absolute power in this realm, don't we?" He appeared pleased.

I hated it when he was happy about anything. "There's an ambulance in front of the House. Did you murder someone else?"

"They're trying to wake me up, I believe," he replied. "You brought us here in the middle of a meeting. I collapsed mid-discussion with the Supreme Priest. I can't figure out how to return to my body, once we're here."

I wasn't about to tell him I didn't know either.

"Lyssa." Leandra's voice was in my head, loud and ringing.

I flinched and glanced towards her. Pale blue sparks surrounded her fingertips as she touched my face. I could feel her touch here, in the other dimension, too. Somehow, she was tugging at me to return.

"I have wandered the entire compound. I can see everyone, hear what he or she discusses with anyone else. I had no idea such an ability existed," Cleon continued.

The more I learned and grew, the more he did, too. I didn't know how it was possible or how to prevent him from becoming stronger alongside me.

The door to my room smashed open. Niko strode in, features taut.

"She did this, didn't she?" he snapped at Leandra.

"Did what?" Leandra asked, glancing up, her focus on waking me broken.

"Cleon won't wake up."

I exchanged a look with Cleon, who frowned. We were observers, watching Niko and Leandra as they hovered over my body.

"Fix this," Niko demanded.

"I don't know how," Leandra replied.

"Bullshit. I saw you wake her last time."

Leandra appeared surprised for the first time in the twelve years I'd known her. It wasn't the surprise of someone who was innocent but someone who had been caught doing something she didn't think anyone noticed she had been doing.

As usual, Niko had read someone in a way I never could. I stepped forward, intrigued by the idea Leandra was more than she seemed.

"Do it." Niko pushed her towards the bed.

The normally unflappable woman's hands shook as she rested them on my cheeks again.

I felt her touch in both dimensions and winced as an uncomfortable shock went through me.

"Wake up, Lyssa," Leandra whispered.

Whatever she did, she snapped me out of the other dimension and back into my body. My eyes flew open, and I gasped in air, disoriented by the sudden shift. I sat up and looked around for Cleon before realizing he, too, had probably been sent back to his body.

But he'd been there to see Leandra's power, which meant, she was about to become a target on his radar.

I stared at Leandra, wanting to ask her how she was calling me back from the other place but afraid to expose her in front of Niko or the constant presence of Cleon in my head.

"Once I've made sure Cleon is safe, the three of us are going to have a talk," Niko said, leveling his glare on Leandra. He stormed out, slamming the door behind him as he went.

I scrambled out of bed and bolted across the room to lock the door. "We have to get you out of here," I said, darting towards my closet. "Now, Leandra!"

"Niko isn't a threat," she said. "I can handle him."

"Cleon knows."

Leandra was silent.

I grabbed a bag and began stuffing clothing into it. Leandra joined me in the closet.

"I can't leave you here," she said quietly. "You don't know how to find your way back from the other places."

Straightening, I faced her. "How in the name of Hades do you know where I was?"

She smiled mischievously.

I wasn't the only one interested. Cleon's emotions grew stronger each time I visited the alternate plane of reality.

"Wait. Don't say. Cleon can hear," I said.

"I wasn't going to tell you anyway."

"I'm trying to save your life, and you're still a bitch!"

Leandra rolled her eyes. "You're sure he knows?"

"He was standing beside me when Niko confronted you two seconds ago!" I exclaimed. "You have to go." Thrusting the bag at her, I snatched her favorite pair of shoes off the racks containing a couple hundred pairs. We wore the same size, and we often tried on shoes and clothes together. "Don't tell me where. Don't tell me how. Just go."

I thrust the shoes at her.

She placed everything on the ground, not showing my concern. "You can't be here alone."

"If you want to help me, do it from outside the wall or at least, far away from here."

"And if you become stuck in the other place?"

"I'll figure it out. You have to go. Now!" I pushed her towards the door, anxious to save her, before Cleon sent a platoon of guards to haul her away and torture her, as had been done to my parents.

"Alessandra, calm down," she chided. "Come here." She took my face in her hands once more and pressed her forehead to mine. Another uncomfortable flare of energy bolted through me. *Nod if you can here me,* she spoke into my mind.

I uttered another of Herakles' favorite curses.

Leandra giggled. *I am a nymph, a spirit of the forest, loyal to Artemis. I have protected you, alongside Herakles, the priests and the other girls, since we first met. You called us from the trees to play with you when you came to our forest when you were six, and we stayed when we learned what you were.*

I listened, astonished as the latest secret of my own life unfolded.

Tread carefully in the other places. You will not be welcome in all of them, and I will not be here to rescue you.

My anxiety settled, replaced by outright fear as I realized I was about to be truly alone. "You have to go," I repeated.

Theodocia will help me. I'll find my way to the Silent Queen. In case you're in danger, or face an emergency of any kind, I've left a clue as to how to reach Theodocia in your jewelry box. She will remain in the city as long as you're here. Leandra released me and retrieved her bag from the floor. "Don't worry about me. I can take care of myself," she added with a wink.

I knew what mythical nymphs were, but I didn't know I was surrounded by them or what power they naturally possessed.

"Wait," I told her reluctantly. I grabbed Mrs. Nettles off my bed, startling her awake. "Take her with you. Just in case."

"You'll be completely alone," Leandra said carefully, as if she knew Artemis used Mrs. Nettles to talk to me.

My eyes narrowed. Any other day, I'd do whatever it took to force the truth out of Leandra. I didn't have that luxury today, not when there was too much at stake, namely the lives of those I cared about.

"No one's safe here anymore," I replied quietly. "Not while Cleon is in my head and able to see and hear what I do. I endanger everyone around me. You have to plot to take him out without me knowing. Take her and keep her safe."

Leandra accepted the purring teddy bear, regret on her features. As I watched, the nymph fashioned a pouch out of a pashmina and secured Mrs. Nettles to her back.

I waved to my stuffed animal, and she waved back.

Leandra went to the balcony rather than the door and walked out onto it. She slung a leg over the railing and dropped down into the gardens. Trailing, I leaned over the balcony to watch her then recalled how Cleon could see what I did.

I turned away in anger. If I watched her run to safety, Cleon would know where to find her. Ignorance was the only way to protect others for me, even if it meant I lived in a state of constant uncertainty and fear of the conditions and lives of those I cared about.

"It's not fair," I muttered and leaned my head back to observe the night sky.

Banging came from the front of the villa. Cleon had dispatched his men faster than I expected. I only ever worried when Niko was leading the charge. Since those coming for Leandra were knocking, I assessed Niko was not among them.

I sneaked a glance towards Leandra, who was making her way through the gardens, then closed the doors to my balcony and retreated into the sitting area of my bedroom and waited, tense, for them to barge into my bedroom. The fatigue I experienced after playing with my power in the Oracle's chamber lingered, and I snacked on the candy and baked goods Leandra always kept stocked in our room.

A few minutes later, the door opened, and four of Cleon's elite military soldiers spilled in, weapons drawn. They didn't lower their guns until they were certain I was no threat. No one spoke to me as they searched my room hastily. They tossed clothing onto the floor then upset my bed and yanked all the drawers out of my dressers, as if Leandra were small enough to fit inside.

While irritated, I said nothing, not wanting to draw their attention when Leandra needed as much time to escape as possible. At long last, the men ceased tearing my room apart and exited, unconcerned with the mess they left in their wake.

When they were gone, I rose. Every bone in my body wanted to check the gardens again to ensure Leandra had made it out without being caught, but I forced myself to remain where I was.

Cleon was ... satisfied. The emotion was unusually strong, enough so, I had to pause to consider whose emotion it really was. I picked up clothing from the floor of the closet, waiting for Niko or someone to fetch me so I could be interrogated about Leandra.

No one came, and I listlessly straightened the closet before returning to stand in the middle of my room.

Without Leandra and Mrs. Nettles, it was too quiet. The comfortable room no longer felt welcoming, especially now that I had no buffer between the memorial sprawling across one wall and my thoughts. I crossed my arms, a little lost and a whole lot angry that I had been forced to send away everyone I cared about because of the chip in my brain. My power was not only isolating me, it was becoming a source for Cleon to commit evil. Would it have been better for everyone if I were on the wall next to Cecelia?

I shifted my focus to straightening up my room enough for me to sleep. The mattresses on the bed were askew, so I straightened them, welcoming the distraction physical activity provided. My thoughts went to the other places, the one-off realities, and how I was going to bring myself back when I didn't know how.

Who was the woman in white? Would she help me? Were there more people in the strange world I hadn't noticed during my first two forays into it? Could I communicate with the people in my world from there? Or was a nymph the only one who could contact me?

Another thought, far less pleasant, hovered in my mind. When I was in the state that allowed me to cross into a different dimension, my unconscious body remained defenseless. Recalling Cleon standing over me gave me the chills, and I didn't know why. While I was under, so was he. It was one of the few times I was truly safe from him.

With a grunt, I gave the mattress a final hip check to push it into place and stepped back. Sweating from effort, I was tempted to return to the other dimension and find the woman in white but also afraid of not being able to return.

Turning off the lights, I sat in bed and gazed at the names on the wall opposite me. Some were visible in the pale moonlight originating from the windows on the east side of my bedroom.

It was just us now, the names and me. I owed it to each of the dead to try to use my powers and feared doing the same would place more lives in danger, if not through my direct actions, then because of Cleon's ability to wield my power to harm others.

I had to do something. I was sick of inaction and fear. Without

Leandra and Mrs. Nettles, I didn't have to worry about anyone near me being hurt, since everyone who mattered to me was gone.

If I got stuck in some other dimension, and Cleon was, too, what did I have to lose? I was probably doing my world a favor by taking him off the streets.

My mind made up, I settled onto my back and drew deep breaths until I was immersed in the meditative state where I could slip out of my body once again and try to find the woman in white.

"You stood me up again."

My heart jolted at the unexpected voice. My eyelids flew open, and I sat up.

Lantos was in my room, part shadow, and part man, standing in the corner.

"You need to leave," I said quickly and leapt off the bed.

"Not until we talk."

Crossing the room, I pressed both hands to his chest and pushed him back into the shadows. "Now, Lantos!" I said when he didn't turn into a shadow.

He gripped my wrists and twisted them away without hurting me. I glared up at him. There was a time, when we first met, when I'd found Adonis' best friend to be attractive. That was before I realized who he was and what he planned. But standing in the shadows of my room, with his solid frame so close to mine, I recalled who else I missed during the dark nights and grueling days here.

Lantos would never be Adonis, but his strong body and masculine scent reminded me of the man I was missing.

Cleon was thrilled, which I took to be a bad sign.

"I'm serious, Lantos," I said and wrenched my hands from his grip. "I'd like nothing better than for you to be paraded out in front of a firing squad, but I respect Adonis enough to try to care about his friend!"

"I know you're angry, but you need to hear me out," Lantos replied.

Whirling, I walked away, arms across my chest. "Anything you reveal to me, Cleon will know."

"Nice. So you're on his side now?"

Even now, Lantos was trying to manipulate me. This game never stopped with him, and I was the least prepared to play it out of everyone I'd ever met. "That's not what I mean," I said, calming. "There's a chip in my head, remember? The one you tricked me into letting him plant? He happens to be able to hear and see everything I can."

Lantos was quiet enough I thought he left. Facing the corner, I glared at him when I saw he remained.

He appeared pensive, if not troubled, his green eyes on me. "You're right. I can't tell you." He went to the balcony and threw open the doors, allowing moonlight to flood my room.

I started to relax, hoping he'd take the hint and leave for once.

"It's a shame, really," he said. He paused on the balcony and clasped his hands behind his back. "What I have to say would really help you."

Don't. Take. The. Bait.

Lantos, the king of secrets, knew I was desperate for guidance. "Bring back Adonis," I whispered. "Or let me talk to him."

"Not yet."

I sighed.

"It's for both of your highest benefits," Lantos said.

Suspecting I'd already fallen for whatever game he was playing this night, I grudgingly joined him on the balcony. "I don't believe you. You don't do anything for others without a reason."

"Adonis is my friend," Lantos said firmly.

I rolled my eyes. "I've seen how you treat your friends. If you can't tell me anything useful this night, then leave."

"Aren't you curious what the Oracle told me to pull me into this game?" He glanced at me.

"No," I lied through gritted teeth.

"She told me my best and only friend in the world would die."

My breath caught.

"I have the power to save him. What would you do to save Adonis?" he asked.

"Anything," I said without hesitation.

"Considering she said you're the one who will kill him ..." Lantos lifted an eyebrow in emphasis.

"No. I'd never hurt him."

"You aren't you when you do it."

I struggled with myself, always at a loss when it came to what I felt for the elusive, enigmatic Adonis. "No. You're wrong. I know it."

"Your mind won't always be yours," Lantos said softly. "You'll be corrupted, unless I figure out a way around it."

The logical side of me was in denial, while my heart hammered and my palms grew sweaty. Lantos knew my fear – that Cleon would one day control my mind completely – and was trying to manipulate me into something. I had no way of knowing what.

Stepping in front of him, I peered up at Lantos' handsome face, searching for some sign of the truth in what he said.

"The Oracle told you I'd kill Adonis, because my mind will no longer be mine at some point?" I asked, terrified of the answer.

"The Oracle says nothing directly, but she led me to believe this could be the case." His response was as confusing as that of a god.

I would never hurt Adonis. But if the Oracle saw me losing control ...

Cleon was agitated. How long before his emotion, and potentially his mind, became inseparable from mine? How long until he could not only control pieces of my power, but control *me*?

"What can I do?" I whispered. "How do I stop him from taking my mind?"

"Never stop fighting him. Don't give him or anyone else the opportunity to wrest your power and mind away from you," Lantos advised.

"No shit, Lantos!" I said impatiently. "But *how*? I can't yank this chip out of my mind. I can't kill him without damaging my power. So what do I do?"

"I'm working on finding a solution."

"So you came here to what? To scare me more by telling me Adonis is in danger?" I asked, face hot with anger. "*Everyone* is in danger, if my mind is taken from me, Lantos!" I turned away, furious I'd let myself dare to hope this man might help.

Lantos was quiet while I fumed. "The truth is, Adonis is the one person who can save you. It's why I won't call him back here. I didn't know that several weeks ago, when it might have mattered. I'm stuck with a puzzle whose pieces I'm not equipped to put together. I'm grasping at straws here, Alessandra. I'm doing what barbaric little I can to give you both a chance. I won't put him in the position where he dies, but I don't know what to do to make things right."

Somehow, it didn't surprise me to hear Adonis held the key to helping me. He had been in both of my visions so far, though I didn't understand the importance of his appearance. I wanted him by my side – but not if it meant he was in danger from me, if I lost control, or Cleon, who now knew who the latest threat to his plans was.

"What are you *really* talking about?" I asked, sensing so much more than Lantos was saying.

He looked away. "A little while ago, I learned a secret. I should have known it came too easily. Secrets this large aren't handed out willingly, but I chose to believe it, and I set in motion something I didn't intend to."

"Then you had a moment of clarity," I said, recalling his words in Cecelia's cavern.

"Exactly. Would you believe this player was played?" he winked. "That's all I can say."

Why did I have the feeling he knew something about my visions?

"Played by whom?" I asked.

"That is not for you to know now. Focus on your power, and on protecting Adonis." His tone was firmer than I'd ever heard it.

Sensing Cleon's interest, I began to think Lantos understood the limitations of what he could and couldn't say better than I did.

"I shouldn't have pushed you," I said, even more frustrated with myself for forcing Lantos to reveal something I didn't want Cleon to know. "You can't tell me anything of significance ever again, if you don't want Cleon to know."

"I do want him to know something," Lantos said with an edge in his voice.

I sighed and leaned back against the railing of the balcony, studying the man with more secrets and depth than I was capable of imagining.

"I want him, and you, to know that nothing will ever stand between you and Adonis. He will not allow it. He will destroy anyone who tries to keep you apart, including me. But you must not allow him into your life, until the moment when you feel all hope is lost."

My heart flipped in my chest. I believed him about Adonis knowing no restrictions on what he'd do. Everyone in the political sphere understood how lethal the former head of SISA was. To this day, I didn't know what rumors were true and which ones were embellishments on the truth, because I, like everyone else, would never know exactly what Adonis was capable of.

"All hope is lost?" I asked cautiously. Allowing myself to believe in anything, especially if led to hope by someone like Lantos, was dangerous. But I wanted to believe in Adonis, and our potential future, with all my heart.

"You endanger him otherwise," Lantos replied. "He loves you. He will do anything you ask, and so, you must be the one who asks him to leave."

Love?

I looked away. I wasn't completely surprised to hear this word, and to accept something this intense existed between my Mismatch and me. I was also scared of what it meant to care for someone in a world in which I could envision no scenario where we all survived. I was happy Herakles and Adonis were outside the wall, far enough away not to see what was happening to me, and outside Cleon's reach.

"I won't kill him or let anyone else try," I said softly. "If that means I have to send him away, I will."

"Be careful, Alessandra. Believe it or not, I'm here to help you, when you need it. I'll be close. The shadows are my domain. If you need me, whisper my name into the darkest corner you can find."

Was the man who betrayed me to Cleon, and who betrayed the Silent Queen, seriously offering to *help* me?

Lantos shifted away, out of the moonlight, and retreated to the darker interior of my bedroom. I watched him until the shadows swallowed him and became still again, indicating he was gone.

Unable to shake his claim I was going to kill Adonis, I remained on the balcony and rested my elbows on the railing. Moonlight dusted the flowers and plants in the garden below, outlining everything in silver. I was somewhat comfortable in the other dimension when it came to creating but not quite as confident in my own world. I wanted to pursue the woman in white, to talk to her, but I also feared leaving my body exposed for too long.

I couldn't possibly sleep after the discussion with Lantos and dragged a chair onto the balcony. Rather than return to the other dimension, I began practicing the creation of inanimate objects in this one.

"Shoes," I whispered and gazed expectantly at the place before my feet. A tingle went through me, as if the magic were trying to work. When the sensation faded, I thought hard about how I was able to create in the other dimension. It seemed ... easier there. Unwilling to leave my world when Adonis' life was in the mix, I focused on creating a picture in my head of a pair of shoes, without closing my eyes.

Fibers from the ribbons suspended over everything around me peeled off and coalesced in front of me. They slowly materialized.

Intrigued by the process, I lost focus at the last second. Instead of shoes, a tiny statue appeared before me.

"Mismatch," I murmured sadly and plucked it up. My mind was clearly on Adonis. I had first met him in his grotesque form when I was five, the day I awoke him and named him Mismatch. He came to visit me afterwards, flying from DC to the suburbs where my family lived, drawn to me by the connection we shared. I never knew he was a man during daylight until a few weeks ago. "I won't let anyone hurt you," I vowed.

To protect him, I had to become stronger. I had to listen to Artemis over Cecelia. I had to make a choice to risk everything in order to protect my Mismatch.

Determined to master my power, I held the statue and tried again.

SEVEN
GROTESQUE PRINCE

MENELAUS WASN'T HEALING WELL or fast. With a glance towards the horizon, and the sun dipping towards it, I lowered the axe and gathered my last armful of wood for today. I entered the small house belonging to my elderly host and placed the timber in the hearth before crouching to start the fire.

"You don't have to care for me like this. I am old. If it is the will of the gods that I die, then I die," Menelaus said from his place lying on the couch.

"I enjoy defying the gods' will. Don't you?" I replied and tucked loose newspaper around the logs.

"Some days. And some days, I feel too old to commit the effort."

"I'll leave when you're well enough to care for yourself."

"This is a young man's world. You should be out in it, not stuck here with me."

I paused. "You've seen my wings. Would it surprise you to learn I am not as young as you think I am?"

"Only if you claim to be older than I am."

Smiling, I returned to my duty of lighting the fire before I left the house to transform into my monster form. Menelaus had turned out to be a good companion. He asked for little and possessed a dry sense of intelligent humor I rather liked.

"Why do you stay when you don't have to?"

"You're insistent tonight. Do you not want my help?" I asked with a glance over my shoulder at the man reclining on the couch. His eyes had turned whiskey hued again within the span of a few seconds. This change occurred often enough I'd stopped noting each time it happened.

"I am curious. I barely know you, and you don't know me," he replied.

At times, he also had an odd way of speaking. It reminded me of how the gods spoke in riddles. For twelve years, I had protected an animated stuffed animal belonging to Alessandra. When Mrs. Nettles was possessed by Artemis, which happened on occasion, I noticed the same enigmatic speech patterns.

It was possible Menelaus and I spoke different dialects of Greek, and this was what I heard, but I wasn't ruling out anything after all I'd seen of the world.

"I came to find something that's not here," I replied. "I want to ensure I don't overlook anything before I leave, and yes, I do want to help you."

With the fire trickling to life, I stood.

"Are you sure?" Menelaus asked. His head rested on the back of the couch, and his eyes were closed.

"Am I sure about what?"

"That what you seek isn't here?"

"I dived into the sea several times. You were right. The sea floor has been swept clean by storms." I gazed out the window, watching the sun start to sink beneath the horizon. "I was sent on a fool's errand." I wasn't surprised a goddess had duped me – but I was angry. When next we met, I would have nothing nice to say to Artemis. If I caught her possessing a human, I was going to end this madness with a blow to the throat.

"Maybe you weren't looking for the right thing," Menelaus

suggested. "Maybe it's not a stone plaque you seek."

"Or maybe it doesn't exist, and a certain goddess will have much to atone for when we meet again."

"In all my years, I've never trusted a god," he agreed. "You are too quick to surrender, if you want to defy this goddess."

My eyebrows lifted. In SISA, most men wouldn't risk looking at me, let alone dare rebuke me. My reputation was well earned, if exaggerated, as were most urban legends.

As soon as my ire rose, it deflated when I observed Menelaus' old, crippled form. He spoke his thoughts with blunt candidness. Only two other people in four thousand years had done this with me. One was Lantos, and the other Alessandra, whose face I saw often enough in my thoughts, I believed something was very wrong, or would be soon.

"Maybe you should look harder," Menelaus added. His eyes were chocolate colored again. His voice drifted off at the end as he fell into the kind of blissful sleep only the old and weary enjoyed.

"Maybe I should," I replied. I checked the fire and draped a blanket over him before leaving the cottage.

The fire of transformation flowed through me. I removed my clothing and folded it neatly, then closed my eyes as the sun began to sink beneath the horizon. Before the last rays of Hesperides had died out, I was in my grotesque form, circling the house as I did every night to ensure no thieves or other threats were close to the sleeping Menelaus.

When I was satisfied he was safe, I soared into the air, did a quick flip to warm up my body, and then tucked my wings and dived downward, into the waters off shore.

I had explored every inch of the sandy sea floor for a hundred yards in each direction without finding one trace of any artifact. The sand was swept clear of debris. Using my wings and legs to propel me forward, I went over a familiar stretch, where I was able to identify the old shoreline by the depth changes.

Nothing here. Nothing there. Nothing anywhere. When I came

up for air a short time later, I flung out my wings and floated on my back, eyes on the stars and half moon above. The water was cool, and the sound of the tide rocking back and forth soothed nerves that were starting to feel frayed.

In the long days I'd been here, caring for Menelaus, I'd had too much time to think.

I had been trying unsuccessfully to understand the mind of Artemis since discovering the purpose behind my journey didn't exist. Did she want me away from DC? Did she have a secondary plan in mind for me that required me to be here?

If so, why tell me I needed to learn who I had been? What would a name matter? Albeit curious, I wouldn't waste my time or endanger Alessandra or others with a fanciful, selfish journey across the world to learn my name.

Except I did. One word. That was all it really was. Yet this word held immense power over me, as much as the name *Alessandra* did, as much as the curse that turned me into a monster each night. I struggled to understand how I had changed so quickly, from the butcher Lantos needed me to be to someone who traveled so far for *one word*.

My mind was my own for the first time since I was seventeen, and it was an unfamiliar place. What bothered me the most was not that I didn't know my name, but that I *wanted* to.

The image of Alessandra was in my mind again, never fully gone. She was beautiful, but it was her spirit that had captured my attention long before I understood our connection. She was *alive* in a world where I had become numb to everyone and everything.

When I thought of her, I was torn by conflicting instincts from my two sides. The first was that of the butcher Adonis, who saw her, wanted her and would have done whatever he had to in order to break her and control her, as he did everyone else, so she would become a fixture in his life for as long as he wanted her to be there. Adonis would not have been kind, had Lantos not ordered him to treat her differently from the beginning, when we lured her to my compound in DC.

The second was Mismatch, the primal instincts of a beast parading as a man, who remembered her kindness and was fascinated by her strength and heart. Mismatch recalled the first breath he took after four thousand years frozen as a statue and knew he had her to be grateful for his release from eternity in stone. He would never hurt her and certainly never break her. He would watch over her as he had the temple of Artemis. He would stand by her side, if she asked it, or keep his distance, if that was her preference.

I was stuck somewhere between the two parts of my psyche, neither fully one nor the other, no matter what form I was in, and not trusting myself around Alessandra, because of the discord within me. Adonis wanted to possess. Mismatch wanted to protect. Adonis would hurt her to satisfy his interest and need. Mismatch would rather die than harm her.

Did I come across the world for my purpose, or to protect Alessandra from what I was, because I didn't know what I would do to her? Was I a conqueror and butcher, or a protector and guardian? How was it possible to be *both*?

In the dark night, floating in the sea I used to rule, I had never felt more disconnected from who I was. It was unlike either of my sides not to know. I had learned nothing this journey, except that I was confused, and I doubted I needed to travel six thousand kilometers to figure that out.

An unfamiliar scent reached me across the waters, and I shifted off my back, head tilted and senses alert. Without waiting to find it with my eyes, I launched into the air. Droplets of the sea rained down from my wings as I climbed upward to reach a height where I could see the bay and cottage clearly.

The scent came from the direction of the cottage. Seconds later, a flurry of wings, and a dark body far too large to be that of a bird, shot into the air. It disappeared behind one of the few clouds visible.

Intrigued, I soared upward, chasing the elusive scent and creature. Reaching the cloud, I paused. The scent was gone, and so was the form. I circled and dived through the cloud then twisted in midair and began flying in large circles around the bay area, seeking the strange creature while keeping an eye on the cottage to ensure no one attacked Menelaus in his sleep.

Twice more, I glimpsed the creature playing in the clouds and pursued it. Twice more, it vanished before I was close enough to identify what it was.

I didn't spot it a third time. At long last, my hunger lured me into a different kind of hunt, and I left the bay to kill a wild deer for dinner. When I returned, it was close to dawn, and the creature was nowhere in sight.

Landing near the cottage, I caught the faint scent once more and whirled. No creature broke the peace and quiet of my surroundings – but I sensed it was close. Treading forward silently, I kept my eyes trained just beyond the cottage as the first rays of morning pierced the horizon.

My body changed, and I shook off the fiery pain of the transformation, determined to find out what was stalking me.

As I rounded the corner of the cottage, I stopped.

Menelaus was hunched over near the back entrance, his elderly frame naked.

Surprise shot through me, along with angry realization.

Artemis hadn't sent me here to find a plaque or my name. She sent me here to find *him*.

I stood in silence, observing him as he seemed to have trouble catching his breath. Returning to the front of the cabin, I snatched my clothing and dressed in jerky movements then returned to the backside of the cabin.

Menelaus had managed to pull on his oversized shirt but was struggling with his pants, since his knee inhibited most of his lower body's range of motion.

"Did you plan on telling me?" I asked calmly and knelt. I helped him carefully, as I had been doing for the past week or so.

He chuckled without otherwise responding.

Bending, I scooped him up and walked him back into the house, setting him down on the couch. His features were drawn, and circles lined the skin beneath his eyes, which were dark again.

Uncertain whether I was angrier with him or Artemis for deceiving me – for it was not coincidence she had sent me *here* – I said nothing and poured him a glass of water. Returning to the living area, I sat down across from him and waited with a predator's patience.

"I can fly easier than walk," he said. "Last night was my first flight since I hurt my knee."

"Did you plan on telling me?" I repeated in a low, controlled tone.

"Not at first," he replied. "If you had come and not been kind to me, I was going to let you wonder the rest of your life why your goddess sent you here."

I stood, edgy and angry, and paced a short distance away to keep from saying or doing something I wouldn't regret – but knew to be foolish anyway.

"But here we are," Menelaus said. He shifted his weight with a grunt.

"Who are you? Really?" I asked.

"Menelaus."

I turned and studied him.

"Not named for him," he answered my silent question. "The original."

"How is that possible?"

"How are *you* possible?" he countered.

Before this moment, I had never considered there might be another living grotesque anywhere in the world.

"Sit down, and I will tell you what you need to know," he said.

I debated leaving, suspecting Artemis and the ancient Spartan king before me were conspiring, and I wasn't going to be pleased by the reasons behind their deception. I was too shocked to find another monster like me and too intrigued to walk away. I did as he said and sat.

"You're the Menelaus who lost Helen to the Trojans and started the Trojan War," I said.

"The Trojans started it," he corrected me. "I am he. The Blood-line – *our* Bloodline – extended down through the Mycenaean kings of that time period, as you well know." He displayed his wrist, which bore an identical mark to mine, the hereditary sign of the omega.

"But you aren't a temple guardian." I shifted forward, anxious to hear his tale. "I thought all of the rulers in our Bloodline were turned to stone and forced to watch over the temples."

"Our history is a little more complicated," he said with a patient smile. "At first, this curse didn't exist. We made a pact with the gods and goddesses to protect them when we all arrived ten thousand years ago. Our kind stood as watchful, living guardians during the day, and when Nyx swept across the sky, we turned into our beast forms and left for food before returning to our posts. The gods respected and favored us above all others. We –"

"Stop there," I interjected. "I don't understand. We transform into monsters. Was this not the curse of the Bloodline?"

"What did you think, that we were *humans* who became monsters?" Menelaus laughed hoarsely. "It was passed down through oral tradition that our kind were created when Apollo brought his favorite guardian beasts with him across the bridge between our worlds ten thousand years ago. He combined our ancestors with humans to create the perfect protector who was more suited to this world and could blend in, at least for half the day. But in changing us, Apollo removed our savage, beastly ways and gave us independent thought, which I imagine he's regretted since that day." He laughed again. "In any case, we protected him and the other gods there, in our original home, and again here. We were never of this world and certainly never human. Not fully. We've always been monsters. This much I know."

"The gods didn't curse us into becoming monsters, because we were already monsters?" I asked in disbelief. "We are born monsters."

"Yes." He was quiet, allowing me to absorb this stunning truth.

"Then what is the curse?" I asked when I'd recovered from my surprise. "Being turned to stone?"

His eyes turned light brown as I watched. Menelaus shifted to make himself more comfortable, took a sip of water, and continued. "The traditional role we enjoyed as protectors with free will ended during a time period too old for either of us to have witnessed. Perhaps eight thousand years ago? Oral tradition doesn't specify the point in antiquity when our favored position with Apollo changed. One of our ancestors broke the sacred pact we had to guard the gods in this world and in doing so, angered Apollo. Apollo condemned the Bloodline to stone as punishment. This period was known as the first Dark Ages, which has been forgotten by modern human history."

"I hate the gods," I muttered. "This happened before both of us were born. Why are you not a stone guardian?"

"Because Apollo wished to punish me."

My head was swimming with questions as I listened. Menelaus paused, but my thoughts were racing too quickly for me to know what to ask first.

"Sacking Troy brought the second curse of Apollo upon our bloodline and also brought about the second Dark Ages, where gods fought one another." Menelaus shook his head. "Troy was his prized possession, a city of beauty, light, and wealth. It was said he helped build the walls with his own hands. You can imagine, when my brother and I sacked it, Apollo became furious. I won't tell you what Agamemnon did to Apollo's temples, but our Bloodline has not been forgiven to this day for his actions." Menelaus grinned.

"He'd already condemned us all to stone. What else could he possibly do to punish us?" I demanded acidly.

"The second curse of Apollo upon the Bloodline forced us to serve him, without question, whenever he called upon us. He stripped away what remained of our free will," Menelaus answered. "My brother's punishment for Troy was to become a temple guardian for Apollo and prevent anyone else from doing to Apollo's holy places what Agamemnon did to the temples of Troy."

"The second curse sounds far less damning than the first," I said. "The Crown doesn't appear to favor Apollo now."

"Until he calls upon a member of the Bloodline to do what he commands. We are compelled to obey."

Of all the horrific curses I had heard of, originating from angry gods and goddesses, this combination of curses was potentially the worst. There was no greater curse than to steal one's life and also replace free will with divine commands. If I dwelt on how shady, evil, backhanded and horrific this one-two curse punch really was, I'd explode. I focused instead on the history Menelaus was relating.

"Agamemnon was a successor of mine," I said.

"The bloodline continued through his union with Cassandra, the Oracle of Troy. Cassandra bore him twins. Both were said to have died, but one lived."

Nowhere in history was it recorded that the Bloodline members turned to stone.

How many disappearances of Bloodline rulers had been explained away as tragic deaths to hide the truth of what happened to the rulers of Greece, once the curse took hold of them? I had never thought to inquire into how the disappearance of Phoibe's mother was handled in an era where smart phones and the Internet prevented major government conspiracies from propagating.

Menelaus continued talking. "Apollo banished the Bloodline from power for many years after Troy. The Bloodline went underground for several generations and was nearly lost during the Dark Ages. It reemerged quietly when a member of the Bloodline married another Mycenaean princess, and our family rose again to power, only to fade away from the historical records when the Mycenaean civilization collapsed and the Dorians invaded. We regained power by marrying into an ailing Spartan dynasty, with the permission of Apollo."

As I listened, I realized how differently historians had recorded the events that the man before me lived through.

Menelaus' eyes returned to their dark brown color. "Even when

Apollo was furious with us, we were always favored by the gods. If our ancestors weren't in a position to rule, they were well taken care of," he said.

I disagreed silently. "Are there others like you?" I asked.

"To my knowledge, no. Agamemnon and I were twins. Those in the Bloodline normally birth one child and then disappear, as long as the Fates believe the child will survive," he said. "I don't think Apollo wanted me in stone, anyway. He wanted me to see my world change and collapse, over and over, and to witness how my actions had caused the Bloodline to do his bidding. Gods love vengeance."

I understood this too well.

"*You* are not supposed to be like you are. Did Apollo awaken you?" Menelaus asked.

"No." I was too interested in his story to explain mine. "Did you know of my family?"

"How old are you?"

"Four millennia."

He considered. "I might have their names recorded. I kept track of those members of the Bloodline who came after me and researched those who came before me. The records are incomplete. It was difficult to find the names of our Bloodline before my time."

"I remember my father's name and that of my grandfather."

"And your mother and grandmother?" he asked.

"The Bloodline passed through my father and grandfather. I had no need to know my mother's name. She and my father died soon after I was born." My heart began to beat harder. "I came here to find a plaque with a name written on it. My name."

"That's why you're here?" Menelaus' brow furrowed.

"Yes."

"Artemis sent you to me, so I might tell you your name?" He appeared puzzled. "What could be so important about it that you obeyed her?"

"She called in an oath," I replied. "But ... it was more than that. I *want* to know. If I can remember everything about the past four thousand years, except my name, then isn't it important to find out why I've forgotten it?"

"If you forgot it, or were *forced* to forget it, do you really want to remember it?"

I was quiet, pensive. It was very unlike me to want to share my internal angst with anyone, but if I ever chose to do so, I could think of no one capable of understanding better than Menelaus.

"I am ... conflicted," I said finally. "About what I was, what I am, and what I should become. The beast is my good side, and I fear my human side. I know what that part of me is capable of. Once, four thousand years ago, I needed to be the military commander and the ruthless ruler. Those traits were prized in that era. I do not need that side of me now, but it feels dominant."

"And you think learning your name will resolve this conflict you feel?" Menelaus frowned.

"I hope learning my name will show me the path I was meant to be on before I learned all I know now."

"You want to go back to the beginning."

"I want to *understand* my beginning and therefore, hopefully myself."

"Your time came before mine by a millennia, maybe longer." He appeared thoughtful. "I do not possess this plaque you insist you must find. If a goddess sent you for that specific purpose, it's likely it never existed at all."

"I now believe I was meant to find you."

"Perhaps." He smiled. "Many of the names I have recorded have not been spoken of in thousands of years. Do you really wish to know?"

"I do."

"Is it not enough to learn you are not human at all?" Menelaus pressed, his eyes flashing from dark brown to light and back to dark. "Is there not freedom in being able to choose the name you wish, and to become the man you want to be, instead of being confined by the past?"

"Do you know my name and bait me, or is this a philosophical question only?" I asked, growing agitated with his stalling.

"Neither. I wish only to prepare you in case I don't have the information you seek."

"I will deal with this possibility if it should arrive," I replied.

"My records are in the trunk in my room." He glanced towards the doorway to his bedroom and lifted his eyebrows.

I shot up and crossed the living area, entering his room. "Did you and Artemis plot this meeting between us?" I called as I moved.

"Plot? No. She said she was sending someone to visit me, and that I should not help you, unless you seemed worthy."

"She did not tell me this was a test."

"It would be less like a test, if you knew," he pointed out.

"Has she forgiven you then for Troy, since you helped sack the city of her brother?" I snapped.

"No. And neither has Apollo." Menelaus' laugh was deep and loud and hard enough to shake his frail body.

Spotting the trunk, I knelt and opened it. It contained computer equipment and a box containing several thumb drives.

"Bring all the drives," he called.

"How do you have a laptop when you have no electricity?" I asked.

"There's a generator in my closet. Turn it on, after you bring me my computer."

I placed his laptop beside him, along with the thumb drives, then went to the closet. The generator whirred to life with the touch of a button, and I returned to the living room. Restless, I couldn't sit still when I was this close to knowing the truth about who I was. I paced behind the couch as his slow laptop came to life. Menelaus plugged in one thumb drive, searched its contents, ejected it and inserted another.

He went through five while I paced.

"If you cannot be still, fetch the pouch from the trunk," he said.

I returned to his room and pulled a heavy pouch made of leather the size of a large notebook out of the trunk. I sat across from him.

"What is this?" I asked and placed it on the cushion beside him.

"It's a plaque. Not yours," he added quickly. "I took it from my brother's tomb."

"Where is your brother?"

"He was placed on Apollo's temple in Attica for a thousand years before Apollo moved his primary temple to Rome, then Paris then London. Last I heard, Agamemnon was on his temple in New York."

My thoughts went to the temple guardians who had been decimated when the gods declared war on the human world, five years before. I hoped to free those stone grotesques that were left in DC and couldn't help wondering how many of my fellow Bloodline members had been killed by those they protected.

"You were born exactly four thousand years ago, or within a centuries or two of that number?" Menelaus asked, peering at me over the top of his laptop.

"I would say at least four thousand," I replied.

He shook his head. "My records end thirty eight hundred years ago." He twisted his laptop to show me the chart he had created listing the names and dates of Bloodline members.

My heart toppled to my feet. Until that moment, I didn't realize how much I wanted him to have the answer.

"Artemis might remember," he said. "Have you not asked her?"

"To ask a favor of a god or goddess is to incur a debt I do not want."

"For every one they give, they take ten back."

"Exactly."

"You're a free man."

I glanced up.

"Choose your own name," Menelaus said with a smile. "Who do you want to be?"

I didn't know. "Maybe it shouldn't matter."

"A name is just a name. I would have liked to replace mine with another after the Trojan Wars." He stretched for the plaque.

I handed it to him.

Menelaus removed it from its protective covering with old, gnarled hands and held it up. I had not seen this ancient writing in four millennia.

Agamemnon, who sacked the city of Troy and died a protector of Apollo

"When my brother turned to stone, Apollo made him sit before this plaque for a hundred years before moving him to a temple. Our Bloodline has been sworn to Apollo since that time," Menelaus said. His features softened as he gazed at the chiseled, stone plaque. His eyes had changed again to light brown. "We stood watch over Pythia, Attica and every other sacred city of Apollo. We guarded his temples, his bastards, his cities and treasures. For a thousand years, our Bloodline married his Oracles at his direction. He sought the successor to his first Oracle of Pythia, the strongest Oracle in history, who opened the gate that allowed the gods and goddesses to enter our world."

I tilted my head, my instincts tingling.

"He probably thought he could outsmart the Fates and breed an Oracle sworn only to him, as a member of the Bloodline. The gods are mad with their need for power," Menelaus said. "It never happened in all the time I watched."

"The Bloodline protected Oracles."

"Oracles are the domain of Apollo, and we are their protectors. We protected everything in his domain, until Greece united and wars among gods and clans no longer existed. The Oracles became revered and treasured four centuries ago. At that point, our protection wasn't needed."

I sat back, dwelling on this news. The Bloodline was born to rule and to protect. The more I thought, the less it seemed like a coincidence that Alessandra had chosen me, twelve years ago. Did some part of her know I was destined to protect her?

The weight of my confusion was starting to lift. I was bound by the blood of my being to protect her. I was her guardian, not a butcher.

Of all I'd been told, the one fact I couldn't quite move past was the idea I was a true monster. Never, during the time I had known what I was, did I believe it possible I had never been fully human to start off with.

"Artemis knew I wouldn't find what she claimed I would," I said, struggling with what to think of my journey. My anger towards her softened. She had answered the question I needed answered about who I was, and it had nothing to do with my name. "She knew why I had to be here."

In fact, I no longer cared what anyone called me.

"To break the curses placed upon us all by Apollo," Menelaus said with a nod.

"What?" I asked.

"She sent you here to learn what you have to do to free our Bloodline."

"I don't understand."

"Have you never asked yourself why he is included in the oath you take, before you turn to stone?" Menelaus asked.

"I took no such oath. I became stone the evening I was told I had a healthy son," I replied.

"It's a trick of the gods. After the first curse of Apollo, no one in the Bloodline was willing to volunteer, because no one wanted to be turned to stone for all eternity. The original pact called for us to *choose* to serve the gods as guardians, after we had born heirs. When no one would volunteer, the gods changed the terms and created a secret invocation that tricked the Bloodline members into fulfilling their oaths. They worked through their priests and priestesses to ensure the members of the Bloodline always spoke the invocation, even if it were broken up over the course of a lifetime," Menelaus said.

"I know this. I warned the current member of the Bloodline on the throne not to speak. But I never knew the exact words."

"*Until the debt to Apollo is repaid, I pledge myself to stone,*" he said.

In that moment, I felt more disgust and loathing for the gods and goddesses than I ever had.

"You are here, instead of stone. Apollo chose *you*. Out of the thousands of members of the Bloodline, you were selected to serve him and to repay the debt our kind owe him."

I had never considered the idea Alessandra was able to animate me only because the patron god of Oracles – who was also the patron god of my Bloodline – wished for it to be so. We were destined to meet, destined to bond, destined to fight beside one another in the war that was coming.

"Tell me," Menelaus said. "What service could Apollo possibly need of *you?*"

"Protecting Alessandra," I whispered. "The Oracle of Delphi who awoke me. She's the strongest Oracle since the first, ten thousand years ago. She bears the sign of the double omega."

Menelaus leaned forward, eyes keen. "From the prophecy. The gods have long anticipated the fulfillment of this prophecy."

"I have only heard pieces of it. The second coming of a great Oracle, the double omega, and the end of the worlds," I said.

"The prophecy foretells a great war that will determine the fates of all worlds, not just ours," Menelaus explained. "It does not specify that this war occurs between humanity and the gods. It does specify a great battle the last of the Oracles must fight, and whether or not she wins will determine what happens to all of existence."

I shifted in my seat. The hunch I'd been slowly cultivating over the course of the past week with Menelaus was all but proven by this answer. He knew too many details about the Bloodline, the forgotten past, and the prophecy for him to be one of my successors. I wasn't dealing solely with a member of the Bloodline.

"Why do you hesitate to protect her?" Menelaus asked, further solidifying my instinct.

Whether it was a distant relative or an earthbound god asking, I decided to answer truthfully. "I fear myself around her. I fear what I am capable of and that I will hurt her because of who and what I am."

"We are guardians and kings. We are also beasts. Who better to protect her from yourself than you?" he challenged.

"Is it that easy?"

"It never is when a beautiful woman is involved. I destroyed the greatest city in antiquity over a beautiful woman."

With a half-smile, I gazed at the plaque. It contained nothing I expected to find and hinted at everything I needed to know. My thoughts were on Alessandra and also on Phoibe. "If I can't repay this debt, what will happen if a member of the Bloodline never says the invocation at all?"

"I imagine he would never turn to stone and never die."

"Would he become a monster?"

"It has never happened that one of our kind was *not* turned into his natural form, or failed to speak the invocation. Several hundred years ago, a member of the Bloodline morphed into his beast form after a sea storm destroyed his ship and left him wounded and stranded in the ocean. In one instance, when the Bloodline bearer was a woman, she transformed when her life and the life of her young child was in danger. It's possible trauma can cause the transformation for the first time. Our true nature is dormant but instinctive, even if we transform once and turn to stone the next moment."

From what I knew of the Silent Queen, who had not spoken since I warned her of the curse twelve years ago, she had lived a fairly sheltered life, more so after Theodocia became her guardian. I doubted Phoibe experienced the kind of trauma that might trigger a sudden transformation into a beast, and I hoped to talk to her before anything remotely traumatic had a chance to happen to her.

With another glance at the plaque, I rose. I had answers to questions I never thought I'd understand, and could no longer fight the compulsion to return to DC. Fulfilling the debt to Apollo would save Alessandra and free the Bloodline from stone. Too many lives depended upon me for me not to find a way to mesh the two sides of me, and I dared not spend any more time here than I had already.

"Are you well enough to care for yourself?" I asked the ancient king starting to doze on the couch.

His eyes opened. "I have been here for thirty five hundred years. I'm not going anywhere," Menelaus responded. His eyes closed again, and he leaned his head back.

With a glance at his dogs, I hesitated. The urge to return to DC was strong, but the insistent instinct not to leave Menelaus remained. Was it because I suspected he had channeled a god whose favor and knowledge I might need? Out of loyalty to the only family member I had ever met?

Or … the shrewd side of me that cared nothing for family and loyalty but understood how valuable Menelaus could be on my side of the war that was coming.

"Come with me," I said.

He lifted his head and gazed at me. "I cannot walk."

"We'll travel ten times the distance by night as we could walking by day."

"Won't I slow your progress?"

"Come with me, Menelaus. An Oracle, and a member of our Bloodline, are both in danger."

"The Silent Queen," he said. "I've seen her on the television."

"You can help me break the curse and free our family."

This caught his attention, and he studied me intently for a long minute. "I would like that, but I am not the Spartan king I once was."

"I know what blood runs through our veins. You are every bit the Spartan king you once were, with the wisdom of a sage," I replied. "One more journey. It's all I ask. This time, we won't be cursed for bringing down the walls of the world's greatest city, and the beautiful woman within those walls won't end up in someone else's arms."

He laughed. "You make a convincing case." Shifting into a sitting position, he nodded slowly. "If you wish me to come, we cannot leave before tonight. The man who brings me bread will be by later today. I will send my boys with him."

My belief Menelaus had not exhausted his usefulness trumped my desire to leave immediately. Aside from the opportunist in me that knew what Menelaus brought to the table, I enjoyed his presence. He was the only other person like me in the world, and that meant something to the same part of me that crossed the ocean to find my name.

"Will you pick the best of the herbs from the garden? I will send them with the boys," Menelaus requested.

With a nod, I left the cottage on the shallow cliffs and circled the cottage. The sea breeze ruffled my hair and the herbs in the elevated garden beds. I plucked up a basket and began to collect herbs as requested.

"If you have any more secrets, Artemis, I'd appreciate you telling me without sending me so far away," I said as I worked.

My sense of urgency was growing. Being half beast gave me stamina, agility and strength far beyond that of a normal human, but patience was a learned trait that took great effort. The return trip would pass much faster, now that I had experienced the journey here and knew how to travel efficiently.

I'm coming, Alessandra. I thought. *And I'm pretty sure I'm bringing Apollo with me.*

EIGHT

SILENT QUEEN

"DO YOU WANT HIM MUZZLED?" Herakles asked.

I glanced up from the report in my hands. I could count on one hand the days I'd received good news since leaving the city. Today was one of those rare days. Over the past two weeks, my army had shifted from scraping by to being able to store food in preparation for a long campaign. In a month, we'd have the stockpile of food we needed to survive a winter at war.

Today was a good day.

I nodded once.

Herakles smiled, as he did each time I requested the presence of Kyros-Paeon but refused to allow the god to speak. As little as I wanted to admit it, the physician to the gods was one of the reasons my army had turned a corner. Illnesses and injuries had disappeared. Everyone who should have been actively engaged in daily activities, or preparing for our future, was capable of performing his or her duties. We had reached a point no army in history ever had: our staffing was at one hundred percent.

Even so, I would never trust a parasite like Paeon. He traveled with me whenever I left camp, not to help me if injured, but to prevent him from sweet-talking any more guards into allowing him extra privileges he didn't deserve. People were grateful to him, which I reluctantly understood. But they didn't know what I did about the gods. Keeping him at my side was my way of protecting my people from their kind hearts.

I returned the lengthy report to the low-ranking soldier standing patiently beside me. My armies were in good shape, compared to where we'd been upon arriving here. It was as much a testament to Kyros-Paeon as it was to Herakles, who worked tirelessly to ensure the people were taken care of, while I mapped out our strategy for the next six months.

Herakles led Kyros-Paeon into the motor pool. I didn't miss how others greeted the parasitic god, with smiles and handshakes and on occasion, hugs. While gagged, he responded with eyes that glowed with happiness. He was comfortable here, and he had managed to garner more respect – and sweets, which were rare – in his short time here than I had since leaving the city.

Nothing he ever did, however, would convince me he was genuinely *good*. I would never trust the god who cured my people or any god who came after him. At their approach, Paeon's blue eyes turned brown as he let the human side of him control his body. They had learned quickly I responded better to a respectful human than an arrogant god.

Herakles climbed into the passenger side of my command vehicle. I got in back, and Kyros-Paeon slid into the seat beside me. It was just past dusk, and daylight had not yet completely faded from the sky. Several rainy days had given way to a warm, clear evening.

"Ready?" Herakles asked, meeting my gaze in the side-view window.

I nodded.

We left the compound, trailed by one vehicle with three armed soldiers instead of my normal escort of half a dozen. Tonight was special. We weren't searching for more gods or scouts. We were headed in a direction we never went before – towards the wall.

We're leaving your personal guard. Are you going to kill me tonight? Paeon asked into my head.

I make no guarantees for your safety on any night, I replied.

His hands were free, and he reached up to remove the muzzle. I didn't care what he said around me, because nothing would ever change my mind about the gods. I ordered him gagged around others.

"I can't speak to you as he does," Kyros said.

I didn't have to look at the man beside me to identify it was the human side of him speaking. His voice was always softer and a tad more respectful when Kyros was in charge of his body.

"If you plan on killing me this night, may I have a last request?" Kyros asked.

I pursed my lips. *Unfortunately, your death is not the purpose of our mission tonight,* I replied archly.

"Ah. Okay. We noticed you brought the one driver who doesn't like us, and none of the guards who favor us, so we assumed the worst."

I didn't care for the reminder my own soldiers were discreetly disobeying my orders. In the time he had been with us, Kyros-Paeon had touched the lives of many people. Two weeks was long enough for the remaining men and women at camp to have heard how great Kyros-Paeon was. His reputation was unvarnished, despite his status as one of the gods we were supposed to be hunting.

"Do you not wish to know my last request?" Kyros pressed.

When the time comes, I will consider granting you a last request.

"He thought you might be more open to discussing it with me."

I do not care to hear it now.

"Thank you for inviting us again. We like coming with you. It's fascinating to see what you do." Kyros sounded excited about the prospect of a ride along. His optimism clashed with my realism every time we were around one another. How ignorant did someone have to be, to believe any of us were destined to live happily in a world like this?

I ignored him with great effort.

"You seem so young to know so much about war and ... this." He motioned to the world. "I had a year to go before graduating college when the gods tried to murder us all. I didn't know half what you do about politics or survival. You're probably the smartest person I've ever met."

What else I disliked about being around Kyros: I sometimes had a hard time remembering he was probably going to die by my hand in the near future. I didn't always know how to handle the duality of this man. He was human. Allegedly, the god possessing his body meant him no real harm. I couldn't forget the fact that Paeon was inside the human, though. The god was selfish enough to endanger the life of a human and to refuse to die as he should have if his existence were truly threatened. There was no honor in any creature that possessed another in order to preserve itself.

But ... Kyros was still a man, and I was sworn to protect humans from the gods. On most days, I was too busy to deal with this complication. Trapped in a vehicle with the two of them, I was forced to face my conflicted feelings. Paeon was alive because I was unwilling to murder the innocent human whose body he had overtaken. If the god endangered Kyros, or displaced his soul, I wouldn't hesitate to kill him.

In the meantime, I was left trying not to be curious about the life of someone who had been, by his own accounts, so perfectly normal, he was fascinating to me. I had never known anything about *normal*. Bred for one purpose – to become Queen – I was born into opulence and privilege, wealth and power. College was a foreign concept to me, as was the idea Kyros had grown up with his sister and brother – now both deceased – in a middle class household in southern Virginia. He played sports and went to the mall to hang out with friends. At times, I wondered if learning more about how normal people lived and how they thought would make it easier for me to relate to my soldiers.

"I'm talking too much again, aren't I?" Kyros asked and turned his gaze from me to the scenery out his window.

People who spoke for reasons other than to convey an important message also puzzled me. Handsome, athletic and friendly, Kyros was also far more extroverted than those I was used to dealing with.

Yes, I replied. *When you're a Queen, people tend to say as little as possible to you.*

"Sounds lonely."

I prefer it that way.

"Oh."

He said nothing else. I glanced at him. I didn't quite know what to do with him yet. His chatter gave me insight into how normal people thought, even if his presence usually irritated me.

Kyros appeared relaxed and interested in watching the trees fly by us.

The vehicle reached the edge of the territory I had claimed as mine. The driver turned off the lights and maneuvered through a bumpy, muddy trail to an abandoned highway that used to be Highway 267. The highway was smooth, and the driver gunned the engine as soon as the vehicle behind us reached the pavement.

We raced towards DC at a pace certain to keep us ahead of any bandits or thieves lying in wait on this stretch of highway. The world outside my compound was one of general chaos, where food and life were the primary concerns of every survivor. My enemies were the gods and the political elite in DC. My people were under orders to avoid confrontations with local militias or bandits as much as feasible.

My hair was tied in a tight bun on top of my head to keep it in place amidst the warm breeze battering us through the open windows of the Jeep. Excitement energized me and lifted the fatigue I had accepted as normal. The wall around DC grew closer as we raced towards it.

"I've never been to DC," Kyros said. "Even before the gods attacked us and the wall went up. Did you like it there?"

I raised an eyebrow. *Like? It was my duty to be there.*

"Duty aside. You have to *like* things sometimes, don't you?"

How I feel about something doesn't matter. My duties do.

"On second thought, you're the smartest person I've ever met, except when you're not," he said. "Even Paeon pities you, and he barely has an empathy button."

Pity? Startled, I turned my head to see him. *I'm a Queen. What is there to pity?*

"For one, you don't get to do what you want with your life. That sounds miserable to me, even if you are the richest person on the planet."

I leveled a cold look on him before returning my focus outside the truck. I *had* been the richest person on the planet, before I used ten thousand years of my family's fortune to build an army and city beneath the streets of DC. I did exactly what I wanted with my life and my wealth. I had created the only force in history capable of challenging the gods and political elite on behalf of humanity. How could anyone *pity* me for that?

"I can kind of hear most of what you're thinking, whenever I'm within about two meters of you," Kyros said apologetically and cleared his throat. "Paeon didn't want to tell you, but it doesn't seem right for you not to know. He said he chose me partially because I have natural telepathic ability that's much stronger than most people he's met, aside from High Priests. If you have some way of thinking silently, you might want to try it."

I decided when the time came, I was personally going to be the one to kill him.

Kyros shifted beside me, aware of this thought, too. I didn't care. He needed to understand his position here and mine.

I said nothing. I thought nothing.

Several kilometers from the massive structure, the driver slowed and navigated the vehicle across the crumbling median wide lanes where traffic used to flow in the opposite direction. He guided the truck through a ditch. I clutched the handle bar above my head as the vehicle lurched beneath me.

Crawling out of the muddy ditch, the truck continued down a short slope to an access road, around sound walls built to block the noise of traffic, and then proceeded into an abandoned neighborhood. Our journey smoothed out once again as we reached a road winding through a sprawling subdivision. The driver and Herakles both leaned out of their respective windows to see the numbers on the houses as we passed. No sign of anyone else present on the road was visible, and it was quiet, except for the sound of our vehicles.

The truck rolled to a stop finally, and I glanced towards the driver then the abandoned house.

"Stay here," Herakles said and opened his door. "I'll check it out first." He strode towards the front door, weapon drawn.

"Paeon says something is wrong," Kyros whispered.

Since when does a medicine god know anything about secret meetings? I returned.

"He says he thinks because he *is* a god, he can sense what humans cannot."

My eyes remained pinned to the open doorway through which Herakles had passed.

Was there truth to Paeon's divine instinct? Possibly. Would I trust his gut over mine or Herakles' assurances? Never.

Clenching my fists, I willed Herakles to return safely. Minutes later, he poked his head out of the front door and waved.

I released a sigh of relief and gave Kyros a pointed look.

"He says to be careful."

He cares nothing for my well being, I replied and got out of the car. I didn't know what game Paeon was playing, but I refused to go along with it.

One of the soldiers from the second vehicle trotted behind me as I went to the front door to meet Herakles. I stepped into the dark interior of the house. The soldier remained outside, and Herakles closed the door behind me.

He turned on a flashlight with a red lens and walked through the bottom floor of the two-story house and into a kitchen. One person was present in the vacant kitchen.

I didn't need to see Theodocia's smile; I felt it. With all disregard for formality and propriety, I hugged her. She wrapped me in her arms and squeezed. Her familiar scent – jasmine combined her natural smell – comforted me in a way nothing had since we parted. It wasn't until she was hugging me that I realized how much I'd missed her.

"I'm so glad to see you!" she exclaimed in a soft whisper. "You're skin and bones. Why are you not eating enough?"

"I told her so, too," Herakles seconded from the doorway of the kitchen. He set down the flashlight on a counter, partially illuminating Theodocia and me.

I have too much to do, I replied, unconcerned with my physical condition, so long as I could perform my duty.

"You need to stay healthy."

I smiled and relaxed in her arms. I barely remembered my own mother. Theodocia had filled more than one void when she appeared in my life, and I was grateful to her for becoming a consistent, trustworthy source of guidance and comfort.

"We can't stay long," Theodocia said, reluctance in her voice. "Are you well? Truly well?" She pulled away and peered into my face. Her brown eyes were concerned.

I am well, I assured her. *Are you? Tommy?*

She smiled. "We're both good. Niko won't let anyone near our son, and I'm raising hell for the Supreme Magistrate." Her eyes twinkled with cunning. "They've been slow to react to our insurgency, but I don't know how much longer we can rely on surprise."

The Oracle? I asked. *Has Cleon deployed her again?*

Theodocia sneaked a glance at Herakles before she looped her arm through mine and led us to the side of the kitchen opposite him so he couldn't hear her speak.

"Not on a scale like he did initially. Her power is growing quickly," Theodocia said, voice tight. "Thanatos speaks to me on occasion and I have limited communication with Alessandra's servant, Leandra. Cleon can access the Oracle's magic and we fear, will soon be able to use it on his own."

My eyebrows shot up. *How is this possible?*

"It would take an act of a god. Something was done to her, but I don't know what or by whom. Leandra passes information carefully. I don't know the full story of what's going on in the walls of her villa."

As if I needed another reason to hate the gods. Dread had been hanging heavily on my shoulders, but it was the sense of doom weighing down my stomach that left me scared for the future for the first time in my life.

What of Artemis?

"I have heard nothing from her recently."

The gods are being elusive. I cannot find Zeus or Ares or any trace of them.

"Something is very wrong in all of this," Theodocia said, a frown in her tone. "But I can't identify what. I have heard something that really scares me."

I waited, uncertain what someone with two divine patrons – Artemis and Thanatos – could possibly fear.

"It is said that Alessandra is likely to become corrupted," Theodocia continued even more quietly. "If Cleon could turn her against us ..."

... we would have no chance.

"It's not her will. Of this much, I am certain. She is a prisoner, but the longer she's with him, the harder it will be for her to break away."

The answer seems obvious. We need to get her away from him, I said quickly, not liking this news one bit.

"I've yet to be able to strike on the compound," she admitted. "My DC forces are effective in small groups. We would draw too much attention and give SISA and the military the chance to stop us, if we amassed the amount of soldiers needed to hit the compound."

Who told you this information? I asked.

"I won't say." Theodocia looked away.

I trust your instincts. Do you feel it to be true?

"I do. Based on what I've seen, it's credible."

The news about Alessandra was the last thing I expected to hear. We had understood her to be in trouble, but I never thought any priority would trump my desire to rid the earth of the gods and political elite. Alessandra was a weapon unlike any other. The ultimate weapon, too powerful for me to hope for the best and continue with my plans, if the chance existed she could be turned against us. If what Theodocia discovered were true, we were already in danger.

If we remove Alessandra from his influence, we cripple Cleon, I reasoned. *We can use her power against him. We need to do whatever it takes to pull the Oracle to our side and throw Cleon off balance.*

"I'll need an influx of your best soldiers to make an attempt."

They're yours. Whatever you need. We must have her on our side, outside the wall. Or we have to remove her completely from the board. We can't risk her reaching her full potential and turning against us.

Theodocia glanced towards Herakles.

My forces outside the wall will be ready for a sustained attack later this year, but I hope to start some hazing operations in a month, I went on. *Even if we only succeed in removing Alessandra from the board, we will need to strike before winter. The longer we wait, the more powerful and entrenched Cleon becomes.*

"You'll give me a month to grab Alessandra?"

I nodded. *Take her alive, if possible. But Theodocia, there is much more at stake here than one life. She possesses the ability to destroy everything we've worked for, and the entire world, if we can't neutralize her in some way. I would rather have her dead than give Cleon absolute power.*

"You're right. As always."

We stood in brief quiet. I didn't want our time together to end, as necessary as it was for us to return to where we were needed most.

"We need to tell Herakles," she voiced at last.

I debated with myself silently with a sidelong look at Theodocia. By the creases around her eyes, she was speaking as a mother, not as an impartial observer.

Herakles deserved to know. A good person would tell him. But I was playing for something much greater than the life of one person and the man who raised her.

When the time is right, I'll tell him, I replied.

She nodded. "I'll do everything I can to ensure Alessandra makes it out of the city alive."

I hesitated then asked the question at the back of my mind. *What of Lantos? Have you seen him?*

"Once, weeks ago. There's a lot of activity in the city but few details coming through our network about what's happening at the top. Cleon is working on consolidating his military arm with SISA."

This answer didn't contain the information I sought, but it was probably better that I didn't learn any real details about Lantos. He was a survivor, and he was a man of secrets. I should never concern myself with him. I had already personally experienced how far he would go – betraying *me* – to further his goals.

Theodocia had to know I wasn't interested in Lantos' public appearances. Was she protecting me the same way we were hiding the truth from Herakles? Because the time and place had to be right before the information was revealed?

Whenever I thought of Lantos, my lover for over a year, I braced myself for bad news. Rolling my shoulders back, I decided I didn't want to know any more than what she had revealed. Lantos was involved in his maneuvering, and mine occupied me. Except, every once in a while, I began to think he and I were playing the same game, and I didn't know it yet. Lantos had an uncanny knack of being a step ahead of everyone. I spent my life training for political maneuvering, but the bastard son of a Titan had the gift of secrets enabling him to pull ahead.

Before he burned me, I had admired him and his mind. Being away from him gave me the ability to see how I'd played into his hands, and how I'd allowed my infatuation with him to blind me to the truth of how he was manipulating me. I wanted to hate him but was angrier with myself for displaying vulnerability that could be exploited. I was the last person who should have been the weak link in my rebellion.

The front door of the house creaked opened.

Herakles left his post to greet the guard entering.

"I think we have to go," Theodocia said, hearing the urgent whispers. "Be careful, Phoibe. You and Tommy are the reasons I do everything I do."

My anger and disappointment with Lantos melted. *I'm happy we had this evening to talk,* I replied and wrapped my arms around her for a quick hug.

"Your Majesty!" Herakles called. "Time to go!"

"Be safe." Theodocia said and released me. She ducked out the back door.

I hurried to Herakles, and we rushed out the front.

"I'm going with the decoy car," he said and pushed me towards the vehicle that had followed my command truck. My assigned vehicle was marked. If SISA or the military had found us, they would know to pursue it.

The command vehicle was peeling away from the curb by the time I managed to climb into the backseat of the second truck. We jolted forward. I snatched my seatbelt and hauled it on before twisting to see who was pursuing.

To my surprise, Kyros-Paeon was in the third row of the vehicle. Paeon was in charge. His blue eyes glowed in the light of the dashboard. Pursing my lips again, I leaned to see past him.

Two dark vans rounded the corner, half a block behind us. They were new, uniform in appearance, and too well cared for to belong to random bandits.

The command vehicle stayed on this street, while we turned left and headed back towards the highway. With a combination of relief and concern, I saw the vans chase after Herakles instead of my car.

I faced forward again. The driver ran over a sidewalk and drove between two houses and through several backyards before we reached an access road to the highway. Jarred by the trip, I hung onto my seatbelt and bounced as the truck drove into a gutter and out onto the highway.

Only when our path was smooth again did I release the breath I was holding. No one pursued us. The farther we went, the more concerned I became, when Herakles' vehicle didn't reappear.

Wary of being exposed on the highway or followed, the driver exited off into the forest a few kilometers before the exit that would take us to the compound. Herakles had insisted on creating several back routes to reach the compound, in case one became compromised. Unfortunately, all the secondary routes consisted of dirt roads or no roads. The headlights went on, and we began another journey through mud, over fallen trees, and through uneven terrain in the general direction of the compound.

"Something's ... not ..." Paeon grunted as we navigated what felt like a trench.

The hair of my head brushed the ceiling as I lurched upward.

"Something's not right." Paeon warned in a quick breath.

My attention was on the world visible through the windshield. Branches whacked the truck. The driver and navigator were both silent, their gazes trained on the terrain ahead.

"We have to stop. Now." Paeon said.

Whether or not he sensed the danger at the house, or it was coincidental, I didn't know. I hesitated too long. An odd sound came from beneath the vehicle, and suddenly, my world slowed down almost to a stop.

An explosion ripped through the front cabin. Flames and metal engulfed me, while the warm blood of the two soldiers splattered across my face. A massive tree rose up before us, and then, I saw the darkness of the sky through the windshield. The world shifted fast enough to render me dizzy and disoriented as the truck flipped over backwards, landed on its roof, and then flipped again.

Pain came from my abdomen, one leg and my face. I was helplessly thrown around in the vehicle. My head smashed into the window beside me, and the world became murky, filled with blood and darkness.

Don't let go. Someone had my hand. My eyes closed as the truck went over backward once again. Unable to fight the darkness swooping through my thoughts, I released my will to stay awake and plummeted into unconsciousness.

NINE

ALESSANDRA

"HOW DID I go from my room to here?" I whispered.

I stood in the gardens at one end of the mall, just past twilight. My heart was racing, along with my thoughts. I sensed no danger and witnessed no additional ribbons that might indicate anything other than inanimate objects surrounded me.

I was alone in the balmy evening, standing in a fragrant garden whose water fountains chattered cheerfully.

I'd been in my room, stretching to go for a run on the treadmill in the workout room of my villa, since I wasn't allowed to leave after dark. I blinked and then, I was here. I hadn't set foot in the alternate reality for several days and instead, focused on bringing my power into this world, where it was far more useful.

Twisting around, I scoured my surroundings for any sign Cleon was present, in case he was the one who somehow hijacked my power to bring me here.

If my life were isolated with Leandra present, it became downright lonely without her. What was worse: I didn't trust the servants Cleon had handpicked to manage my household and bring me food.

He wasn't going to kill me. Not yet, at least, but I couldn't shake the fear he would try something else.

Perhaps it was his presence in my head, which seemed a little stronger every day I awoke. The incremental increases in his control were troubling, but not as much as realizing – after two weeks had passed – his claws were sinking deeper into my mind.

No one was around, which left me more deeply puzzled. If he weren't playing with my power, and I hadn't intended to transport myself, then what happened?

I tracked back mentally to what I was thinking about when I was stretching. My mind had been on the forest where I grew up and how I used to go running with Herakles.

My surroundings didn't resemble the forest in northern Maryland, though.

My eyes rested on the hollowed out hole where the Silent Queen's palace used to be.

The lady in white, I thought, interest spiking. There was a second forest, albeit a small one, past the crater. I had pursued the woman in white through the garden where I stood now, past the Silent Queen's former residence, and into a thatch of woods beyond. I hadn't thought to look for her in my world.

I started forward at a jog, suspecting I wasn't going to have much time alone before Cleon noticed I was somewhere not on his schedule, or before one of the Cleon-loyal servants raised the alarm. The compound was littered with cameras. Niko would have no problem spotting me. He was delighted by the opportunity to tranq me, whenever it came around.

Crossing the mall, I went around the crater and to the expanse of grass separating the buildings from the forest growing inside the fence. I picked up speed and followed a familiar path, the same I had originally traveled in the other plane. Reaching the point where I'd tried to talk to the woman in white, I stopped and looked around.

Stars were overhead, and the leaves of the oaks and maple trees around me whispered and rustled in a warm breeze. It was hard to see far in the darkness.

Flashlight. One appeared in my hand, along with another tiny statue of Mismatch. I sighed. Whenever I used my power in my world, I managed to produce a Mismatch toy simultaneously. It was a physical sign of how much I obsessed over a man-beast I barely knew.

Studying the statue, sorrow fluttered through me. I tucked it safely in my pocket with the silent promise of adding it to the rest of the toy Mismatches and flipped on the flashlight.

"Are you here?" I called quietly.

The alarms began to wail throughout the compound.

Where are you? Why are you there? Cleon's voice was becoming louder than my own internal monologue.

"I just need five minutes alone," I grumbled.

The lady in white didn't appear. Was this area at all significant? Or just where she happened to be when I saw her last? Was I transported outside my room, because I needed to be here, or because my power acted out?

A flicker of white, so faint I wasn't certain I saw it, came from the place where the woman had stood the other day.

Already, I could see the flashlights preceding the group of soldiers bolting in my direction from the compound. If I returned without making them hunt for me, I'd get off easier.

The flicker returned and flashed out of existence.

Or I could stay here and try to talk to her. Rebelling was easy when I knew I was probably going to be tranq'd either way.

"Hey, trees. Do this Oracle a favor and give me some time to myself," I said, half-jokingly. When they didn't move, I assumed my magic didn't quite work like this.

I sat down on the ground, determined not to waste my trip out of my villa. It would probably be my last for some time, if Cleon were angry enough, which he felt like he was.

The ground rumbled and shifted beneath me. Tentacle-like shapes beneath the surface snaked past me. I yanked my hands away from the earth, startled by the strange movement. Trees groaned, and I started to smile.

The trees were rearranging themselves. They closed in around me in a protective circle, using their roots to pull and push them into position.

"Amazing," I whispered and raised a hand as leaves drifted down to me amidst the shuffling of the great trees.

When the trees stilled, the green ribbons that gave them life automatically returned to me. I absorbed them with no small amount of awe. Not only had my command been seamlessly obeyed, but my power had also done what was necessary and then returned to me without me intentionally controlling it. I felt at odds with my magic most of the time. It was so intangible, so completely beyond my ability to understand and sometimes, to accept. I couldn't begin to comprehend how it worked or why it worked in some instances and not others.

This time, it was almost effortless to use it. I didn't try to control it, and it had flowed naturally to do as I bid it to.

All the effort I'd been putting into using my magic the past two weeks, since Cecelia fell into a coma, was paying off.

"Thank you," I said to the trees. Another Mismatch statue was at my feet, and I plucked it up and put it in my pocket.

There was a lesson in the statues, or perhaps, a reminder of how important he was. A shout from outside the safe confines of my trees disrupted my train of thought.

"Someone get a chainsaw or axe!" one of the guards bellowed.

I stretched onto my back and closed my eyes, determined to find the lady in white.

It was easier to slide into the gray world belonging to Hades than it had been before. All round, my magic was becoming easier to use.

A mirror was opposite me, a direct reflection of where I was, except that world was filled with vibrant colors. I was on the wrong side – the black, white and gray side – of the curtain without knowing how to enter the correct side on my own.

I walked towards the mirror and pressed my hands to it. Unlike a real mirror, it gave with the softness of the veil separating me from the other world. I couldn't pierce it, though I tried several times in several different ways.

"Hey, Cerb -" I started and turned my back to the mirror.

The massive, three-headed monster was already behind me.

I swallowed hard and backed away. "I feel like we got off on the wrong foot. I'm Alessandra, and I'm here to –"

Before I could complete my sentence, one of the monster's heads smashed into my torso and forced me through the veil.

I smacked into one of the trees on the colorful side of the curtain separating worlds.

Grimacing at the impact, I nonetheless waved at the monster. I wasn't going to chance pissing off a creature that had a choice between dragging me to Hades' underworld, eating me, or sending me on my way by telling it to stop being so rough. As before, Cerberus turned and disappeared into a dark hole in the gray mirror facing me.

"Thanks," I said with a grimace and straightened.

Aware I didn't have much time before Cleon's soldier cut down all the trees, I glanced at my still body then floated through the tree fortress onto the other side.

A dozen ghostly military police were gathered around the fortress. A couple of them sought some way of entering the tight ring while most appeared to be waiting for something. I wasn't about to stick around and see how they decided to decimate my hiding spot and began walking deeper into the forest, in the direction where I'd seen the flicker of light.

"Are you here?" I called again.

A flash of light came from my peripheral, and I whirled. The train of the lady in white's dress disappeared around a boulder inset with a dedication plaque at the center of the forest. Without stopping, I passed and darted around it.

The lady in white was facing my direction, expecting me. Her unusual beauty left me speechless for a moment as I tried to determine what made her beautiful. Her features were too heavy for contemporary beauty standards. Perhaps it was the odd glow around her, how she carried herself, or the ethereal silk dress perfectly draping over her body. The combination was mesmerizing.

With a shake of my head, I dispelled the odd enchantment surrounding this woman.

"Hi, again," I said and drew closer to her. "My name is Alessandra, and I think I'm supposed to talk to you."

As before, she didn't speak.

Her baffling silence and glowing presence reminded me of a video game I'd played in my early teens, where I was questing to find information from mysterious figures I stumbled upon during the course of my journey.

The earth rumbled again, and I glanced over my shoulder. This time, the sensation was caused by a bulldozer rather than the trees moving.

"Please," I said, returning my attention to the woman in white. "Can you help me?"

"You have everything you need to help yourself," she replied in a rough, husky voice as strangely alluring as her appearance. It wound its way into my ears and through my thoughts.

"I don't really need any more fortune cookie advice," I replied. "I don't know how to use what I have, or even if it would work in my situation, since I have a parasite clinging to my power. If I don't figure myself out, the entire world – every world – is going to cease to exist!"

She smiled.

"I could really use some specific advice, not a riddle," I pressed.

"I am the first. You are the last. I saw you, ten thousand years ago."

I. Couldn't. Breathe. I stared at her until the sound of a tree crashing down beneath the force of a bulldozer reminded me of my situation.

"You're the first Oracle of Delphi. The one who opened the door for the gods to come through," I managed at last.

"Pythia."

"It's an honor, Pythia."

She laughed. "In my time, and for eight thousand years after, we were known as the Oracles of Pythia. It was a sacred city of Apollo on the coast where I was born."

"Oh, sorry." My cheeks grew warm. "I'm sure I should have remembered that from school."

"I prefer to recall a simpler time, when we were respected and certainly not tortured."

"You've been wandering around for ten thousand years?" I asked, horrified by the idea I, too, was destined to roam the earth as a spirit of some sort.

"No. Hades cast me out recently," she replied, amused. "Perhaps because he did not appreciate you trespassing."

"This is why I need your help," I retorted.

The first Oracle of Pythia laughed again. "Ignore the gods. They cannot harm our kind. They complain much but it is all wind. Hades cast me out recently, when I told him even he could not survive what was coming, if he did not free me. He cares nothing for our problems, but he will not let his wife risk harm when she visits our world for several months a year."

I smiled despite my growing sense of urgency. I could easily believe the elegant, graceful woman before me could handle anything – even the ill-tempered god of the underworld.

"I can guide you, but you do not need my *help*, Alessandra," she continued. "Artemis has always looked out for us on behalf of her brother Apollo."

I glanced back and shivered, a little scared about leaving my body exposed when Cleon's men were using a bulldozer.

"You should be concerned," the first Oracle said.

"I am. Those idiots will probably run me over."

"No. Because of him." She elegantly extended her arm to point.

I followed the line of her finger.

"This parasite can never control your full power, unless he is in your body," she continued. "When you are here, or in any other plane of existence, he – or another spirit – can replace you. You must take care not to stay too long or go too far from your body."

Coldness streaked through me. Cleon's spirit, yanked out of his body when I left mine, was hovering around me. He appeared as concerned as I was about the bulldozer and less interested in possessing my body. If he knew he could possess me and have all my powers, he would have done it long ago.

"Is this what you saw, when you envisioned me ten thousand years ago?" I asked.

"I saw much worse."

At the hushed note in her voice, I met her gaze. "The end of the world?"

"Among other things."

My heart began to race. "Did you see how I can prevent it?"

"I foresaw it is possible to prevent it. I foresaw those working to help you who may lead you to corruption instead and I foresaw the impossible."

More riddles. "What's the impossible?" I asked.

"I cannot say."

"Because you don't know, or you *do* know and won't tell me?"

"Because this battle is one you must fight, and the choices you make will determine the outcome. I foresaw many choices and many potential outcomes. Only you will decide which one comes to fruition."

My chest was tight, and my heart pounded so hard, the sound filled my ears. "I don't understand."

"You will." Sadness was in the first Oracle's gaze. "I can give you two pieces of advice. The first, you possess everything you need to overcome and to win. The second, what is part of you, you cannot harm. The answers you seek, and the danger, will not be outside you, anymore than your power is."

Mnemosyne had told me the same about not being able to hurt Adonis, the day I faced off with him during the first of my trials. He and I were connected, because I brought him to life when he was a statue.

But the *danger*? She made it sound as if I were the real threat to the world, not Cleon or the gods or anyone else. Or did she mean Cleon would possess me and turn me into a weapon?

I had more questions to ask her, but my worried eyes returned to my body. Cleon was bending over me, and I started forward, alarmed by the first Oracle's warning.

"I'll come back. Don't go back to Hades!" I shouted over my shoulder. Without waiting for her response, I vaulted back towards my body with the ground eating strides that allowed me to pass distances ten time faster in this plane than in my own.

Reaching Cleon, I glanced in the direction of the bulldozer ripping down the trees.

"I would appreciate these odd excursions more, if they didn't occur during meetings," Cleon said, facing me.

I searched his features. If he heard or saw or otherwise knew the content of the discussion I'd had with the first Oracle, he showed no sign of it. I didn't let myself relax, not when he was standing between my body and me. Could two spirits fight in this plane? Or would it be like walking through walls and trees, and our blows would pass through one another?

"Send us back, Alessandra. I have business to conduct."

"Okay. Get away from my body," I said as calmly as I could.

A flicker of something went through his gaze and vanished just as quickly. Cleon stepped aside, and I closed the distance to stand beside my body. As I stood, looking down at my physical self, I began to wish I had asked the first Oracle how to return to my world. Leandra had been the one to pull me back before, and I had no idea how she did it.

Aware of Cleon's intent gaze, I waded into the middle of my body and stood there stupidly.

One of the trees – as ghostly as the other physical entities in my world – crashed down beside my body.

"Holy Zeus!" I exclaimed. "They're going to kill us both!"

"This is why Niko handles you, not the rest of these fools," Cleon growled.

"Where is he?" I demanded. "Tell him to stop this!"

"He's on an important mission."

The bulldozer rammed another tree. It began to fall. If the first one was close, this one was going to be dead on.

"C'mon, c'mon, c'mon!" I shouted and stretched out to try to force my spirit back into my physical body. "Let me in, gods dammit!"

The sense of the earth shifting was followed by the very physical sense of air reaching my lungs. I opened my eyes as the tree began to fall.

I was stuck between worlds, able to view what was happening from the outside while also living through it. My surroundings seemed more faded than usual, and I could also feel the solid ground beneath me and the scrape down one arm caused by the first tree that grazed me as it toppled to the ground.

I gasped. Hearing my breath catch grounded me fully into my world, and I lifted my hands to snatch the tree's ribbons.

Green ribbons swarmed and engulfed the tree, responding to my panic. The tree paused mid-fall. I pushed it over with one hand, and the tree settled gently to the ground beside me. The ribbons snaked back to my body.

I didn't have time to be relieved or to release the tension causing me to grind my teeth hard. The oblivious soldiers on the other side were busy ramming the next tree. I guided it out of the way with a single thought then bounced to my feet. Creating a secondary exit with magic by moving two trees beside me, I left the safety of the fortress and stood outside, trembling from effort and from nearly being crushed to death.

As much as I despised Niko, I had a feeling Cleon was right. The mercenary-turned-army-commander was never this clumsy. He might tranq me first and ask questions later – or never – but he would never risk dropping a tree on me.

Because he's disciplined and loyal.

I straightened. The thought wasn't mine – of this I was certain. But if Cleon had responded, he was reading my mind now, and no longer limited to the images I saw.

Another tree smashed to the ground, no farther than twenty centimeters from my leg.

"Holy ... just stop!" I cried at the men and women about to bring the forest down in their ill-planned attempt to reach me.

Abruptly the bulldozing ceased, along with the movement of Cleon's soldiers. No sound but the summer breeze and rustling trees remained. Oh – and my heavy breathing. I didn't know which part of my evening was the worst, but nearly being crushed by a tree ranked pretty high.

When the bulldozer didn't start up again, and no soldiers rushed me with tranq guns, I cautiously emerged from around the fortress.

"I'm cooperating!" I called and raised my hands.

No one shouted for me to drop to my belly with my hands above my head. No one spoke at all. I eased around the final trees standing between Cleon's men and myself, and my arms lowered of their own accord.

The bulldozer and soldiers were frozen in place. Humans normally had three ribbons above their heads. These still did – but the ribbons were wrapped in green sheaths. I had never lashed out at anyone before. I was careful not to, because I didn't want anyone hurt. These people were alive still, but completely immobilized. I approached the nearest one.

He was frozen mid-shout, a radio in one hand and his eyes on the driver of the bulldozer, as if he had been trying to flag down the driver. I reached out to touch his skin and withdrew with a scowl.

His skin was cool and malleable, like rubber. Definitely not human. I had somehow de-animated all of these people with a simple command.

Incredible.

"A little freaky, I think," I said and stepped away.

We can use this.

"Not if I don't know how I did it in the first place."

Realizing I was talking to Cleon – whose words had seemed like my own thoughts – I clamped my mouth closed. I purposely did not think about the first Oracle, afraid of revealing what she had shared with the one person capable of using it against me. Instead, I crossed my arms and turned all the way around to observe the statue farm I'd created.

The Silent Queen will soon be captured. Cleon said.

"What?"

That's where Niko is tonight. Leading the attack. We were tipped off about her location.

I tried not to think about Theodocia, Leandra and the Silent Queen, who I'd met only once.

It's only a matter of time before we finish off the rebellion, Cleon added. He was pleased. *And then she'll be more willing to negotiate.*

I didn't know what to think. To say I didn't believe most of what that man told me was an understatement. The amount of misinformation circulated within this compound alone kept me from putting my faith in anyone but Leandra. Without her present, I wouldn't be able to confirm or refute the information, either. Would Niko tell me the truth, if I confronted him during our next sparring session?

No.

Was that Cleon or my mind that answered my question? I was having a harder time distinguishing his voice from mine.

I began walking back towards my villa. "I'll release your soldiers when I'm home," I told Cleon. "I don't feel like being tranq'd tonight."

I blinked. When I opened my eyes, I was back in my room. Disoriented, I bent to touch the floor and ensure I hadn't been yanked into some other dimension. The marble was cool beneath my fingertips. The servants had left the door to the balcony open, as I requested. Even knowing my Mismatch was gone, I couldn't help hoping he would magically appear on my balcony.

"Release the soldiers from whatever I did to them," I directed my magic aloud. "I'm sure you'll tell me if it worked." This sentence was directed at the ever-present Cleon. He didn't respond, but he seemed unusually cheerful this evening, even for him.

The more I dealt with him, the more desperate I was to dislodge him from my mind.

I placed the newest Mismatch statues with the others on the mantle above my hearth. My collection was over two dozen strong. Each time I used my power, I inadvertently created a new grotesque statue.

I rearranged them restlessly, my mind on Theodocia. I had admired her since the first time our paths crossed. She was strong, an incredible warrior and sure of herself, and I wanted to be like her. I tried hard not to think about what happened if Cleon were telling the truth, and the Silent Queen was dead with her rebellion soon to follow. They controlled the only entity capable of standing up to Cleon's army and, down the road, the gods when Cleon was handled.

Movement came from the corner of my eye, and I twisted away from the mantle. A sense of not being connected to my world crossed through me as I studied the form lingering in the shadows of one wall.

"Lights," I said and moved towards it.

The chandelier overhead burst into brilliant light, and the image across the room remained.

I walked towards the mirror that hadn't been present at any other point in my life. At least, not while I was in my world. The black and white reflection was a remnant of the other world, not mine, and yet, I saw my reflection in the gray world, along with the reflections of everything else in my room.

My image faded suddenly, replaced by a gaping hole leading

deeper into Hades' domain. Cerberus emerged, towering high enough for his heads to reach the top of the cathedral ceilings of my bedroom.

I stopped in place, waiting to see what he did. The beast sat on its haunches, remaining on his side of the curtain, protecting the gateway to Hades. He wasn't looking at me, and I followed his gaze with my own.

My heart sank. All six of Cerberus eyes were staring at the memorial wall of my room.

"No offense, but if you're going to be there all night, its going to be harder for me to sleep," I said.

The creature ignored me.

Crossing my arms, I reassured myself with the ability to feel my body as normal. I was in my world, and I could now see into another world. I wished with all my heart it wasn't Hades. As if my memorial wall, and the heavy weight of those I'd murdered, didn't already haunt me.

A tingling at the base of my skull gave me no uncertainty about who had just entered my villa. Seconds later, my door opened, and one of the servants walked in.

"Excuse me," she said.

"Leave me alone," I replied.

Silence.

When she didn't speak or close the door, I turned to find her gone. Realizing what I'd said, and how my words gained more power with the passing of each day, I cursed under my breath.

"Wherever you went, you can come back!" I called.

The servant materialized. She was pale and trembling. With a long look at me, she backed away slowly, until she was out of my room completely.

"Sorry, not-sorry," I mumbled, well aware of who she was loyal to.

My room, as much as it tormented me, was also my sanctuary. Rather than allow Cleon to enter my private space, I left and went to the foyer, where the man I wanted to see least waited for me.

"What do you want?" I asked bluntly.

"A demonstration."

"No." Pain shot through me, fast and sharp enough to cause me to stagger into the wall.

Except this time, I wasn't the only one hurt. Cleon dropped to one knee.

The pain stopped, and we stared at one another. Neither of us expecting for him to be affected. He tapped the pain mechanism again, and we both flinched.

I pulled my knife free and made a tiny cut on my hand.

My palm bled – and so did Cleon's.

"This might complicate matters," he said, gazing down at his bloody hand.

The image in my head wasn't mine but his. He had planned – at some point – to put me up on the wall where Cecelia was. My dismembered body was in his mind and projected into mine – along with his satisfaction.

"Good luck with that," I said and straightened. "Looks like you can't hurt me anymore."

"Perhaps not physically," he agreed.

Nothing ruffled his feathers, not even the realization his favorite toy could no longer be played with. It was when he started to smile that I grew concerned.

"Your show at the edge of the compound gave me an idea," he said. "What better way to incapacitate in important pawn I may one day need?"

"I'm not doing it, whatever it is," I said. "You've run out of ways to force me to obey you."

The image of Theodocia flashed through my head. I pushed it away, not understanding why my mind chose to think of her at this moment.

"Perhaps you need a different kind of encouragement," Cleon replied. "Bring her!"

I tensed, expecting the worst.

Two of his guards entered through the front door, dragging someone with them.

My breath caught in my throat. "Theodocia," I said.

They dumped her on the floor. She was bloodied and motionless, unconscious.

"Turn her into a statue, as you did the soldiers in the forest," Cleon ordered.

"Um, no."

"I would rather not kill her, when I plan on using her against her Queen. But I will, if you won't obey. I can't risk her escaping."

I shook my head. "I'll turn all of you into statues," I said and held my breath. I envisioned the rubbery forms of the soldiers.

The men with Cleon went completely still, frozen in place.

Cleon, however, remained fine.

"I believe this is what the first Oracle meant by indirectly warning you that you can't affect me," he said with a smile.

Not good. "What else did you hear?" I snapped.

"Enough."

Was he bluffing? Had he read my mind after the fact, or had he been there, spying, when I spoke to the first Oracle? Cleon was a master politician, and I didn't have the experience with liars required to determine if and when he was telling the truth. One thing was clear. I couldn't risk going back to the other plane, in case he had overheard *everything.*

"You can turn her into a statue, or I'll kill her right here in front of you." Cleon reached over to one of the statues and plucked the gun free from the soldier's hand.

I reacted instinctively and tried to push Cleon away.

Nothing happened.

I stretched for his ribbons and gripped them, then twisted, not caring what kind of pain I put myself in, if Theodocia survived.

Still nothing.

Dropping my hand, I stared at Cleon in surprise. One of my green ribbons floated above his head.

Soon after Adonis and I first met, we were forced into a duel, in which I wasn't able to hurt him, because my magic was the source of his reanimation. He was alive because of me, and my power had somehow integrated into him and bound us together. I was warned then that I couldn't hurt my own creation, and again by the first Oracle.

Why did Cleon also possess my green ribbon? Was it an unexpected side effect of the chip in my head, melding our minds together? Was it a protective measure my power innately executed, in case something happened to him?

Even if my magic was off the table, I could still hurt him physically with my knife and fists, enough to free Theodocia and perhaps, send her away. I started forward.

He fired the gun, and a chunk of marble beside Theodocia's head exploded.

I stopped.

"Proceed, only if you want her dead," Cleon said firmly. "It's in your best interest to turn her into a harmless statue no longer capable of threatening me. When circumstances are ideal, I'll unfreeze her."

I racked my mind, infuriated to realize no matter what plan I came up with – he'd know it instantly. I didn't want Theodocia dead, and I didn't want her interrogated and tortured. I had the potential to summon all the power in the universe – and couldn't do anything to protect those near me.

I was left with one real option.

"Fine," I said through gritted teeth. "Turn Theodocia into a statue."

My green ribbons swept past her, and her body became lifeless and still.

"And free my men," Cleon directed, lowering the weapon.

We both waited to see if his command worked.

It didn't, which was a tiny, bittersweet victory for me.

"Free his men," I repeated the command.

They began to move again, and I glanced towards their reflection in the mirror. Cerberus was watching us. What did that asshole want? Wasn't it enough he smacked me around whenever I accidentally entered his territory?

If Cleon noticed, he said nothing. He returned the weapon to the soldier and motioned for the two to remove the Theodocia statue.

Without another word, he left.

My anger had nothing to do with Cerberus, who was watching me still, and everything to do with being helpless to stop Cleon. I stood in the foyer, struggling to rein in my mixed emotions and to create some semblance of a plan without tipping Cleon off. Every once in a while, the discussion I'd had with Lantos returned to me, and I couldn't help feeling as though I should have learned more from him during our exchange, that he knew much about what was coming.

I was tempted to return to the other world and talk to the first Oracle about everything, but scared as well, in case Cleon had overheard the secret the first Oracle told me.

My situation was impossible. Unless ...

Sleep. Cleon had to sleep at some point. When he did, could I plan without him being aware of my thoughts?

"Coffee. Lots of it," I said quietly. Cerberus kept pace with me as I headed to my bedroom. "What do you want?" I growled at him. "I'm not coming over there any time soon!"

He didn't speak and didn't disappear.

Before I reached my bedroom, I could smell the invigorating scent of coffee. The minute I entered, I spotted the mugs of goodness on the table near the window – along with another statue of Mismatch.

Cerberus settled down to wait. I began drinking coffee, determined to outsmart Cleon some way.

TEN

SILENT QUEEN

I AWOKE with a jolt and clutched desperately at the space around me, seeking a handhold as the vehicle tumbled out of control. My surroundings spun, and I was unable to focus on any one thing or understand the feedback my senses were sending me.

"Ssshhhh!" someone hissed.

Hands pressed me back while the night sky spun sickeningly overhead.

You're safe.

I struggled and then went still, sucking in deep breaths and trying to focus. The ground beneath me was solid and warm and most importantly – stable. I was no longer in the truck, no longer rolling through the forest with glass shards pelting my skin and my neck being whipped every which way.

For a split second, I was back in the car again. I tensed, and the same hands pushed me back to the ground. The sensations abated, and I lay still, breathing heavily in the otherwise quiet night. Stars stretched overhead as far as I could see, unencumbered by trees. I strained to identify where we were. The forest around our compound was thick, and trees surrounded the road we'd been on when the truck blew up.

But no trees were close to us. Twisting my head to see what was beyond my immediate surroundings, I realized we were in a stadium, near one sideline, in the shadow of the seats nearest us. The moon was high and to the east, appearing to rest at the top of the stadium wall.

"We got away, but they might still be close by. We have to be quiet." Kyros was hunched over me.

I was bruised and sore. The pain I'd experienced in the vehicle was gone, and I quickly evaluated my physical condition before sitting up. I inched away from him and rested my back against the wall of the stadium.

Kyros-Paeon appeared every bit as beat up as I felt. My clothing was shredded and bloodied, and my hair tangled and matted. With trembling fingers, I touched my face and neck then my right side, recalling the puncture from the car.

You cured me! I said, glaring at him.

"Of course. It's what we do." Kyros was in charge. His brown eyes were twinkling as he glanced at me before looking out again over the large field.

No god – even one who heals – can be trusted. He will turn on you, Kyros.

"Look, lady," he returned with some exasperation. "I get that you have an issue with gods. But Paeon saved you and your ..." He motioned to my stomach.

My breath caught, and I tensed.

Kyros rolled his eyes. "He says I wasn't supposed to mention the fact you're pregnant. But he saved all our lives and you should respect him for that. He didn't have to do it."

He did it because he wants something. I owe him nothing for helping me and if you tell anyone – ever – about my child, I will kill you myself. I returned icily.

"Considering that was your plan anyway, I'm not exactly threatened by the latest reminder you plan to murder me at some point," Kyros returned. "Just ... relax. Okay? You can be pissed at Paeon and me – or both of us – when we're safe."

If I had a knife ...

"As a reminder, I can hear your thoughts," Kyros said.

To Hades with a knife. If I weren't so sore, I'd kill him with my bare hands.

He sighed, as if he really, truly didn't know how terrible the gods could be. I wished I could convey the knowledge to him somehow. No human deserved what suffering Paeon was likely to inflict upon Kyros before this was over.

"You're welcome," Kyros murmured. "Did you know it's a girl?"

Some of my anger melted, and I rested a hand on my lower abdomen. A girl would make for five queens in a row, assuming we both survived the next few months.

I didn't know, I answered. *She's healthy? The bomb didn't hurt her?*

"They both are healthy. You're carrying twin girls."

Twins. I had never heard of anyone in the Bloodline birthing twins. How was it possible, when only one could rule? Would they both bear the curse, if I couldn't rid the Bloodline of it during my rule?

Restless to continue my war, I wiped my face and sat up straight, testing my body. *Where are we?*

"Oh, about twenty kilometers from where we were supposed to be," Kyros said with a snort.

You carried me twenty kilometers?

"Yeah. I played football in college. You're pretty light." He flashed a smile. "And Paeon can instantly heal any exhaustion, strains or muscle fatigue I feel. We make a good team."

I pursed my lips. He already understood, without a shred of doubt, what I thought of his *team.*

What of Herakles and the others in our van? I asked.

"Those with us didn't make it. *We* wouldn't have made it, if not for Paeon. I don't know anything about Herakles' condition. When we got out of the car, all we could think about was helping you and getting as far from our attackers as possible."

So there were attackers, not just a bomb.

"Yeah." Kyros frowned. "SISA and military."

I wanted to believe Lantos would never send his people after me with the intention of hurting me, but I didn't know him as well as I once thought I did. He was a lesson about not trusting anyone – a very painful one. Anyone posing a threat to his or Cleon's plans was likely to be killed, no matter what emotional attachments were once believed to be present.

It was my fault for falling in love anyway. I knew better. My duty always preceded any personal interest. A queen could never let her heart lead, when it was her shrewd mind preserving the Bloodline and the family's elevated position in the world.

Did Theodocia make it back inside the wall? I asked.

"We don't know," Kyros replied. "Sorry. We've been concerned with keeping you alive and out of the hands of the uniforms."

Deep inside, a part of me softened when I realized what Kyros had gone through to protect me despite how I treated him and Paeon at camp. Was it possible to distrust the god and admire the human, even if they were trapped in the same body?

Thank you. The words were difficult to admit.

"You're welcome. You can put a knife in our back when we get to camp, if it'll make you feel better."

I settled another cold look on Kyros, who smiled in return. *I will look you in the eye when I do it,* I assured him. *I'm not a coward.*

"I know," he said. "Do you feel well enough to leave the stadium?"

I stood in the shadows of the box seats of the stadium. My body was healed, aside from the occasional bruise and lingering muscle stiffness. Considering what I'd been through, I was in near-perfect shape. It was hard not to feel grateful when my children and I were not only alive but healthy hours after surviving an explosion.

I'm fine, I replied.

Kyros stood and handed me a bottle of water. "The only thing Paeon can't do is rehydrate me. We figured that out the hard way a few weeks ago." He laughed. "That was rough."

Something about this human tugged at the tension that was always curled at the base of my belly. I wanted to do something that I never did ever. I wanted to let my guard drop a little when he was around. His informal manner would never survive court or the political scene of DC. Easygoing and friendly, Kyros often rubbed me the wrong way, because he didn't seem to understand how serious our circumstances were or what was at stake. Like Herakles, he was trusting and soft inside, which was a recipe for being killed.

Was he a genuinely nice guy, or was he an absolute idiot? The line between the two was blurred with him.

"I may be a Virginia farm boy, but I'm not stupid," he said. "I understand what's at stake. I guess I just have a different perspective than you do."

Displeased with his ability to read my mind, I narrowed my eyes at him and then struck off down the field, towards one of stairwells leading out of the field and into the stadium.

"Do you know where we're going?" he asked, trailing.

Yes. I glanced at the night sky to orient myself. Herakles had taught me to navigate by the stars as soon as we established camp. He was always preparing everyone around him for the worst-case scenario. For once, I was grateful for his attention to what sometimes seemed to be the smallest, most mundane details I didn't usually concern myself with.

I needed him to be okay, not just for myself, but also for the sake of my war. Herakles belonged at my side, the human, compassionate face of the battle against the gods. I liked him. I didn't want him wrenched out of my world as everyone else always seemed to be.

Kyros said nothing, and I led us into the stadium, through the silent hallways winding around it that once housed restrooms and eateries, and out into the quiet night. We paused at the edge of the expansive parking lot.

Do you sense anything? I asked, lingering in the shadows of the stadium.

"Now you believe me," he replied.

Twice was enough to prove the point – even to me – that he had an ability I didn't think he should.

"Feels good," he said after a moment. "I'm pretty sure we lost them about a kilometer from the stadium."

I strode into the parking lot. He drew abreast of me, and I gave him a sidelong glance. Built like a linebacker, Kyros carried himself with upbeat confidence and walked with a gait that bordered on a swagger. His dark eyes were bright and alert.

Skeptical after a lifetime where I was taught I could trust Theodocia and Tommy, and no one else, I found it hard to believe he was a good person. Good people with no hidden agendas didn't belong in this game, in the control of a god, in this world at all. Survival depended upon ruthlessness and strategy, and in general, good people were not known to possess these traits.

"Every once in a while, you think something nice, and I start to thank you. Then you think something really offensive, and I'm left wondering why I would ever consider thanking you at all when I know what's coming," he said quietly. "Good people can be survivors, too, and gods can be genuinely benevolent. Not everyone is out to get you or to betray you."

Anger lit my blood. He was aware of Lantos or at least, that someone I trusted had recently turned on me. He had to be since I thought about Lantos more when Kyros-Paeon was around than when they weren't. It struck me then that the timing of my Lantos thoughts made little sense, given the son of a Titan was just as likely to be an enemy of Paeon as I was.

Why, then, did I always think of Lantos when I was near Kyros?

"We better pick up the pace." Kyros-Paeon's gaze was to the

north and the abandoned cityscape in that direction. "And find cover."

I didn't need a second warning and jogged towards the forest hedging the parking lot dead ahead of us. Kyros kept pace with me easily. We reached it and ducked into the shadows of the trees, just as headlights appeared from the northern side of the parking lot. A caravan of armored, military vehicles drove close to the stadium and stopped.

How do you do that? I asked, sinking deeper into the forest.

"I'm not sure." Kyros sounded puzzled. "Paeon says he can't do it on his own, and I know I can't. There's something in our chemistry."

If you tell me one more time that you make a good team, one of us will not make it back to camp.

Kyros chuckled. "I'm just happy you listened. I definitely don't want to be blown up again."

It was my turn to roll my eyes in the darkness of the forest. A familiar form emerged from one of the vehicles, and fury warmed me from the inside out.

I told Theodocia he should have been killed long ago, I said at the sight of Niko.

"It can't be easy for her to kill her baby-daddy," Kyros replied.

I'd kill my children's father in a heartbeat.

"You say that now, but what about when you see him again?"

Pain radiated through me, the kind with no physical source. I never wanted to see Lantos again. When I had the city under control, he was among the first people I'd send before a firing squad or have hanged or worse – send to the House. He had betrayed me worse than Niko ever did Theodocia, and he'd pay the price for it.

So why did the thought of him disappearing from the face of the planet – forever – hurt, when I had every right to end his life?

Thankfully, Kyros chose not to respond to these thoughts. As if sensing my pain, he was quiet. I watched Niko for a moment, vowing to send an assassin after him the first chance I had, and then stepped away from the edge of the cement. The only good to come out of

Niko being here: if Theodocia were in danger, he would help her. Theodocia always doubted this about Niko, but I saw the way he looked at her, the few times all three of our paths crossed. He wouldn't let anything happen to her anymore than he would his son. If she were in danger, or if she didn't make it back to the wall, he would distract or bribe his men to give her a chance to escape, if not outright order his people to help her.

What would Lantos do, if he knew I were here?

He would let me die, if it suited his purpose.

If I let myself think about him, I would break down and cry, which was rare for me. Theodocia brought out the only drop of good existing in Niko, and I ... well, I brought out Lantos' betrayal. What did that say about me?

We need to go. They won't stop until they find me. I said to Kyros. I turned away from the scene before me and reinforced my emotional state with the reminder of what happened when I chose my heart over my duty. Resolve solidified inside me, and the pain withdrew without leaving completely. It lingered in the shadows of my mind, waiting for me to allow it to confuse me again, which I wasn't going to do.

My path was set. I would fulfill my oath to free humanity or die in the process. There was no room for Lantos or emotion or doubt or torturing myself with thoughts of what might have been.

"We'll stay ahead of them," Kyros said.

Picking my path through the forest, I reached a sidewalk marking a running trail and began walking quickly down it, fueled by the anger in my blood.

"I know what you think of my opinion, but for the record, you're amazing and strong," Kyros said. "You're also human. You're too hard on yourself."

I'm not a mere human. I am a queen who happens to be cursed by the gods. I will behave as required to fulfill my duties without any concern what you think about it.

He said nothing else.

I marched until my anger ebbed and was replaced by more tempered determination. My pace slowed then, and I became fully aware of my surroundings. Owls, crickets and other nocturnal animals were active in the woods hedging the sidewalk. The summer night smelled of trees. It was clear and breezy but humid enough that I was sweating after an hour of walking.

We passed a sign marking this trail as following an old railroad path, and I checked the sky again to ensure the trail was leading us in the direction we needed to go. Without a map or my cell phone, I couldn't gauge our exact path. At some point, we were going to need assistance to find camp. I was confident I could get us to the general vicinity, thanks to Herakles' basic survival lessons.

We walked for two to three hours in silence, without passing anyone, and with no sign of Niko following. At that point, Kyros spoke.

"Not to be a downer, but could we stop for a break? Healing as much as we have the past few hours drains Paeon and also me."

I glanced up and noticed the dark circles around his eyes for the first time. I was torn briefly between pressing on to reach camp as soon as possible and stopping, because my companion requested it. Being tired was constant for me anymore, since I found out I was pregnant. I had a feeling if I said no, Kyros was too good-natured to object.

If it were only Paeon, I would continue, but it wasn't. The man beside me housing two spirits was at least half human, and he had risked his own life to protect mine.

Very well, I relented.

"We think there's shelter that way." He pointed.

I stepped aside to let him lead us in the direction he indicated. We left the path onto a dirt trail emptying out into the parking area of what was once probably a great estate, before the gods firebombed it five years prior.

Kyros made a sound of disappointment at the sight of the

destroyed mansion and approached the garage, which was equally damaged.

"I guess it's as good as we'll find," he said. "Wait here. I'll see if I can find blankets or something." He struck off towards the house.

I circled the garage and spotted an empty pool a short distance away. The quiet estate was situated on several acres of cleared land. A herd of deer grazed on the expansive lawn. My eyes fell to the jungle gym not far from the pool and then to the sole tree visible in the yard, close enough to the house to provide shade during summer picnics and far enough for its branches not to pose a threat if hit by lightning during a summer storm.

On a hunch, I approached the tree and spotted the wooden boards hammered into its trunk to create a ladder. I craned my neck back to see the tree house with satisfaction.

I would definitely feel less exposed up there than sleeping in the middle of a field. Testing the boards closest to me, I determined they were safe enough to support me and climbed the tree.

The tree house was empty, its interior small. Spider webs filled the open windows, and dust was thick on the floor. I entered and sat down in the middle, relaxing for the first time since leaving camp to meet Theodocia.

"Phoibe?" Kyros called. "I mean, Your Majesty?" This was followed by a sigh. "Well, how am I supposed to know protocol for dealing with royalty?"

I started to smile at the sound of him arguing with himself.

"Yes, I remember. We don't want her pissed enough to murder us."

Leaning out of the tree house, I summoned him telepathically.

Kyros was at the back door of the destroyed mansion, his arms filled with linens. He looked up when I called him and then smiled before starting towards the tree house. Flinging the linens over one shoulder, he scaled the ladder with ease and entered the space that had not seemed quite so confined when I was alone in it. He hunched over to prevent his head from hitting the roof and jostled past me before he sat.

"Sorry."

I moved over to give him more room. The difference in our sizes was more pronounced in the tree house. His feet were going to stick out the door when he lay down, while I was perfectly comfortable with extra space for my limbs.

"I couldn't find any blankets, but these towels were sitting on the dryer. It was the only thing in the house not completely destroyed." He handed me a thick, plush towel. "These are nicer than blankets anyway. Nothing like what I had growing up."

I was accustomed to the best of everything. I had never had a reason to believe towels came in different qualities from which I was used to. I rolled the towel up and placed it on the floor of the tree house then stretched out onto my back.

Never did I imagine sleeping on the floor would feel this good. I released a deep sigh. My bruised body relaxed of its own accord, as if it, too, needed a break after the stressful night.

"Thank you for stopping," Kyros said and stretched out beside me. "We were starting to feel sick."

What were you doing with your life when Paeon possessed you? I asked.

"Working in a town where everyone was trying to cooperate to survive. I was on the hunting and chopping wood teams and basically any task needing brute strength. I was a terrible hunter, though. Killing animals isn't really my thing, which is probably one of the reasons Paeon and I get along so well," he replied.

Every time he said Paeon's name, I wanted to snap at him. But I didn't, and I managed to listen without criticizing their relationship. It was a first for me, and it was difficult.

"Why do you hate him so much?" There was a smile in Kyros' voice.

Because his kind are selfish.

"You said you were cursed. It seems more personal."

I rolled onto my side, placing my back to him and effectively ending the conversation.

"Okay then. Sleep well."

I stared into the darkness. Of all the thoughts running through my mind, the one concerning me most had nothing to do with making it back to camp and everything to do with the idea I almost hoped Paeon wasn't like the rest of the gods. That maybe, being a healer rendered him more compassionate, less likely to play games or possibly, gave him the ability to sympathize with others instead of using them and cursing them as the rest of the gods did.

Was it Paeon I wanted to be different, or Kyros? Or ... the combination? Dealing with Kyros was sometimes maddening, until I recalled he was the kind of person I was supposed to be protecting with a war I couldn't get off the ground. It didn't seem right to despise humanity and protect its members at the same time. This was a very *gods*-like attitude to have. My problem wasn't Kyros as much as his nonchalant attitude towards being possessed and allowing a god to do as he pleased with a human host.

This was a personal war, one I was waging for the hundreds of members of the Bloodline preceding me as well as for the humans who didn't understand how dangerous the gods were.

Kyros ... well, he complicated the black and white view I had developed towards what I was doing and why, and I didn't like the challenge to my principals he represented.

Closing my eyes, I started to drift to sleep. I was jarred out of my doze by the sudden sense of being back in the truck, and rolling over and over and over and over ...

I snapped awake and recalled where I was. Relaxing, I tried again to fall asleep.

Fiery adrenaline raced through me, as if my system were reliving the explosion. I became fevered and agitated, caught in the state between sleep and consciousness. The sound of something ripping nudged me farther away from slumber. It was followed by a strange physical sensation in my shoulders. They were ... pulling out of my body. The explosion was tearing me apart ...

"Um, Phoibe?" Kyros' voice reached me across the darkness of my mind. "I mean, Your Majesty?"

His scent was strong in my nostrils: sweat, human and rain. My skin became sensitive and the brush of the towel against my cheek felt like fire and sandpaper. I wrestled with myself, unable to awaken fully and reassure my flighty mind that I wasn't burning in the explosion.

"I think you need to wake up," Kyros said.

He burst into full color and clarity in my mind, which would not have been surprising, if my eyes hadn't been closed. I could see everything painted on the back of my eyelids, clear as midday. The edge of fatigue in his voice was joined by alarm. I heard and saw him shift closer, reaching out to shake me awake with an expression bordering on baffled.

My eyes snapped open, and I stared up at the ceiling of the tree house. I saw every splinter, every piece of dust, and every minute detail of the wood two meters above me. The summer breeze against my skin made me jerk in unexpected awareness. My body contorted in an uncontrollable spasm. I was being torn apart from the inside and healed so quickly, I had no idea which sensation I felt: fire or coldness.

At last, the episode passed, and my body ceased bucking – but I didn't feel remotely normal. The sound of leaves brushing against one another outside the tree house was nearly a shout in my ears, and my sense of smell was so intense, I wriggled my nose to prevent a sneeze that was forming.

What's happening to me? I asked Kyros, twisting to see his face.

He had moved across the tree house from me. "Um. It's kind of hard to explain," he said after a pause.

I struggled to sit up, weighed down by what felt like a heavy blanket around my shoulders. Something whacked Kyros in the leg as I moved, and I froze.

My skin was gray. My nails had turned into claws. I touched my face and uttered a broken sound. My features were lopsided, and my hair was gone. Shifting forward, I started to fall backward before the long, thick cord of my tail balanced me. Wings flared out on either side of my body, smacking Kyros again. My shredded clothing was at my feet.

What did you do to me? I demanded, rounding on him.

"This isn't us," he said quickly.

No one else has been near me! What did you do?

"We *can't* turn you into anything else, and if we could, it wouldn't be a gargoyle."

Gargoyle. A vision of the creature that visited me when I was six flashed into my mind. He, too, had possessed wings, gray skin, a tail … and resembled one of the grotesques perched on the corners of temples in New York.

He had warned me of the Bloodline's curse.

Had he been talking about *this*? Would I turn to stone this night? What would happen to my daughters?

I'm a monster! I shrieked in silence.

"It's not that bad."

How can you say that?

Kyros cleared his throat. "Paeon needs to talk to you."

I didn't answer and stared at my talons, struggling not to panic. If I were a monster, were the twins in my stomach also monsters? What had happened? More importantly, *why*?

"Hear me out." Paeon's voice was lighter, less emotional than Kyros.

Too shocked to know what else to do, I waited and grappled with my self-control before I completely lost it.

"Nothing is wrong with you," the god claimed.

My jaw dropped, and another strange, beastly sound came out.

"The Bloodline members are all like you."

Cursed by the gods! Tears filled my eyes. I managed to stand despite the awkward weight of wings. My tail acted to balance me out of instinct when I felt like I was about to fall.

"It's not what you think."

I felt suddenly claustrophobic in the tiny tree house, overpowered by the details and scents and trapped with one of the gods I hated with all my soul. Staggering to the door, I grabbed the doorframe and tried to turn. One wing made it out while the other flared behind me, knocking me off balance. I tumbled out of the tree house.

My wings stopped my fall in mid air. They stretched out on either side of me, flapping to keep me aloft with no conscious thought from me. I hovered in the air outside the tree house, not liking the sense of having nothing solid to stand on.

I wanted to cry, to scream, to tear Paeon apart with my claws and the fangs resting on my lips. If the tree house overwhelmed me, the night was much more unnerving. My senses were a hundred times more active and sensitive, registering the smallest movement and sound for hundreds of yards in each direction.

I tossed my head back to stare at the sky. If ever I needed my patron goddess, Artemis, it was now.

What's happening to me? I screamed telepathically into the night.

ELEVEN
ALESSANDRA

"YOU'RE SLOW TODAY. You don't look sick."

Gods, Niko was driving me crazy. He was as unrelenting as usual. After two nights with less than three hours of sleep each night, I was in no shape to handle him in the ring or out. Light headed, and panting after ten minutes of sparring, I leaned against the ropes of the boxing ring.

I didn't answer him. My mood was fickle, and I didn't want to tell him to join Cerberus in Hades and earn myself a punch or two. The ever-present, three headed dog monster had become my only companion. He didn't need sleep either, and he sat or paced or stood behind the curtain separating my world from that of Hades. All. Day. Long. I had never had a pet in the forest, but I did now. I didn't have to worry about feeding or walking him, which was nice.

"What's wrong with you?" Niko yanked my chin up while dragging me from my thoughts again. He studied my face.

"Nothing!" I tried to pull away.

He ignored me. "You're weak, too. Are you sleeping?"

I sighed.

"So you're not." he grumbled and released me, stepping away.

"I'm having issues," I replied and straightened.

"*What* issues?" he retorted. "Villa doesn't have enough servants or shoes for you?"

"You have no idea what I'm going through!" Anger flared within me, warming my blood and clearing my mind temporarily.

"C'mon." He motioned me forward. "Hit me if you can. It'll help."

"You're my therapist now?"

"I don't give a shit how you feel, kid, but you gotta be physically ready to deal with the world, and you aren't."

I was agitated enough at him to give him a good thirty minutes of sparring before I ran out of energy again. Taking a break in my corner, I sipped water and studied him. He was ... Niko. Regular, irritable, quick-to-snap Niko.

We hadn't sparred yesterday, because he was hunting insurgents. I had dreaded our session today, certain he would beat me to a pulp for my involuntary involvement in helping Cleon disable Theodocia. Forty minutes into our hour session, he hadn't dropped the hammer, and I was getting edgy.

"You're not mad at me?" I asked him at last.

"You'd know if I were."

"Do you even know what I'm talking about?"

"It's likely I won't care."

"Theodocia."

He glanced up. "What about her?" His tone remained the same, but I sensed it took effort.

"I put her into this frozen-rubbery state of immobility," I said. "She's a gummy statue."

One eyebrow lifted.

He doesn't know. Whether this was Cleon's assertion or my realization, I couldn't tell.

I had Niko's attention, which was not always a good thing. He lowered his water bottle and approached, a predatory gleam in his eyes.

I knew he loved her still. Another thought that was both Cleon's and mine. *If he hits you, he hits me. Do not let that happen.* This was distinctly Cleon's order. I shared his concern. I didn't really have the intention of getting my ass beat by a pissed Niko, who was just as likely to cause permanent damage as not, if he were pushed to the point where he stopped checking his blows.

"This is your fault!" I snapped at the unwelcome voice in my head.

"What's my fault?" Niko asked.

"Not you," I replied. "Maybe you should talk to Cleon about this."

"You can tell me. Or I can make you tell me."

Before Niko, I never would've folded to such a threat. Herakles had instructed me how to fight. The one lesson he neglected: how to deal with someone who was so much stronger than me, I didn't stand a chance. Herakles was cut from the same mold as Niko, but he was gentle and patient, whereas Niko didn't care at all for my mental or physical welfare, beyond what he was paid to care about. Even the butcher Adonis had acted with restraint when it came to me.

"Cleon sent you out to catch the Silent Queen. While you were outside the wall, he ambushed Theodocia," I replied. The images in my mind were Cleon's, and I began to think there was a small benefit to being connected with him. If he knew what I did, then wouldn't I understand when he was lying from here on out? "He was going to kill her, but I turned her into a gummy statue instead."

Emotion disappeared from Niko's features. He stood absolutely still for a moment. I shifted my weight, uncertain if he were going to walk away or attack.

"She's the leader of the insurgency. He was doing what he had to," he said after a tense pause.

"Is that what you'll tell Tommy, when Cleon kills his mother?" I said.

The words were out of my mouth before I realized how stupid they were.

I said NOT to get punched, Cleon snapped.

I was halfway out of the ring, unwilling to face Niko after his initial threat about his son.

Not only did the former mercenary not attack, but he didn't emote, either. He was watching me, as if trying to decide whether or not I was telling the truth or maybe, what to do with me.

"Two o'clock tomorrow. If you aren't up to your usual activity level, it will not go well for you," he said. Spinning, he snatched his towel and left the ring.

I released the breath I was holding.

That went well, Cleon said.

"No, it didn't," I replied. "If he's too angry to blow up, someone is in trouble."

You doubt his loyalty.

"Never," I said, thoughts on Niko's son. I had nothing to offer him in exchange for his loyalty whereas Cleon held the upper hand. The compound was the safest place on Earth, and Tommy was in the middle of it.

What that meant for Theodocia, I was afraid to imagine. I could see Niko leaving her where she was for the time being – or maybe forever. Cleon didn't want her dead, so she was, in a twisted way, safe. Maybe having her close was doing Niko an indirect favor, since she wouldn't be in harm's way on the streets while Cleon quelled the rebellion.

Was this my reasoning or Cleon's? The Supreme Magistrate did nothing out of good faith or benevolence, and I doubted Theodocia was *safe* when she was anywhere near him.

Fear caused my heartbeat to accelerate.

For the first time, I couldn't identify whose rationale it was. I was no closer to dislodging Cleon from my mind. If anything, he was becoming more entrenched. My thoughts were an open book to him, and his were becoming indistinguishable from mine.

"Cleon wants to see you. Now." Niko poked his head in from the locker room, cell phone in hand.

On cue, my escort filed in from outside the gym. I slung my towel around my neck and grabbed my water bottle before reluctantly trailing the armed guards out of the gym and to the House.

We met in Cleon's office again, on the second floor. Instead of sitting behind his desk, he was seated with a tumbler of cognac at the sitting area of his office, beneath a portrait that made me roll my eyes.

"I take it that's new," I said and shook my head. In the fashion of royal portraiture, Cleon had been painted solo, standing, and wearing a military uniform filled with medals. "Were you even in the army?"

"I'm the Commander-in-Chief of the military and SISA," he replied. His words ricocheted in my head, and I dropped my gaze to him. "Sit."

I did so and watched him pour more amber liquid into his glass tumbler. Tilting my head to the side, I shifted uncomfortably in my seat.

"You have a headache," I said, able to feel what he did, now that we were a meter apart. "You're weak. Dizzy, and the back of –"

"Enough."

"Side effects of this joining?" I asked allowed, echoing his thoughts.

"Dr. Khan assures me I'm well," he replied.

"But you don't believe her."

"I wanted to discuss something important," he said, ignoring me.

"I can't imagine what."

He gave me one of his looks that said he was trying to be patient, while he ordered me silent with his thoughts. "I wanted you to know why I'm doing what I'm doing."

"I do know," I replied. "You want to take over the world."

"That's sort of a side benefit," he said with a smile. "There's much more to it. I'm saving those who deserve it from a larger threat."

What in Hades was he talking about? I knew him to be a little crazy but this assertion sounded outlandish, even for him. His mind was silent on what he meant, giving me hope we weren't fully integrated into each other's consciousness yet.

"Many years ago, I was granted an audience with the Oracle, as many wealthy and influential people are," he began. "I don't know what most people ask her. Maybe about their fates or fortunes, but I asked her something different. I've always wanted more. More power, more money, and specifically, more knowledge I could use in my pursuit of power."

Cleon's soft, low voice and deceptively non-threatening manner had always deflated my anger and irritation, whether or not I wanted it to. I relaxed back into the plush, leather chair. I had no intention of believing a word he said, but I studied him, seeking some sort of weakness or tell or other red flag I could use to dismantle what he had done to me and what he was planning to do.

"Among the questions I posed, I asked her how to become the most powerful person ever to exist," he continued. "She led me to Niko, who is the sole reason I survived the gods' wrath and elevated myself to this position. And then she told me something I didn't understand at the time, or for several years afterward. She said I was asking the wrong question, that it wasn't about becoming the most powerful person to exist. She said only one person could ever wield such power – the Oracle – and one day, I would understand what that meant. The question I should have been asking was how to control the most powerful person on the Earth. Then she gave me a number. Four twenty-five."

I was waiting for him to say something horrible – that he had done something to cause the Oracle to sink into her coma. When his story stopped, I leaned forward, able to experience the racing of his blood as anticipation set in.

"Okay. What does it mean?" I asked.

"Five years ago, everyone of significance in the world was gathered in one place, for a ceremony that occurs only once a generation, during the coronation of the ruler of Greece. It was the Silent Queen's fourteenth birthday, the day she claimed her rightful title, the day everyone of importance in the world was gathered in one place, to include Zeus and almost all – if not all – of the gods and goddesses, who were certain to be in our world for the event."

I listened, unable to help my fascination. His emotion was high as well, and I shifted in my seat, hating the sensation of two people in my mind.

"Four twenty five. Fourth month, twenty fifth day," Cleon explained. "The day of the coronation. The day the gods purportedly attacked the earth. Over the course of twenty four hours, eighty percent of the human population was destroyed, and the gateway to the gods' world was closed."

"Cecelia foresaw it," I guessed. "She warned you, but you didn't know that's what it was."

"I thought the same. I wasn't present in New York, because the former Supreme Magistrate and I didn't see eye to eye. He considered me to be competition, and he banished me to an unimportant political position in northern Maryland. I was within reach, but far enough not to challenge him. In any case, I wasn't in New York when the political elite and the wealthiest people in the world were murdered," Cleon said. "I came here, to this compound, with the help of Niko, a semi-loyal mercenary on my payroll. I did what anyone would do when faced with what we thought was the end of the world. I went to the Oracle, and I asked her what was happening. Her response: *four twenty five. Now you know what power is.*"

I frowned. Was he saying what I thought he was? That the gods weren't behind the Holy Wars? "I don't understand," I said.

"I think you do."

"Um, Cecelia warned you what the gods would do. She wouldn't do this."

"How certain are you?"

I laughed. "I would trust her over you any day!" I exclaimed. Yet the image in my head was of Lantos when he, too, warned me I didn't know Cecelia as well as I thought I did. Why would I ever entertain anything spoken by either of the lying politicians?

"If the gods were cut off from their power source, how could they have done this?" Cleon asked.

"They were cut off *after* she closed the gate! She closed the gate to protect us from them."

"Think about this, Alessandra," he said with tried patience. "Who had the better reason to attack humanity? The gods, who were venerated and worshipped, and who have suffered alongside humans since that day? Or the Oracle who was a slave to man and god?"

"Whatever lie you've created ... I can't even ... no!" I managed. "Humans have been preparing to rebel against the gods and return us to the Old Ways for years! They found out, retaliated and before they could cross back to their world, the Oracle trapped them here."

"But why trap them here? Why not let them return and close the gate then?"

"Maybe because she was pissed about what they did? She's still human."

He sat forward, irritated. "Are you capable of seeing this perspective at all? On four twenty five, I realized there was one person who could have launched such an attack, and it wasn't the gods. On four twenty five, I also came to understand that if I wanted her power, I had to control her. From the day I reached this compound five years ago, I began researching how it was possible to control someone with absolute power, and I came to the conclusion that I had to be able to control that person *before* she reached the height of her power." He studied me. "Did you believe the chip in your head was developed on a whim overnight? That level of technology took years to create and close to a billion drachma in research, custom technology and favors to gods."

"You could've been developing it to put in her head," I reasoned staunchly. "It's not like she's able to defend herself where she is now!"

"You really believe she's defenseless? Helpless? You and I both know where your power comes from, and how you can slide into the other dimensions or planes or worlds or whatever these alternate realities, without your body."

I wanted to think it was his thoughts polluting my mind, but some part of his wild claims – however tiny – struck a chord within me. He really was making sense. Cecelia didn't need her body in alternate planes, and she could still affect our world from those places. But everything else he said was ridiculous! "I'm not about to buy into your insanity, Cleon!" I said.

He winced and touched his head. His dull headache was at the back of my mind, but whatever other pain he felt, it wasn't conveyed to me.

"It would not have had any use to me in her head," he said with a controlled sigh. "My goal in binding your mind with mine has not been solely about power. It's been about preserving the desirable elements of our society from what she started. Zeus stepped in before she could finish. He's siphoning the power from every other god trapped here to give *you* the chance to stop the Oracle from destroying everything that remains. But we're running out of time, and he's running out of power."

It was the most ridiculous story ... no! It was a *delusion* so intricately crafted, it could only come from someone who had fallen into the void of insanity long ago. He hid the signs well; I never suspected this level of madness dwelt beneath the smooth-talking, brilliant politician's façade!

I stood up, disgusted with his claim about Cecelia, a woman dismembered and enslaved in agony by people like the one sitting in front of me. "Enough," I said.

"If you'd listen to the voices, you would hear him tell you the same," Cleon insisted.

I froze.

"Yes," he said. "I can hear them, too. The whispers Lantos allowed into your mind the day our minds were linked. You've actively blocked them, but I've spent quite some time listening to what they're trying to tell you."

"Do you think the gods would *admit* to trying to destroy the world, when they need your help to return to theirs?" I challenged. "Of course they're going to lie about their intentions. Of the two of us, you should know a liar when you hear one."

"Clearly you aren't ready for this conversation." Cleon stood. "I am trying to save what I can of those deserving humans, through your power."

"Deserving? You mean those rich enough to afford whatever price you dictate! You want to rule over a handful of rich people."

"I want to create a colony, a utopia, to start humanity anew, with principals and wealth," he said. "You can't disagree that eliminating poverty would only benefit the world."

Was I really having a discussion about utopia with this madman? "You want to eliminate the *poor*. Not poverty," I corrected him.

"In any case, when you realize I am trying to act for the general benefit and proliferation of our species, you'll stop fighting me and the gods, and you'll face the real threat."

I stared at him and then laughed, incredulous.

"Listen to them," Cleon said and strode towards the door. Opening the door, he glanced out towards the guards. "Return her to her villa. She doesn't leave again until I allow it."

Of all the discussions I thought I would ever have with Cleon, this was not one. I bolted from his office with more eagerness than I'd ever left his presence with. Just when I didn't think he could surprise me more, he came up with the most incredible delusion I had ever heard!

That the Supreme Magistrate – who tried to murder the Silent Queen, Theodocia, and anyone else in his path, who was using my power to hurt innocent people – believed his creation of a utopia for wealthy people wasn't as crazy as the gods destroying humanity ... He was completely insane! He sincerely believed himself to be the good guy in this scenario.

Was he trying to brainwash me? Place these thoughts into my head, so when our minds fully merged, I accepted his delusion faster and didn't fight him? Why else would he possibly reveal something of this nature?

I hurried back to the villa, consumed by Cleon's bizarre theory. He did nothing without considering how his actions would better his position. What did he possibly hope to accomplish by turning me against Cecelia? By flat out lying about why the gods had lashed out at humanity and started the Holy Wars?

Only when I was standing in my bedroom did I let out the scream of frustration bottled up inside me. My eyes went to the names on the memorial wall, and any credence I might have one day been willing to allow Cleon vanished.

A man who murdered over three thousand people as a demonstration of his power could never be believed about his true motives!

Unless I wanted Cecelia to see what I could do as well as Artemis and the insurgency, he said telepathically.

"I thought you were working for the gods," I pointed out. "Artemis is a goddess."

I wouldn't say I was working FOR them. I'm working for the cause of humanity. The gods are a threat, just not the primary threat.

Maybe it made a little sense.

No, it didn't! The acceptance I felt was his, wasn't it?

"I hate you," I whispered and clutched my temples. Tears of anger were in my eyes. Most of the time, I could pretend I either wasn't losing my mind to a madman, or that I still had time to find a way to stop him. "Get out of my head!"

Was it already too late? I had already witnessed the expansion of my green ribbons to him, and physical sensations I experienced were transferred to him. Had my denial of my power and adherence to Cecelia's guidance only enabled the merging of our minds? If I tried harder early on to dislodge him using my magic, would I be in this position?

Cerberus was watching, which only made me angrier.

"I'm tired of this," I said. Swiping at my tears, I went to my nightstand and hauled open a drawer. I snatched the smallest of the knives I kept there and yanked the sheath off. "This ends now!"

Stop! Cleon commanded.

With a deep breath, I felt for the telltale scars at the base of my neck with the fingers of one hand then positioned the tip of the knife with the other.

Stop! This time, there were so many voices, I jerked.

I ignored them and plunged the knife into the base of my skull. Agony shot through me. It wasn't just my scream I heard, but Cleon's as well in my head. I sagged to the ground. Before I fell unconscious, a familiar sensation raced through me.

A vision exploded into my mind, absorbing my pain and substituting my reality with another.

I STOOD in the Oracle's caverns beneath the compound. My future body was there, frozen in place. The glass of her protective bubble had been lifted, and I was touching Cecelia with one hand. Unnerved to see myself, I circled me. I didn't appear to be a gummy statue, but I wasn't animated, either, as if my body was here and my mind was elsewhere. The alternate plane? Another vision? I didn't know.

"They breached the walls," an unfamiliar voice said quietly.

Turning, I peered into the darkness engulfing the back part of the caverns, where I'd had my brain surgery weeks ago.

"Do whatever you have to in order to keep everyone out of here," Lantos said. His features were pale and for once, he wasn't amused or smiling or pleased. He clutched his hands behind his back and stood a short distance from my inanimate body.

The soldier who warned him left, and the soft sound of the elevator door sliding closed was all I heard.

Recalling Lantos' assertion that there were clues and hints in my visions, I circled myself again then walked around him before striding to Cecelia.

What was happening between Cecelia and me? Who breached the walls?

"Is it working?" Lantos asked.

I looked around, not spotting the small frame of Tommy until he emerged from the shadows.

"I don't know," Tommy replied. "Thanatos can't hear me right now."

"Then I guess we wait."

"For what?" he asked, looking up at Lantos.

"Betray them all, die a hero," Lantos said almost too quietly for me to catch. "We wait for someone to murder me."

"Okay." Tommy said nothing, and his eyes returned to Cecelia. It didn't surprise me that the son of Theodocia and Niko seemed comfortable with the concept of murder, though I did pity him for not having the innocent childhood Herakles had tried to give me.

"You know what to do when that happens?" Lantos asked with a tight smile at Tommy.

He nodded.

Nothing in what they said or within the scene in front of me gave me any kind of insight into what I needed to know about this vision. Did I want this to happen, or was I supposed to work to prevent it? When was this supposed to occur? Why was I touching Cecelia? For an energy transfusion?

How was I supposed to determine any of this?

I began circling Lantos and Tommy, my mind full of questions. Where was Theodocia? Why was I down here? Why were *they*? What in Hades was a twelve year old child supposed to do, who would murder Lantos, and why were Tommy's parents allowing him to hang out with such an untrustworthy character as Lantos?

Before I could circle them completely, the scene changed suddenly.

I squinted beneath the blinding midday sun. The breeze felt of fall – cool where the sun was warm. Explosions ricocheted in the distance, and the report of gunfire was close.

"We have until dusk. No longer," said a familiar voice behind me.

Herakles! I whirled, thrilled by the idea of seeing him in my vision. He stood with a small group of people behind me. I approached them, orienting myself. I stood on a hill a short distance from the wall, over-looking the battle taking place between the Silent Queen's troops in purple and the combined SISA-military forces in black. The wall around DC was breached, with the fiercest of the fighting occurring around the gaping hole. Smoke rose from several points within the city.

Wearing her crown the Silent Queen stood with Herakles and several of her commanders, observing the battle with intense interest. My heart leapt in my chest at the sight of my scarred, red-haired protector. I yearned to throw my arms around him and feel his strength as he hugged me, to return with him to our forest in northern Maryland and never, ever leave again.

He bore new scars, and there was a steeliness to his gaze I had never witnessed. My eyes slid from him to the petite queen beside him, and I gasped. Her belly protruded, a clear sign of the advanced stages of pregnancy.

"We've made contact with our people in the city. They're close. We're monitoring the signs given us by the Oracle," one of the commanders reported.

What signs? Did he refer to Cecelia or me?

"Heavy casualties reported already," another said grimly.

"I can handle that," said the man behind the Queen. He was tall and built like a football player with dark eyes. He didn't wear a uniform, and he appeared out of place with the others. Something about him was different. Before I could determine what, Herakles spoke again.

"Niko hasn't reported in," he said.

Niko? I opened my mouth to speak before recalling they couldn't see me.

"What of the Oracles?" he asked one of the commanders.

"We can't get near the caverns."

No one can, the Silent Queen said. *Tonight is the full moon. Our world ends at dusk. Either we succeed now, or everything we've done is in vain.*

They fell silent, and I turned my attention in the same direction as theirs. More questions pelted my thoughts. I couldn't even determine what day this was let alone identify the signs I was supposed to see.

My pulse raced, and I paced, circling the oblivious people to find some hint as to when this was. It wasn't as if they carried newspapers or absently displayed their phones or tablets, where I could spot the date!

Think, Alessandra! I yelled at myself mentally. I racked my thoughts. Full moon. Fall. These clues narrowed it down to three, maybe four months during the year. I wasn't able to tell if this was happening this year or perhaps a year or two down the road. Everyone looked the same, but wouldn't they, for a couple years?

Someone groaned, and I glanced towards the group then back.

The Silent Queen was clutching her stomach with one arm. Herakles supported her.

"They're due at any time," said the man who was out of place. "You shouldn't be here, Phoibe."

This is my army, my war. If this is the last day of the world, then I belong nowhere else! She retorted.

The man didn't respond. His eyes turned bright blue abruptly. Fascinated, I shifted closer.

"I can't stop the babies from coming," he said. "And they *are* coming." He and Herakles exchanged a look.

On what was the last day of the world? I studied the Silent Queen's strained features, equally concerned. How did she feel, knowing she would give birth today of all days? She groaned again. Her eyelids fluttered, and she sank into Herakles' arms.

I wanted to help, to do something. Stepping forward, the vision melted away, and I was somewhere else again.

Everything was black, white, and gray. I stood next to a river, at the edge of a field.

"Alessandra."

My heart leapt in my chest. "Adonis!" I turned to face him. My gaze scoured his perfect, noble features. Every cell of my body ignited beneath his direct look. He had a way of seeing through me, of making me feel both isolated from the rest of the world and no longer alone.

"Did it work?" he asked me.

Suddenly, I realized he was looking past me. I stepped back, away from the secondary form of future-me, which was in color. Cerberus trailed future-me, as if he were about to throw me out of his dimension again. In the distance, I saw the full color mirror of the forest. Future-me was a vibrant slash of color in a world with none.

But Adonis was gray.

"I don't understand," I said, simultaneously with future-me speaking to Adonis.

"Your body and mind aren't yours. We didn't know how else to reach you," he replied.

"But you're ... you're ..." Future-me couldn't finish the sentence.

I watched, and fresh pain tore through me. Lantos told me Adonis would die because of me, and I'd seen him here in another vision.

Had I killed him? Had Cleon, with my powers? And who possessed my body and mind? Cleon?

TWELVE

MY CHEST TIGHTENED, and my stomach dropped so fast, I felt ill. The vision started to fade.

"NO!" I screamed and clawed my way back.

It stabilized in time for me to hear future-me speak.

"I won't let Thanatos take you," future-me said. My face was ashen, my eyes red with tears. "I won't let it end like this."

"There's no other way it can end," Adonis said. He stepped forward and cupped the cheeks of future-me with his hands. "Alessandra, you must return."

"I refuse to accept that!"

"It's too late," he said softly.

"I won't leave you here! I can't lose you both!" future-me exclaimed.

Both? Who else had died?

"It's done," he said calmly, quietly. "But if you don't reclaim what's yours, if you don't fight this, all is permanently lost."

"You're my Mismatch. I can't do this without you."

"You're strong enough to do this. I will always be your Mismatch, no matter where I am. I have always loved you, even if I haven't always known how to say it."

His words shredded my insides.

I was crying. Future-me was outright weeping. Panic coursed through me as I sought some explanation. Lantos had claimed these premonitions could be prevented, but how did I prevent something when I saw only the end result?

The vision blurred and faded. Too distraught by what I'd seen, I could only watch Adonis slip away, as intangible as smoke, until only the darkness of my mind remained. My thoughts were everywhere at once, and the indecipherable murmuring of the gods and goddess wove into them, further confusing me about what to do.

I won't let him die, I vowed. Whatever I had to do, whomever I had to fight, I would never let my Mismatch die.

Three times. His death had been prophesized three times, twice in my visions and once by Lantos.

Listen to us. The voices were back, faded and faltering. *We will help you save him. Mismatch is the key.*

I pushed them away, hating the gods and goddesses anew for not only destroying the world, but also allowing Adonis to die.

My eyes opened, and I blinked rapidly. My bedroom was quiet. It was nighttime, and the lights in the bay window were on. Unlike dreams, the visions didn't lessen in intensity upon awakening, but lingered with full clarity, playing in continuous loops in my head. Tears warmed the sides of my face, and I stared at the ceiling.

Adonis would die. I didn't know when, or even if the three premonitions I foresaw existed in the same span of time. I had seen no hints about how Adonis would die or when Lantos and Tommy would stand in the caverns. The last day of the world, however, was possibly the easiest to discern, assuming I had the chance to talk to Herakles or the Silent Queen about what I saw.

As I lay still, I began to calm. This time, I hadn't foreseen the end of the world. I had witnessed efforts to prevent it. Whether or not they were successful, I didn't yet know, but it had to mean something, if I didn't see the world on fire, being swallowed by darkness.

I told myself this without remotely understanding if it were true. I had to believe the future could be changed, the world wouldn't perish, and Adonis wouldn't die, or I wasn't going to have any reason to fight the Fates, the gods, and Cleon.

"Next time you try to kill yourself, stab yourself in the jugular," Niko said from his position seated beside my bed.

I wiped away my tears and sat up, twisting towards him. A wall of dizziness caused me to slump, and I blinked away tunnel vision to keep from passing out.

"I wasn't trying to kill myself," I mumbled and straightened. "I was trying to dig that damn chip out of my head."

"Which would've killed you."

"And Cleon. Maybe that's what needs to be done," I snapped.

"Then who will stand up to the gods, defend humanity, bring back the Old Ways and all that shit you told me you wanted to do?"

"What if the price of doing those things is too high?" I asked. The image of Adonis standing on the banks of the River Styx was forefront in my mind.

"You only pay the price once. Then it's done."

Niko had no way of knowing what I was really talking about. I stretched to feel the back of my head. A bandage was secured to my head by staples. "I'm guessing I didn't succeed," I said and lowered my arm.

"Almost. I'm sure when Cleon awakens, he'll be pissed, and you'll be permanently attached to the wall of the caverns."

"He's unconscious." I tilted my head, looking inward.

Niko was right. I didn't feel Cleon's presence in my head at all. It was the first time in over two months where I was alone in my mind, except for the whispers I worked hard to ignore. Thrilled, I scrambled out of bed. Dizziness drove me to my knees. I took a deep breath and then stood.

"You have to take a message to someone," I said to Niko anxiously.

"I can't remember ... who's my boss? Is it you?" he replied. "No?"

Ignoring him, I scribbled down what I could recall of the visions onto a piece of notebook paper and ripped it out. "This is for the Silent Queen and Herakles."

Niko remained seated beside my bed, occupied with his phone, unconcerned.

"Niko!" I snapped.

"I'm in the middle of a game of *Angry Nymphs*."

"If you agree to do this, and we go now, I can un-freeze Theodocia."

"She's fine where she is."

I struggled to come up with some reason, any reason that would motivate Niko to act. It was impossible to threaten someone who had one priority in life and I couldn't get near what he cared about most. "What will it take for you to deliver this letter?" I asked finally.

"You have nothing I want."

I chewed my bottom lip. Whether or not my visions would all come true, I had to warn Herakles and the Silent Queen about the apocalyptic vision while Cleon was unconscious.

How did I buy the loyalty of a mercenary, when I had nothing to ...

My eyes fell to the Adonis statues on the mantle, and I gasped. "Gold," I breathed. "How about gold?"

"It'd take more gold than you could hide in the pocket of one of your dresses," Niko answered with a derisive snort.

"I can do that."

He glanced up then back. "You can't pay me from the Oracle's treasury without Cleon finding out."

"I won't need to." Crossing the room, I held out the letter. "Deliver this to the Silent Queen or Herakles, and I'll pay you with a room full of gold."

"That's not how this works. I'll need a substantial deposit to betray my current boss."

I drew a breath and focused on an image in my head of a trunk of gold appearing at the foot of my bed. The sound of another Mismatch statue clattering to the marble floor preceded Niko's puzzled expression by a second. He stood and pushed me out of his path and strode to the trunk. He opened it, and I neared, holding my breath in anticipation.

"Really?" he asked and picked up one of the gold bars.

It was in the shape of Mismatch. All of the bars in the trunk were. My cheeks grew warm. "It's gold, isn't it?" I replied.

He replaced it. "You made it out of thin air?"

"It's not exactly how it works," I replied. "But yes, I used my power."

Niko dropped the lid of the trunk and faced me, assessing my features intently. "What else can you do?"

"I'm still figuring that out, but pretty much anything I want to."

"Then why don't you escape?"

"Because Cleon's mind has merged with mine. He can control my power, and he's going to use it to control or blow up the world." I held out the letter again. "You have to agree before Cleon wakes up. He can see and hear what I do and think now."

Niko didn't move.

Come on, I urged him silently.

At long last, when my hope faltered, he snatched the letter and started towards the door.

"Do you know where the army is?" I asked, trailing.

"I have an idea."

"So did you purposely *not* capture the Silent Queen, or did you not know when you tried a couple of days ago?"

"I'll send someone for the trunk," he said over his shoulder. "Don't show them what's in it. I'm not the only mercenary in the ranks." He opened and closed the door behind him.

Relieved, I stood in the center of my room, clutching my newest

Mismatch statue and wondering if I had the ability to save him. The longer I was quiet, alone with my own mind, the more I wished I'd learned more about using my power from Cecelia, so when it came to the rare instance when Cleon wasn't in my head, I could act. My thoughts returned to Herakles and the Silent Queen, somewhere outside the wall. If I could create a trunk of gold, and accidentally teleport myself places, could I intentionally leave DC?

I waited ten minutes to give Niko a head start then went to the door and opened it. The two guards outside shifted to intercept me. I stopped.

Gummy statues, I thought.

They solidified and froze. I hurried past them towards the foyer.

"Take me to the Silent Queen and Herakles," I ordered quietly.

Nothing happened. I remained in my villa.

Irritated, I raced through the villa and went to the front door, willing the guards there to turn to gummy statues before I ripped the door open and hurried outside.

"Silent Queen and Herakles!" I said again, standing in the quiet night, beneath a dark sky. I breathed in the summer night, closed my eyes, and tried again. "Silent Queen."

I felt the shift this time. The breeze changed direction, and the scent of the city faded, replaced by the earthy smells of the forest. My insides melted, and I sighed, unaware of how much I had missed the smell of my former home. How had I ever taken the peace and trees for granted?

I opened my eyes. Expecting an army encampment, I was perplexed when I saw not the smallest hint of civilization. I was in the middle of the forest. No glimmers of streetlights or other manmade sources of light pierced the darkness.

Had my power backfired? Where was I?

Gentle tapping reached me, and I strained my senses to identify where it came from. Finally, I looked up and yelped.

The creature peering down at me from its perch in a tree branch had bright blue eyes in a lopsided face. It was too small to be

Mismatch. With the same sinewy musculature and gray skin, I quickly realized it wasn't some sort of monster waiting to eat me.

"You scared me," I said quietly. "It *is* you, Your Majesty. Isn't it?"

She blinked at me, responding with an unhappy yowl before her voice rang out clearly in my mind.

How did you know?

"This is your royal curse, I believe," I replied.

She leapt from the branch and landed lightly on her feet in front of me, her wings flaring out to soften her landing. A little taller than me, the Silent Queen's nightmarish appearance made me back up a step.

It happens every night, she said, sounding uncertain. *You know about this?*

I laughed. "Yeah. There's someone else like you out there. Same Bloodline and everything."

She tilted her head to the side. *Who?*

"Adonis. Mismatch."

What?

Surprised she didn't already know, I explained their relationship quickly.

Her response was to utter several foul curses that reassured me Herakles was alive and well, if he were spreading his creative swearing to those around him.

"I don't have much time," I said, interrupting her angry outburst. "I kind of have to ask you something. I had a vision of the world ending, and I know what day it is, but ..." I cleared my throat, uncertain how to ask a queen about her sex life when I'd never kissed anyone.

Did you say the world ending?

"Yeah. It's, uh, on the day you give birth to ... your kids," I said awkwardly. "I don't know what year that is, but it's in fall, on a full moon."

She was silent, still enough to resemble the stone statues her family turned into.

"Could be this year or maybe ... whenever you ... um. Have a boyfriend or something."

I'm pregnant with twins now.

"Oh." I was about to ask who the father was when I realized just how much that wasn't my business. She was a *queen*. Who did the richest royal in the world date? "You wouldn't happen to be due in fall, would you?"

I am.

"Wow." Surprised this prediction was accurate, I fell into silence, thoughts on the other visions. Adonis dead. The apocalypse. Me frozen in the caverns. The walls breached. Was there a sequence to what I foresaw? At least two of the events appeared to happen on the same day, but I wasn't able to tell when the others occurred.

Close to panicking, I clenched my hands together. Herakles would tell me to focus on what was in front of me, and to take everything one step at a time.

Just because the Silent Queen was pregnant, and due when my vision claimed she would be, it didn't mean everything else would come true as I foresaw. Adonis wasn't going to die.

What else did you foresee? The grotesque queen asked me.

I described the scene of her on the hilltop without mentioning my other two visions. She listened intently, tail flicking back and forth.

"I'm sorry there's not more." I looked around. "Where's Herakles?"

At camp, hopefully. The Supreme Magistrate's army attacked us on the way back to camp. I changed into this for the first time and panicked.

"You're normal," I assured her. "Relatively. I mean, normal for the Bloodline."

She growled.

"Is Herakles okay?"

I don't know.

I frowned, concerned about my former guardian.

How did you find me?

"I don't really know," I admitted. "I told my power to take me to you, so I could warn you, and it did. It's not always this reliable."

We have heard you are not well?

I cleared my throat. "I am, but Cleon used technology and favors from the gods to merge our minds."

She was quiet for a moment. I assessed she was shocked. *We had heard there was a problem, and he was able to influence you, but not to this extent.*

"Well, it's worse than you think. He can control my power, and I can't stop him. I don't know if I will have my mind and power completely under control by the time you attack the city."

I'll move up our schedule. I had planned a spring attack, but if you foresaw the walls coming down in four months, I'll make it happen. In your original vision, there's a chance you weren't able to warn me. In any case, a vision is not a guarantee of the future, only a warning.

Her confidence helped some of the tension release its grip around my chest. "Cleon believes he's on some sort of mission to save the world, not just rule it. I think you should know he's convinced the Oracle is the enemy, not the gods. He's gone completely mad. If he murders her and fulfills the third trial ..."

He will have access to your full power. I understand. We will take precautions.

I didn't exactly like the way that sounded. I doubted Herakles would allow anyone to harm me, but I was guessing the tough Silent Queen would do whatever she had to in order to achieve her goals. She was similar to Lantos and Cleon in this area – far more experienced in the political arena than I ever cared to become.

Should I have been more willing to sacrifice people in order to accomplish my goals? I wanted to think there were enough people like that in the world already. Too many of them, actually. Three people willing to sacrifice anyone and anything would strip this world bare.

I wanted to become something different, even if I didn't know yet what form that took.

You have not completed the third trial yet?

"No. It's why my power hasn't completely manifested. When it happens, I may not be in control."

I'm sorry. This was softer. *I fear we are both facing challenges we never expected.*

"Yeah," I agreed.

We stood in comfortable quiet, each of us lost in our respective thoughts. I had only met the Silent Queen once, but I liked her a great deal from the single interaction. The politician side of her I was less certain about.

"Cleon has Theodocia," I said, aware Cleon could awaken at any time. "She's a prisoner at the House."

The Silent Queen tensed. *What of the rest of my insurgency?*

"I don't know." I paced nervously. "I have to go. I want to check on Herakles before ..."

Cleon stirred in my mind seconds before his voice rang out. *Where are you?*

I closed my eyes and silenced any thought I had about where I was and what I'd been thinking.

"Villa," I breathed.

The breeze and scent of the forest dissipated, replaced by the quiet whir of the air conditioning and traces of pine cleaner left over from the maids.

Opening my eyes, I didn't have a chance to register my surroundings. I could actually *feel* Cleon in my head, as if the chip in my brain was alive and wriggling. Disgusted, I froze. His initial disorientation about what happened and where he was gave way to anger.

Some things are about to change, he promised me. *Starting with the independence I've allowed you so far. I've waited for you to come to a point where you might see things my way, but I can wait no longer.*

I shook my head without freeing my mind of the wriggling. I'd been granted too much freedom, and it was affecting his ability to lead and meet with people who could further ...

It wasn't my thought. Another image was in my head, this one of Cleon. Too fuzzy for a vision, too crisp to be a dream, I determined it was a memory.

I RESTED my hands on the railing in front of the Oracle's display case.

'Four twenty five,' said the Oracle. 'You will understand what true power is.'

I SHOOK MY HEAD, and the memory faded.

"I can't handle you in my head," I said to Cleon and squeezed my temples. "You're confusing me."

The sound of someone banging on the front door jarred me from my attempt to distinguish whose thoughts were whose. My hands fell to my sides, and I sucked in a deep breath. I read in Cleon's mind why he had sent the guards to fetch me.

Four armed soldiers entered, each carrying a tranq gun that was drawn and ready. As if I had every put up a fight. Cleon knew well enough I would never purposely hurt anyone. Except Niko. I might smack him, if I could do it without him retaliating.

I lifted my hands like a good criminal. I left the villa in their company and walked quietly to my fate. The back of my head pulsed with warm pain, and I purposely kept my thoughts and mind trained on my surroundings and nothing else that had occurred this day.

How horrible was it that I wasn't safe in my own mind? No one else was either, if I failed to prune my thoughts and allowed my mind to drift to those I cared about.

I looked up at the sky, as I did every time I was outside at night. I kept hoping I'd see Mismatch, framed against the moon or coasting among the clouds. Whenever he failed to appear, my heart sank. Maybe Niko wasn't the person I wanted to punch most in the world.

Maybe the shadow titan was. Not a warrior, Lantos would probably dissipate into shadows if I tried to hit him.

My escorts led me to the House. This time, we didn't go to the public rooms on the first floor or the offices on the second. We went all the way up to the third – and uppermost – floor, which appeared to consist of living spaces. According to the images of Cleon's playing through my mind, the hall was trifurcated into three apartments. More guards stood outside the first door and lined the corridor inside, before we reached the second door. The second hallway was much shorter, and at the opposite end, several more soldiers stood before another metal door leading to a third space.

This is your new home, Cleon said into my mind. *I am on one side, Lantos on the other.*

"Gods. The only way to make it worse is if you put Niko in my closet," I muttered.

That can be arranged, if you run wild again.

One of my escorts flung open a door, and I entered. He closed and locked the door behind me.

My new apartment was fully furnished and decorated in bland, neutral colors. It was nowhere near the size of the villa. I explored my new home quickly. The apartment consisted of two bedrooms, two bathrooms, a tiny office where racks of clothing had been placed, kitchen and living-dining room combo. It was hard to be disappointed with it, when I had only ever known a room I shared with another girl before arriving to the villa, but I did miss having my own balcony.

Cerberus was there, watching me. Even Cleon couldn't get rid of the mirror leading to the underworld or my new pet. I had to assume my view into Hades realm would be permanent.

I crossed to the picture window in the living area and touched the window to open it. A light shock swept through me, and I cursed.

"Did you electrify my windows?" I asked Cleon.

Since my welfare depends upon you not doing anything foolish? I absolutely sealed your apartment. It's not electricity, but one of Lantos' abilities.

"Gods-damn Lantos," I muttered. I touched the window again, only for a second shock to knock me back a step, stronger this time than the first. Whatever Lantos had done, it wasn't electricity. His power, derived from his Titan father Lelantos, had always had the ability to cage mine. It was how Herakles and the priests at the orphanage originally hid me from the gods and repressed my power, and Niko and Cleon used it at will to control me.

You are confined to your apartment. Cleon seemed content.

"No shit. For how long?"

Until I determine you may leave.

I hated my life. The impetuous side of me wanted to drop into the other world and seek out the first Oracle for advice, while the rational voice in my head reminded me of the danger.

I'm planning another demonstration in two days.

"You should already know I won't cooperate, and you can't make me, since hurting me hurts you."

I may not need your assistance at all.

I chewed on my lower lip. I didn't want to imagine Cleon could siphon off my power and use it, but I wasn't seeing any other explanation that would make him this confident.

I drew near the window and peered out. I had been out-maneuvered, manipulated, and trapped the minute I set foot outside my forest. The sense of helplessness inside me was growing, as the walls seemed to close in around me.

What was I supposed to do, when anything I tried was instantly transmitted by my own mind to my enemy?

If you agree to listen to the voices of the gods, I'll free you for an hour tomorrow, Cleon offered.

"How could I possibly refuse?" I replied sarcastically.

I'll leave that option on the table.

Another image flashed through my mind. He was seated in his office, across from two men in suits.

"No," I breathed. "The last thing I want to do is see what you do. It's enough to have your thoughts polluting my mind."

You need to hear this.

I couldn't push him out of my mind. I started to panic, when I understood what was happening and peered at the two visitors through Cleon's eyes.

The discussion with the political representatives from northern Maryland was not going well. Before this, he had never had any reason to suspect Zeus' power was starting to fail. According to the two men, the safe zone was retreating several meters every day.

"Several meters?" My words were spoken through Cleon's lips.

"Yes, sir," one of them answered. "We have reports from our contemporaries south of DC of the same thing."

I shook my head and exited Cleon's mind, stunned by the claim. Was it true, or was he trying to manipulate me somehow with this information?

It's true. This is why I need your power, to create pockets of safety for those willing to pay me for it, he said.

Cecelia's magic was fading, if she couldn't safeguard the protected zone any longer.

You refuse to listen. Cleon was angry. *She's not protecting us – Zeus is!*

"Shut up, shut up, shut up!" I turned on the television and cranked up the volume, until I could no longer hear my thoughts or Cleon's.

When I was stressed, I tended to eat. I summoned a bowl of popcorn drenched in caramel. The bowl appeared on my coffee table. At its center was another of my Mismatch statues.

"Where are you?" I whispered and plucked up the figurine. "Why were you in Hades?" The visions were fresh in my head. It wasn't the first time I'd seen Adonis on the wrong side of the curtain separating our world from that of Hades.

I went to the side of the apartment, where Cerberus sat on his side of the curtain. He lowered his head, as if expecting me to attempt to cross over.

"Relax," I said. "I'm looking for someone, not trespassing."

Darkness filled the space behind him. It was impossible for me to know if Adonis was there or not. Thinking about my friend being dead filled me with raw, cold fear at a primal level.

Was Lantos right to facilitate Adonis leaving? Would I kill him, if he hadn't gone?

THIRTEEN
SILENT QUEEN

ALESSANDRA VANISHED before my eyes without completing her sentence.

I remained where I was, in case she reappeared. Five minutes passed. The sounds of night filled my ears, and I gravitated back towards the tree. I felt much safer in the branches, out of reach of any predators and likewise hidden from people. I had no idea what they would do, if they saw me. As a child, I had reacted to Mismatch with delight and fascination. As an adult, I had terrified myself peering into a pond last night. My reflection was unrecognizable.

My stomach growled, and I scowled. Leaping upward, I returned to the branch on which I'd been perched when Alessandra suddenly appeared. I'd been hungry since I first transformed the night before, panicked, and flew away from Kyros. I didn't expect to return to a human form with dawn, or to be turned back into a monster when dusk fell.

Alessandra's seconding of Paeon's explanation – that this was the true nature of the curse of the Bloodline – resonated within me, as if part of me already understood this to be the case. I had believed we turned into stone grotesques, and this was the curse. Mismatch, when we met twelve years before, had said as much. I never thought twice about why he was an animated monster, but I did now.

I found myself astonished for the second time in the past several months. First, Lantos betrayed me. Now, I discovered Adonis was a member of the Bloodline. A man I was leery of, because of the butcher he was rumored to be, I couldn't have been any more shocked than when Alessandra revealed the truth. Theodocia had never spoken well of him. He was universally feared, and his methods of torture were renowned within the elite political circle to which we belonged.

I settled onto the branch, unable to reconcile the butcher of DC with the kind creature that sought to warn me against the curse so long ago. That we had spent the past five years in DC, and he never spoke to me again, struck me as odd. How had he attended security meetings and never addressed me directly? As the security chief of SISA, he was entitled to pass through my royal guard at will, and he had never made any attempt to visit, either. Nor had he settled on my balcony, as he did twelve years ago, in his beast form.

What had prevented him from returning as he promised to do so when I was a child? I packed my bags minutes after he left and waited for days for him to return to take me away, as he swore he would.

Alessandra's hasty explanation only inflamed my curiosity – and managed to pierce through the callous I was normally adept at maintaining around my emotions.

Adonis ... Mismatch ... whoever he was ... he abandoned me when I was six. I still recalled that pain – of having a friend and hope briefly and then losing both without explanation.

My stomach felt like it was eating itself. The scent of a rabbit reached me, and my mouth watered. I clenched my jaw closed, horrified by the idea of killing an animal with my bare hands and eating it raw, as if I were ... well, a beast. I was afraid to test my nighttime body. No matter what Alessandra claimed about this being *natural*, I couldn't fathom how I had been a normal human for the entirety of my life and suddenly I wasn't.

What of my children? Did they transform when I did?

Were they safe from whatever was happening to me?

Questions left me frustrated, and fatigue wore me down. As a human, I was completely naked, and I'd sat down at the base of this tree yesterday and sobbed most of the day away, alone, and scared. The confidence I felt leading an army disappeared when I considered no one would ever follow a monster.

A new smell hit me, and my nose wrinkled. I hunched back against the trunk of the tree and held my breath. Able to see at night almost as clearly as I could during day, I searched my surroundings, until I spotted movement.

Humans smell unappealing, I thought. A split second later, I realized it was likely a survival mechanism so I didn't try to eat someone.

"Your Majesty?" The summons was accompanied by the too loud movement of someone without discipline walking through the forest.

Kyros wasn't close enough to hear my thoughts. I didn't know if I wanted him to be, either.

A second human's smell reached me, and I twisted. This man navigated the forest with stealth. Not even my acute hearing picked up on his movement until he was within three meters of me, but I could see him. Herakles was alive, though he wore bandages across one cheek. The mouthwatering scent of fresh blood wafted to me, as if he were hurt during the escape from our meeting with Theodocia.

"Is she here?" Herakles called to Kyros.

"I sense her but can't see her."

Herakles stopped almost directly beneath my perch. I didn't move.

He looked up, and his features softened into a lopsided smile. "Hey, there," he said.

It wasn't the reaction I was expecting. If I saw someone who looked like me in the tree above my head, I'd run away as fast as I could.

"Come on down, Phoibe," Herakles said. He removed his back-pack and crouched.

I don't want you to see me like this, I told him.

Kyros reached the massive ginger and spoke my words aloud.

Herakles snorted in response. "I brought you dinner." He pulled a fat, juicy, raw steak from a bag and held it up.

Gods, I had never smelled anything so delicious!

"Come on," he said again. He threw the steak into the air.

I snatched it on instinct and tore into it with my fangs. Before my human side had a chance to be appalled, I'd ripped the steak apart and swallowed without chewing.

Herakles tossed another up to me, then a third. After inhaling the large chunks of meat, I immediately felt stronger. My stomach no longer complained, and my head cleared. I crept forward on my branch then dropped to the ground near them, bracing for their reactions.

"Still prettier than I'll ever be," Herakles said and indicated his face. He tossed the last of the steaks into the air.

I leapt two meters off the ground with little effort and snatched the food with my mouth, gobbling it up.

"You okay?" he asked.

I released a sigh.

"Kyros told me what happened. I've seen your kind before," Herakles continued. "I can't imagine what you're feeling, but we're here to take you home."

I can't go back like this.

Kyros verbalized my words.

"Of course you can. Do you have any idea how uplifting this will be for morale?"

I made a strange sound of objection that needed no translation.

"But it will," Herakles said. "Who would you rather follow into battle? A little girl half your size, or a monster?"

Offended, I hopped up, caught myself with my wings, and returned to my branch.

"I mean that nicely," Herakles said. "The armies will follow you either way, but seeing their commander-in-chief strike fear into the enemies with one look ... it's priceless."

"We agree," Kyros said. "This might not work in the political arena, but it will with the military."

What they said made sense – to an extent. Was I ready to be a monster, though? To accept this as my fate and show others what I was? Did this mean the curse was upon me, despite the measures I'd taken to prevent it from befalling me? Were my unborn heiresses the reasons why I had changed?

"She's thinking," Kyros said to an expectant Herakles.

Herakles dug out a canteen of water from his backpack and tossed it up to me. I accepted it and drank my fill with some awkwardness, not accustomed to the fangs that were in my way.

I reviewed what Alessandra had told me, both of this curse and the day the world was going to end – in four months, when I was due.

"What?" Kyros asked, picking up the thoughts.

Say nothing of Alessandra to Herakles, I warned him. *Or I will eat you one night.*

He didn't even blink, accustomed to my thoughts of murdering him. "That other part though. That sounds important," he said.

I know when we must attack, and what will happen if we don't.

"Whatever you're talking about, let's do this at the encampment," Herakles said, glancing between Kyros and me. "The forest is infested with SISA and military patrols."

Some part of me balked, and I backed up closer to the trunk of the tree. Was it instinctive for the beast side of me to want to remain hidden, or was this my fear?

"We might want to make ourselves comfortable," Kyros said and pulled off his backpack. "She's not ready."

Herakles studied me, and I studied him. I didn't understand how accepting he was of my appearance, or how he could look at me with warm compassion when I was still on the verge of panicking.

"Okay," he said. "When you're ready. I brought you clothes just in case." He perched on the trunk of a fallen tree.

Kyros settled onto the ground.

Why did you not heal Herakles? I demanded, waiting for the other shoe to drop and for the man-god to reveal his true intentions.

"He didn't want us to," Kyros said. "He despises gods almost as much as you."

Herakles uttered a few of his more creative curses. I didn't blame him. All things considered, his adopted daughter was basically a goddess. What did he think of her power? Was he as confused as I was sometimes when confronted with the human face of Kyros, knowing he was also possessed by a god?

When they were comfortable, I ventured out of the tree once more and crouched nearby. Twisting to Kyros, I motioned for him to tell Herakles what I needed my second in command to know.

Kyros explained what I had learned about the last day before the apocalypse. To my dismay, Herakles was already made aware of my pregnancy. Nothing caused the former Olympian so much as a flinch, for which I was grateful. He listened carefully, shifting forward in interest.

When Kyros finished, quiet fell over us. I began to relax, grateful for their acceptance and company and for my content stomach.

"Four months will be cutting it close," Herakles said after a thoughtful silence. "We have one wall buster missile, and I've been working on a recruitment plan with Commander Ronos. With your permission, we'll move into the second stage and start actively recruiting."

I nodded my assent.

"We haven't heard from Theodocia since the meeting," he said. "I'd like to return to the city to find her and assess her insurgent capabilities."

Herakles going to the city – and discovering what was happening to Alessandra – would derail my second in command when I needed him focused here, on the army and our war.

Kyros glanced at me, aware of my thoughts. I didn't bother threatening him again; by this point, he understood.

Send the person you trust most in your place, I said to Herakles. *I need you here, preparing the army. More so, because I'm about to become a part-time commander, if I'm a monster at night.*

Kyros obediently relayed my directive.

Disappointed, Herakles nonetheless nodded. "When I get Theodocia's numbers, I'll have a better idea of how many we need to recruit to have a chance against the military."

My army was healthy – but relatively small. In addition to my royal guard, its members included those disillusioned men and women we'd found in the city and recruited from around the Atlantic seaboard. Many others were hardened survivors, criminals, and mercenaries. I doubted we were at a tenth the strength of the military, let alone military and SISA combined. In the morning, when I was human again, I'd return to the attack strategy I'd been building over the past few weeks. With roughly a quarter of my forces inside the wall already – acting under Theodocia's command as a guerrilla insurgency – we had a leg up, but would suffer in a head-to-head clash.

I was too easily distracted by my beast senses at night to brainstorm further. It was hard to sit still, when my instincts wanted me to explore every sound and follow at least one of the animal scents wafting through the air or perhaps, just to fly into the night sky.

Why aren't you surprised by what I am? I asked, training my gaze on Herakles and then waiting for Kyros to verbalize.

"I've seen one of you before. Adonis," Herakles said with a scowl. Dark emotion crossed his features, and he fell silent, tense where he had been relaxed before my question. He couldn't have known Adonis long, and even he didn't like the butcher.

Would I become like Adonis, now that I was a monster, too?

Herakles drew a breath. "He's Alessandra's protector now," he said quietly. "I hope she doesn't need him in DC. I hope she's safe enough to wait four months, so I can protect her before danger reaches her."

Kyros frowned and gazed at me. I read what he wanted to say in his eyes. The human side of him had a good heart, but I needed Herakles with me. It was for his own safety as well as the army's benefit. What would the people's champion do, if he discovered the Supreme Magistrate had hurt Alessandra? Run into the city and get himself killed!

No, I ordered Kyros.

He looked away. His disappointment troubled me, because I had the sense he was disappointed in *me.*

Why should I care what one person thought?

More sensitive to emotions and stimuli, I rose and paced. Craning my neck back, I eyed the dark sky and had the sudden urge to fly.

I'll return, I told Kyros.

Without waiting for either of them to respond, I leapt upward and unleashed my wings. Bursting above the treetops, I experienced a thrill of euphoria as my powerful wings instinctively knew how to propel me upward. My shoulders soon burned from the effort, but my beautiful, gray wings remained sturdy and strong. I paused to catch my breath and gazed down, startled by how far up I was. My eyes roamed the area around Herakles and Kyros for some sign of the patrols of which they spoke.

No one was near, and I suddenly understood Herakles' point about the military advantage being a monster could bring to the table. With my enhanced senses and ability to fly, I was the perfect scout. No one would ever ambush us again. Being this high caused my stomach to turn, but when it became more natural, I'd be able to travel great distances and conduct reconnaissance with skills no human could match. And if I found a god possessing a human ...

The mere thought caused me to flex my talons and test the whip-like tail. There was no denying I was a predator. Common sense told me that my fangs, claws, and barbed tail would easily overwhelm the natural defenses of pretty much every other animal – or human – in existence. My advantage at hand-to-hand combat just obliterated every other attempt I'd made to learn how to fight from Herakles. All the blocks and punches in the world wouldn't stand up against my new, personal arsenal.

Less certain about how the armies would react to a monster queen, I felt somewhat relieved to learn I could still contribute, that I wouldn't be stuck in a tree for hours at a time, waiting for dawn, until I could resume my activities. At night, I would become a warrior or scout. During the day, I'd rule as a queen and commander.

The longer I thought about it, the more excited I became about the prospect of helping the army – and my cause – in a manner I hadn't thought possible before.

I flew for a short time, growing accustomed to my wings, and gauging what they could do, before I noticed the line of yellow on the eastern horizon announcing the sunrise. Circling the trees beneath whose canopies Herakles and Kyros waited, I coasted down from the sky and landed lightly near them.

Both were sleeping. I plucked up Herakles' backpack and circled a thatch of brush to await the sunrise. He had packed practical clothing for me, consisting of cargo pants, a t-shirt, boots and socks, bug spray, and the lucky knife he'd given me. I set everything out then caught sight of something else in the bottom of the bag. Removing it, I lowered the backpack.

A picture of Alessandra and him had been tucked at the bottom of the pack. He looked almost identical, but she was several years younger, grinning widely with her arms around his neck.

I didn't notice the difference in her appearance until this moment. When she magically appeared beneath my tree, she had seemed pale, her eyes haunted and her manner flustered. I didn't quite understand how it was possible for her mind to merge with Cleon's, but it was clear she was under duress of some kind. I trusted my instincts too much to feel guilty about abandoning her to her fate, though I was troubled by the change between the vibrant, fearless young woman I recalled meeting in DC and what she was becoming.

I sensed Kyros' approach and replaced the picture.

"You have to tell him," he said.

You don't understand what's at stake, I replied.

"You keep saying that," he responded. "Because what? I'm a human-god combo, and therefore, I can't understand what someone like you, elevated beyond us mere mortals and gods, is doing?"

Because I can't manage armies by myself, and Herakles is the glue required to keep everything together, I replied, glaring at him.

"That might be true, but you also have this irrational fear of being abandoned by everyone. I think this is why you won't tell him. You don't want him to leave you."

I turned away, irritated.

"If you tell him, he may decide the best way to help her is to attack in fall, as you've planned," Kyros pressed.

It's not your concern.

"It *is* my concern. I'm part of this now, whether or not you want me to be."

I'll tell him when I determine the time is right.

"What if something happens to her between now and your attack? He deserves the chance to make this decision for himself. I mean, she's his family! You know firsthand what it's like to be ditched by everyone you care about."

A god will never understand! I retorted.

"He doesn't," Kyros replied promptly. "But I do. I saw my sisters murdered by bandits, and my mother and father were killed in the initial fireball attack. I know what it's like to lose someone, and I know what it's like to regret not having the chance to protect them or say farewell."

The raw note in his voice struck me hard. The picture of Kyros in pain did not sit well with me. I didn't want Herakles to feel what I did about Lantos, my mother, Mismatch, Theodocia and everyone else who had been ripped out of my life. I didn't want anyone to feel that way.

I'm sorry for your loss, but I'm in a different situation. I have a duty to fulfill, I said more calmly. *I can't afford to jeopardize it, or more innocent people like your family will die.*

"If you gave people a chance, they might surprise you." This time, anger was in his voice.

Kyros marched away, back towards where Herakles slept. Twisting, I watched the possessed human. He was good at disrupting my plans, whether it was by his mere existence, or the fact I sensed he was, in part, correct. I didn't trust people, because of my position as a leader and Queen, but also for the simple reason I didn't want to be hurt anymore. Because that's how it always ended: with me alone, hurt, and still responsible for the fate of humanity.

Sunlight crested the sky, and fire raced through me. I closed my eyes and banished Kyros from my mind while I changed from a monster into a human. Shuddering at the sensation of my body tearing itself apart and putting itself back together again, I gritted my teeth until the transformation was complete.

I stood naked and alone in the forest. My dulled senses were a relief after the onslaught of my night. Dressing, I found myself stuck on Kyros' assertion that Herakles needed to know about Alessandra's danger. Theodocia had claimed the same.

When I was ready, I left the private area and returned to the others. Herakles was awake and brushing away any sign we were present with a branch of leaves while Kyros watched.

The two glanced my way, and I lifted my chin another notch. I was ready to return, now that I understood I posed no threat to others and that becoming a grotesque was part of my curse that might help me meet my goals.

Neither of them spoke, for which I was grateful. I waited for Herakles to finish. I was drained from staying awake all night. I learned yesterday that I slept best in the morning. Unfortunately, today, I had an army to manage.

"This way," Kyros said and started through the brush.

I trailed him, while Herakles followed me. A four-seater, all-terrain vehicle waited for us, a hundred meters away from where we'd been. It was hidden beneath a layer of branches and leaves. Herakles and Kyros cleared it away and Herakles climbed into the driver's side. Kyros hopped in back, and I sat in the passenger seat.

We moved through the forest as fast as possible, following an old four-wheeler path that hadn't been cleared in years. Branches smacked the frame of the vehicle, and I kept my hands and legs far from the door, just in case.

Half an hour later, we reached a highway. Herakles kept to the drainage ditches. The jarring ride left me nauseated – a combination of movement and morning sickness. Exiting the ditches for a familiar dirt road, Herakles drove us through several back roads before we arrived at the outer perimeter of the camp.

He slowed, and two guards in purple emerged from the forest near the fence. With a quick glance at us, and they opened the gate. Herakles waved as we passed through and drove us into camp via the back entrance before finally stopping in the motor pool. I sat perfectly still, uncertain if my stomach was going to revolt when I moved.

Kyros touched my shoulder. I didn't feel his magic, but I experienced its effects. My stomach righted itself immediately. I released my death grip on the roll bar overhead and moved away from his touch to exit.

Two of my other five top commanders waited a respectful distance away.

"What do you want us to do with Kyros?" Herakles asked, rounding the vehicle. He handed me a notepad.

My desire to throw him back in the barn – tied to a chair – was nowhere near the level it had been when we left several days ago.

Find him a bunk, I scribbled on the paper.

Herakles said nothing, but he didn't have to. This was good news to the army that had fallen in love with the cheerful, possessed human.

"Your Majesty," one of my commanders stepped forward. He bowed his head before continuing. "We have a visitor."

I raised an eyebrow, uncertain what that could mean and worried another Kyros-Paeon had showed up at my camp.

"He's requested to see you specifically."

Herakles joined me and waited for my decision.

I nodded.

"I'll accompany you," he said.

The commanders turned and strode away, towards the squat former anchor store housing the common areas. They led me into the back offices, past my room – which I desperately wanted to visit for a quick nap – and into a break room we had converted into a meeting area for senior staff.

I paused in the doorway, my gaze falling to the visitor on the opposite side of the room. He stood rather than sat, and he was neither armed nor tied. But ... that didn't surprise me about Adonis. He wasn't going to let anyone bind him, and he didn't need weapons for those around him to understand how dangerous he was. He radiated command and lethality unlike anyone else I had ever met.

Gazing at one another, I didn't know if I should have been excited to see the one person who understood what I was going through – or wary of the butcher who never should've known where my camp was to start with. With his direct blue-green gaze and royal command of the room, I began to wonder how I had never suspected what and who he was before this.

"Leave us," he said to my escort with the command of the prince he had been.

My commanders obeyed without so much as a look at me!

"No," Herakles growled, glaring at Adonis.

I glanced up at him and rested a hand on his arm. His jaw tightened, but he relented. Herakles left and closed the door behind him.

Adonis studied me. There was nothing soft about the man, no

smile lines around his lips, no warmth in his eyes, no excess weight in the lean musculature of his frame.

"You must have questions," he started.

What are you doing here? I asked.

"I was hunting in the area last night and sensed you."

The little girl he abandoned wanted to demand to know why he hadn't returned all those years ago, but I didn't feel ready to open the box of emotions this topic was certain to stir up. My feelings were much closer to the surface, now that I was pregnant.

He tilted his head, and his eyes rested on my lower abdomen.

You can hear my thoughts, I grated internally, infuriated. Would he tell his friend, Lantos, about my children? I would kill him before he spoke!

"Yeah," he admitted. "I don't know where to start. Twelve years ago? Four thousand?"

Another thick silence fell. I assessed him, not liking the idea of creating a bridge to a man I had no reason to respect.

Except he was family. A distant predecessor of mine, the butcher and confidante of my betrayer was also the only family I had left in the world.

Start from the beginning, I decided finally and reached for a chair to sit. *But be brief. I have problems awaiting me.*

"I have a feeling I'm the right person to help you with them," he said, the corner of one side of his mouth lifting in a half-smile.

Not about to trust him, just because the same curse ran through our veins, I folded my hands in my lap and prepared to listen.

FOURTEEN
GROTESQUE PRINCE

BEFORE I SPENT several days with the Silent Queen, I had little insight into her personality. I recalled meeting her as Mismatch when she was a lonely, isolated child, as well as the few times we had crossed paths in the political circles in DC. She was on Lantos' level, not mine, so those circumstances of our co-existing anywhere simultaneously were rare and normally consisted of high-level security meetings of the political elite.

Phoibe exhibited the best traits of the bloodline: intelligence, ambition, discipline, willingness to sacrifice for her goals, consideration of those she cared about and coldness towards the rest of the world. She was a born leader, bred and raised to rule, and she'd learned to survive the DC political climate at a young age.

She also inherited the trait that made her out of place in this world. Her ambition blinded her to the cost of achieving her goals. While displeased initially to see Herakles at her side, I quickly assessed this pairing was for the best. Herakles' experience, genuine warmth and grounded personality softened Phoibe's drive to rid the earth of the gods at all costs. She knew when to defer to his judgment and when to stick to her own. If she were considering altering her plan, it was because Herakles had likely urged her to do so in private, despite the natural animosity he and I shared when Alessandra was caught between us.

I'd been invited this morning to her weekly conference with senior staff.

You believe this to be the best plan. She was studying the edits I'd made on her initial strategy for a two-pronged attack against the military and SISA security elements in DC.

"I believe it to be the only plan with the resources at your disposal," I replied.

Her commanders were studying the proposed changes as well, along with Herakles, who seemed more interested in watching me than reading what was in front of him.

"This has merit," said one of her commanders. "A simultaneous attack following an incredibly risky diversion."

"It's more of a concentrated attack, disguised by two diversions," I replied. "The main objective is to chop the head off the snake by crippling the leadership at the compound. Her Majesty's objective isn't necessarily to destroy the military but take it over. The first distraction will draw the Supreme Magistrate's forces one way, and the attack on the wall a second way, freeing up the area we need to move around in. Our main forces will arrive into DC via the Metro system, on trains scheduled to bring food from the Maryland farms and weapons from their NOVA ammo depot. They'll converge at Metro Center, then move through the tunnels to the compound where the Supreme Magistrate is holed up. When the diversions erupt, the forces beneath the ground will take the compound."

"A modern day Trojan Horse, using the subway system," Herakles said.

"Yes," I said.

"How do you know we can take the metro cars? The military has the stop they use heavily guarded. Even if we took it by force, they'd alert the others," Herakles stated.

"And the other stops are sealed," one of the commanders added.

"We unseal one stop per line in advance and overtake the extra cars not in use. Theodocia's forces in the city can access the control points for each line. Her people will divert the cars coming in. After the cars leave the loading points, we divert them to maintenance tracks and replace them with cars filled with our forces," I explained.

Silence fell. Herakles was studying the layout of the metro system with interest.

The others in the room glanced at me frequently and then at the Queen. No one trusted me, and I didn't expect anyone to. With full numbers on the SISA and military personal located within the walls, in addition to detailed information on their standard protocol, strongholds and likely reactions, I was too useful for them to write off completely.

These numbers are much higher than we thought, she said. *We'll be facing the Supreme Magistrate at half-strength even with these distractions.*

"Half strength compared to a tenth is evening the odds," I pointed out. "And we won't be looking solely at using manpower to fight this battle. There are some with otherworldly abilities who are willing to help us."

She lifted her eyes and pinned me with a look. *I hope you mean Alessandra, because I will not partner with the gods to fight Cleon.*

"If you want to win this war, you'll partner with whomever you must," I replied.

Not like that.

The others were silent. I sensed they didn't need to hear our full discussion to understand what it was about. The Silent Queen's war on gods was a solid principle in recruiting those who fought for her. I had never met a body of people more similar in opinion than she and her commanders were when it came to the gods.

We cannot rely on the Oracle, either, she added. *This will be a battle among humans.*

And beasts? I countered telepathically. *You and I are not humans.*

She didn't respond, though I sensed her entrenchment. My thoughts went to the figure seated along the wall, among the lower level leaders of her organization. The god-possessed Kyros was listening to our words, frowning. I hadn't been able to assess what he had said or did to be counted among her allies, rather than her enemies, but it had to have been great, for the army as a whole loved him.

You are confident once we take the compound, we won't have to worry about the military attacking? She asked.

"I am. This is the best way to achieve your goal of amassing the largest military possible for the purpose of facing the gods."

Phoibe tapped the paper in front of her. *I like this.*

Good. Maybe now you'll tell me what is it you're hiding about Alessandra? I asked.

Phoibe looked away. She said nothing of the Oracle unless I asked and even then, her responses were monosyllabic. Something was wrong. I'd spent five days here, helping her learn to hunt, fly and fight in her grotesque form. It was five days more than I planned on spending, but I was also having a difficult time justifying my departure, when I saw how far she had to go in order to prepare her army for a war in four months. The better prepared she was, the higher the chances of success.

And ... she was family. The only real family I had, aside from Menelaus. Both of them were descendants. I didn't exactly know how to balance loyalty to blood and the burning desire I had to find Alessandra and ensure she was safe. Herakles seemed convinced she was, and Lantos possessed abilities no other god or man did. In theory, Alessandra was safer on the DC compound than anyone else in the world.

Yet this knowledge didn't help the restlessness at my core, and Phoibe's intense focus on suppressing her thoughts and reactions whenever I brought the Oracle up was an indication something was wrong.

"Excuse me, Your Majesty," a soldier opened the door and bowed clumsily. "We have a situation at the front gate."

Herakles started to stand, but I beat him to it. "With your permission, I'll go," I said to her. *Your people aren't comfortable expressing their opinions while I'm here.* I added telepathically.

She nodded.

The tense silence of the boardroom was soon behind me. The soldier at the door scrambled out of my path and then darted ahead of me, as nervous as everyone was when they caught sight of me. I was allegedly under a sort of house arrest, but Herakles was the only person in camp who would dare step in my path. Accustomed to the general aversion others had of me after my time at SISA, I welcomed the solitude resulting from my reputation. It allowed me space to evaluate and think without distraction.

I strode through the former department store acting as their headquarters and out into the afternoon heat. It was balmy and bright, and her camp was a beehive of activity. The soldier led me to the motor pool, and we climbed into an armored vehicle to drive the two kilometers separating the front gate from the center of the sprawling encampment.

As we approached, the front gate positioned behind a trench and razor wire opened to reveal a single figure standing outside the fence line. I recognized the man before we were close enough for me to see his features. When he spotted me, he smiled. My instincts went on high alert, and I skimmed the surrounding forest for signs he had brought his army with him.

I couldn't begin to fathom what Niko was doing here. The breeze brought no one else's scents to me, and no dangerous shadows lurked in the forest. Niko was alone and armed, though he was no match for the multiple weapons currently trained on him. The vehicle stopped at the gate, and I got out.

"Close the gate behind me," I instructed the soldier I passed as I crossed through the protective barrier.

He obeyed. I waited until I heard the sounds of the locks sliding into place before I approached Niko. The brash head of the military was my polar opposite, and just as dangerous. I had a great deal of respect for him and understood never to trust him with anything of value.

"I didn't expect to see you here," he said.

"Likewise," I replied.

"Guess who has your old job?" His gaze glinted. "What was it you told me once? Someone like me would never be the head of SISA?"

"Gaining a position by default and winning it by merit are two separate situations," I said coolly. "I'm well aware SISA is under the control of the military."

Normally, he was the first to anger when we traded barbs, but this time, he continued to smile.

"I made a deal to bring you all this." He held out a piece of paper. "A certain Oracle paid me in gold to ensure it made it. It took me some time to slip away."

I despised a man who could be *bought*. No one was lower in my mind. I accepted the paper and opened it.

The apocalypse is coming. It occurs the day the Silent Queen gives birth to twins. Adonis is dead.

The hastily scribbled words relayed the panic of the person who wrote it. My beast senses picked up on the faint scent of Alessandra, and I ran my thumb across the sentence about me.

"I'll admit, I'm a little disappointed to see you alive. I assume she means you will be dead soon," Niko said in satisfaction.

"Her visions have started."

"Yeah. The episodes are sporadic and take them both out. Makes my job interesting."

"Both?" I repeated. I re-folded the letter and placed it in my pocket.

"She and Cleon."

I tilted my head, not understanding what Alessandra's visions had to do with the Supreme Magistrate.

Niko studied me. His smile became broader. "You don't know," he said softly.

"Assume I don't. I've been away for a few weeks."

"Thank the gods for today." Niko glanced at the sky. "Destroying your world might be the best day of my life."

I waited for his explanation.

Eager to twist a knife in my gullet, Niko spared no details. By the time he finished the tale of what had happened to Alessandra in my absence, and dwelt on the many ways Lantos had turned on everyone, I was tense. Niko was too thrilled by the brutal truth – none of my instincts flagged his words as lies.

He finished, grinning. I remained silent, unable to recall a time when I had experienced anger this deep.

Niko sensed it. His eyes sparkled as he studied me. "Best day of my life," he repeated.

"The Silent Queen knows," I guessed.

"I assume. Theodocia did, and they communicated on occasion."

Phoibe's secret was worse than I thought. Herakles didn't know, or he wouldn't be here. I didn't care for him, but he would never let anyone harm Alessandra. Every instinct in my body wanted me to leave now, to go to Alessandra and ... I didn't know. I wasn't able to think clearly after all I'd heard.

"Where is she?" I asked after a long silence, in which I grappled for control of myself.

"The House. She and Lantos are confined to quarters," Niko said. "That means nothing to Lantos. He leaves as he chooses."

"You're being helpful. Why?"

"Maybe I want to make it easier for you to get yourself killed."

"Or you figured out who might be left standing."

"What can I say?" He shrugged. "I have a price. Alessandra can make gold out of thin air, enough for a hundred lifetimes. And I wouldn't mind seeing you dead, if you charge into the House and try to free her."

"Have you destroyed the insurgency's abilities?"

"Why not come inside the walls and see for yourself?" Niko asked.

"I intend to. Soon."

"I'll be ready."

"No, you won't," I countered. "If you have any desire to stick around once Cleon is gone, you'll step aside when you see me coming."

Niko and I sized each other up. He was an incredible warrior. We had fought enough for me to know this. But the weakness of his I'd choose to exploit would never be inside the ring, and he knew this as well.

"There's another way," he said.

For the second time today, he surprised me. "Meaning ..." I prodded.

"Cleon wants you for some reason. He won't tell me why, but I'm sure it has something to do with Alessandra," Niko said. "I'll sneak you in."

"What's the catch?"

He shrugged. "Maybe I like the idea of an asshole winding up in the dungeon under the House. With their minds connected, Cleon will know you're there when she does."

"That's not material enough to motivate you."

Niko chuckled. He shifted, and I sensed he was uneasy. I understood him well enough to know he didn't care about the half dozen weapons trained on him. He was here because Alessandra paid him, but I suspected even that wasn't enough for him to risk his life for anyone. I mentally reviewed the details from the portfolio I'd created on him during my time at SISA. I had assessed long ago, when I first profiled him, that there were two real weaknesses with Niko, and they had nothing to do with his physical prowess and bank account.

"Tommy or Theodocia?" I ventured.

He shifted, and some of the amusement left his features. "I heard something about you. Something really interesting about how you're a monster or a god."

"Monster is most accurate," I replied.

"Who can fly."

"Yes."

"I might need a favor down the road," Niko said.

"In exchange for taking me to Alessandra."

"In exchange for taking you inside the walls. If you want access to the House, there's a second price. When you do see her, tell her to un-do whatever she did to Theodocia."

I didn't possess the details about what had happened, and Niko was being unusually cagey. "You want two favors in exchange for helping me see Alessandra and turning me over to Cleon after," I repeated in a hard voice. Did he know I'd do anything to see her again, even if he asked me for a dozen undesirable favors?

His smile and answered my question before his words did. "She destroyed four thousand lives for you. I'm pretty sure you'll do whatever I want for her."

At that moment, I wanted to murder Niko. It wasn't entirely because of him. He was basically the messenger in this scenario, one with the ability to help me reach the House without being arrested first. My anger was close to the boiling point, and I loathed Niko's smug smile and confidence.

It would be much easier to reach her, and Lantos, if I could do it in broad daylight. At night, I could fly into the compound, but I'd draw attention the moment I tried to creep into the House, the most fortified, safeguarded, and closely monitored building in the world. It wouldn't stop me from smashing in a window to reach her. But I'd rather assess if what Niko said was true about her mind and Cleon's colliding before I busted her out and risked hurting her.

I also needed to talk to Lantos face to face. I had trusted him. I wasn't completely willing to believe he'd betrayed me, not when his motives were often times beyond the scope of a human like Niko to understand. It was possible there was a solid explanation for what Lantos had done. I was going to give him the benefit of the doubt, and if I found him unworthy, I'd kill him where he stood. That he and Alessandra were imprisoned in the same building would make it easier for me to maximize the one shot I had at entering the House.

"All right," I said.

"I'm headed straight back."

I dwelt briefly on Phoibe's situation before my thoughts settled on Alessandra. Phoibe was surrounded by good people and capable of taking care of herself. I wasn't able to say the same about Alessandra. "I need to go somewhere first. I'll be thirty minutes."

"You'll understand if I don't stand here in the crossfire of my enemies," Niko replied wryly. "I'll be at the main road." Turning, he walked away, unconcerned with the weapons trained on his back or the anger radiating off me.

I released the breath I was holding and strode into the forest.

I was infuriated enough that I didn't feel capable of facing Phoibe before I left, not when she had kept something this important from me. I stalked off into the woods towards the cabin Menelaus and I had discovered our first night here. He and Apollo were my secret. After seeing Phoibe's hostile reaction to any suggestion of the gods helping her take the city, I had initially decided to keep Menelaus hidden.

Several minutes later, I reached the cabin. The previous occupant of the isolated home had lived completely off grid. Solar and wind power provided electricity, and a well ten meters from the wood cabin provided water. A small paddock had housed some sort of animals at one point before rotting.

I leaned against the fence. It was a very rare day in my life when I felt as if I was going to lose control. In fact, I couldn't recall a time ever when rage bubbled within me as it did after hearing Niko's tale. I was torn between anger with Lantos for turning on me and with myself for leaving Alessandra alone, despite knowing how the twisted politics of DC worked.

Niko was as likely to turn me in the moment I set foot in the walls as he was to take me to the House. But my own safety was the smallest of my concerns. I was capable of anticipating danger and acting in my self-interest with skill no man could match. And if he was telling the truth, and I would be permitted to see Alessandra, I wasn't going to pass up the opportunity.

A sliver of self-doubt returned, and I wrestled with my two sides. Right now, they were both urging me to go to her and to destroy anyone who had tried to hurt her. The unity left me struggling even harder to control the fury inside me. I squeezed the wood in my hands hard enough for it to snap. Dropping my arms, I rolled my shoulders back, seeking to calm myself.

"What is it?" Menelaus was standing in the doorway of the cabin.

"Bad news," I replied. "Alessandra's in danger. I'm returning to the city and have to leave you here. If I'm not back in a day, introduce yourself to Phoibe. But do so carefully. She holds no favorable views of the gods."

"It is fortunate I am not one."

I glanced at him. Apollo didn't yet feel safe revealing himself to me, and I wasn't going to risk alienating him when I would need his help later.

"If you do not return, should I tell her to find you?" Menelaus asked.

"No. Stay with her and keep her safe. She needs the type of guidance only an ancient king who brought down the walls of Troy can provide."

Menelaus nodded. His warm gaze was concerned.

"Take care," I said quietly.

"And you."

I left him, troubled about the future, yet convinced I was leaving Phoibe with the only person who could help her more than I was able to. Jogging through the forest, I returned to the dirt road leading to the encampment and strode down the opposite direction, towards the main road.

Niko was waiting. He had brought no soldiers with him and stood leaning against a black van, arms crossed. He pushed himself away when he spotted me and climbed into the driver's seat. I opened the passenger seat to find a black SISA uniform, complete with hood, waiting for me.

"Figured it'd make you less conspicuous," Niko said.

Already, I'd accepted I was going to my doom. I got in and maneuvered into the back of the van. He began driving while I changed. I returned to the passenger seat when I was finished.

"What happened to Theodocia?" I asked as we headed towards the walls of DC.

"Cleon ambushed her." The response was clipped enough to reveal his unhappiness about the circumstance.

"I meant, what did Alessandra do?" I clarified with a half-smile.

"She turned her into a gummy statue. Dosy's alive, but has the consistency of a tire."

"Alessandra's come into her power?"

"Eh." Niko was quiet, thinking hard about the answer. "She's fighting it and has been. The safe zone is starting to recede, and Cleon's desperate to create this utopian safe zone filled with the elite and weather away whatever happens next, but can't wield her power well enough to stop it. And she's ... confused."

"I would be, too, if I had more than one voice in my head." My hands tightened into fists instinctively. I *did* have more than one voice in my head, but I wasn't about to tell Niko I'd been struggling with my own identity.

There was a pause. I sensed more before Niko spoke. "It's not just that," he said pensively. "I have no desire to understand this insanity about power or magic or energy or whatever this is." He waved a hand at the unseen forces about which he spoke. "But something's going on beyond what is supposed to be happening. The Oracle is in a coma. Cleon is fading and obsessed with either the insurgency or the safe zone. Lantos is playing an erratic game no one understands, and Alessandra is on the verge of being lost. They're all part of a bigger picture, and I don't know who could be calling the shots – but someone has to be."

"The major players are too preoccupied to be manipulating the board," I said.

"Exactly. And Lyssa ... her visions have her spooked, and her power has something to do with Thanatos and Hades."

As strategic a thinker as I was, even I was unable to assess what was going on beyond the obvious. Niko's astuteness came as no surprise. It was his uneasiness that concerned me. When a street thug, whose survival depended upon the speed of his ability to read people, took a step back and couldn't piece together what the danger was, then the problem was either immense or complex.

With gods and power in the mix, I was guessing both.

"How quickly is the safe zone receding?" I asked.

"It's sporadic. Some days, it's a kilometer or five or ten. On other days, no loss occurs. On the rare occasion, it grows."

"Almost like someone is trying to prevent it from receding."

"It's not Cecelia or Cleon or Alessandra, and they're the only people capable of fighting anything unseen."

"Lantos?"

Niko shook his head. "If he knows, he's not looking in that direction."

"In which direction is he looking?"

"I can do a lot of things, but tracking a shadow isn't one of them. When he wants to be seen, he's in his apartment, doing absolutely nothing. When he doesn't ..." Niko shrugged. "But in our discussions, he's not at all concerned about the safe zone."

We drew near a checkpoint. Neither of us spoke as we crossed through two checkpoints before reaching the heavily guarded entrance of the wall. Niko drove through slowly with a wave at his men then picked up speed as he headed through the city towards the compound at its center.

The city looked much like it had when I left ... until we reached an area cordoned off by police tape. A gaping hole ran for several blocks before the cityscape began again.

Seeing my long look at the collapsed area, Niko spoke for the first time since we started driving.

"Your girl did that," he said. "Messed her up."

I didn't have to imagine Alessandra's distress; I'd experienced it in some form every day, whenever I tried to rest, only for the image of her to flash through my mind.

"Everyone agrees she's stronger than Cecelia," Niko added.

"She's the strongest since the first," I replied. "That is her prophecy."

"Maybe you can fix her."

Niko wasn't capable of caring for anyone outside his son and ex, but even he had to understand Alessandra was the key to everything.

He drove us to the compound. We entered with no difficulty, and Niko parked in the general lot a short distance from the mall, around which the buildings were arranged. We left the van and began walking towards the House, the largest of the remaining buildings.

"You may want to see Lantos first," he said. "Cleon can see everything Alessandra does. He'll alert security the second she spots you."

Niko was genuinely concerned about something. At the moment, I cared too much about the woman on the third floor of the House to find out what.

Niko left me at the back entrance of the heavily guarded house. I wore a uniform similar to my old one, complete with the red patch on the shoulder marking me as a commander, which ensured no one challenged me. Several checkpoints inside the House slowed my progress considerably. My blood was boiling, my skin crawling with my growing sense of dread.

Finally, I made it through the final set of guards monitoring her hallway and stood before her door. My heart pounded hard in antici-pation, and I was on edge enough that I paused to breathe deeply, so I didn't snap if I heard a loud sound.

Niko's advice returned to me. As much as I yearned to walk into

Alessandra's apartment, the rational side warned me I had one shot today, and I needed to talk to Lantos first.

With reluctance, I left her door and passed through another set of guards to the section of the House where Lantos was loosely confined. His door, too, appeared to be locked from the outside. As I stood there, I felt sorrow replace much of my anger when I considered my only friend in the world had betrayed me.

I walked into his apartment and closed the door behind me, senses on alert.

"I'm not due for my meeting for an hour," Lantos said from the breakfast nook a short distance away. He glanced up at me from his tablet then back.

Spotting the camera in the corner of his apartment, I didn't remove my mask.

"I'm not here about your meeting," my voice carried a note of unmistakable tension. The muscles of my frame were taut, stiff, as I considered my personal failing in trusting Lantos. "I came to see a friend, but I'm not certain he exists anymore."

His bright green eyes fixed to me. "Adonis," he breathed after a moment.

"I have little time," I said. "Because we are ... *were* friends, I wanted to give you one chance to tell me why you've done what you've done. I urge you to think and speak quickly. Your candidness determines your fate."

"I assure you, there is an explanation." He stood and moved towards me then stopped when he saw me tense further. "Adonis, I need you to know what I'm doing is for the benefit of everyone, including Alessandra. My actions appear –"

"Like you betrayed the man you called your brother?" I finished with calm I didn't feel.

"And like I betrayed everyone else," he said. "The truth is much more complicated."

"Tell me. Now."

"I can't." He searched my features. "I know how this looks, and I know how this sounds. A secret was revealed to me, so that I could take action. But it is not my secret to reveal. I consider you to still be my brother. I have, and always will, do what I feel I must to protect you."

I absorbed his words. He was sincere and firm. I wanted to believe he had a reason, but with the overwhelming information Niko had revealed, it was difficult to believe anything could be worth what Lantos was willing to sacrifice.

The human side of me, who viewed Lantos as my savior, was too hurt to want to give him the benefit of the doubt, while my primal instinct was more rational. Lantos was a politician, and a damned good one. He was always manipulating the environment and people to better his access, position or power. But he had always needed my help, too, when it came to the political game, which I had learned the same way Phoibe did – as a child-ruler of a vast empire. I always knew the possibility existed for Lantos to manipulate me, if the circumstances warranted it. I'd also thought I would be aware of it, since my instincts were better than his.

As the long silence stretched between us, I couldn't help wondering what I was more upset about: my own failing to catch the warning signs about Lantos, or the fact he had done what I had always understood him to be capable of doing. He was not acting out of character. Before Alessandra, however, we had been an inseparable team.

I entered expecting to be able to decide with ease whether or not I would kill Lantos. Five minutes later, I was mired in an inner battle between understanding who and what he was, and denial anything in the world could make up for what he'd helped do to Alessandra.

"I can forgive your betrayal of me," I said at last. "But Alessandra ... Lantos, I can't turn the other way."

"How do you think I felt, knowing I'd probably lose you to do what I had to?" he replied bitterly.

"Yet you did it," I pointed out. I drew near him, scouring his features. "Tell me the truth. Is it worth it?"

"Yes," he said without hesitation. "Hurting you is the hardest thing I've ever done. But it was necessary."

I didn't doubt that he believed his own words.

"What's worst: I'm not done hurting you," he said with a harsh laugh. "If I don't continue down this path I'm on, much worse will befall you than anything I can and will do to you."

"You're hurting me to *save* me?" I asked.

"Yes. No," he replied. "But it's not just you. It's complicated. I'm trying to fix something I broke." His gaze rested on the wall separating his apartment from Alessandra's. "I promise, one day, I'll tell you everything, Adonis. But I can't today."

I was quiet, pensive, unable to shake the ominous sense about the secret Lantos was unwilling to share. His betrayal, while unexpected, made more sense, if he believed he was working to *help* people choose the lesser of two evil paths.

But it didn't justify what he'd done in secrecy, to someone I cared about. If he had a legitimate reason for hurting Alessandra, why had he not come to me?

Did it matter what his reasoning was, when his choices were already made and acted upon?

The discussion had taken a turn I didn't expect and, in doing so, revealed more than Lantos was willing to admit directly. Niko's hunch that there were more forces at work here than those that met the eye was confirmed. Lantos was operating independently of the other players in DC. Whatever his agenda was, it was not self-driven, which meant, he was not operating out of self-interest this time.

I was too emotionally charged to guess what, or who, could motivate him to leave the course he'd been on or to imagine what his purpose and end state were.

"*One day* is too late, Lantos," I said finally.

The light in his gaze faded. "I understand," he said quietly.

Turning away, I strode toward the door.

"Adonis," he called.

I paused.

"I mean this when I say I still consider you a brother. If you ever need my help, I won't ask any questions."

What good was the offer of assistance from someone who had already told me the worst wasn't over yet?

Who had such an influence over him that he was willing to say such a thing, when his actions were the source of the damage? The man who could read secrets out of people's minds wasn't an easy target for anyone. Whatever he was doing, he was likely executing the directives of a god, or perhaps even his father, to whom his loyalty was greater than it was towards me.

I nodded once and exited his apartment. Wary of the scrutiny the guards were giving me, I didn't stop to clear my head as I wanted to but returned to the corridor sectioned off from both ends of the hallway.

Alessandra's door was locked from the outside. I unlocked it and stepped inside, my senses pricking with awareness.

The apartment was quiet, neat and clean. Her scent was in the air, and it managed to clear my mind of the turmoil of emotions remaining from my encounter with Lantos.

"Alessandra," I called and closed the door behind me.

A quiet pause was interrupted by the sound of a door whipping open. The beautiful woman emerged from what appeared to be her bedroom and stared at me. Smaller than me and toned, she appeared in general good health, though slimmer than she had been. Emotions played across her features too fast for me to gauge which one would win. The air around her rippled with energy and power, to the point her aura blurred the edges of her surroundings.

I couldn't feel her. Even this close. The connection we shared was battering against my chest, trying to reach her, but unable to. My inability to feel our bond supported Niko's claim about Lantos going rogue, and lessened my satisfaction with Lantos' explanation further. This was why she hadn't contacted me – and I had been too immersed in my sense of betrayal to ask Lantos to lift the wall between us.

"Who are you?" Alessandra asked, eyes narrowed.

In the strange silence between us, I peeled off the SISA mask.

Alessandra snapped her eyes closed. "You can't be here. He knows. You can't be here!" she whispered in a strained voice. She whirled away from me and paced to the window, staring out.

I trailed and paused behind her, close enough to feel her body heat and the waves of energy radiating off her. Because she brought me to life, I was immune to her magic. "Alessandra."

"You can't be here!" she said again, this time with an edge of desperation in her voice. "You have to leave!"

"I'm not going anywhere, Alessandra."

I rested my palms lightly on her arms. She tensed, her breath catching audibly. Seconds later, she twisted and flung her arms around my neck.

"I knew you'd come back," she whispered fiercely.

I hugged her against me hard, uncertain when any physical sensation had struck me to my core as her touch always did. The smell of her hair sent my beast side into euphoria, and the need to claim and protect what was mine rose hard and fast within me. Before I left, we had started down a path that unnerved me, because of how deeply I felt, and how much I feared I'd hurt her. With her body pressed to mine, I was able to feel where I belonged. Every other worry or question or doubt vanished. I had wanted to hold her like this many times before I left but respected her too much to be forward in what I felt.

Tension melted from her frame. I held her tightly, absorbing and memorizing every sensation. Every breath, the softness of her skin, the scent of her shampoo, the firmness of her frame.

"How did you do that?" she voiced.

"What?"

"When you touched me, he was gone."

Unreasonable anger surged at the reminder Cleon had overtaken her mind, with the help of Lantos. I suppressed it with effort.

"I don't know," I replied. "What we have runs deeper."

"I thought you were dead," she repeated. "I saw you, Adonis. I saw you in Hades."

My pulse quickened. No man, especially one who had been alive for four thousand years, was immune to concern when an Oracle admitted to foreseeing his death. Sensing her distress, I squeezed her. "I'm alive and plan to stay that way," I said.

She released me enough to pull her head back and meet my gaze. Her blue eyes were large and filled with emotions I wanted to remove and destroy permanently, so they never disturbed her again. Her features were flushed.

We gazed into each other's eyes, lost to the rest of the world, speaking a silent language only the soul understood. Being with her like this was so natural, it was difficult for me to restrain the part of me that wanted more. My concern now was her well-being, not the satisfaction of the primal needs thrumming through me.

"You're not okay," I said and cupped her cheek with one hand.

"No," she replied. "You're in danger around me."

"I don't care."

Her blush deepened under my intense look, and she hugged me once again.

Banging on the door sent a ripple of anger through me. "Niko sneaked me in. I knew they'd figure it out quickly but had hoped it took them a while to react."

"Cleon saw you when I did. I can fix this for now," she said.

The banging became muffled. I glanced toward the door. A thick sheet of metal walled off the front of the apartment from us. The creation of the wall had been effortless for her.

"I won't let them hurt you," she added. "But you'll have to leave before Cleon arrives. My magic doesn't work on either of you."

I smiled, touched by her concern, if not amused by the idea she feared anyone could hurt me. Her breathing was quick and shallow. I didn't need our connection to understand she was struggling with herself, or perhaps, her power. Bending, I scooped her up and walked to the couch. I sat with her in my lap, and we shifted until she was comfortable. I pushed a strand of hair from her features.

"Did Niko blackmail you?" she asked unhappily.

"I wouldn't call it blackmail. I was happy to pay his price," I replied.

Her eyes narrowed, and anger flared deep within them.

"He asked for a favor unique to my skill set and one of you," I continued. "He wants you to undo what you did to Theodocia."

"I *knew* it!" Her anger faded, replaced by a reluctant smile. Tilting her head, she peered past me, at the metal wall. Her look grew distant for a fraction of a second before she blinked the spell away. "It's done."

"That easy." I didn't display my surprise. When I'd left her, she had little handle on her magic and no ability to use it without great effort.

"Yeah," she said. "It's gotten both easier and harder. Easier, because I can do anything. Harder, because Cleon can use it, too."

"You're the strongest since the first oracle."

She nodded. "Yeah. She told me."

"You've spoken to her?"

Alessandra hesitated. "I can slip out of our world, Adonis. I can go to an alternate reality. More than one, I think, and I can venture into Hades' domain at will. The first Oracle was sent by Hades to help us, though I don't know she understands exactly how."

My thoughts were on Apollo, trapped in the body of Menelaus. It wasn't coincidence that the first Oracle was present in some regard, and so was the patron god of Oracles and the Bloodline.

"Did you find what you sought, when you left?" Alessandra asked and relaxed in my arms.

"Not exactly," I replied. "The world outside these walls is very different. The gods are dying, and they're overtaking human bodies to try to survive."

Her eyebrows quirked. "Dying," she repeated. "You've witnessed this?"

"I have. The Silent Queen has been hunting and killing them. Neither of us can understand how or why the gods are in the shape they're in."

Her expression fell, and I didn't understand why. The tension of her body didn't leave completely, and a shadow similar to that I saw in Lantos gaze lingered.

FIFTEEN
ALESSANDRA

I HAD to send Adonis away, for his own benefit, and I couldn't find the words to do it. I'd wanted to stand here like this with him almost since we met. I clung to him instead, never wanting him to leave me while knowing our time together was short.

"I don't want that to be true," I said, focusing on what he said rather than what I felt. My thoughts were grudgingly lingering on one idea planted by Cleon and Lantos alike, and I hated the path it took me down. I was at a crossroads.

If the gods were dying, how was it possible for what I wanted to believe about their involvement in the Holy Wars? Adonis was opening a door I'd been struggling to keep closed – the door to a different version of events than that I had been led to believe about the gods' involvement on Earth. The priests who raised me at the orphanage had hated them and were determined to bring back the Old Ways.

Was it possible they weren't the first to act upon their beliefs that the gods were more of a nuisance than benefit to humanity?

"You bear no good will towards them. What troubles you about them dying?" Adonis asked softly.

I was caught for a few seconds in the beautiful shade of blue-green of his eyes. His strength and warmth grounded me while simultaneously frightening me a little, as always. Seated half on top of him on the couch, I couldn't help wishing this moment would never end, that the chaos in my mind wasn't going to return when our bodies no longer touched.

For two weeks, I'd been trapped in this apartment, swirling slowly down into a level of insanity that left me unable to distinguish my thoughts from Cleon's, or my experiences from his. Sometimes, I sat in his office and spoke to high level officials and sometimes, I watched television endlessly in my living room. I didn't know which of us was which anymore.

I hadn't, until Adonis touched me and yanked me out of the mental free fall I'd been in for days. Without Cleon's mind merged to mine, I understood where I was, *who* I was and even what conversations and thoughts had been mine.

Adonis caused a different kind of free fall, where my heart – rather than my mind – was tumbling into the abyss. I rested my fingertips on his face, not quite able to believe he was here, even though the warmth of his skin assured me he was.

Registering Adonis' question, I lowered my hand before my fingers reached the full lips I ached to touch. "It's complicated," I replied, thoughts on Cleon's firm belief the gods weren't responsible for the Holy Wars. "Lantos ... he gave them the ability to talk to me, but I've been suppressing them. Cleon won't let me leave this apartment if I don't talk to them."

"Maybe you should."

I studied Adonis. I could ignore the advice of everyone – except for Adonis and Herakles. Adonis was the former leader of the religious police, SISA, but I had never thought him particularly fond of the gods, especially given his Bloodline's relationship with the deities who cursed them.

"If you do not feel comfortable speaking to just any god, I know one who will listen," he added at my silence.

I hesitated. "You think it's necessary?"

"I think there's no downside to understanding who your enemies may or may not be."

"Makes sense." The guards had pierced the outer door and were starting on the metal wall I put between us. Instinctively, I gripped Adonis' hand, unwilling to let him go, especially not before I warned him. "I foresaw your death, Adonis. Twice."

"Tell me exactly what you saw."

I filled him in on the visions. Whereas I'd hidden parts of them from Phoibe and Lantos, I revealed everything to Adonis. He listened, head tilted in interest and eyes steady on my face. When I was done, he remained quiet.

"I can't believe you're here." My cheeks grew warm again. I wanted to ask him if he thought worse of me after the incident in the city where I murdered over three thousand people, but I couldn't. I couldn't handle disappointing him.

"I belong right here," he said and cupped my cheeks in his hands.

"But you can't stay," I insisted. "I can't protect you. I couldn't protect Theodocia or Leandra or Mrs. Nettles." Tears blinded me, and I wiped them away, humiliated to cry in front of anyone.

"I don't need protection, Alessandra."

I loved the way he said my name. Low, soft, deep with reverence I'd never considered giving much of anything in my life.

"If you will consider meeting with one god in particular, I think he can help," Adonis added.

At that moment, he could've asked me to murder another three thousand people, and I would have agreed without a trace of independent thought interfering with the decision. I gazed into his eyes, hardly able to believe he was sitting here with me, and we were touching in a way far more intimate than we ever had. Something akin to adrenaline was blazing in my blood, leaving me self-aware, my skin too sensitive, to sit here long without exploding or squirming.

"Okay," I whispered.

"He may be able to interpret your vision. I see pieces of information in it, but the bigger picture eludes me."

"Me, too."

The grinding whine of a massive drill sent both of us covering our ears. The floor and ceiling trembled, and the metal wall began to shake. I tried to brace it, to will another layer of metal over the existing wall, with no effect. My heart began to race, and I recalled too clearly Lantos claim I would be the reason behind Adonis' death. Cleon wanted Adonis dead, because he understood the threat to our bond.

"Cleon's here," I shouted about the drilling. "He's blocking me! You have to leave!" I scrambled off the lap of the man I was pretty certain I loved and willed all the lights in the apartment out. Certain to keep a death grip on his hand, I identified the darkest corner.

"Alessandra," Adonis called.

"I can't leave the room because of that asshole Lantos!" I exclaimed in frustration. "But he owes us both for betraying us. He'll do what I tell him to!" Towing him to the corner, I leaned into the darkness and did as the shadow titan had once directed me. "Lantos!"

Adonis took my arm and turned me to face him. His features were grim. He understood he couldn't stay, not if he wanted to survive this. He said nothing, though, and we stood in awkward silence. He was calm. I was panicking.

"I can't lose you," I said.

"You won't. I'm not going anywhere. Nothing that comes through that door -" The ferocity in his low growl was pure Mismatch.

"You have to go. If you don't, you *will* die!" I said urgently. "If you're gone, I don't care what happens to the rest of the world!"

His jaw was clenched tightly enough for the muscles to tick. He was gripping my arms tighter, and emotions churned in his eyes.

"Please," I begged. "For me. We will find a way to be together, but it's not here and now. If you die, I will chase you into Hades, and everything else will be lost. I'm safe here. No one can hurt me."

"One condition." He released a breath. "Meet me tonight on the wall where I saved you once before."

I couldn't. I *wouldn't,* not if it meant I placed him in danger.

"I'll be there." It took every ounce of what I'd learned from Cleon and Lantos for me to look Adonis directly in the eye and lie – and it broke my heart to do it.

With the drill screeching in our ears, and our fates doomed at best, I could think of no other moment in history where I wanted to be than here with my Adonis. Our look grew too long. Did he sense the thought going through my mind – that this might be our last time together?

Did he know I would destroy my world to save him, and had already considered destroying myself for the same reason?

More tears burned my eyes. I deserved far worse than their fire after all I'd done. I didn't know what to say, and by his silence, neither did he.

Adonis leaned forward and kissed me. The second his soft, warm lips touched mine, I froze. My mind went completely blank, and the fire racing through me turned into an inferno whose source was the base of my belly. Having never kissed anyone, I didn't know what to do. His lips guided mine with gentleness at odds with the intensity of what I felt, and I timidly responded to the light pressure of his lips. Leaning into him, I rested my body against his.

Adonis' warmth and strength ... his dark, masculine scent ... his flavor ... I wanted to disappear into him. My instincts were screaming at me to do so much more, but I didn't understand what that meant. Herakles had raised me with absolutely no knowledge about the opposite sex, aside from where to hit or kick a man to disable him quickly.

Someone coughed loudly enough for us to hear over the sound of metal grinding against metal.

Adonis lifted his head from mine. My eyes opened, and I stared at him, breathless and unable to hear much of anything above my heart beating.

"Pardon me for disturbing you," Lantos said from behind Adonis. "I believe someone called for me."

Adonis' hands dropped from my face to take my hand, and he turned away. If he hadn't moved, I'd have been stuck there for eternity, gazing up at him in absolute awe. Any doubt I had about what he felt vanished in the flames of need raging in my body.

Lantos didn't look at Adonis directly but focused on me.

"Yeah," I managed in a faint voice. "Can you take him to safety?"

"I can," Lantos said.

Adonis' jaw was clenched, and the glare he leveled on Lantos was cold.

"You have to go," I said and pushed him towards Lantos. "Please. I'll meet with whomever you want. Just go now!"

Lantos and I exchanged a look, both of us aware of the danger Adonis was in if he remained. Adonis knew as well. He squeezed my hand and walked towards Lantos.

"If you betray us again ..." he began.

"I won't betray *her*," Lantos replied.

Adonis was tense, but he appeared to accept this, while I was left startled. *Now* Lantos decided to protect me? After he'd already inflicted the worst damage possible? Was this part of his attempt to right some wrong he wouldn't discuss? And what did he mean by he wouldn't betray *me*? Was he planning to turn traitor on Adonis?

"We don't have much time," Lantos said with a glance at the metal wall.

I squeezed Adonis' hand.

"I'll be back for you," he said to me without taking his eyes off his former friend.

Adonis shifted towards Lantos. I braced myself for the return of Cleon to my mind, and turned away, eyes closed.

The second his hand slid from mine, I crashed to my knees. Cleon was there, his consciousness merging with mine until I didn't know if I stood in my living room or in the hallway outside, pacing anxiously.

Thank the gods, he was thinking. *What happened?*

The drill stopped immediately. I willed the wall away and

wobbled to my feet. My head was filled with too much for me to manage without a major headache.

Cerberus was in his mirror again, watching me, as always. This time when I looked at him, I thought about how far I'd go to rescue Adonis, in life and death. There were no limits.

Wiping my eyes, I climbed to my feet. Now that I was reconnected to Cleon, we were sharing information again. I could keep nothing from him, and he could keep nothing from me. His relief was forefront in my mind, followed by anger and concern. He had thought I was dead or similar, though we both knew if I died, so did he.

He would also know about now that Niko had set this all up.

"If Adonis comes near here, I will have him killed," he said, standing in the ruins of the destroyed wall of the front of my apartment.

"You're getting worse," I said and faced him. The strange pains that had plagued him since shortly after we were united continued to grow. I sensed it without feeling it, which puzzled both of us, since we had been able to experience the physical sensations the other did for several weeks now. This pain was unique to him. It showed in the tightness of his features, his blanched skin, and the general weakness of his body. I could tell his hunger from mine, and I read in his mind he hadn't eaten in four days.

If anything happened to one of us, it would probably kill us both. Neither of us, however, had any idea why he was suffering.

"I'm ready to listen to the gods," I said. Speaking aloud was unnecessary with our minds linked, but I did it to try to put some space between us.

"Good." He turned and motioned to one of what appeared to be two-dozen guards crowding the hallway. "Grab Niko and his son. Take them to the basements. Put out an alert for the Supreme Priest." He was thinking of Adonis, but he didn't mention him. "Move this shit." He motioned to the equipment they'd used to breach the door and then flinched, one hand going to his head.

Two soldiers hurried away while another five shifted into the apartment to lift the large drill.

Cleon came to stand beside me. "I'm thrilled Adonis talked some sense into you."

"It's not just that."

He met my gaze, accessing my thoughts as if they were his. "Then let's go see her."

"Oh, so now I'm allowed out of my room?" I snapped.

"If anyone had ever tried to convince me of how bizarre the brain of a teenage woman was, I'd have never believed it," he said and shook his head.

"Can't be worse than being in the mind of a delusional psychopath!"

"They're pretty similar."

I hated him. He didn't exactly hold the highest opinion of me, either. We were like a couple married for fifty years. Nothing either of us said or thought surprised the other anymore. We'd both sunk into a state of agitated apathy towards one another.

"We're not going to meet *him* tonight, no matter how much you want to," Cleon added.

"I wouldn't put him in that kind of danger," I snapped. "We have to see Cecelia."

He stepped aside and motioned to the gaping hole in my wall. "After you." He was triumphant, aware I'd been swayed to do what he wanted me to since he dragged me into his office to discuss the gods. "Their voices are easier to hear at twilight."

I said nothing and walked through the mess into the hallway. The soldiers fell away when Cleon motioned them to, and I strode through the adjacent hall and to the stairs.

Ten minutes later, we were outside. I breathed in deeply, and my whole body felt like it was coming back to life after a long slumber. It was muggy and cloudy, the air as thick as soup. I didn't care. Fresh air was fresh air. After two weeks trapped in my apartment, I rejoiced in the cement and exhaust characterizing the city's air. It was late afternoon.

As one, Cleon and I struck off towards the Oracle's caverns. Our strides synced, and we walked in step, our bodies adjusting to one another's. I chose to ignore how little left of me was truly *me* and instead, sifted through our combined thoughts about the Oracle. Where we were in disagreement, it was easier for me to identify my mind from Cleon's. He was ready to charge in and wrestle the Oracle's power away from her, which sounded insane to me, since neither of us had a handle on the source of my power or hers, and no one knew what happened to us if she lashed out. She retained her full capabilities, even if she was weak, whereas I wouldn't until she died.

It was the one area where I was unusually apprehensive and restrained and Cleon shed his patience and plotting for the purpose of instant action.

"That was really your first kiss?" he asked, entertained.

I flushed. I had been trying very, very hard not to think about Adonis at all, let alone dwell on how incredible his kiss had been. Lantos was taking Adonis to safety, which gave me a little time to do something stupid without the shadow titan interfering. A thrill raced through me at the thought of kissing him again but was soon followed by profound sorrow.

I couldn't see him again. Ever. Not while Cleon was in my head.

"At least you won't go down in history as the Oracle who's never kissed a man," Cleon said. "Of everything at stake, and without knowing if we can stop the apocalypse, how is that the most important thought on your mind?"

"Stop it!" I snapped. "The only reason I haven't blasted you to the moon is because I'm not ready to give up yet."

He was quiet. Our combined concern grew stronger as we reached the guard shack atop the caverns until the energy of my magic was bouncing between the politician and me. We entered unchallenged and rode the elevator down to the cavern.

I breathed in the giddy, familiar scents with relief, enjoying the tiny piece of peace they offered.

Cleon stopped a meter from the elevator. "I understand now." He closed his eyes, and I felt his inner contentment, echoed inside my own being.

Can you hear me? Cecelia's soft voice sent a jolt of awareness through me.

I looked towards her then at Cleon, who was smiling and oblivious.

How can you talk to me without him hearing? I asked.

I have had thirty years to learn to use my gifts. She said no more.

I approached her prison inside the glass bubble on a wall. I wanted to ask her about the suspicions Cleon and Lantos shared, but I hesitated. When I saw what humans and gods had done to her and to her predecessors, I found it harder to condemn her for wanting to destroy everyone.

I couldn't let that happen, even if I pitied her and understood why she was so angry.

The protected zone is shrinking, I said carefully.

I am weak, Alessandra. If you do not help me, I will not survive much longer to assist in protecting what's left of our people.

And this time when she spoke these words, which I'd heard many times, I couldn't believe her. Adonis' words returned to me, as did the vision of the future where I stood here in this chamber, frozen in some sort of altered state, while Lantos and Tommy looked on. Cleon hadn't been in the vision, but nothing else about it gave me any hint as to what was happening, when, or why.

I didn't know whom to believe, but I was leaning towards the lying asshole politicians who manipulated and trapped me, not because I had any faith in them, but because of the information Adonis provided about the gods dying. I replayed the visions I'd experienced over and over.

The apocalypse and ghostly Adonis.

Lantos and Tommy standing here.

The Silent Queen going into labor outside the walls.

Adonis appearing to me in Hades.

Were they even in the same potential timeline, or fragments of multiple paths leading to multiple potential futures?

I don't know what to believe, I said, in case Cecelia was reading my mind.

Give me strength, so I can save us all, was her reply.

I had touched her in one, and I'd been frozen. Was this vision a warning of what *not* to do?

My heartbeat was racing, my palms sweating. Cecelia had a quantum computer to help her sort through her visions and powers. I had martial arts training and ... Cleon. While he was brilliant in his own twisted way, I didn't think he could offer the type of support I needed right now.

"I can't hear your thoughts." Cleon joined me at the railing, his gaze sharp.

"Maybe it's the cavern," I mumbled.

"She's talking to you, isn't she?"

I tried not to react. Being a shameless liar, Cleon spotted my tells.

"Do not do anything without me," he said quietly. "You have no idea what you're dealing with, Alessandra. You may hate me, but you know I know how to handle power and those ambitious enough to do anything to get it."

He was right. It took a psycho dictator to know one.

"What is she saying?" he asked.

"She says she's weak."

He left the railing to check the readouts on the screen on the wall nearest the glass petri dish. "According to this, she's still in a coma. She shouldn't be talking to anyone."

"Well, she is."

What can I do to help you? I asked Cecelia.

What we planned, the last time we saw each other when I was fully awake, she replied.

I gripped the railing.

"What's she saying?" Cleon asked, watching me closely.

"Nothing really," I lied.

"Now is not the time for games, Alessandra."

I can get rid of him, Cecelia said. *Permanently. I can free you.*

My eyebrows went up.

"She's not to be trusted," Cleon said.

"Neither are you."

"I want to protect humanity."

"You want to *rule* a select colony of approved humans!" I retorted. *How can you free me?* I asked Cecelia telepathically.

He's bound to you, but I can break the connection, after I regain some strength.

By an energy exchange, I said, recalling what she asked me to do before.

Why do you hesitate to help me? You once were eager to, she said, sounding disappointed.

"Because I have no idea who to trust." I looked pointedly at Cleon. "He says you started the Holy Wars and Zeus is safeguarding the protected zone, not you."

You believe the man who stole your mind?

"No," I snorted. "But I have a reason to believe there might be a different version of events."

They have polluted you. This was prophesized.

My pulse raced. I didn't know if what she claimed was true or not. I could think of one person to ask, but I wasn't risking Cleon stealing my body, if I dropped into the alternate world to find the first Oracle again.

"Did you have anything to do with the Holy Wars?" I asked.

I closed the gate to prevent a worse fate.

"So you were protecting us," I said. "Right? You didn't launch the fireballs five years ago and wipe out humanity. You reacted when the gods tried to hurt us."

I acted to prevent a worse fate, she repeated.

"I don't understand. You closed the gate to prevent a worse fate, destroyed most of humanity or ... you did something else?"

The deaths of billions were unintended. I did what I had to.

Coldness settled into my core. "That's not an answer!" I retorted. Herakles and Adonis would probably tell me that this really *was* an answer, an indirect confession. She wasn't denying anything, as I suspected she should be, if she were innocent. Growing alarmed, I gripped the railing harder. "Did you hurt all those people?"

Cleon waited expectantly, and I ignored him.

Cecelia was silent.

"You didn't. You wouldn't," I reasoned aloud. "I mean, how *could* you?"

I glanced at the monitors, unable to tell if she'd fallen into her coma again or if she'd ever really been in one.

"She's gone. I can hear your mind again," Cleon said.

"I don't understand," I said, looping the conversation around in my head again. "She didn't admit to anything but she said whatever she did was necessary to save us from a worse fate."

"There is no worse fate. If Zeus loses his grip on the protected zone, chaos will rule briefly, the gods will die, and all this will be followed by permanent darkness," Cleon said. "You've foreseen this."

"I don't know what I've foreseen! My visions are incoherent." I sought some explanation, some reasoning behind whether or not Cecelia had done this. "She said the deaths were unintended. Maybe she had a vision about what was coming and couldn't, or didn't, stop it."

"Or maybe she didn't try, or she was the one to burn the world to the ground," Cleon said.

I didn't want to listen to him, didn't want to believe Cecelia was capable of doing what they thought she was. I was starting to panic internally, to question everything I'd ever been told by Cecelia, to review every word Cleon and Lantos had said to make me doubt her. Artemis hadn't spoken out against the Oracle when she advised me to use my power, but wasn't her encouragement yet another nail in the coffin of what I was beginning to believe was the truth?

"The thirty nine hundred deaths under your belt were unintended, too," Cleon pointed out. "As were the deaths of your parents. But someone killed all those people. Someone collapsed the buildings around them while they slept, and someone pulled the trigger that took your parents' lives away."

With the scents of the cavern, and Cleon in my head, I was starting to feel ill. It was impossible not to listen to him; his speech was echoed in his thoughts, which were *my* thoughts.

"Those deaths were your fault," I said through clenched teeth. "You forced me to hurt them."

"You *chose* to hurt them for some higher purpose," he replied calmly. "Cecelia did the same."

He was right. I had a choice between becoming a monster, and surviving another day to help what people I could, or being chopped up and ending up on the wall where Cecelia was now, where I couldn't help anyone I loved.

"The only difference is we don't know what Cecelia's higher purpose is," Cleon concluded.

"Maybe she was salvaging what part of humanity she could, so we weren't all destroyed."

"Justify it however you please," he said. "As long as you believe me."

"I don't ..." But I did. Or more accurately, I had enough doubt in my mind not to believe Cecelia over Cleon as I had before.

"I can feel the difference."

I said nothing, not wanting to admit the truth. It was harder for me to deny Cecelia was not the innocent party I had assumed her to be. I wanted to know more about what Adonis told me, about what was happening outside the walls and why and how the gods were dying.

"Listen to them. They'll tell you," Cleon advised.

At times, I heard the urgent whispers at the back of my mind. At sunset and sunrise, they became clearer, until I could distinguish individual voices among the murmuring.

I didn't trust them any more than I would Cleon. I believed

Adonis, and I believed Pythia, which was what I'd started calling the first Oracle. The only way for me to see her, though, was too dangerous.

"We could make a deal," Cleon said.

Gods, I hated this! I had no privacy anymore!

"If talking to her is what it takes for us to become allies, then I'll agree to behave better in the alternate world than you do in this one."

I rolled my eyes at him. And then his meaning struck me. Studying him, I saw no deception in his features and read none in his mind. We were connected, but I was convinced one day, he'd find a way to hide his thoughts from me, because that was how good of a sneaky politician he was.

"Seriously? You won't steal my body and go on some crazy Cleon rampage?" I asked cautiously.

"The longer it takes me to sway you to my side, the worse off the world becomes. I will cut you a break. Once."

"Why didn't you offer this sooner?"

"Because you had to be near the tipping point, or nothing anyone said would ever convince you. As displeased as I am about the reappearance of Adonis, he managed to open your eyes, when nothing I ever said would."

It was a lot, coming from him. He believed what he was saying. I hesitated a moment longer, a little too freaked out by the idea of him tricking me and taking over my body.

"Okay," I said finally. "I need to know."

"Not here. I don't trust her."

I walked towards the elevator, chewing on my lower lip in consternation as I juggled all I'd learned today.

Cleon was quiet as we left the caverns and returned to the balmy afternoon. He left me at my villa's doorstep, along with four soldiers. Surprised he wasn't confining me to the House again, I eagerly climbed the stairs.

"Give me ten minutes," he directed me.

I was tempted to drop into the alternate world as soon as I

entered the house but decided against it this time. We had a luke-warm truce, and I didn't want to aggravate the perpetual tension between us.

My bedroom was as I left it and clean, as if the maids had been contacted ahead of time about ensuring it was ready for me. I stopped in my doorway to gaze at the memorial wall.

Choice. Cleon had claimed I chose to murder all those people. It was true, in a sense. I had blamed him for forcing me to hurt them, but was he to blame at all? Obviously, if I hadn't been placed in that situation, I wouldn't have done it. Would someone else choose differently? If I were a better person, would *I* have chosen differently?

I closed the bedroom door behind me and crossed to my bed. It was too quiet for me, too calm. Even Cerberus was gone, though the window to Hades remained no matter where I went. I had seen Adonis there twice in my visions and still didn't know what I'd done to send him there.

Cleon was soon ready.

Closing my eyes, I breathed deeply and slid into the alternate world to find Pythia, accompanied by a man I didn't want anything to do with.

As usual, I ended up on the wrong side of the mirror and waited for Cerberus. He emerged from the underworld. I waved and braced myself, and he knocked me into the alternate world filled with blooming color.

"I'll get it right some day," I called to the beast. He sat on his haunches, glaring at me with all six eyes, as if he didn't believe me. "Thanks in the meantime."

"Are you talking to that thing?" Cleon sounded irritated already. "Let's go. I have something to do tonight."

With a long look at my body, I led Cleon away. Using the travel ability that let us cover great distances quickly, we were soon in the forest at the edge of the compound. No flashes of light caught my attention, and Pythia didn't emerge.

"Let's start looking," I said.

SIXTEEN
MERCENARY

"C'MON, KID."

I paced in the small bay in the basement of the House, where Theodocia was stored with stacks of boxes in a little used cell in the prison. She showed no signs of life, and was therefore not an escape risk. As a result, she'd been locked in a room consisting of shoddy lighting, no cameras, rusted hinges on the door and the moldy scent of cardboard from boxes exposed to the leak in the corner. She was propped up against one wall.

Her creepy condition was something out of a haunted house and did nothing to make the trip down to the torture chambers and prison area any more appealing.

Perhaps my discomfort came equally from another source. I was acutely aware of how I could very well wind up here permanently in one of the cells reserved for those people Cleon held a personal vendetta against. I never challenged any of his orders to round up random people and bring them here. Ambassadors and political elite, I understood. The teen boy I dragged down here from the inner city? I had no idea what he'd done to piss off Cleon. Angering the politician often resulted in a life sentence.

My skin crawled with the awareness of my potential fate as I stood in the prison. My choice was made long ago. I'd jump ship when Cleon was no longer the man I thought he was, capable of protecting the only thing that mattered to me. With Alessandra's growing powers, and Cleon's increasingly erratic behavior, I saw the writing on the wall. The protected zone wasn't going to be protected much longer, and Cleon had no power to change that. In addition, the only people I needed to be cautious of, who I couldn't battle physically, were corralled on this compound. I could survive anything outside the walls, and I wasn't going to risk Tommy disappearing in a poof of Oracle-created smoke or Cleon's lunatic magic.

This compound, and everyone in it, was doomed. I wasn't about to stick around to see how bad it got.

I listened to the endless chatter of security teams through the earpiece I wore. Accountability of all military assets was the last consideration, once all hell broke loose and Cleon ordered people to hunt me down. As his chief of security for five years, he wasn't going to take my betrayal lightly.

"Any day now," I muttered to the Oracle confined upstairs. Adonis gave his word. I'd never trust him with a weapon, but I knew him to be compromised in judgment when it came to Alessandra with a reputation for following through on his promises.

I wasn't interested in gods or magic or Oracles, and Theodocia's state reinforced the belief I wanted nothing to do with any of it. Allegedly, she was alive, but her skin, clothing, hair and everything else – down to the blood on her battered face – were cool and had the resiliency of gummy candy.

Checking my weapons again with light touches, I paused to gaze at her. It was rare when I experienced any sort of internal disquiet. My window to free her was narrow, and I couldn't exactly carry her out like this. As a gummy statue, she was twice as heavy as usual, not to mention awkwardly stiff. I couldn't carry a three hundred pound log out of the basement without disabling my ability to fight.

Impatient, I began pacing again. I always hesitated to place pieces of my plan outside my control, such as by asking Adonis to have the Oracle free Theodocia. There was too much potential for things to go wrong. Perhaps the Oracle was completely insane, thanks to Cleon, or Cleon reacted before Adonis had a chance to reach her. That whole mess wasn't predictable, but it was also my best chance of undoing what had been done to Tommy's mother.

I reached up to tap the earpiece and ask one of the guards on the top floor what was happening, when I heard a groan.

Theodocia wobbled and then collapsed.

Good girl, I thought. I didn't give myself time to feel relieved and crossed to her. "Can you stand?" I asked and peered into her face.

As if she hadn't been frozen as a statue, blood oozed from several cuts in her face and one place in her abdomen. She appeared dazed.

"Never mind." I stood and pulled her to her feet then slung her over one shoulder. She groaned again, this time in pain. I didn't have time to assess the damage. I had to get her out of here before we were both in trouble. Drawing one weapon, I eased into the hallway. As the commander of the military, and temporary commander of SISA, I had unprecedented access to the security systems on the compound and had created a blind passage starting in the hallway and leading off the compound by turning off or rerouting the cameras along my path. No one would see me leave from the tightly monitored security stations, and I had a short buffer between now and when Cleon reacted to my betrayal. If anyone else crossed my path, I had enough weapons to take care of the job.

It was a perfect plan.

Which was why I was waiting for something to go wrong. One of the many life lessons I'd learned the uselessness of good planning, when so many factors were outside my control. I didn't make mistakes – but the rest of the world did.

"*All security personnel to their posts!*" shouted someone into my earpiece. "*Find General Niko ASAP. Use whatever force is necessary to prevent him from leaving the compound.*"

"*I see him! North entrance!*" someone cried.

"All response teams to the north entrance!"

I smiled. In my preparations, I'd paid off a few of the mercs-turned-soldiers to cover for me. I didn't need much time, and their assistance had been bought with one of the bars of gold Alessandra had paid me to deliver the cryptic message about the apocalypse to the Silent Queen's camp.

"No! He's on the east side!" claimed a second familiar voice of one of the men I'd paid off.

Moving faster, I went to the back stairwell known only to those who worked here and ran up the metal stairs to the ground floor. Whipping open the door, I continued down the path leading to the backside of the House, where the staff break and restrooms were located, along with the kitchens. The halls were vacant.

"Niko?" Theodocia rasped. "Where's Tommy?"

"Shut up, Dosy."

I hurried past the door leading to the main break room and then slid through the kitchens. Three of the cooks were present. One glanced towards me and paused in his task of unloading the industrial dishwasher.

I pointed at the dishes with a hard glare. He took the hint and returned to his job without alerting the others.

Reaching the staff entrance, I exited into the humid day.

Sticking to the back lots of the compound, I kept to my planned route, weapon drawn and eyes roving my surroundings. No sooner had I reached the corner of the parking lot than the alarms blared. I quickened my pace and ducked behind the protection of one of the maintenance sheds.

"Niko." Dosy squirmed.

"Tommy begged me to save you, but I can still drop you here and tell him you were already dead," I snapped. "Be still and quiet." I lowered her to the ground then went to the front of the maintenance shed and snapped the lock open with a sturdy kick. The chances of anyone looking for me here first were slim, now that those I'd bribed were scrambling the emergency response teams in every direction but mine. Still, I wasn't about to lower my guard, sit down and discuss the plan with my ex over afternoon tea. We had to keep moving, no matter what.

I started one of the golf carts used by the elite to navigate the sprawling compound and exited the shed.

I drove around the side – and hit my brakes fast.

Theodocia wasn't alone.

"What in Hades are you doing?" I snapped and launched out of the cart.

The stunning blonde servant with an attitude who had worked for Alessandra backed away quickly and raised her hands. "I stopped the bleeding," she said.

I glanced at Theodocia. A leaf was on her cheek. "With that?" I demanded.

"I'm a nymph, remember? I can do things with nature. A grunt like you wouldn't understand."

"You're right." Ignoring her, I went to Dosy's side and lifted.

"Take me with you, Niko," the teen girl said.

"Um, no."

"I can help you."

"By ... nymphing?" I snapped and lowered Dosy into the back of the cart. "Covering me with leaves?"

"Or by telling you the fastest way to reach the city beneath, so we aren't murdered by your own men," she said.

I straightened, eyeing her. She appeared as I'd last seen her, in her servant's robes, though they were smeared with dirt, and her hair was lumpy. Dark circles lined her eyes, and she carried a backpack. "You've been here the whole time?" I asked.

"I had to stay." She averted her eyes.

The last thing I needed was someone claiming to be a mythical creature that was clearly hiding a lot. Mentally calculating response times and how long it would take for someone to spot me, I climbed into the driver's seat. "Good luck!" I placed the cart in gear and started to drive off.

"Niko! I can help you!" she cried. "Dosy's unconscious, and she will be until I wake her. I used magic to knock her out!"

What I would give for a world without magic. Hissing a sigh, I slowed then stopped the cart. Twisting, I glanced at Dosy, who was out, then up at Leandra. She didn't appear to be bluffing, and if I made it off the compound, and Dosy didn't awaken ...

A shout came from the direction of the House.

I waved at Leandra reluctantly, suspecting any friend of Alessandra's possessing magical abilities was going to be more trouble than she was worth. Leandra climbed in beside me.

"There are rules to this," I said and shifted into gear again. "If you lie to me, I'll kill you. Don't talk to strangers, and don't make a move I haven't approved. If I suspect you of anything, you're dead. Do you understand?"

She nodded. "Don't take the southern exit," she said.

"Why not?" It was my planned route of escape.

"I asked the trees to help hide us. If we go the southeastern –"

"*Trees?*" I echoed. "You want me to go a different route because ... *trees?*"

"If I'm wrong, and I can't get us to the city before we're caught, you can murder me!"

"When we're free, you're going to tell me what a nymph is," I directed her.

Gripping the steering wheel tightly, I waited until the last minute to change our course. I skipped the eastern entrance and headed towards a stretch of trees near the southeastern staff entrance.

"Tell me why you didn't escape," I said, not trusting her, despite her connection to Alessandra.

"Someone told me to stay."

"Who?"

Leandra was hugging her backpack. She didn't answer.

"A tree?" I asked with a snort.

"A ghost."

I rolled my eyes. Allowing her to accompany me was probably a mistake. If this escape route backfired, she was dead where she sat.

We reached the forest.

"You need to send another email to the trees or something?" I joked darkly.

"They're moving, aren't they?"

"What? They're not ..." I stopped, eyes on the flora that was shifting around us. Rather than step out of the ground and walk to a new spot, the trees glided from one spot to another, through the earth, as if they were floating through water.

"Over there." Leandra pointed to a spot where the trees were creating room.

It wasn't the first time I'd seen magic used, but I would never be comfortable with something I didn't understand and could never control. Uneasy with the display, I slowed instinctively and drew my weapon. Halting a short distance from where she indicated, I climbed out of the golf cart and stared at the trees that appeared to be alive.

"What're you going to do? Shoot one?" Leandra snapped, seeing my gun clenched in my hand. "Hurry up! The entrance is here."

"What entrance?" I faced her.

"Do you really think we didn't install a secondary entrance to the city on the compound?" she retorted. "How else do you think I was able to slip by your guards all the time?" She dropped to her knees and placed her palms on the ground. Blue sparks lit up the space around her palms, and the grass and soil peeled away from the spot, revealing a metal door. "Hurry!"

The alarms all over the compound wailed. The trees had formed a wall between us and anyone who might pursue. Beginning to suspect I'd never be free of weird, magical beings, I snatched Theodocia's unconscious form from the golf cart and strode to Leandra. She climbed down a ladder whose top rungs were all I could distinguish in the dark hole. With misgivings heavy in my gut, I put my gun away and followed her.

Reaching the abandoned sewer tunnel beneath, I stepped back

while she darted up to seal the entrance once more. She leapt down and started down the tunnel, in the direction of the city outside the compound. I jogged after her.

"The trees aren't coming?" I called after her.

"I don't know how Lyssa tolerated you," Leandra said with a frustrated sigh.

"Where are we going?"

"To our headquarters."

"I thought we destroyed the underground city," I said as we walked.

"You destroyed a couple of sections. Mama's army just moved to the part you missed."

I hadn't missed them on purpose. I had an idea of where Dosy was located for much of the time, thanks to Tommy and his unnatural connection to a god. More than once I'd walked in on him mid-conversation with Thanatos. I purposely didn't target the strongholds or the way stations where Dosy spent much of her time. But I also didn't know the full layout of the mysterious underworld, so it was beyond me to understand how large Mama's operating area was.

Leandra led me through the dark tunnels with minimal light. Her step was sure and quick. I followed closely, not about to be left or lost in the dark. Whether she knew this path because she was constantly traveling it, or her unusual nymph – whatever that was – ability helped her see in the dark, she didn't hesitate once to enter new tunnels I didn't sense until we turned down them. I was blindly following her and becoming tenser the more lost I became in the underground maze.

Dosy didn't stir, and Leandra didn't stop. We walked for close to an hour, until even my sense of direction was clueless as to how far we'd gone from the compound or which direction we were headed or where we might be relative to the city above. No sounds of pursuit reached me. It was our destination, rather than who might pursue us, that left me leery.

As I walked, I listened to the chatter of those soldiers coordinating search parties. None of them mentioned the walking trees or the entrance to the underground. Their focus was on the eastern and southern exits, with the response teams scrambling between the two. With some reluctance, I admitted Leandra's instincts had been right. If I had fled through that gate, I'd be caught by now, and Theodocia and I would both be in cells in the dungeon under the House.

"All hands return to base."

The command caused silence to replace the flurry of chaotic messages. I listened hard, as confused by the directive as everyone else on this channel.

"Emergency response as well?" someone finally asked the question on my mind.

"What part of ALL HANDS don't you understand, soldier?" came the quick reply. *"ERTs deploy immediately to Site Persus and assume defensive positions."*

I stopped walking.

"Countdown to Persus attack: T minus one hour, forty five minutes."

I checked my watch. The heavily military jargon sent a streak of uneasiness through me. What was Cleon thinking?

The military maintained several clandestine sites outside the wall, one in each cardinal direction, to include a missile-launching site called Persus. Our *Persus* rockets were designated as surface-to-surface projectiles and had been placed within range of the Silent Queen's camp as soon as we discovered where it was. It was a precaution only, to prevent her from making a move on Washington DC before Cleon had accomplished the first phase of his plan, whatever that was. He told me enough to do my job without revealing his true agenda. I suspected he understood killing the only surviving member of the Bloodline wasn't smart.

The voice over the earpiece was ordering the emergency response teams to take up defensive positions around the site with an attack planned in less than two hours.

"Say again," said the commander of the EST.

"*Obey your order, soldier.*" This voice was Cleon's. "*Operation Bloodline is in effect.*"

And this was the codename given to the super secret mission to take out the Silent Queen.

"What're you doing?" Leandra called. "You'll get lost down here, if you don't keep up!"

My boss is going to launch a shit load of missiles at your boss, I answered silently. What was Cleon thinking? He had told me multiple times this was a last resort operation. He wanted us to keep hazing the Silent Queen, to keep her boxed in and busy fending off our recon teams, so she didn't have a chance to coordinate a large attack. If he wanted her dead, he would have destroyed her a few weeks ago. What had changed?

It had nothing to do with my escape. Something else had happened, if he were ignoring my betrayal and setting his targets on the Silent Queen. Nothing I'd heard today, before I maneuvered Adonis into freeing Theodocia, gave me any insight into what Cleon was doing or why he had suddenly changed his mind about the Silent Queen.

I began to smile.

What happened to the Silent Queen was irrelevant to my interests – with the exception that I knew one person who would trade me a ticket out of the city to hear this secret.

I started forward, listening intently to the exchanges as the EST dropped their current mission to find me and prepared to move out to the western site a few kilometers outside DC.

"I hope you don't plan on sleeping too long, Dosy, or I can't use this information for my benefit," I whispered.

SEVENTEEN

ALESSANDRA

"IS THAT YOU?" Cleon asked.

I glanced up from my seat on top of the boulder in the middle of the forested area where I had met with Pythia twice. The glow of light, emanating from the compound's floodlights, brightened the shadows of dusk.

"Is *what* me?" I replied.

"I'm experiencing mild vertigo."

I tilted my head. "I don't feel it," I said. "Is it part of the illness you won't admit exists?"

"No." He stood again, and my attention turned from my thoughts to the relative location of my body. If he made a run for it, I'd hear it in his mind first and could then outrun him. Even reading his thoughts, I didn't feel comfortable trusting him. He was able to keep his illness from me, and I didn't know how. If there were a way for someone in our circumstances to deceive or trick me, he'd be the one to figure it out.

I paced and roamed a circle around the boulder, alert for any flickers of light indicating Pythia was here. As always, Cerberus was reflected in the black and white mirror opposite me, watching me curiously. I didn't know how to assure him I wasn't ever going to purposely trespass.

Although, one of my visions was of future-me in Hades, with Adonis.

"I am no closer to figuring out our visions," Cleon said, sounding puzzled.

My cheeks grew warm. Whenever I thought of Adonis, I felt his lips pressed to mine again. I shook my head, embarrassed to know Cleon felt it, too. "They could be pieces of four different paths," I said, equally frustrated. "Or ... one path."

"A warning."

"Yeah. One that's too disjointed to fully understand."

"But we can understand it," he insisted.

I glanced over at him.

"I have never met a riddle I couldn't solve," Cleon said. "I think the problem isn't that we don't know the answer, it's that our minds have the potential to uncover it, if we both stop resisting the full integration."

My heart began to beat harder. "By full integration, you mean we lose our separate identities and become some kind of joined Frankenbrain."

"I wouldn't put it so inelegantly, but yes." He was frowning. We shared identical distaste for the idea, for two completely separate reasons. I thought he was a psychopath and wanted nothing to do with his mind, and he viewed me as ignorant, backwards and uneducated. "But we each maintain a unique piece of the puzzle. We think differently, and our differences complement each other."

"You mean you couldn't survive a day without your butler, and I'm not going to win a chess championship," I said icily.

"Yes."

"What if we don't have to merge our brains? What if we just ... cooperate more?" I suggested.

"It's preferred for certain."

I rolled my eyes.

"This is awkward." At Pythia's husky voice, we both spun to face her. She was studying Cleon intently, if not a suspiciously. "This must be the parasite."

Cleon's look cooled.

"Yeah," I said with a half smile. "We have a problem."

"Aside from the fact your minds are inseparable?"

Until that moment, I held out some hope this was reversible or at least, I wasn't going to be joined with Cleon forever. From the flicker of surprise in his thoughts, he hadn't thought this as permanent as it was.

"The technology wasn't intended for a long term –" he began.

"Even if the technology wasn't intended for this, you won't have a choice soon," Pythia said. "Did I not warn you against leaving your body unprotected?" She addressed this to me.

"Yes, but that's why I brought him with me. We have a truce. He knows we needed to talk to you."

"He wasn't the only threat to which I was referring."

Cleon understood before I did, and his knowledge spread to me a fraction of a second later.

"Perhaps you can convince her. She's on the ledge. She just needs that final push," the Supreme Magistrate said.

I studied Pythia, wanting her to refute his confident claim of who my enemy was. When she did not speak, I did. "Is this true?" I asked. "Did ... *she* start the Holy Wars? Did she nearly destroy humanity? Did Zeus save what he could of my kind?"

"The truth of matters like this is always complicated," Pythia said softly. "I made a mistake when I opened the gateway to allow the gods onto Earth. I replaced the Old Ways, in which humanity ruled itself, with a group of selfish dictators of extraordinary supernatural power. It was one thing for them to exist and create from their place in the universe and another for them to live among us. That's one bridge that should not have been crossed."

"Then you accept responsibility for destroying humanity," Cleon said.

Pythia and I both gave him looks.

"Before I could correct my error, I was struck down by none other than Zeus, over the protests of Apollo," she continued. "There has never been a threat to their rule of the Earth, until one Oracle figured out how to block the bridge. She couldn't undo what I had done, because she didn't have the strength, but she could start an initiative that extended across dozen Oracles. Each of them fed some of their power into building a wall between the world of the gods and ours. And finally, one had the strength to hammer the last nail into place."

"Cecelia," I said.

"Correct. Except, when the time came to act, she acted not out of the desire to help humanity, but to punish everyone. What her true motivations are, I don't know. If not for the god who struck me down, humanity would be gone. My enemy is who kept you alive, knowing when you came of age, you could do what I had not, and what Cecelia won't: put an end to this chapter of human history."

I felt sick to my stomach. "Then why was she helping me?"

"*Was* she helping you?" Pythia challenged.

"She was teaching me control, so I didn't destroy everyone by unleashing my power."

"She was trying to clip your wings, and keep you under her thumb, until she had the ability to outmaneuver you. It's similar to what I did," Cleon said. "You look at her and you pity her. You don't see her brilliant, manipulative mind. You related to her, and she used this. It's why she wanted a power transfusion, and why she encouraged you not to learn or use your magic."

"To harness my power, I'd have to kill her first," I said, thoughts on the third trial I had not yet completed.

"All the more reason to keep you in check," Cleon said wisely.

They made too much sense. As much as I didn't want Cecelia to be my enemy, it was looking as if she were going to be the next name on my memorial wall instead of Cleon.

"How do I kill her?" I asked quietly.

"You have to touch her, and then you'd have to overpower her,"

Pythia said. "With her guard up, it's virtually impossible. You can't access the full power you need to beat her in a direct confrontation, and she's likely safeguarding her body in a manner which would prevent you from reaching her to try."

"If I can't get to her from my world, can I from here?"

"You understand too well," Pythia said. "How long have you been here, waiting for me?"

"An hour. Maybe two," I answered. "We came to ask you about my visions, but stopping Cecelia seems more important."

She was looking into the distance, towards the compound. "What of them?" she sounded distracted.

"How do I know which ones I want, and which ones lead to total annihilation?"

"With a gift as strong as yours, the visions will follow a sequence or pattern or contain meaning only you can understand. A single vision may tell you nothing, but looking at the larger picture created by several will reveal clues you wouldn't see otherwise," she said. "Is there a common theme? Location? Sequence of events?"

"Adonis," I said. "He appears in three of them, and he's always dead."

Cleon drew nearer. Our minds were working hard to identify other trends.

"What else?" Pythia asked.

We were quiet, our thoughts bouncing back and forth through one another's minds. Cleon was stuck on the vision I hadn't wanted to look at too closely, the one of me in Hades speaking to Adonis. The more he dwelt on this particular premonition, the more I began to see what he did.

"Adonis is the key, but I don't know how," I said. "Lantos is convinced I'll kill him, and he appears in Hades to ... find me? Warn me?" I looked at Cleon.

"It has to be *warn*," he said. "Based on what he told you, his death isn't an accident."

"He dies because ..." My eyes went to Cerberus. "... because he knows I can see him, no matter what world I'm in, which must mean, my body and my mind are separated."

"Good," Pythia said. "What else?"

I closed my eyes. I felt so close to understanding.

"Adonis is sent to Hades to warn me in one vision. In another, I am with Cecelia ..." I started.

Cleon picked up the thought. "... in the caverns, where Lantos stands and claims he will die a hero for betraying everyone ..."

"... while Tommy – who can speak to Thanatos – looks on ..."

"They're not watching me, but something happening in a place where only Tommy can speak to one of the gods present."

I gasped suddenly, and the visions clicked into place. "They all occur on the same day, in reverse order in which I foresaw them!" I exclaimed.

"Adonis is killed in the morning. The walls are breached around noon, while Lantos is standing in the cavern with us. At dusk, the world ends," Cleon said.

"To stop this sequence, Adonis can't die," I said and glared pointedly at Cleon. "This is the warning, isn't it? Lantos said Adonis was the key, and he also said I'd kill Adonis when I wasn't in control of my body."

"I would guess this is correct," Pythia said. "It is not always possible to discern the *why* behind what we foresee, only the event itself. Somehow, the death of Adonis causes a chain of events that results in you being unable to stop Cecelia."

Neither Cleon nor I were able to understand how this was possible. It was implied from the vision that Adonis' death was purposeful.

"Lantos," I said. "Lantos kills Adonis. It's why he and Tommy are in the cavern."

"*Betray them all, die a hero,*" Cleon recited the words Lantos had spoken. "We are frozen, and he can't reach us any other way then to send someone you care about into Hades."

"It's not me directly who murders Adonis. It's his best friend because of me. Because my mind is lost." My heart was pounding.

"So if Adonis lives, we have a chance to stop the end of the worlds."

"Yes," Pythia said.

"That seems easy," I said, growing excited. "We just tell Lantos, and he won't kill Adonis."

"Lantos never should have been involved," Pythia said. "I spoke to him a few weeks ago. He knew too much, and he was going to become an instrument through which Cecelia could bring about the apocalypse."

"You were his moment of clarity," I said. "She twisted his mind like she did mine."

"I ... stepped out of line to help," Pythia admitted. "Cecelia, you and I have all seen the same sequence and interrupted it in different ways."

"She knew the only way to get to Adonis was either through me or Lantos."

"She chose the weaker of the two of you."

I felt sick to my stomach. I'd been chatting daily with Cecelia before she fell into her coma. She knew all about the friendship between Adonis and Lantos, because I told her. Before I could discuss this further with Pythia, Cleon gasped and leaned against a tree.

"She's found the next weak link," Pythia said, eyes on him.

"What's wrong?" I asked Cleon, irritated he chose now to have issues, when we were making such headway.

"Vertigo." He was unsteady and clinging to the tree.

"Someone has his body," Pythia said.

Cleon paled, and I stared at her. "What?"

Cleon pushed himself away from the tree, headed towards the compound, and then collapsed where he was. "Go," he said urgently.

I hesitated, not wanting to leave him only to discover he'd planned to take my body while I was distracted.

"I will stay with him," Pythia said, sensing my fear.

After a long look at him, I bolted and moved through the brilliantly hued world with speed that wasn't available to me in my own reality. The moment I stepped foot into the mall, I stopped. The flurry of activity was unreal, with lines of troops on the lawns, helicopters buzzing overhead and the shouts of commanding officers competing with the blare of alarms and voices over intercoms and radios.

I started past the formations, headed towards the house. Halfway there, I sensed something out of place, a tickle to my instincts, and turned away.

Cleon strode among the formations, flanked by officers with stars on their uniforms. Disoriented, I tried to process how he could be in two places at once, before Cleon's thoughts surfaced loudly in my mind.

That's not me, he said.

His alarm was second only to mine, and I rushed to the side of Cleon's physical body, not understanding how his body was here, walking, when his mind was with Pythia. As if feeling my presence hovering, Cleon looked directly at me.

I stepped back. This Cleon's eyes were blue, not brown like the real Cleon's. Blue like ...

Cecelia's eyes.

He smiled and moved on.

I remained in place, trying to quell the tumbling emotions and thoughts that weren't fully mine. Cleon was urging me to do something, to retake his body, to ... I didn't know. I had never seen or felt him this upset.

My gaze turned towards my villa, and I raced across the lawn. The front door was open, and soldiers lined the hallways while another half a dozen tore the villa a part. I floated through the walls towards my bedroom, terrified of what I'd find.

"Please be there," I whispered to my body.

Reaching my bedroom, I stopped to scan the damage. The bed was overturned, the mattresses shredded, and the rest of the furniture tossed around as if by a hurricane. I ran around my bed twice, searching for my body, before lifting my eyes to the soldiers tearing apart my closet.

Our magic works here, Cleon reminded me.

I reacted instantly to the jarring reminder and turned everyone in my room into a gummy statue. Shaking and desperate, I searched the entire room for my body before floating into the hallway. I turned all the soldiers into statues, lifted all the furniture in the villa and attached it to the ceilings, and searched everywhere.

"Where is it?" I cried, panicking.

I explored the entire villa again and returned to my bedroom, sucking in breaths fast and quick.

"She's been here." Cleon's voice made me whirl. His human body strode into the room, faded and ghostly. None other than Lantos accompanied him. "She might still be."

"If she is, I cannot see her," Lantos said.

I glared at the Supreme Priest. How long was he in on Cecelia's plan? Why was he working with her, when he had been the first to dime her out to me?

Did he know with whom he was dealing at all? Or did he believe he was talking to the real Cleon?

"Alessandra, if you're here, it's only a matter of time before I find your body and possess your power," said Cecelia through Cleon's mouth.

I picked up the dresser with my power and hurled it at her.

The real Cleon panicked. The dresser bounced off the green ribbon around Cleon's body and smashed into the wall beside his body instead of hurting him directly.

It wasn't *her* ribbon I saw but mine. In choosing her host, Cecelia had picked one of the two people in the world I couldn't hurt with my magic. Cold fear shot through me. How was I supposed to stop her? Where was my body?

"She's here," Cecelia said. "Any luck finding Adonis?"

"None. He disappeared."

"How can a human simply disappear on a compound this big?"

"You called off the searches before the sweeps were complete. He obviously slipped through to the city," Lantos said.

Lantos was lying. He knew exactly where Adonis was, because he had been the one to take him away. I studied him, unable to understand his secrets.

"First Niko, then Adonis, and now Alessandra. If I didn't know better, I'd think you had something to do with their disappearances," Cleon rounded on Lantos.

I held my breath.

"Too bad you see me in your final vision, or you could just kill me off," Lantos said with a confident smile.

Any concern I had for him vanished. He could handle himself in any situation.

Cecelia wasn't pleased by the answer. She glanced around again. "Find her body!" she shouted to the soldiers outside the door.

Lantos stepped aside as she stormed out. When certain she was gone, he stepped into the middle of my room. His smile and confidence seemed to fizzle, and his features became haggard.

"Your body's safe, Alessandra. Adonis is as well. I took him far away, so neither of us could hurt him," he whispered. "I am trying hard to undo a great injustice I helped create. This is my fault, and I am sorry."

I stood before him, beginning to understand. By listening to Cecelia, he had thought he was helping prevent the inevitable, while in truth, he was furthering her agenda. I had fallen into a similar trap.

For the first time since meeting Lantos, I pitied him.

Cleon appeared at my side, staggered, and then darted after his body. His emotions were a frantic mess interfering with my ability to focus.

"She's ordered a strike on the Silent Queen's compound," Lantos continued. "It will start soon. If you can help her, please do so." Genuine regret was on his features.

Operation Bloodline. Site Persus.

I didn't have this inherent knowledge, but Cleon did. The details of the operation were as familiar to me as if I designed it myself.

"Where is my body, Lantos?" I asked, alarmed to learn it had been hidden by the master of secrets, who could transverse a shadow world no one else on the planet could. "How did you know to hide it?" And what was he talking about when he seemed to be saying he wanted to right something he'd done wrong.

He didn't hear me.

"Betray them all, die a hero," he murmured.

My breathing quickened. He had said the same thing while waiting with Tommy in the caverns in one of my visions.

"What does this mean?" I whispered.

A gunshot rang out, and Lantos staggered.

I cried out and scrambled away, then realized I was safe in the alternate reality.

Lantos fell to the ground in the middle of my bedroom. His eyes darted to the shadows under the bed nearby. Blood poured out of a wound in his neck, and he grabbed at it with both hands, desperate to stop the gushing blood.

"In my premonition, I was in Alessandra's body." Cecelia was in the doorway. "You've disrupted the sequence of events I chose. Thirty years planning, and you did the one thing I couldn't plan around."

Lantos opened his mouth and tried to speak. Nothing came out.

"Unlike your friends, I don't take betrayal well." Cecelia lowered the weapon. "I definitely won't trust you to lead me to her body without tricking me. You already changed the future, Lantos. I don't need you anymore."

She turned and left him to bleed out.

"No, no, no!" I knelt beside him and reached forward, wanting to help him, before recalling I couldn't physically touch him. Sitting back, I wracked my mind for what to do. Lantos hands fell away from his neck, and his eyes took on an empty look. "Dr. Khan!" I cried.

Seconds later, the befuddled physician materialized in the doorway. She was in a bathrobe with wet hair, as if I'd caught her just after a shower. Looking around in surprise, she hesitated only a blink when she saw Lantos bleeding in the middle of the floor. Dr. Khan hurried forward and knelt beside him. She reached out immediately with one hand to apply pressure to the wound.

I paced anxiously. I had wanted his name on my wall at one point, or thought I did. Watching him die, and knowing Adonis would be heartbroken by his death, I couldn't help thinking it was wrong to wish him dead. He had, in his own twisted way, tried to help me.

Within a minute of touching him, Dr. Khan sat back. Her white robe bloomed red from blood, and her features were drawn.

"No, no, no!" I repeated and dropped beside her.

The blood created a pool around them both, extending for two yards in every direction. Lantos' eyes were blank, his face blanched.

"I'm so sorry," Dr. Khan whispered to him.

Tears stung my eyes, and I stared at his lifeless form.

"Both our bodies are lost," Cleon said. He was seated on my bed, slumping.

Conflicting emotions immobilized me. I didn't know what to feel about losing the one person who seemed to know what was going on, even if he used that knowledge to further his agenda. Now that he was gone, would the bond between Adonis and me be restored? Would I need my spirit back in body first?

I looked from him to Lantos. Where exactly had he taken my body? And Adonis?

Movement across the room caught my attention, and I stood, startled to see Lantos in the black-gray-mirror leading to Hades. He stood beside Cerberus in much better condition than how he'd left the world.

He lifted a hand and waved to me. I waved back. With one of his characteristic smiles that made me wonder if he knew this would happen, he turned away and walked into the gateway leading into the underworld. Cerberus trailed him, and the gateway closed behind him.

Numbed, I didn't know what to do.

"I do. We murder her," Cleon said.

Pythia was present, emerging from a wall. "Come with me. Quickly."

I wiped my face. Was it wrong for me to want to be as far from there as possible? Did this emotion somehow cheapen Lantos' death or disrespect him? I had seen his spirit enter Hades, which I took to be a good sign.

Disturbed, I followed Pythia through the villa and back to her forest. This time, a third form was present, and my heart melted.

"Mrs. Nettles?" I asked, grateful to see her.

"Not quite," Pythia said with a smile. "Artemis has been hidden in her body, spying on the titan's son who is now dead."

I frowned.

"Mrs. Nettles is fine," Pythia assured me.

Distressed by the murder I'd just witnessed, and struggling with what emotion I should feel, after Lantos' betrayal, I sat on the boulder.

"I have limited power," Artemis said through Mrs. Nettle's tiny body. "What is left, I promise to use to help you."

"You have always helped me," I said. I fell quiet. My mind was wrestling with what I'd learned about the Holy Wars and the person who manipulated me the most. "Is all this my fault? Because I'm not strong enough?"

"It is one path of many," Pythia answered.

"Cecelia put all this in motion long before you were born," Artemis said. "She manipulated Lantos into betraying you all, in her favor, and would have continued to ruin your chances of making everything right, if the first Oracle hadn't interfered when she did."

It wasn't easy for me to accept I needed the help of gods when I'd been raised to believe they were a blight on humanity.

"I have to stop her," I said, mind on Cecelia. A different emotion was settling into my breast: fury. Lantos was a politician. His betrayal had stung, but Cecelia's? She'd been trying to weaken me from the start under the guise of helping me. And if she succeeded, she brought about the apocalypse.

"Only you can," Artemis said. "On our world, there are many gods and goddesses with many different powers. We balance each other out. On this world, there's only one with absolute power, and only her equal can face her."

Everything I'd learned about who I was and what I was supposed to do was wrong. This was not a battle against the gods, but between two Oracles.

"Not wrong. Just not as straight forward as you thought," Pythia said, reading my mind. "To send the gods home, you have to deal with the immediate threat first."

"Cleon was right."

Artemis laughed. "I wouldn't go that far. Selling life and survival to those elite able to pay for it?" She shook her head. "He wants to rule over select chosen individuals and cares nothing for the rest of the world."

"You will need the help of the Silent Queen," Pythia said.

I blinked out of my heavy thoughts. "Lantos said Cecelia's launching an attack this evening on her base of operations. How do I warn her?"

Pythia and Artemis exchanged a look.

Artemis fidgeted in her bear form. "I have warned my brother. He will tell her." Her voice sounded fainter, as if she were under some kind of strain I was unable to see. "We need to focus on you and finding your body."

"Lantos hid it," I said.

"Did he say where?"

I shook my head. Adonis was gone, too. For a few minutes today, I hadn't felt like I was overwhelmed and sinking beneath the weight of my world.

"We must find it soon. None of us survive long in spirit form only," Pythia said, concerned gaze on Artemis.

"You're dying," I said, recalling what Adonis had told me.

"I am. We all are. Zeus is the strongest, and his energy is directed solely at protecting those humans and members of the pantheon he can," Artemis said. "I cannot stay long. I must be careful where I exert myself."

"Thank you," I said with difficulty.

"Thank *you*. You will be the one to send us all home."

I didn't share her faith in my abilities. I blinked – and Artemis disappeared. "Are you leaving me, too?" I asked Pythia.

"I can't stay with you for long, but I'm not leaving quite yet."

I sank into silence, thinking hard. Cleon was calming, assured his body wasn't being abused, though he was weak. I didn't know Lantos well enough to guess where he'd hid my body. I couldn't search everywhere on the planet. I didn't have that much time. I needed someone I could trust to help me navigate the physical world. Adonis was out of the question.

Leandra. Could she talk to me? Sense me with her nymph abilities? She and the other nymphs were groomed to help me bring back the Old Ways. Thirty women with supernatural abilities, loyal only to me. What better way to find my body, so I could face Cecelia?

"Take me to Leandra," I said to my power.

"It works differently here. You can travel quickly, but not teleport, as you can with your physical form," Pythia said.

"I'll be back." I turned away from her and raced across the compound and to my villa.

Dr. Khan had covered Lantos' body with a sheet. I looked away quickly and went to the jewelry box in my closet. Leandra said she'd left a clue how to find her beneath the city streets. I used my magic to lift the lid and saw a leaf resting on top of several priceless pendants. I picked it up with magic and rotated it in the air.

"What is this, Leandra?" I whispered.

The sound of soldiers entering my bedroom disrupted my focus.

Releasing my hold on the leaf, I expected it to sink to the ground. Instead, it remained in the air. A second later, it floated upward, towards the ceiling and lazily whirled its way out of the closet, out of my bedroom, and into the early evening sky. Intrigued, I trailed it across the compound and to the southeastern, staff exit. The leaf diverged from the road and floated through the forest. It came to rest on the grass at the center of the woods. As if feeling its weight, the grass rolled away to reveal a door.

"Perfect," I whispered. I lifted the leaf with my power, and the grass rolled back into place.

Standing in the quiet forest, I tried not to think about the possibility something horrific happened to m physical body or that it was lost in the shadow world. I didn't let myself dwell on how I'd been misled by everyone or how my visions foretold the end of the world, and I had no way of protecting Adonis when I didn't know where he was. Already, the future was changing, because Lantos was gone. If Cecelia knew Adonis was the key – which I had to assume she did – I needed to find him first. Or I had to disable and kill Cecelia to unleash my powers. With Leandra's help, maybe I could do both, and if the Silent Queen wasn't derailed by the attack, I could go to her and Herakles, too. We would hit Cecelia from inside and outside the walls in a way she didn't expect, thanks to my power.

Sending the leaf to rest in the brush nearby, I left the spot. I was starting to form a plan or ... *we* were. My mind struggled to differentiate between my thoughts and Cleon's. Cleon's knowledge of the military and operations was going to come in handy, and I would use every ounce of power available to me to disrupt Cecelia's plans.

EIGHTEEN

MERCENARY

AT LONG LAST, we turned down a tunnel with a light glowing at the other end. Leandra's pace quickened, and we reached a door flanked by two bright lights and four guards.

Their weapons went up when they spotted me.

"No!" Leandra cried. "He's with me."

No one spoke. I was pretty certain by now everyone in Mama's insurgency knew who I was. If my picture weren't plastered all over the walls after how many of their troops I'd arrested or flat out murdered ...

"He has DC Mama," she added.

"DC Mama. Cute," I said. "What do you call the real Mama?"

"NOVA Mama," she snapped.

The insurgents lowered their weapons. One of them reached over to open a door.

Leandra darted through, while I moved more slowly, glaring at the four insurgents. The door closed behind me, and I paused on the other side. I was expecting more tunnels or perhaps, compartmentalized pockets of underground rooms and chambers, which the army had discovered before.

The underground city, however, resembled a small town complete with roads, buildings, and electricity powering massive lights lining the walls to create a sense of daylight.

My first thought – none of my intelligence indicated the underground city was this huge and well equipped – was quickly replaced by the hair on the back of my neck rising. My visual examination could wait. I had to deal with the ten insurgents whose weapons were trained on me.

"We need a medic," Leandra said to one of them. "Mama's hurt."

Without waiting for a secondary command, a soldier darted off, into the city.

She faced me and planted her hands on her hips. Her expression was one I recognized from Theodocia, right before she drew her weapons.

"I brought you your leader. That should grant me some preferential treatment," I said.

"I don't think she'll exactly be overjoyed you're here, no matter what you did."

Sensing the hostility in those around me, and gauging my chances of surviving a fight were decent but not guaranteed, I carefully lowered Theodocia to the ground at my feet then stood and began removing my weapons with deliberate movement to keep the insurgents from opening fire.

I pinned Leandra with a look. "Do what you want with me," I said and dropped two knives into the growing pile. "But I'm the only person who knows where Mama's son is. I don't have to tell you how unhappy she'll be, if something happens to him."

I smiled, confident of my chances. It was a solid bluff, because Theodocia and Tommy were both favored by the same god. Dosy would have no trouble finding Tommy wherever he was, with Thanatos' help. But the woman standing in front of me, and those with her, didn't know any of this, which I was counting on to provide me the leverage I needed to survive this encounter.

"We can't let you walk free," Leandra said after a tense silence.

"You'll be imprisoned until Mama is awake. I'm pretty sure her plans for you will wipe that smile off your face."

"Sounds good." I had endured worse than prison in my life. In the meantime, while I waited for Dosy to wake up, I'd plan my next move.

"Take him," she directed one of the insurgents.

"On your knees!" the stocky man belted.

I obeyed and placed my hands on my head. The ring around me closed in. One of them slung his weapon over his shoulder and hand-cuffed me with my hands behind my back. I sensed the blow seconds before it landed. Another insurgent smashed the butt of his rifle against the back of my head, and I dropped into the state between awake and unconsciousness. I was aware of being jostled, moved, and kicked but not able to pull myself out of the state.

I didn't fully regain my senses until the movement stopped, and the coldness of a cement floor pressed against my cheek. From the warm pain radiating through my body, Dosy's men hadn't been content with simply jailing me. They'd taken my earpiece, too. But I was confident I had all the information I'd need to buy my way out of this situation.

My six-by-six cell was lit by a single light bulb hanging from the ceiling and reeked of raw sewage. The door was closed, though I heard the brush of a rubber sole against cement from someone outside. I sat up and rested my head back against the wall.

"Hey!" I called. "Get Theodocia!"

No one answered. I was pretty certain my ex would want to talk to me in any case and closed my eyes. From somewhere, water dripped. The circulation in the cell was poor, the air stuffy and old. I was in one piece, my hands bound and connected by a chain to the wall behind me.

Not long after I yelled, the door cracked open, and my ex appeared.

"You're a real piece of shit, Niko," Theodocia said icily.

"You're welcome for the rescue," I replied with a smile.

She sighed, fed up with me already.

"You find Tommy?"

"Of course I did," she snapped. "What were you thinking? Dropping him off in a cemetery all alone?"

I relaxed, relieved. "He likes dead people, and Thanatos likes him. I figured he was safer there than anywhere."

She opened her mouth, closed it, and then shook her head. "Either that's the most thoughtful, sweetest thing you've ever done, or it was the stupidest."

"Funny how you can't tell with me, isn't it?" I replied, unable to stop my smile.

"What are you planning?" she demanded. "Are your troops getting ready to attack us?"

"No. And yes." My goal had been to drop off Theodocia to her people in exchange for safe passage out of the city, then to leave this forsaken area with Tommy and live in a mountain somewhere, safe and away from everyone. Now that I was a prisoner, I was working on a new plan.

"Was this part of some elaborate scheme to find out where the bulk of the insurgency was?" She was pacing, features creased in concern.

I snorted. "Nope."

"Then what?"

"I'm a survivor, Dosy. You know that."

She stopped and faced me, frowning fiercely. She was cleaned up and armed. Bruising marred her features from the rough treatment she'd experienced at the hands of my boss. The woman before me was tough enough to take a few punches.

"Something happened," she assessed. "That's why you moved Tommy last week."

I wasn't surprised he told her, though I didn't like the reminder I couldn't do much of anything without Theodocia eventually finding out. "I want to take him to safety outside the walls."

"Outside?" she repeated. "How is it safer out there?"

"I'd love to tell you all of Cleon's secrets and the inner workings of his plans, but I need some assurances."

"I knew you wanted something!"

"The same thing I always want. To make sure my son survives this disaster."

She chewed her lower lip, pensive. "Letting you go would be a mistake."

"Letting me go, knowing I'd protect our son, sounds smart to me."

"Out of the question. He's safe here."

"Sure. Until a certain Oracle implodes and takes out DC," I countered. "Or Cleon claims her power and does the same. The safe zone is dying, and I don't plan on being here when it's gone."

She was silent.

"I don't give a shit about your insurgency, your cause or your boss," I added. "I've only ever done what I do for Tommy."

"I know that, but I've never – and will never – trust you, Niko. You'd turn on me for enough money."

"Yeah," I agreed.

She drew a deep breath. "You're going nowhere, and you *will* reveal what I need to know about Cleon's operations, no matter what my people have to do to you to get the truth."

"I can handle the fire, Dosy. You know that better than anyone." I rested my head back against the wall again. "When shit hits the fan, you'll know where to find me, and you know my price."

"You're not the only one who can take care of our son," she told me firmly.

"But I am the only one who will abandon every other cause, moral, and principal in existence to protect him. I don't give a shit about gods, politicians or oracles or whatever it is you're fighting for."

"I'm fighting for a better world for everyone, including Tommy!"

"Yeah, I don't care," I said.

For the first time in twelve years, since we first split up, I had the distinct sense she was hearing me, if not considering my offer to leave and protect Tommy outside the walls. Normally, we fought much harder, to the point we were close to blows. I wasn't feeling my normal animosity towards her. Not because she didn't deserve it, but because I was relatively certain we both wanted the same thing for once, and she'd see that soon enough.

"We're evacuating the city. I might leave you here for your boss to find," she said.

"You want a piece of information to prove I'm not here to do Cleon's bidding? Fine. Here's a freebie," I said, unruffled. "The military is launching a missile attack on the Queen's compound at dusk tonight."

Her breath caught. "That's in half an hour!"

"Then you probably want to hurry," I advised. "I might be willing to tell you one of Alessandra's visions in exchange for a decent meal and water."

"Alessandra's visions have started?"

"And they're not good." I'd overheard Alessandra discuss them with Cleon. The whole compound was bugged, and I personally oversaw the Oracle's security. I knew about Leandra long before they suspected I did.

Theodocia lingered for another moment before striding out of the cell. As soon as the door closed, she shouted for a messenger.

I had high hopes of being out of this cell, and on my way with Tommy, within a few days. Once I told Theodocia what was going on, I'd be resentful if she didn't see the need to move our son to safety. We both knew I was the best person to take care of him in a world where survival depended on who was stronger. As unusually calm as I'd been with this interaction, I was starting to ratchet up again, to feel the urgency and need to act now to ensure the safety of my son's life. I could do nothing while trapped here underground, and I fared a better chance of making it out of the DC area if Cleon and Dosy weren't both hunting me.

While I never dreamed of Dosy accompanying Tommy and me, I was counting on Dosy's insurgency to provide cover for our escape, until we was several hundred kilometers beyond the furthest military outpost. Only then would I feel completely at ease being far enough that even Cleon couldn't get to me. By that point, he'd be fighting wars on two fronts: one with the gods to secure the protected zone and one with the insurgency. I'd be of no interest to him.

I shifted to my feet and stretched my sore body the best I could. I wanted to be prepared for whatever decision Dosy made: torture or a deal. Either way, I'd get what I wanted. My greatest concern was leaving the walls before everything here went to shit.

Several minutes later, the door opened again.

"Start talking," Theodocia ordered. "What has Alessandra foreseen?"

"Only the end of the world."

She paused studied me briefly before she entered. "You son of a bitch, Niko. You won't just tell me what I need to know to stop this, will you?"

"It's called negotiation, sweetheart. The rest of the world isn't as black and white as you like to paint it," I replied.

Theodocia punched me in the jaw. Ignoring the flare of pain, I caught myself against the wall behind me and pushed back to my feet. She straightened a strand of hair that had fallen into her pretty features and then looked me in the eye.

"What are your demands, and what is the nature of the knowledge you possess about Cleon, Alessandra, and the military?" she asked.

"You might want a piece of paper to write all this down."

She pulled a notebook from a cargo pocket. "I'm listening."

For once, she really was.

I told her everything, and no part of me regretted betraying Cleon, now that he couldn't do a gods-damned thing to help me protect my son.

NINETEEN

SILENT QUEEN

ANY WORD FROM ADONIS? I wrote in Herakles' notebook, puzzled as to how the other living Bloodline member had disappeared after going to meet Niko at the gate.

We walked through the motor pool for a random inspection, checking to ensure the vehicles were being maintained, lined up and in their assigned spots. It was close to sundown, and I was growing antsy about hunting on my own tonight. I'd yet to kill my own dinner. As instinctive as it was to fly and twirl and soar in the sky, maneuvering through thick forests and reacting to the sudden movement of prey was going to take me longer to master. Adonis had been guiding me the past few days.

Herakles read the words slowly. "None," my trusted advisor said. "But the commanders have signed off on his plan. We're calling it Operation Troy."

I wasn't surprised. The plan was well thought out and solid, and it would give us a distinct advantage we wouldn't have otherwise with our numbers.

Send word to Theodocia. If Niko imprisoned Adonis, I want him returned. I scribbled. My reasoning had as much to do with Adonis' unique talent as it did my general distrust of Lantos' lackey. I wasn't yet convinced Adonis didn't have a secondary motive for showing up at my camp when Lantos had spent weeks searching for me.

Herakles waved over one of the soldiers following us and issued quick instructions. I continued onward, inspecting the vehicles visually.

"Something's wrong." Kyros' soft warning came from a short distance away.

I glanced at him then back. *What do you sense?* I asked.

"Someone's at the front gate."

As much as I hated to admit it, I knew to trust his instincts. I waved him forward.

Speak to Herakles for me, I directed him. *Tell him to go to the front gate himself.*

Kyros obeyed, and Herakles ran to the vehicle stationed on the road and used to run new guard shifts to the compound gate.

"Thank you for trusting me," Kyros said.

I ignored him.

"Don't you want to know who it is?"

He was the first person to show up unwelcome to my compound, followed by Adonis, then Niko. I was starting to grow concerned about the secrecy of a place my enemies had no trouble finding.

"Okay. I'll let him tell you," Kyros said, amused.

I walked a short distance until I reached the end of this row. Tilting my head back, I glanced towards the eastern horizon, which was beginning to grow dark. Whoever my guest was, he had better hurry, or I was going to have to meet him in the morning.

Kyros trailed me as I started down the final row of vehicles. Not ten minutes passed before the sound of Herakles' truck drew my gaze. He drove right up to me, instead of halting at the truck's assigned place, then stopped fast enough for the vehicle to kick up dirt. He leapt out, and my eyes settled on the old man with dark, olive skin and white hair in the car with him.

"Your Majesty," Herakles was breathless. "You need to hear this." His features were pale.

"Your Majesty." The elderly man exited the truck more slowly and limped towards us, supported by a cane. His eyes were the shade of whiskey. "It is an absolute honor to meet you at last."

What could this man possibly have to say that alarmed Herakles so much?

"Only that your camp is being targeted. They will strike at dusk," the old man answered.

I blinked, not expecting him to hear me. *Who will attack?*

"The military. And we have ..." He peered up a the sky. "... maybe half an hour."

My heart felt like it flipped over in my chest before it began to race.

Who in Hades was this man?

"Menelaus." He offered a stiff bow. "I am a friend of Adonis." When my eyebrows rose, he chuckled. "Or ... if you do not care for Adonis, I am not a friend of his," Menelaus said. "We must go, either way."

"How do you know someone is going to attack us?" Herakles demanded.

"Apollo," Kyros answered quietly.

"The god?" Herakles asked.

Menelaus laughed. "Yes. Because I am Menelaus and I am also Apollo."

I glared at him then at Kyros, who took a step back and cleared his voice, avoiding my direct look.

How do you know this information? I asked Menelaus-Apollo.

"Zeus revealed it to me."

So he speaks to everyone but me?

"You are killing our kind. We will not let our king address you directly, until we are certain of your motives."

So the gods had learned a thing or two about my opinion of them.

I didn't know if Kyros told them of my intense hatred of Zeus, or if the slaughtering of their kin had cemented the truth.

Apollo was the brother of Artemis, who had tried to safeguard and guide me throughout my life. If there were a god I didn't despise, it was Artemis. But I had no direct dealings with her brother before this evening, and no insight into what his ulterior motives could be. If Menelaus were possessed, in the same way Kyros was, then Apollo was immediately my enemy. Unfortunately, Apollo had one advantage that was probably going to prevent me from taking his life or leaving him behind.

Apollo is the patron god of Oracles, is he not? I asked Menelaus.

"Yes."

Anyone with potential access to Alessandra was of interest to me. Hence the reason Herakles was so easily accepted into my organization. Apollo was a major deity, not one of the smaller gods and goddesses I'd hunted and murdered. It was possible this god could help me, not as much as Ares or Zeus, but in ways I didn't yet know.

Having two possessed humans around me was enough to spur my anger. I set my hatred aside and looked to Herakles. He didn't need to hear or read my words to understand my meaning.

Herakles spun and bolted towards the main building.

A trickle of fire went through me, and I glanced at the sky again. A sliver of the sun remained above the horizon. The timing of my transformation was terrible.

"You are ready to change?" Menelaus asked me.

I shot Kyros a look.

"I didn't say a word," he said.

How do you know about this? I demanded of Menelaus.

He lifted his gnarled hand and twisted his wrist to me. Like Adonis, he bore the faint sign of the omega, the birthmark of the Bloodline.

I snatched his hand, barely believing my eyes. *How is this possible?* Menelaus was a member of the Bloodline? My second thought was far darker. After cursing us to suffer, one of the deities had the nerve to possess a Bloodline member?

The sirens blared, alerting the compound. At Herakles' insistence, we had staged many drills and educated all soldiers and civilians about which protocol should be followed with each kind of alarm. There was no mistaking the one sound my people had never heard: that calling for a full and immediate evacuation.

"I'll explain later," Menelaus said.

At once, the motor pool exploded into activity. Soldiers in different stages of dress, carrying fly bags, poured into the vehicle staging area and raced to their assigned vehicles. We didn't have enough vehicles to transport everyone, and those members of the infantry lined up in small formations of twenty. As soon as one formation hit twenty, their leader signaled to one of the commanders and bolted out of the compound. The commanders were tracking numbers to ensure everyone made it off. The orderly evacuation was as efficient and fast as Herakles had trained those executing it to be.

A strange wail overhead drew my gaze to the sky. Something streaked above us. Seconds later, it smashed into the main body of the mall and exploded.

"We have to go!" Kyros said and pushed me towards the command vehicle awaiting me.

I go last! I replied. *When my people are safe, I'll leave!*

Another missile crested the treetops and smashed into the headquarters building. Debris sprayed twenty meters into the air, and flames flashed.

Fire was trickling through me more insistently, warning me I wasn't going to have time to drive anywhere before the transformation came. I tried to fight it, determined to oversee the orderly evacuation of my army.

Herakles joined us. "We have to go!" he shouted.

Tell him – I started to direct Kyros.

As if knowing I wasn't going to leave, Herakles scooped me up in his arms and ran to our vehicle at the center of the motor pool. Furious, I nonetheless waited until he set me down to give him a stern look and shake of my head he ignored.

"Get in!"

Menelaus was hobbling quickly towards us with the aid of Kyros. More missiles rained from the sky, followed by deafening explosions and the ground shaking. Shouts between commanders and among those being evacuated were joined by the screams of the injured and dying. Debris sprinkled out of the sky, along with chunks of cement when the parking lots were hit. Dust clouds left thin films of gray everywhere.

It wasn't supposed to be this way. I was supposed to lead this army to the walls and knock them down in four months, and then rescue humanity from both men like Cleon and the gods who abandoned us all. Frozen in horror and surprise, I could only watch as chaos broke out. The orderly evacuation turned into a free for all, as people fled the camp in vehicles and on foot, desperate to be away from the missile fire.

I watched my army scatter and die, helpless to protect anyone. I didn't know what to think or do, and my stomach twisted with nausea as I realized I was losing a war before I had a chance to start it.

In that moment, I began to understand how poor my chances of fighting had been. With ten times the people, fifty-meter walls, and a corrupted Oracle, Cleon's advantage was no longer something I could ignore, not when I was experiencing firsthand what a few missiles could do.

Kyros twisted to see over his shoulder, hearing the sounds of people in pain. I started forward, determined not to leave anyone behind, and then stopped as familiar fire smashed through my system.

"Phoibe ... get in!" Herakles shouted above the war zone around us.

My body began to morph. My clothing grew too tight, and fire raged within me. Fighting the sensation, I closed my eyes and willed myself not to change, at least, not yet.

The magic didn't listen. Wings tore through my clothing, and talons through my shoes. Within seconds, my skin was gray, my hair gone, and my sensitive senses ringing from the bombing. I stretched my wings and shook off the last of the clothing clinging to my frame then threw my head back with a roar of fury.

An eerie silence fell between missile strikes, and I *felt* those around us back away. Any hope I'd had of not revealing my other self to my army was gone. I was too angry, too overwhelmed by the sounds of explosions and scents of war, to care. Propelling myself upward, into the air, I hovered to see the damage below and let out a second roar, this one of pain.

The destructive power of the missiles left me stunned. We had taken gradual, slow losses over the past few months, but this was something entirely different. The power of one rocket could have decimated half my army, if we hadn't had advanced warning. What would an outright war do, when I had so few advanced weaponry?

One of the missiles had hit the nursery section of the strip mall. My mind filled with images and sensations only my beast side was capable of seeing, and I stared, unable to process what was happening.

Let us stop this.

The light gray wings of Menelaus swept by me as he darted upward into the sky, twirled, and then made a beeline in the direction from which the missiles had come. I hesitated only a second before the beast side of me took over. Compelled by fury and sorrow, I raced after Menelaus. For the first time since transforming into a beast, I freed the primal side of me whose intensity had previously scared me. I was a woman of great control, meticulous thought and careful action. To release everything, to give up my control, had never happened before in my adult life.

The queen would never do what had to be done this night. But the beast would. I *felt* the depths of my strength, fury and bloodlust when in my secondary form. So I freed the monster from the careful control I exerted over every second of my life and flew after

Menelaus, towards a brightly lit area outside the walls, where the military had set up camp to destroy me.

Vengeance consumed me, along with the images of the dead men and women I was supposed to protect.

What happened next was a blur of blood, night, and uncontrolled emotion.

IN WHICH DIRECTION WE WENT, and what exactly we did, I didn't know with certainty until the next morning when I awoke with a cloudy mind and parched mouth. Moving caused me to groan from muscle soreness, and I blinked away sleep to try to make sense of my unfamiliar surroundings.

I launched away from where I lay before alarm fully registered. Scampering back, I glanced down at myself then at the pile of bodies I'd been lying on. My skin was stiff from caked blood, and I was naked. No less than ten men were tossed in the pile, all dead, all bearing horrific fang and claw marks, as if they'd been mauled by a group of bears.

Oh, gods! I thought and glanced down at my hands. Dried blood was packed under my nails and had stained my blonde hair pink. I swallowed hard. My heart thumped against my chest. I stood.

Fifty men. There had to be at least that many corpses strewn around the military's camp. The surface-to-surface missile launchers remained in their original positions, and additional neat stacks of rockets sat beside each one. Blood splattered everything from the soaked dirt to the sides of the vehicles to the tents. No one else moved anywhere in camp.

Numbed to the damage, and afraid to look too long at the carnage for fear of vomiting, I picked my way through the bodies and mess. I didn't want to consider why I was full when I knew I hadn't hunted any animals last night. The violence displayed around me soon drove me to my knees.

I retched even harder when I saw how much blood I threw up. Tears stung my eyes, and my throat burned as I emptied the contents of my stomach. This was not morning sickness. This was disgust.

"Phoibe!" The shout came from the other side of camp.

I finished throwing up and stood carefully. My legs shook, and I had the urge to run as far from this place as possible. My anger was completely gone this morning. All I could think about was how I had not only murdered tens of people, but I'd *eaten* parts of several of them!

My thoughts shifted as I awoke fully and made my way towards those searching for me. Had I gotten here in time to stop the complete destruction of my army? To give my people a chance to escape?

Where was Menelaus? Did I dream him coming with me?

The night was too hazy for me to recall details with any sort of certainty. My stomach turned again, and I snapped my gaze up, beyond the piles of bodies.

"She's here!" Unfazed by the massacre, Herakles spotted me long before I did him. He raced towards me, blanket in hand. With no consideration for my title or standing in the world, he draped the blanket around me and swept me up into his arms. His concerned gaze searched my face. "Are you okay?"

He was surrounded by dozens of dead, and he wanted to know if *I* was okay? I didn't think I'd ever appreciated him as much as I did in that moment.

I started to squirm. The jolting sensation inside me made me suck in a breath and go still, lest I threw up all over him. When I'd conquered the urge to vomit again, I nodded.

Reaching two of our vehicles, he set me down on the ground and went to one truck to grab a pack.

"Kyros!" he belted loudly enough to be heard across camp. Kneeling, he pulled out a bottle of water and handed it to me. "I'm no doctor, but you look okay. No worse than Menelaus. He took a couple of bullets."

I sat up straighter.

"He's alive and recovered, thanks to Kyros," Herakles added. "I brought you clothing and enough wet wipes to take off all the blood. I can make you breakfast quickly, too." He pulled a portable stove out of the pack, along with sausage, eggs and bread.

How he was so calm and accepting of my transformation and massacre, I had no idea.

My thoughts went unexpectedly to the insistence of Kyros that I tell Herakles about Alessandra. Guilt fluttered through me. Herakles had never once let me down, never once questioned my orders, and never once failed to help or guide me. His actions and heart were pure, much more so than mine.

Notebook? I wrote into the dirt.

"I'll find one in a minute," he said and placed a small frying pan on the stove.

The army? I scrawled next.

"We're estimating a twenty percent loss of personnel," he replied quietly. "It would've been eighty percent, if you and the old man hadn't stopped the missile fire."

So we had succeeded at some level. Twenty percent loss was huge, but it wasn't as bad as I thought when I hovered over the camp last night. I was relieved and a little surprised. My beast side had thought nothing of stopping the missiles but of seeking revenge against those attacking us. Was it possible the two sides of me were more integrated than I thought? That I didn't need to be in control of my monster to remain ... me?

"For the record, I was right." Herakles gave a tight smile. "The army *loves* the idea of following a monster. Grotesque. Whatever."

I pursed my lips in what he would recognize was mild disapproval. He retrieved a notebook and pen from the interior of the vehicle and handed them to me. I watched him make me breakfast amidst the corpses of our enemies.

I had to tell him about Alessandra. I didn't want to, and a bad reaction from him would hurt my efforts, but he deserved to know. As breakfast cooked, I wrote him a note about the Oracle he considered to be his daughter. I made an effort to keep it short and to use small words, but the letter stretched for two pages. When I finished, I moved behind the truck, with the wet wipes and clothing. Torn about whether or not to reveal the truth, I cleaned myself up and pulled on clothing before deciding I had to do this, because a good leader would tell her most trusted advisor the truth.

Returning to the other side of the truck, I sat. When he handed me a plate, I handed him the notebook.

"You wrote me a book," he said, glancing down at it. His eyes were glued to the two words at the top. *About Alessandra*

I stood and walked away, leaving him in peace. My hands trembled as I ate, and I watched his expression change in a way that caused me pain. I forced myself to face him, because I deserved to hurt after hiding the truth from him.

"You did the right thing," Kyros said softly from behind me.

Did I? I replied bitterly. *What if he walks?*

"What if he stays?" he countered. "Your army still has the best chance of rescuing his daughter."

Not after last night. We lost our supplies and home.

"Almost everyone survived. Not only that, but they know *you* saved them. "

Hearing the truth, I was still inconsolable. I should have predicted the attack or ordered an evacuation after Adonis disappeared. I had saved most of my army, but I had also not been the one who prevented their danger in the first place.

"They're soldiers. They understand," Kyros said.

Not all of them are soldiers. They're volunteers whose lives were destroyed by the gods. I owed them more than to let fire fall from the skies and finish them off.

"You did the best you could."

It wasn't enough. Anything short of complete victory would never be enough to justify everything humanity had lost, and would lose, in the war to come.

"You're just full of it," Kyros said with a laugh. "You hurt?"

I ignored him.

He touched my upper arm, and a flicker of warmth shot through me. "Bruises and scrapes are now gone. Along with the bruised ribs." His hand dropped.

I released the breath I'd been holding. My body moved more easily after his touch, and I rolled my shoulders back.

Did you heal all the wounded already?

"As many as possible. We evacuated according to Plan Pegasus, whatever that is. I don't know where all the different backup sites are. We wanted to find you first then travel to see the rest of the army."

I had a feeling Herakles was regretting his kindness. He stood, bristling. He didn't look at me but tore the pages from the notebook, crumpled them, and threw them then the pad of paper into the forest. He strode off, towards the woods, and away from me.

I started forward.

"Ummmm no." Kyros caught my arm. "Give him some time to breathe and think."

I hated the twisting feeling in my gut but did as he suggested and stayed where I was.

"What next?" Kyros asked.

We rebuild. But we do it smarter. Multiple sites instead of one main one, similar to how Dosy set up the insurgency. Turning, I gazed up at him. Dark circles lined his eyes, and he wore a smile.

"Okay. Leave Herakles a truck, and we'll start."

I lifted my chin.

"Or ..." He sighed. "You can make the decision."

I glanced in the direction Herakles had gone. I wanted to go after him, not because I hoped he would remain with my cause, but because I cared about him.

We'll give him an hour or two, then do as you suggested, I decided. *Where is Menelaus?*

"Sleeping. He didn't handle the stress of last night as well as you. Claimed he's too old for this shit."

I had a few choice words for the Bloodline member I didn't know existed, and even more to say to Apollo. As I looked out over the destruction Menelaus and I had caused, I focused on how well prepared and supplied the Supreme Magistrate really was. Adonis had believed we would fail quickly and absolutely if we faced Cleon's forces directly, and I began to agree with him. They had nearly destroyed us from twenty kilometers away.

I was spooked. For the first time since leaving DC, I felt like my eyes were open to what I was doing. I had always considered my war with Cleon to be secondary to my true purpose, but how was I going to defeat him and retake his army, when a few missiles had sent my forces into hiding? My supplies were gone, my people scattered, and my staffing down twenty percent.

What would I do to win? To defeat Cleon? How far would I have to go in order to end his tyranny and restore the government to the people, before I could attack the gods?

"I know someone willing to help you reclaim the city." Paeon was back, as displayed by the bright blue eyes peering out of Kyros' face.

I pinned Kyros-Paeon with a look. *I need help toppling Cleon before I can face the gods, and I need real answers about what's going on, to include why they're possessing people.*

"You want to work with us then destroy us."

Yes.

"Oddly enough, I think a few gods might be willing to listen to your proposal. Would you consider a modification to your truce? Namely, will you consent to allow us to return to our home rather than slaughter us?"

Opening the bridge is outside my control, I replied.

"For now. But once you take the city, and with your intent to either work with the Oracle or kill her, if she can't or won't help you, there might be a window where we can return home."

Every cell of my body rebelled at the idea of working with the gods. My jaw clenched, and I was tense enough that I wanted to turn back from this path already.

Why are you willing to aid me, when you know I might turn on you? I demanded. *I hate your kind, and I will not stop until you all are gone from the Earth.*

"Let's just say there's more going on than you know yet. We're trapped her. Did you ever wonder who has the power to trap us, and why?" he asked cautiously.

I don't care. I'd see you all murdered in your beds.

"Then let's stick to our original deal. You at least try to open the bridge to send us home, or don't interfere with us if we find a way to return home, and we'll help you through the wall."

I hated, *hated* the idea of working with the gods.

These were emotions. The beast side of me. Instincts I couldn't allow to cloud my judgment. Not when the lives of my army depended upon me to protect them and lead them to victory. Last night had been a wake up call in many ways, to include the stark reality that I was playing in a sandbox while Cleon focused on conquering the entire desert. He had sent sixty men and three missile launching vehicles to take me out, and he'd almost succeeded.

If I stood any chance of taking the city, I needed the help from beings far more powerful than I was.

Very well. I said. *We will cease hunting your kind, and I will expect you to participate in my war.*

"Done." Paeon smiled.

You speak on behalf of Zeus now? I snapped.

"In this matter, yes. He sent me to broker a peace with you, and I've finally succeeded."

When your kind leaves, you'll release Kyros, I added. *And any other human you've enslaved or possessed.*

"We will."

Nothing about this sat right. Even understanding I now had the potential key to victory on my side, I wanted to vomit again from forcing myself to work with those I hated most in the world.

But my war against the gods didn't matter, if I couldn't take the city, usurp Cleon, protect what remained of humanity, and rescue, or destroy, Alessandra.

We're done, I said, at my limit with negotiating with the gods. *Bring back Kyros.*

Paeon's eyes turned to brown, and I started to relax when Kyros' smile returned.

"He is so happy right now," he reported.

I'm not.

My thoughts weren't as much on the Bloodline as on my unborn twins. Assuming any of us survived the apocalypse, would they still suffer from the curse as my family had for ten thousand years? By choosing to work with the gods, was I sacrificing the fates of my own children?

Sick to my stomach again, I tossed what remained of my breakfast.

"For what it's worth, I think you made the right decision," Kyros said.

What does a football player from rural Virginia know of war, curses, and defending humanity? The words were much harsher than I intended, but I was feeling emotionally raw from the rough night and fear for my babies.

"Not much," he replied softly, unfazed. He held my gaze. His dark eyes were filled with compassion and warmth, neither of which I deserved. "You're doing your best."

It wasn't enough. I moved away, unable to understand how he thought the best of me, even now, after I'd sold out my principals and potentially condemned by children.

From this point, I was able to see the tops of the walls surrounding DC. My goal mocked me. Not only could I not reach the walls without suffering the massacre of my army, but I didn't know if I'd be able to execute Adonis' brilliant plan now that my forces were scattered.

I felt helpless and alone. Tears of frustration pricked my eyes as I thought about the massive undertaking before me in reestablishing my army.

"I understand why you did what you did."

At Herakles' measured voice, I swiped my tears away hastily and turned to face him. He remained a short distance away, gaze stormy and features flushed.

"You are still my best hope at rescuing Alessandra," he continued. "I will stay, as you requested, but only on one condition."

I waited.

"No more lies. About anything."

I nodded.

"I found help," he said. "Technically, they found me. I guess they've been trying to find me for a couple of weeks."

Startled, I was about to have Kyros ask him what that meant, when the slender forms of two dozen young women slid into view from behind trees. A dour priest in brown robes accompanied them.

"Alessandra had more than me as her protector," Herakles explained. "Her sisters are nymphs. They possess abilities we might be able to use in your war. They would like your permission to join us."

In all my experiences with gods, I had never met a nymph. The women with mythical powers were quiet and still enough to be part of the natural world from which they drew their abilities.

While I would deny Herakles nothing at this moment, my logical side also understood the value such people could provide. If their powers were anything like what I'd read, it was possible we would never again worry about tainted water, finding food, or being discovered in the forest by our enemies.

I nodded my agreement. The women moved with otherworldly grace and silence to surround Herakles. One of them giggled, and suddenly, they were all trying to hug him. He managed to smile and hugged the nymphs back, murmuring words I couldn't make out. That he cared for them was clear, and I couldn't help feeling a pang of envy. I'd give anything to have Theodocia here to hug me or to feel as if I weren't so alone in my war, especially after alienating my trusted advisor.

"Things are looking up," Kyros said with far too much cheer.

Maybe, I allowed. I wasn't so certain the gods were going to follow through with their promise or be of much use if they did.

Feeling once more as if I were isolated from the rest of the world, I turned my back on the happy reunion before me and went to the vehicle.

Kyros joined me. "Let's go find our army!" he said.

I glared at him. Secretly, buried too deep inside me for me to admit their existence, relief, and gratitude towards Kyros softened my anger.

"We better go." His mood darkened. He was gazing out at the forest. "Something is coming."

Fetch Herakles. I wasn't sticking around to discover what Kyros was talking about. His instincts had kept me alive, and I'd trust them again and again. Exhausted, I climbed into the passenger seat of one truck and rested my head back.

Somehow, we managed to pack all the nymphs into the trucks. We left the scene of my massacre, but I couldn't shake the heavy feeling sinking into me.

Last night was just the beginning, and I viewed what was to come with trepidation.

TWENTY

ALESSANDRA

"I'M TIRED of being weak, afraid," I whispered, distraught by the thick column of smoke rising towards the sky. Pythia and I stood atop the walls surrounding DC, gazing out over Northern Virginia. I assumed the smoke came from the Silent Queen's compound and could only hope Herakles and the army had evacuated before the attack. Not knowing how he was – this was torture. As with the situation with Adonis, I couldn't afford to be selfish right now. The fate of the worlds was on my shoulders, and I had to become the Oracle I desperately needed to be. The two of them were safer away from me than in DC, and I had to focus on doing what it took to keep them protected.

"None of us knew what would happen. The paths I foresaw were too many. They have been narrowed down, and now you must make the best choices you can," Pythia answered.

"Did you see what happened after this?"

"Did you see what happened after this?"

"No. I cannot have visions now that I am dead, and what I foresaw has changed. Lantos was always a wild card, but I didn't foresee him hiding your body from Cecelia."

"That could end up being a bad thing, if he hid it somewhere where I can't find it," I said, frowning."

"You have a chance to forge a new path. And in every circumstance, I saw you have the power to change the course of the Fates. The apocalypse is one option of many, but it will take a great deal of effort to avoid it."

"This isn't a great pep talk," I said.

"It's a new day. Anything is possible. The apocalypse is not inevitable, and sometimes, that's as good as it gets."

"Correction. This is the *worst* pep talk ever," I mumbled.

She smiled.

I tested my strength again. "I can still use my power, even though my body is missing."

"As long as you have a body, you're grounded to the source of your power, to our Earth."

"I can bring the walls down right now." I funneled energy into my feet and beyond, into the walls. The cement began to shake.

"Not yet." Pythia said. She motioned to the forest at the base of the walls. "Zeus built the wall to protect the people inside. Until you have a plan to save humanity, you'll want to avoid exposing those who remain to the dangers outside the walls."

I peered over the edge, not understanding. Movement occurred in the trees hedging the wall. Interested, I strained to get a better view of what it was. Something huge, if its movement caused the trees to bend as they were.

"Manticore," I breathed. "Cleon ... Cecelia unleashed all the monsters."

"And that's not all." Pythia pointed.

Several humans were huddled with what appeared to be rope. A closer look revealed rotting flesh that fell off their bodies, and missing limbs.

"What in Hades?" I asked, disgusted.

"Gods and goddesses who have possessed human bodies. They

need new bodies to survive, or they need to draw off Zeus' power, which is centralized in DC."

Monsters and zombie-gods outside the walls, and an all-powerful tyrant inside. Which was worse?

"I have to find my body," I said with a shudder. "We're running out of time."

"Yeah," Pythia agreed. "My parole is almost up as well."

I studied her, and fear floated through me. I could still here the whispers of the gods and goddesses at the back of my mind. The door Lantos had opened between them and me remained. If Pythia left soon, I hoped to retain some divine guidance. "Then let's get started. Teach me what I need to know to destroy everyone."

She lifted an eyebrow.

I flushed. "Sorry. That was a Cleon thought," I said sheepishly.

"You're scaring me."

"Yeah. Me, too," I admitted. "Teach me what I need to know to *save* everyone."

With a nod, she turned away and floated to the bottom of the wall, on the protected side. I glanced once more down at the possessed bodies and monsters moving within the forest, and then followed.

All I had to do was save the world. Once I did, I'd have Herakles and Adonis back, and the death of Lantos – and anyone else who didn't survive this game – would be for a purpose.

Betray them all. Die a hero. Maybe, just maybe Lantos knew how important his life and death were.

THETA BEGINNINGS MINISERIES

Silent Queen
Mercenary
Shadow Titan
People's Champion

SILENT QUEEN

I HAD WAITED my entire life for this night. Even if I were able to draw a full breath in the voluminous gown I wore with its tight girdle, I would still be breathless.

The lights overhead were too bright, and sweat trickled down my legs and gleamed on the faces of the clergy in front of me. None of the dignitaries, politicians, royalty from around the world, acolytes or other honored guests dared complain about the air conditioning going out two hours before the ceremony. Like me, the most powerful and influential people in the world stood in quiet anticipation, prepared to witness an event so very few ever did.

I suppressed the urge to sneeze. The air was clogged with incense and smoke emanating from burning orbs filled with herbs held by priests. The coronation ceremony was performed in the oldest temple in New York City, the temple belonging to Apollo, the patron god of the City. Built around two hundred years ago, it was cozy and showed the signs of being renovated recently: modern, track lighting, pristinely whitewashed walls, and a gold altar whose corners were sharp and unscathed surfaces polished to a shine. The walls, ceilings and floors were all adorned in royal purple, and my personal guard lined the perimeter.

My hands trembled, and I struggled to stand perfectly still under the weight of my attire and my own agitated excitement. Now fourteen, I was officially of age to assume my duties as the Queen of Greece and following in the footsteps of my mother, grandfather and every other royal member of the Bloodline.

Someone sneezed, shattering the solemn silence of the ceremonial chamber. The bursts of sound came three more times.

I didn't look directly at the offender, but it was hard not to smile.

Tommy, the son of my confidante the High Priestess of Artemis, Theodocia, was probably too young for the ceremony. All of six and a half years old, he was like a little brother to me. I wouldn't hear of him missing today. He and his mother were my family. No one dared shush him, not when it was understood I wouldn't approve of anyone who did.

Theodocia – my friend, advisor and mother figure since her arrival into my life seven years ago – stood before me flanked by two High Priests, one serving Apollo and one serving none other than Zeus. Behind them were three rows of other high level members of the priesthoods, each one representing a different god or goddess.

Theodocia was trying hard to maintain the deadpan expression worn by every other attendee, but her brown eyes glowed with pride. Seeing her joy filled me with such warm emotion, I wanted to cry, so I stared at the mark of Artemis on her forehead instead of meeting her gaze.

One of the two priests jerked and went rigid. His eyes became glassy and his face blank as the god he served possessed his body in order to communicate with us. A flicker of unease worked its way through me when I saw the lightning bolt tattooed on his forehead.

Zeus himself had possessed the priest. From what I knew of my family's history, it was a very rare honor for the chief god to oversee the ceremony. I didn't know what to think of this, not when my own feelings about the honor being bestowed upon me were mixed. To be a member of the Bloodline was to have the ability to harness untold influence over mortals and gods – and coupled with a debilitating curse. All the wealth my predecessors had been hoarding for ten thousand years couldn't buy our way out of our destinies.

Long simmering anger threatened to spike at the appearance of Zeus, the god with the power to end the curse that suspended the Bloodline bearers in a state of living death lasting all of eternity. My emotions were already difficult to control tonight. I wasn't certain if my sense of duty would prevail when confronting the god with whom I'd been furious since learning my fate. I simultaneously hated what he had done to my family and loved him for blessing mortals with life, and the warring emotions distracted me to the point I forgot to offer any sign of deference before he spoke.

"Hello, Phoibe, my sweet child." The head of the Greek pantheon greeted me quietly.

Hello, Father, I gave the traditional address which my family alone was permitted to give. I dropped into a deep curtsey. The sounds of rustling and movement filled the chamber as everyone around me hastily did the same.

"Still you do not speak." He sounded both gruffly disapproving and amused.

No, Father, I replied mentally, fully aware the gods and goddesses were able to hear me.

The possessed priest shifted closer to me and knelt.

"You cannot escape your fate forever, young one," Zeus said through his human puppet. "You know this."

In a kneeling curtsey, I stared at the floor at my feet. My heart pounded hard in my chest, and it became even more difficult to draw a breath. If he was aware that I knew of the curse, he would also understand how angry I was with him. His knowledge should not have surprised me, given he was the most powerful of the gods, but I didn't expect him to scold me. How could he believe I, or anyone else, would ever welcome such a fate? I could never forgive him for what he'd done to my family, and yet, my eyes filled with tears at the prospect of displeasing the mighty Zeus.

I'm so sorry to disappoint you, Father. I said. I truly regretted upsetting him – and my weakness turned the direction of my anger inward.

"I admire your spirit, Phoibe," he added. "For now, your defiance amuses me. But be warned this will not always be the case. You cannot defy the will of your gods forever. You are too young yet to understand the importance of the gift bestowed upon your family."

I clenched my fists and kept my head down, so he couldn't see the anger in my eyes.

"Rise, Queen Phoibe. Your family bears the mark of the chosen," he said, referring to the birthmark shaped like an omega on my inner wrist. "You do not kneel like a mortal."

I stood slowly, set my shoulders and lifted my chin.

The High Priest of Zeus stepped back from me.

"Let it be known and recorded I have given my personal blessing to this ceremony, and to your new Queen." Zeus' voice rang out loud, rich and deep. "The relationship between the Bloodline and the pantheon has never been stronger than it is today. No mortal, or god, will stand between my chosen children and me, and those who dare to dishonor this sacred bond will earn my wrath." He faced me again. "Your reign, Queen Phoibe, my Silent Queen, will be unlike the reign of any other member of the Bloodline. For this reason, you will be the first ruler blessed with the appointment of two holy guardians from among the members of the pantheon, whom you may call upon as you would a mother or father. You know the first, Artemis, who has so diligently cared for you since your birth."

Theodocia, now also possessed by the spirit of the goddess she served, stepped forward.

"My daughter. You need only ask, and I will provide," she said.

My anger melted. Artemis had been with me since I was a child. Where I experienced confusion and anger whenever I thought of Zeus, I knew only love and admiration when it came to Artemis.

She dipped her finger into the anointing oil and drew a bow on my forehead before stepping aside with a deferential bow to Zeus.

Surprised by the honor of two patrons after his warning, I waited for Zeus to reveal who my second guardian was.

Another priest moved in the third row, indicating he was likely a minor god, and I strained discreetly to see his mark to identify which one. His name would hopefully help me interpret what it meant when Zeus said my reign would be unlike any other's.

An inverted torch was tattooed on the forehead of the High Priest moving towards us.

No, I thought forcefully enough I was afraid I spoke the word aloud.

If the chamber were quiet before, it became a graveyard when everyone present realized whom Zeus had chosen.

The High Priest bearing the torch stopped before me, and I gazed up at him. For the sake of my station, I didn't let my horror bleed through to my expression. But I felt coldness to my core.

"Thanatos," Zeus announced.

Thanatos, who knew neither mercy nor failure.

Thanatos, whom every mortal and immortal faced eventually.

Thanatos, the God of Death.

I glanced at Theodocia, wishing she weren't possessed by a goddess, so she could give me one of her warm smiles. I never felt as alone as I did that moment, surrounded by dignitaries and deities, facing Thanatos. Death would come for everyone at some point, but there was nothing like standing before him and feeling my own human frailty.

Why him? Was this an omen of what was to come?

My breathing was harsh in my ears. Hearing it, I squared my shoulders and forced myself to focus on my carriage and position rather than what was before me. I looked Thanatos in the face and forbade myself from quaking in his presence.

"You need not fear, my child," came Artemis' soft voice. "I will be with you every day of your reign."

"As will I," Thanatos seconded.

The silence grew too much as I stared into the eyes of Death.

What does this mean? I asked finally, unable to control my emotions long enough to rationalize what was before me.

"That is up to you," Zeus replied for our ears only. "This comes at the petition of someone we all hold dear to us, the Oracle of Delphi. She has revealed to me a portion of the future. Upon hearing what she has foreseen, I approved her request. You will need Thanatos, my queen."

I had never met the Oracle. She lived in Washington DC, at the compound housing my secondary palace, which I would travel to after my coronation ceremony. Only upon becoming the Queen of Greece could I take my place as the official third member of the Sacred Triumvirate, alongside the Supreme Magistrate and Supreme Priest, both of whom were in attendance today.

Zeus continued. "The Queen of Death does not have the same ring to it as Silent Queen does for certain. Perhaps you should remember this, if you ever decide to call upon your patron."

Never, I thought before I could stop myself. In the distant past, before the world was conquered and divided up, my forbearers led great armies across the Middle and Far East and into Europe, Asia and Africa. They tamed the world before Greece fell from power and the Bloodline was reduced to a symbol of the unity of gods and mortals rather than a military powerhouse. In another time, perhaps I would have welcomed Thanatos at my side.

But I was unable to imagine how I was supposed to benefit from such a patron in this day and age and could only view his presence before me as a reminder I, too, would one day lose my mortal body and be forced to surrender to the curse of the Bloodline that would render me immortal and frozen in stone for all time.

What had the Oracle of Delphi foreseen? What could the future possibly hold that required Thanatos at my side?

It took every last piece of my willpower not to back away when Thanatos claimed the anointment oil from Theodocia and reached out to me. But I did close my eyes. The fingertip that drew the sign of the God of Death on my forehead was cold and sent a streak of fear through me.

"Let his presence in your life be a reminder to you, my young queen," Zeus cautioned quietly. "The Fates, while temperamental, have a preferred path for each of us. There will come a time when you must face yours."

Yes, Father. It was all I could think of to say. I was too overwhelmed by the idea Thanatos himself was supposed to become a fixture in my life, in the same way Artemis had been. Not only this, but the most powerful people in the world had witnessed his appointment. How was I to maintain the influence of the Bloodline when everyone knew I'd been touched by Death?

This time, I wanted to cry for a very different reason.

"It does not escape my notice I am being appointed a guardian to the Bloodline, the only creatures with souls who defy me when I beckon." Thanatos' tone was terse. "Through the grace of Zeus, your predecessors never truly die, Queen Phoibe. If you are at a loss as to how I have been assigned to you, I am even less satisfied. I believe it to be a personal insult."

His reluctance and bitterness convinced me he spoke the truth about not knowing why we were put together. I sensed his last comment was meant for Zeus, who was never under any obligation to offer an explanation to anyone for any action he chose to undertake. But Thanatos was right. The members of my Bloodline technically didn't die. We faced a destiny worse than anything the God of Death could do to us. Of any god or goddess in creation, Thanatos was the last deity who ever should have been appointed as my guardian.

Which made this experience more unsettling. If the god chosen as my patron didn't know why he was selected, and resented the sacred Bloodline for rebuffing his power for ten thousand years, what exactly was in my future that would require the two of us to co-exist, if not cooperate? Artemis' influence was inextricably entwined in my life, personified by Theodocia, who had become like a mother to me.

The goddess guided Theodocia's decisions and actions, and the goddess spoke to me regularly through Theodocia as well.

No part of me believed I would ever have such a warm relationship with the God of Death, even if my circumstances hadn't already excluded me from his influence. He would never become a father figure, and he held only one purpose and role in the pantheon: to guarantee Hades a steady supply of souls for the underworld.

His baffling appointment was a bad omen, any way I considered it, and I found myself yearning for the ceremony to be over so I could consult with Theodocia.

Without another word of objection, Thanatos stepped away. I centered myself the best I could before opening my eyes.

The ceremony continued in the same subdued, tense manner. Zeus removed the jewel-laden crown of Greece from its place atop a plush, velvet pillow. He placed it on my head and held it as two of my servants raced forward to adjust it. When the heavy crown was secured, Zeus then handed me the scepter of Greece, a gold rod inlaid with filigree and writing and topped by brilliant purple gems. It was heavy and cold to the touch.

He moved away, and I concentrated on holding the scepter without affecting my balance. At fourteen, I was considered frail in stature despite my ravenous eating habits and physical activity.

The two priests and Theodocia took simultaneous deep breaths. Their glazed expressions faded, and they began to move naturally once more. Likewise, the gods and goddesses released the holds on their respective clergy members in the three rows behind them.

No one spoke for a long moment, as if everyone in the chamber were trying to figure out why Thanatos had been appointed my patron. Finally, the High Priest of Zeus stepped forward.

"May I present to you, the Queen of Greece, Sole Protector of the Bloodline, mortal daughter to the gods, ward of Artemis and Thanatos, and member of the Sacred Triumvirate, who has been extraordinarily blessed by our Holy Father," he announced.

The men and women present in the room all bowed and curtseyed. All I cared about was trying to read the features of Theodocia. She had her public face on, but the skin around her eyes was tight. She was worried. If not for the reception following my official succession to the throne of Greece, I'd take her aside and talk. However, my first act as the queen couldn't be a selfish one. I'd been schooled since I was four about how to behave in accordance with my royal birthright. Duty always came first. Later, we would talk.

A harp began playing. It was my cue to exit the ceremony.

Turning, I waited for my servants to straighten the long train of my gown before I paced gracefully down the purple carpet towards the chamber's exit. The crown of Greece was heavy on my head, the scepter threatening my balance with each step. I moved slowly. My audience had enough to talk about already without me tripping and providing more gossip for them to spread.

Reeling from the unexpected twist to my coronation ceremony, I followed two priests of Apollo blindly through the temple and into the basement, a space large enough to host everyone present, for a low key, celebratory soiree. My assigned position was on a simple bench on a dais at the center of the room. I walked as elegantly as possible given the uncomfortable weight of crown, clothing and scepter and took my seat while my servants fixed the bunched up dress and train. Only when I appeared flawless did they allow the others to enter, in order of perceived importance.

One by one, men and women approached the dais, bowed or curtseyed, offered a few words of congratulations, and then stepped away to form small cliques and enjoy the three thousand year old wine imported from Greece for this event.

Managing to nod my head in acknowledgement after each person spoke, I barely heard any of their words. The marking of Thanatos on my forehead burned with coldness to the point it hurt, and I began to wonder if his appearance had a more ominous meaning than I originally thought. Was the Oracle of Delphi trying to tell me I'd be the first of my Bloodline to die a real death? I had never thought about a true, natural death. Such a heavy thought left me as distressed as I became whenever I thought about spending eternity in stone.

Suddenly, I could think of nothing I wanted more than to meet the Oracle and ask her why she petitioned Zeus to insert Thanatos into my life, and why Zeus had agreed.

Pensive, I reacted mechanically to my subjects. Once each person paid homage to the Crown, they all moved away and began talking and eating amongst themselves, no doubt discussing how, of all the gods and goddesses out there, Thanatos had been chosen as my secondary guardian. How would world leaders react?

And the people? I held no true power over the people of the world, even if I were raised to consider every man, woman and child to be a subject under my guardianship. What would they think of their Silent Queen and her deathly benefactor?

So concerned and confused was I, I didn't notice the latest subject to approach me until he spoke – into my mind.

You are too young for such worry.

I blinked and focused on the man standing in front of me. Whoever he was, he was young and striking, with brilliant green eyes, olive features, dark hair and a dazzling smile. I spent a lot of time watching movies with Tommy, and I'd never seen any actor more handsome than this man.

"But perhaps it is not misplaced," he added quietly out loud.

I lifted my chin a notch, unimpressed with his tricks, despite his incredible looks. He wasn't a god. They rarely took human form for any period of time. But normal humans weren't able to speak to me through my mind, which left a hybrid – a demigod – who was classified as neither human nor god, and therefore, treated with general aversion by the rest of the world.

"You remain as smart as always," he said.

Who are you? I demanded.

"A concerned subject," he replied and bowed his head in an elegant display of deference. "One who bears a message for you."

I waited.

"May I approach?"

I knew without looking my personal guard was always present. Four soldiers followed me wherever I went, outside of my personal quarters. They were as discreet as shadows and moved like lightning when required. No demigod was a threat when they were around.

With a single nod of my head, I granted the stranger's request.

He drew nearer and knelt in a deep bow near the top of my feet. His frame was lean, his cologne pleasant without being overwhelming. When he met my gaze once more, I was almost too mesmerized to ask him what he wanted. At fourteen, I had a life very unlike that of normal teenagers, but it didn't mean I wasn't aware of handsome men and didn't often wonder what it would be like to have a boyfriend.

It didn't seem likely, given who I was, that I ever would. My mother's marriage was a match arranged by the clergy for the sole purpose of producing an heir to carry on the Bloodline. There was no room in my future for love or pursuing handsome men, according to the priestesses who tutored me. I was born with a humbling, important purpose, and I'd been raised to view fulfilling my duty as the ultimate, and only, achievement that mattered.

But the beauty, and charismatic smile, of this stranger made me wish I was normal, if only for half a day, so I could be like every other teenage girl or better yet, like the princesses who fell in love with their princes in the fairy tale movies I watched.

I didn't like that feeling. I was one of the wealthiest people on the planet, enjoyed the favor of gods and mortals, and had been blessed by Zeus himself; there was no room for the sense of longing, of envy, I experienced as I gazed at the demigod kneeling before me and knew I would never be a princess from a movie who found her perfect prince.

And yet, I couldn't suppress the emotion tumbling inside me.

What is it you wish to tell me? I asked him, eager to leave him and the strange feelings he caused behind.

"Do you have time to speak in private with an old friend?" he asked.

I studied him. Something was vaguely familiar about his eyes, but I didn't fully recognize him. *I'm afraid I don't know you. However, if you wish to petition me for an audience, you can inform one of my priestesses.*

"What're you doing here?" Theodocia's voice was level and tight. She approached from the direction of the door, bowed her head to me, then pinned the stranger with a glare.

"Docia," he said and smiled at her. "I thought you'd be happier to see me."

"You have no business with Her Majesty, Lantos."

I blinked. Lantos?

My Lantos?

It was the second major surprise today.

Theodocia started towards the guards.

Wait, I told her.

She stopped and faced me.

You're Lantos? I asked the man, scrutinizing him.

"The same Lantos who used to sit beside you and watch cartoons. The same Lantos who saved your life when your priestess tried to smuggle you out of your quarters. And the same Lantos who brought you Theodocia," he said.

The same Lantos who left me without warning and never returned, I said, frowning.

"Yes. That, too," he said, smile fading.

"What is it you want?" Theodocia asked.

"To warn and help you."

"Out of the goodness of your heart?"

Lantos ducked his head but was smiling.

"I didn't think so," Theodocia said.

I almost asked her how they knew each other so well, and why she never told me Lantos brought her into my life to begin with. Aware we weren't in private, where we might speak freely, I resisted the urge. Day one of my reign was by far the most bizarre day of my life.

"We are defined by our positions, are we not, Queen Phoibe?" Lantos addressed me. "We must be diplomats first, people who understand the need to give and take and to negotiate."

I found myself nodding. More questions hammered my brain, such as, where he had been for the past seven years and why he never came back to see me again. As a child, I hadn't questioned who or what he was. He was a shadow that spoke to me and befriended me when no one else did. I didn't know he had a form, or at least, I hadn't known that before he mentioned the man who rescued me from the sidewalk after I tried to flee the High Priestess who treated me as a captive rather than a child.

That was seven years ago, before Theodocia, when my life was a nightmare, and Lantos had been the only good part of it. And then he did what everyone else before Theodocia did and inexplicably abandoned me.

You're really Lantos? I spoke to him but looked at Theodocia.

"Yes," she said reluctantly.

"I am," he said.

I rose. *We will speak in private.* Without waiting for anyone to object, I strode past him, through a crowd that made a path for me, and into the hallway. It, too, was crowded, so I continued walking until I found the courtyard where the priests grew herbs at the center of the temple.

The full moon hung overhead, visible through a thin layer of yellowish smog. It was quiet and dark, and the garden was lit by a few lamps ensconced on the outside walls of the building. I stopped at the center of the walkway and turned to wait for them.

"I appreciate your attention, Your Majesty," Lantos said, stopping a little too close for my comfort.

I gazed up at him, uncertain what exactly I felt, aside from a sudden flush of anger.

I slapped him. *You abandoned me.*

"I understand," he said and touched his cheek. "I deserved that. Trust me, Phoibe, it took my world almost ending to keep me from returning." The somber expression on his handsome face was sincere.

It sapped the strength of my anger away. I felt myself starting to fall into his green eyes again.

"I sent you Theodocia, didn't I?" he added.

"You didn't *send* me. Artemis did. If I remember correctly, she forced you to bring me to Phoibe when you didn't want to by threatening to expose your secret," Theodocia said calmly.

I raised my eyebrows.

"Technically," Lantos said.

With a shake of my head, I moved around him to join the person I trusted most in this world.

"I've always looked out for you. Even your guardian can't refute that," Lantos said. "I'm here for you, Phoibe. To warn you."

"Against what exactly?" Theodocia demanded. "This place is locked down by the royal guard, the military and SISA."

"It won't be enough."

Theodocia stared at him.

Enough for what? I asked.

"The end of the world. Sort of."

I studied him. I didn't remember my Lantos being a madman but I never thought he'd abandon me either. I did recall how well he loved games, from board games to hide and seek to playing tricks on my caretakers. Was this a game to him?

"By midnight, everyone in this building will be dead and the city will be under siege." Lantos spoke to Theodocia this time.

"From what?" Theodocia pressed. "What could possibly defeat our security?"

"Nothing human, for certain," he replied. "But this attack isn't from humans."

I was starting to become concerned. First Death as my patron and now Lantos with an ominous message.

"I had a conversation with the Oracle of Delphi," Lantos said when neither of us spoke.

"And you rated her attention how?" Theodocia challenged.

"It wasn't an authorized visit," he admitted. "But I can move through shadows, as you both well know. I spoke to her on a matter of a different nature, and in the course of our conversation, she gave me a warning for you and for Artemis. She's the Oracle. She knew of my connection to both of you and asked me to come here and save the life of the Queen touched by Death."

My throat grew almost too tight to swallow at his mention of Thanatos. *Why would she send someone like you to warn the Queen of Greece?* I demanded.

"Because she thought you might trust me more than a complete stranger. Who else would be here in this garden talking to you?"

"Lantos, do you really want us to believe the *gods* are going to attack this place, after the Queen just received a blessing from Zeus?" Theodocia asked.

"I do not know what the danger is exactly," he replied. "The Oracle was reluctant to tell me. She said it would not be of a humanly nature. This, to me, indicates an otherworldly type of threat. I don't have all the answers, Theodocia, but I do have a way out of the City."

I had never heard of any situation this unusual. I was the Queen. But I didn't know what the right thing to do was. Studying Theodocia, I waited to hear her thoughts on Lantos' claim.

"If there is a threat," she started slowly, "We're going to leave through our means, not yours. With the queen's approval, you will either be arrested and forced to accompany us, or you will leave this place immediately."

Lantos smiled and held out his hands. "Arrest me. I don't mind handcuffs." He winked at me.

I didn't understand what he was inferring and glanced at Theodocia, confused as to why someone would want to be arrested.

She rolled her eyes. "Gladly." Waving to the guards lurking in the shadows, she glanced at me. "With your permission?"

I nodded.

"Arrest this man and prepare for an immediate departure of Her Majesty," she directed.

"By air," Lantos added.

Theodocia studied him. "Very well. By air."

One guard cuffed Lantos while another darted away to inform our cadre of personal assistants.

"He goes with us." Theodocia told the guard before she turned to me. "I need to grab Tommy. Would you like to come or remain here?"

I will stay, I said. I didn't want to slow her down. The crown and scepter were causing my muscles to start to ache, and I couldn't move fast or well in this dress.

"Quickly," Lantos urged.

"Stay between them," Theodocia said to the guard. She strode away, back into the temple, leaving me with Lantos and the guard.

I found myself studying Lantos once more, recalling how good of a friend he had been to me when I was younger. Theodocia once told me that it was almost impossible to understand the depths of anyone's heart, even when we cared for someone and believed we knew them. I had loved Lantos for loving me when I had no one else. How had I not known he would abandon me?

Why did you leave me? I asked him.

He glanced at me, away, then back. "I had little choice."

You could have told me farewell.

"You were a child, Phoibe." His expression held genuine warmth. "How could you have understood if I said I had to leave and never come back?"

I thought about Tommy and what it would be like to try to explain to him if I decided to leave him forever. We lived an extremely isolated life. He had no real friends, aside from me, and rarely left my apartments. He wouldn't understand – at least, not at the age he was.

I would have understood later in life, I told Lantos defensively.

"I believe you," he replied. "Maybe this is as much about me as it is about you. Maybe I felt like I was doing you a favor by leaving you in such a way you wouldn't want anything to do with me ever again."

His words bothered me. I didn't fully grasp his meaning – but I sensed there was more to what he said. Theodocia, who had more life experience, would no doubt understand, and I made a mental note to ask her.

"I've been asking myself why here and now," he said and looked around, as if waiting for a monster to leap at him from the shadows. "Then it hit me. This is the one event every generation where the Sacred Triumvirate, and every other person of influence and power, is located in one place. Every twenty to thirty years, there's only a three to four hour window when world leaders, every deity of consequence and the richest people in the world gather ... right. Here."

Again, I was left trying to understand what he was really saying. The coronation tradition had not changed in ten thousand years. What he said was correct, but how he said it left me uneasy.

"We should hurry," he finished in a whisper, his eyes on the full moon.

Something in his expression scared me. We stood in silence for a full five minutes, waiting for Theodocia. I heard the distant thump of a helicopter, a sign Theodocia hadn't just requested our transportation but had to have called in an emergency order for them to be in the air this fast.

She, too, felt something was wrong. Her relationship with Lantos troubled me, not because he brought her to me, but because she had never spoken to me about him. I had told her when I was younger about my shadow friend. I wanted to believe she didn't bring up meeting Lantos because she didn't want to upset me. However, after witnessing their exchanges, I had a feeling there was more than a simple meeting between them.

While young, I had learned the hard way, at a very young age, how to read people and to be cautious of their true intentions. I was in a position many envied and which led many more to try to use or influence me. I had dealt with enough people to know Theodocia's reaction to seeing Lantos was born of deep distrust, the kind someone had to earn. Even so, she believed him about the threat. I struggled to reconcile how she could both trust and distrust him, or perhaps, trust his warning without trusting *him*.

It seemed likely they had dealt with one another on many other occasions. I was not entitled to know Theodocia's personal business, but this wasn't on the same level of Theodocia dealing with the father of her son.

Whatever was between Lantos and Theodocia, it seemed to revolve around me. I didn't expect Theodocia to keep these kinds of secrets from me.

"Chopper's coming," Theodocia said, returning to the courtyard with Tommy in tow. She had an overnight bag slung over one shoulder. "This way." Her gaze lingered on Lantos, and her jaw ticked. But she didn't object to him accompanying us.

We hurried through the temple and behind it to a common park area inhabited at night by the homeless. My personal guard closed in around me as we crossed the street. Unable to hold the scepter upright any longer, I let my arm fall to my side then picked up my skirts in a very un-royal way in order to quicken my pace.

The deafening sound of the helicopter prevented us from speaking as we waited for it to touch down in the center of the small park. Theodocia left Tommy with me and trotted to the head of my guard, who stood at the helicopter. Releasing my dress, I took his hand, and we waited with my royal guard.

Theodocia soon waved us over, and we joined her at the helicopter.

Twenty minutes later, we were in the air over New York City. The passenger cabin of the helicopter was opulent, designed for a queen, with comfortable, dark purple leather bench seats that reclined, an in-flight entertainment system, small bar, and very private. A secondary cabin for staff and guards was at the rear of the helicopter.

Theodocia, Lantos, Tommy and I sat in the spacious main cabin, which was almost as quiet as the temple had been.

"Are you the queen now?" Tommy asked, gazing up at me with his large, green eyes.

Shifting my gaze from the City visible out my window to the little boy beside me, I started to relax. We had taken off without any sign of danger. I wondered if Lantos were here for some ulterior motive rather than to warn us as he claimed.

I am, I replied to Tommy. Like his mother, he could hear my words in his head.

"Just like the cartoon?" he asked.

Just like the cartoon, I confirmed with a smile.

"Wow."

Seated across from me, Lantos smiled. "It's rare for such a gift to be passed down," he said to Theodocia. "Will your son follow you into the service of the gods, or his father's less honorable footsteps into the arena?"

"My son is none of your concern," she replied firmly.

There it was again. Another indicator the two knew each other better than I would have guessed. I knew the name of Tommy's father, but not his profession.

Why are we here? I asked, pinning Lantos with a look.

"I was about to ask the same thing," Theodocia said.

"As I explained, I'm not completely –"

"Fire," Tommy said. He had his face pressed to the window nearest him.

I instinctively glanced out my window and started to ask Lantos another question when what I saw beneath us silenced me.

We were high enough in the air to see the entirety of the city. From some point below us, around the same elevation as the smog, streaks of lightning and fireballs formed and flashed downward. They smashed into tall buildings and were followed by massive explosions, rendered silent by the noise cancelling insulation of the helicopter. First a few streaks fell and then hundreds, if not thousands, of bolts of lightning and fireballs barreled out of the sky. The City erupted into pockets of fire and smoke.

"I'm assuming that's why," Lantos said in a whisper.

Brilliant flashes of light pummeled the City as we watched.

"Mama," Tommy's voice was shaky.

"Move away from the window," Theodocia said hoarsely.

Tearing my gaze away from the surreal scene beneath us, I reached out for him and pulled the little boy into my lap. Theodocia twisted away from us to speak as quietly as she could into her mobile, no doubt contacting the royal guard commander in the rear cabin of the helicopter.

Everything will be okay, I told Tommy without understanding what we were witnessing. *What else did the Oracle tell you?* I asked Lantos.

He, too, appeared shocked as he stared out the window. "The end of the world. But I thought she was ... I mean, who would say such a thing seriously? And if it were true, how could she not warn everyone? She swore me to secrecy and sent me to save you."

Why? I asked. While I was considered one of the most important people on the planet, so were many of those in my company at the coronation ceremony.

"I've spoken only once to her, but I came away believing the Oracle says what she wishes and nothing more," Lantos said, meeting my gaze. "She does not need to explain her actions, visions or advice to anyone. She said I must warn you today, after your ceremony, but before the end of the reception."

And you agreed, even though it sounded crazy?

"We made a deal," he said vaguely. "Not one I care to discuss. I warned you in exchange for something I needed."

Lantos hadn't come here because he cared. Why this disappointed me, I didn't know.

"She said nothing more," he finished.

"It's not just happening here," Theodocia said. Her ear was pressed to the cell phone. With her free hand, she tapped the touch screen controlling the entertainment system. The televisions in the walls of the cabin lit up, each of them with a different station.

"... this just in," one newscaster was saying. "*The Gods Must Be Crazy* sitcom has been cancelled this evening. Instead, we'll be covering the events in New York. It appears as though fire is being cast from the sky ..."

"We interrupt *The Bachelor – Olympian Edition* for this important news update. Seconds ago, in Los Angeles ..."

" ...fireballs over St. Louis? Arty, where are the reports ..."

"... lightning struck down the world's largest statue of Zeus in Miami, Florida ..."

"*American Oracle* will not air tonight, though you can still vote for this year's winner online. Please stay tuned for an emergency message from this station."

Baffled, horrified and stunned newscasters struggled to explain what we were witnessing. Theodocia began flipping channels. On every station, across the country, news tickers and reporters were popping up on the screens with breaking news of the attacks.

I don't understand, I said as I stared numbly at the reports from around the country of fire and lightning falling from the sky.

"The gods have turned on us," Lantos said.

I looked from him to Theodocia. My mentor didn't disagree with him.

That's not possible, I objected. *Zeus himself attended my ceremony!*

"And brought with him the omen of death," Theodocia said. "I don't know what this is, but Artemis would never forsake you, my queen. Even now, I can hear her whispering to me to protect you. She promises never to abandon you. I can't think the gods would do this, either."

"Look at the city below. This is not the work of men, priestess," Lantos said roughly. "And you, little queen. Your Bloodline is cursed by the very gods who pretend to be your patrons. How do you believe them capable of enslaving ten thousand years worth of privileged, *chosen* rulers but not turning on the humans who disappoint them? History is filled with instances where the gods withdrew their favors and lashed out at those they were supposed to protect."

My mouth fell open in a gasp. Theodocia's sharp intake assured me she hadn't been the one to reveal my family's secret.

"How can you possibly know of the curse?" she questioned.

"I have my ways," he said. "What's important is realizing what's happening here. This isn't the work of people. The Oracle may have been speaking the truth when she claimed the end of the world is here."

His words struck me hard. I'd struggled not to begrudge the gods for the curse they placed on my family. Theodocia, ever a dutiful priestess, was constantly cautioning me against speaking out against the gods and advising me to control my anger towards them. But whenever I thought of my mother, who had been turned to stone when I was four, how did I *not* consider the gods to be cruel at the very least? How did I not feel fury towards them for forcing my own mother to abandon me when I needed her most? The older I grew, the more difficult it was not to feel that anger. I understood so much more as a young adult than I had as a child. Such as how unnecessary it was for my family to suffer and how any number of gods and goddesses could put a stop to the curse – but didn't.

And now? When they turned on the people I was duty sworn to protect?

I was a symbol without power. My royal guard was forbidden by the other members of the Sacred Triumvirate from growing to more than a hundred members. I had no ability to be the guardian I was meant to be and yet, watching the City I'd called home my entire life being destroyed by the very gods who cursed my mother, who cursed *me*, to an eternity of living death, I began to think Lantos made more sense than anyone else in my life at that moment.

Only the gods could destroy a city, a country, for selfish reasons. Only the gods could stop such destruction, if they chose to. I knew from my family's history that the gods rarely dealt with the consequences of condemning humans. If destroying everything suited them, then they wouldn't think twice about doing it.

The day I discovered my true fate, I had started to hate the deities, with the exception of Artemis. This night, that hatred was solidifying. How many of my subjects were going to be massacred tonight? For what purpose?

"Perhaps you will be known as the Queen of Death because your reign will oversee the destruction of humanity." The words were uttered by none other than sweet Tommy, whose eyes were glassy and face was blank.

The phone fell from Theodocia's hand as she stared at her son in horror. Lantos appeared surprised as well.

I recognized the possession of a god when I saw it and tightened my grip around Tommy, not about to let the poor boy be taken away.

Who are you? I asked cautiously.

"Thanatos."

Why are you doing this?

"I am here to collect souls and carry them across the river to Hades," he replied through Tommy's childish voice. "The underworld remains open, even when the bridge to our home is gone."

My brows furrowed. *What bridge?*

"The one the deities use to pass between our world and yours. The Oracle has closed it."

The Oracle's diverse powers were somewhat familiar to me from knowledge passed on by my tutors. Many thousands of years ago, the first Oracle of Delphi had been powerful enough to build a bridge, thereby allowing the gods and goddesses to move between our dimension and theirs. But I didn't recall my tutors discussing the ability for anyone to close the sacred bridge.

"This is godly vengeance?" Lantos asked.

"I do not know. I am only here to collect souls," Thanatos replied. He faced me, and I shrank back a little when confronted by the empty eyes of Tommy.

Theodocia managed to speak at last. "I swear by the bow of Artemis, if you hurt my son –"

"Your son is touched by the gods, as you are," came the sharp response. "You know I could not possess him if this were untrue."

Theodocia's face was flushed, and I saw the profound confusion in her eyes. As a priestess, she was duty bound to honor a god who chose to possess a body to pass on a message. As a mother, she wouldn't let Tommy out of her sight.

She was about to explode, and I wasn't certain if she'd cry or if she'd lash out at someone with the skills she'd been learning from training daily with the royal guard.

"I did not give you a blessing upon your coronation. I am permitted, I believe," Thanatos said, his attention returning to me.

Please don't hurt Tommy, I pleaded. I had never heard of a god possessing someone so young. Priests and priestesses were normally apprenticed at the age of eighteen.

"My blessing. Do you wish me to bestow it?" Thanatos repeated.

What kind of blessing? I swallowed hard.

"Death."

My pulse quickened. I looked at Theodocia and then at Lantos. Neither spoke.

"What do you mean?" Theodocia asked.

"The ability to kill and to become invulnerable to death, save by my hand directly."

I will not become the Queen of Death, I replied. *I am already immune to death, am I not?*

"You are. Look upon the City, heiress to the Bloodline, and tell me you do not wish for the ability to bring those responsible to justice."

"You want her to take on the gods? You cannot put that kind of responsibility on a child!" Theodocia exclaimed. "And besides, it's blasphemy to speak of such things!"

I am not a child, I argued. *And I bear the gods no good will, not after tonight. These are my people, Theodocia. I am supposed to protect them.*

"But you weren't born for revenge. You were born to lead and to protect! Thanatos is too quick to offer you the blanket ability to commit murder in whose name? His?" She shook her head. "The Bloodline monarchs are guardians, not mercenaries. If this is truly an attack led by the gods, then who else will humanity have to turn to but the one woman who can bridge the gods and us? Thanatos must have some ulterior motive to offer you this!"

Theodocia's dose of truth was as welcome as it was troubling. I was groomed to lead, to balance compassion and necessary action, to act as a mediator between heaven and earth, and to focus on my duty as a reigning monarch first and foremost in every situation. What did a queen do in this situation, when the gods were attacking her people, and she had no army to defend them?

What did I do, if Theodocia was right, and Thanatos' offer was born of some hidden agenda, one that might serve the pantheon of which he was a member, rather than help me as he claimed he wanted to?

"A queen has many difficult choices to make. This is but the first," Lantos said quietly.

I studied Theodocia, wishing we had some privacy so we could openly discuss my options. In truth, I felt like I had none at all. The feeling of helplessness was overwhelming. This was my first day as the queen – and I was failing the ultimate test.

What good am I, if I can't protect my own people? Can't stop the gods who favor me? I asked her, hoping no one else heard my desperation.

"We don't know that you can't mediate between them," she replied. "Someone decided to save you. This, to me, means you have the favor of the gods still."

"The Oracle sent me, not the gods. It's foolish to assume anything when it comes to them," Lantos pointed out. "Thanatos is sharing his power over death. Take his offer, Phoibe."

"No," Theodocia said quickly.

The two began a heated discussion, and I tuned out to gaze down at the blazing city below us. In a matter of minutes, most of the city was destroyed or burning. If the gods could do this to New York, what would they do to the rest of the country? The world? Even if I accepted Thanatos' gift, what was one person against the wrath of the gods? How did I stop them?

At one time, my ancestors ruled over the known world and controlled vast armies whose goals were to conquer and then to defend all they'd taken.

Thanatos' gift, while useful, wasn't going to stop the gods from destroying everything I'd ever known or from taking someone else I cared about away from me. My ancestors had the power to protect those they loved and the lands they possessed. I had wealth built up over thousands of years, influence over mortals and was favored by the gods. How did I turn what I did have into what I would need to protect my family, my people?

How did I stop the people I loved most from suffering? My eyes drifted back to Theodocia. I'd lost my mother when I was four. I couldn't lose the woman who righted my world, whose arms I'd collapsed into and sobbed the first day we met. There were thousands of children who had a Theodocia in their lives, someone they loved with all their hearts.

The gods were taking their mothers away, too, right before my eyes, on the first night of my reign, and I could do nothing to stop them.

My forefathers and foremothers commanded great armies. It was how the balance used to be kept. The gods never did anything like this when my ancestors were in power. Why can I not do the same? I asked.

Theodocia and Lantos fell silent.

"What are you saying? You want to take over some country's military?" Lantos asked after a pause.

Is it not in my blood to rule? To conquer? To protect?

"Phoibe, you're smart, and you're the heiress to the Bloodline.

But heading an army? What do you know of such a feat?" Lantos asked. "Whose army would you take over? No country would just hand control of their military to you!"

Then we build our own army. We find every person who lost a loved one this night, every person who wants revenge and who is angry at the gods. I replied. *We ask them to fight for me, to seek revenge against those who did this to us.*

"You're better off accepting Thanatos' gift."

Why else was I spared, if I'm not destined to right this wrong? I frowned, my face growing warm in quiet anger.

"You don't get a vote here," Theodocia snapped at him. She tilted her head and closed her eyes. I recognized her stance. She was listening to Artemis. When Theodocia's eyes opened, she appeared puzzled. "Artemis says the queen must be the one to decide our course of action." She was frowning. "Phoibe, please. Do not accept Thanatos' gift. You know the gods give nothing without requiring something in return. The Bloodline has suffered enough."

She was right in every way. I leaned back against my seat, pensive. To accept Thanatos' blessing was to make my already hellish destiny worse without offering me what I needed now: the ability to stop the destruction of humanity. The gods were not benevolent; they were calculating, and they did nothing without reason.

"Give me the gift," Theodocia said in a hushed voice. "I will become the sword of your vengeance."

I hadn't thought of this option – but I liked it almost immediately. Theodocia would be immortal, alongside me. We'd be together until Thanatos decided otherwise. I wouldn't fear losing her.

But you might be made to kill, I objected. *You know nothing of what it means to bear the curse accompanying a gift from the gods.*

"I won't let you suffer more than you already do, Phoibe. I would do anything for you. For Tommy. For Artemis," she replied. "If Thanatos' gift means I can defend my children, and help you protect humanity, then I will gladly bear whatever curse I must."

My children. She considered me one of her own. My gaze misted over at the inclusion.

"I do this of my own free will, Phoibe. Let me help you."

You have always helped me, I responded. Indecision kept me from accepting her offer outright.

"Let it be so," Thanatos said via Tommy.

I didn't object. I was torn. If I could have prevented the curse from taking my mother, I would have. But the order to stop Theodocia would not form, and I knew the selfish reason why. If we were both immortal, I would never be abandoned again. I'd never lose her if she were protected by death from Death.

Crippled emotionally from a young age by my fear of abandonment, I didn't know what to do when faced with a situation that might guarantee the person I loved most in the world would always be with me.

Tommy stretched out a hand to his mother. She obediently knelt before the possessed child. He traced the symbol of an inverted torch onto her forehead, and then Tommy slumped back against me, released from the clutches of the god.

Uncertain this was the right course of action, I hugged him hard and buried my face into his shirt. The little boy was quaking and breathing erratically. He blinked rapidly and clutched at my arm.

You're okay, Tommy. I promise. I won't let anyone hurt you.

A rush of air filled the cabin, accompanied by the scent of smoke and burning metal.

I lifted my head in time to see Theodocia shoving Lantos out of the helicopter and into the dark night sky. With a gasp, I watched him disappear. I stared at my guardian as she closed the door.

She sat heavily, her hands shaking.

What have you done? I asked.

"He's a demigod. He's not dead," she replied. "And if he is, it wouldn't matter. He will betray you, Phoibe. He is the worst kind of man."

I studied her, uncertain what kind of changes to expect from someone bearing the touch of Thanatos and wondering if her callous act and words were caused by Thanatos or her history with Lantos.

"Artemis said the same thing Lantos did, that the gods are angry, because the Oracle has trapped them here. But she said there is too much happening for her to know the full truth, and that we must act in a way that will position you to challenge the gods one day."

In the same way as my ancestors? I asked, genuinely surprised the goddess would approve of an idea to challenge her and the other deities.

"I don't know how else it would be possible," Theodocia replied. She held out her arms for Tommy. He crossed to her and crawled into her lap.

How do we build an army to challenge the gods?

"I don't know." Theodocia shook her head. "Artemis said to take you to DC, which is under the protection of Zeus, so that's where we're headed. We need to reach safety first and figure out where to go from there."

Did you really just throw someone out of a helicopter? I asked in delayed shock.

Theodocia glanced at me then at the door. "Yeah." She, too, seemed baffled. "I'm not sure what came over me. I wanted him gone, and so ... I threw him out."

Because you wanted to or because Thanatos' blessing did something to you?

"I'm not sure."

I didn't say what I was thinking, that she'd disliked a great many people before this without throwing them out of helicopters. Not only that, but she'd done it in front of her son, who she was normally extremely protective of.

It was possible Thanatos' gift had a side effect of dulling her sense of compassion. The God of Death was known for having absolutely no mercy. He claimed the lives of deities, demigods, and humans with the same unbiased zeal. I didn't know how his blessing would affect Theodocia, but I was definitely going to keep an eye on her from here on out.

She hugged Tommy and slumped back against her seat. There were lines around her eyes and mouth, and her breathing was shallow, quick. She was too strong to show the depths of her worry, but I sensed it nonetheless. I *felt* her building panic and clenched my hands in my lap. I was too wired even to notice the weight of my crown anymore. I was too worried to dwell on Lantos' fate. The friend I remembered as a child had to have been my imagination, because the man who came to warn me was nothing like him. The sense of loss I experienced when he left me seven years ago was missing, replaced by emotions I was having trouble controlling.

The world was crumbling around us.

Nothing seemed real except for my anger at the gods. A piece of me was vindicated to know I wasn't alone in feeling forsaken, but mainly, I couldn't stop thinking about how I was supposed to protect humanity against all-powerful deities when I had no means to do so. My ancestors would be appalled and ashamed to know the Bloodline had been reduced to a ceremonial, symbolic, useless entity at the mercy of lying politicians in whichever country had the mightiest military. Greece had not been relevant on the world stage in a thousand years. Despite being directly linked to the gods, its monarchy was a sign of the past, a piece of living history, in the minds of most people.

Maybe it was time for that to change. Maybe, by defeating the gods, I'd save those who came before me, as well as those who succeeded me, from the living death that awaited the heirs and heiresses of the Bloodline.

But how did anyone challenge a god?

As the helicopter took us closer and closer to DC, Theodocia and I could only stare at the television monitors. We watched, entranced, as the widespread destruction of cities spread from the US to other countries around the world. She was on the phone for almost the entirety of our trip. Each time she hung up, her phone rang seconds later, and she was once again speaking to someone else about what was happening. I half-listened to her terse voice as she coordinated our arrival with my security team and responded to the inquiries and reports from the offices of other government officials. My own staff in New York had yet to check in, though the skeleton crew we kept at the DC palace reported they were safe.

Finally, Theodocia turned the ringer off and threw the phone onto the bench beside me. My most trusted friend and advisor doubled over and covered her face with her hands in a rare sign of being overwhelmed.

"Mama?" Tommy asked, going to her. "Are you okay?"

"Yes, baby," she whispered.

But she wasn't, and even Tommy knew it. He sat down beside her and rested his head against her shoulder. I waited for her to share what else she'd learned from the latest round of calls.

"It's worldwide," she said at last and sat back. Her eyes were bloodshot from stress. "Every world leader in attendance at your coronation was wiped out, including the Supreme Magistrate, Supreme Priest and the highest ranking military officials. There's no one to declare martial law. Everything is ... breaking. Social order, first response efforts, the country's infrastructure. Everything."

I listened in rapt horror, once again drawing a blank about how I was supposed to carry out my duty and obligations to the world.

"Zeus is protecting a corridor along the eastern seaboard encompassing Maryland, DC, NOVA and the rest of the metro area," Theodocia continued. "But the city itself is barely staying on this side of chaos."

Would there be anyone left to challenge the gods by the time this attack on humanity was over? Was I already too late to protect those I could? Familiar, deep-seated fury kept my mind focused on what was happening.

"We're about thirty minutes from landing. DC airspace has been declared a dead zone. The military commander I spoke to gave us permission to fly to your palace and the SISA commander charged with internal security in DC flat out refused. But, technically, he has no say, since the military is monitoring the airspace around DC," Theodocia added with a sigh. "I'm afraid if we fly in, someone will shoot us down, because the two entities aren't on the same page. I don't know what to do, Phoibe."

What does Artemis advise? I asked.

"She's not responding at the moment. Her last words were to go to DC, and she'd protect you. Her silence leads me to believe we might be on our own."

How can she offer to protect us when her brothers and sisters are destroying everything? I asked in frustration.

"This isn't a question we have time to try to answer," Theodocia responded. "Our biggest concern is how we're going to get you to safety. Do we attempt crossing into DC airspace and hope the military and SISA are talking, or do we land outside the protected area and pray we aren't burned alive by lightning and fire?"

We go as far as we can in the helicopter, I replied. *This makes the most sense to me.*

"Me, too. It's also potentially the most dangerous course of action." She picked up the phone connecting the cabin to the pilots. "Take us straight in as originally planned. Do what you can to avoid detection," she said to the pilot.

She hung up and leaned down to grab the bag she'd brought with her and set it beside me.

"In case things get messy, you can't run in that," she said and lifted her eyebrows towards my dress. "Come here, Tommy. Let the queen change clothes in privacy."

Both of them turned away, and I stood. Three servants had helped me into the extravagant ceremonial garb. I wriggled, maneuvered, tugged and ended up accidentally ripping the silk bodice and at least one layer of skirts. When I was free, I breathed deeply for the first time in several hours and then changed into the more practical clothing Theodocia had brought with her. I pulled on the slacks and long-sleeved sweater before sliding my feet into shoes. I didn't want to think about what might happen if we had to make a run for it.

I carefully removed my crown and wrapped it in the layers of my dress and then tucked it into the bag, next to the scepter.

Finished. I said.

"The fire's stopped," Theodocia said in a hushed tone.

I leaned forward to see out the window. The lights of DC were brilliant in the clear skies ahead of us. Behind us, fire and lightning continued to rain down upon the rest of the country. The helicopter began to descend until it was skimming the tops of the tallest trees of the forests of northern Maryland.

The phone linking the cockpit and the cabin rang. Theodocia grabbed it and listened for a few seconds.

"Seatbelts," she said. "Pilot says it might get a little rough." She hung up and quickly strapped in Tommy then herself.

I tugged on my seatbelt, too. Heart hammering, I then stared out the window, watching DC grow closer and closer and praying we made it to the palace in safety.

The pilot began to alter our course and elevation with speed that made my stomach turn. Tommy laughed at the jolts and sudden turns while Theodocia and I exchanged looks of worry.

Just as we reached the northern most part of the city, the helicopter ascended suddenly and fast enough for the air to feel like it was starting to crush me before we stabilized. Theodocia gripped her seatbelt, and I was braced against the cabin door.

Flashes of fire appeared again. This time, they weren't falling from the sky but originating from the ground into the air and heading straight for us.

The helicopter pitched to the right, careening until my window faced directly down at the ground and I was kept from face planting against the door by my seatbelt.

Theodocia! I said, alarmed. *This isn't working!*

"Damn SISA!" She stretched for the phone to the cockpit. "We're going back to - "

Before she could finish or order the pilot out of DC airspace, an explosion ripped through the tail end of the helicopter. Fire licked the outside of my window, and the scent of jet fuel filled the cabin. The window beside Theodocia cracked and then shattered, spraying us with glass that cut our exposed skin.

The helicopter started to free fall into a downward spiral and plummeted towards the city below. The sickening sensation of tumbling out of the sky was made worse by my inability to tell which direction I faced or how close we were to smashing into the ground. Pain radiated through me as the seatbelt snapped me back against the seat. I couldn't move, and the scenery outside the cabin became a dizzying blur of night-city-night-city, over and over.

With each rotation of the cabin, my head was flung from side to side, and I smashed it into the window at least twice before I started to lose consciousness. The bag containing my crown and scepter smashed into me on one round, into Tommy on another, then into the walls, windows and floor.

Tommy was sobbing, Theodocia shouting, and the city below quickly growing closer. Someone – was it me? – was screaming.

My body went limp of its own accord as I struggled to remain awake and aware. Our crash was inevitable, and it wasn't possible for any of us to survive impact. I fought the darkness fighting to pull me under, despair and fury filling me.

In that moment, the meaning of Thanatos' appearance in my life struck me with more force than my head smacking into the window again. The God of Death had the ability to kill without mercy – or to stop death from occurring at all. Perhaps the Oracle hadn't requested his guardianship in order to help me fight an enemy, but to prevent me from dying this night. She sent Lantos to warn me of the impending attack by the gods. I was saved, so I could in turn, save my world from the gods.

She wasn't going to risk letting me die here. Was this the grim future she had foreseen? The reason she chose him?

Thanatos! I screamed mentally. *Do not let us die!*

I tried to wait for his answer, but the dark edges of my mind began to close in on my thoughts. Pain radiated through me from too many places for me to count. My surroundings became fuzzy then blurry. In a brief flash of clarity, I saw the double yellow lines of a highway, close enough for me to touch, half a second before my world went completely black.

MERCENARY

I WATCHED the world burn with glee. Fresh off a paid mission over-seas, I had spent several years building up a reputation and career as a personal bodyguard for drug dealers, heads of criminal organiza-tions, mob bosses and anyone else who paid upfront, asked no ques-tions and didn't care how many bodies piled up. They were the only kinds of jobs I could find after my two year murder trial ended five years ago. I was acquitted – compliments of the politician who hired me to make the hit landing me on trial – but I was also blacklisted from any sort of legitimate employment anywhere, thanks to a Supreme Magistrate determined to punish my former employer and anyone who worked for him.

So when I saw the words, *Supreme Magistrate feared dead,* scroll across the screen for the fourth time, I laughed. I continued to grin as the news stations in Washington DC, where I lived, scrambled for coverage of what was happening around the world. Whenever they managed to grab a live feed from another city, it ended up flat lining once the other station was struck by the gods' fury.

"The gods show their true colors at last," I said, smiling. Earlier in the evening, the gods had begun to attack humanity, everywhere but within the DC area and Maryland, an area reportedly protected by Zeus. The newscasters weren't able to identify how far this safe zone extended, but they claimed Zeus' priests had contacted them directly and assured them that DC would be spared whatever wrath the gods were displaying across the rest of the planet.

My eyes glued to the television screen, I loaded magazines into the weapons I spent the past hour cleaning and piled my favorite knives on one side of the coffee table for a quick inspection before I left my apartment.

The world had descended into absolute madness. I couldn't conform to a society where my natural violent tendencies were condemned but this ... this was chaos. This was *me*. An environment where only the merciless survived? I was born for this! The fatigue I experienced from nine months overseas disappeared when I began to consider all the possibilities.

My cell rang, and I grabbed it.

"Yeah," I said gruffly into the phone.

"Good evening, Niko." The polished voice was quiet.

Wariness crept into my excitement. "What do you want?"

"Are you watching the news?"

"Who isn't?"

"Then you should know what I want."

I had been hoping this particular man had been killed by the gods. I squeezed the hilt of a knife hard enough for my knuckles to turn white. Setting it down, I leaned back and allowed the sofa cushions to support my weight. "Humor me," I said.

Cleon, the wealthy politician I allied with seven years ago, called when he needed my particular skills. We had a deal of sorts, one I wasn't able to buck, when he alone knew what to hold over my head to make me comply with his demands. The good: he called infrequently, and it had been eighteen months since we last spoke. The bad: the jobs he hired me for were rougher than any of my other gigs. All the scars I had earned since we met were from jobs I did for him.

"I thought you would be pleased to know the Supreme Magistrate won't be crushing either of us beneath his heel anymore," Cleon said.

"You never call to discuss the news."

"Very well, Niko. I try to make our exchanges pleasant as my way of showing you I appreciate what you do."

I rolled my eyes. It had taken me some time to figure Cleon out. I was constantly surrounded by men whose reputations for violence were a source of pride. I had developed a sixth sense when it came to people and surviving strangers. Like me, Cleon was a different animal. Brilliant, driven, and obsessive, he was also capable of generosity and kindness. He fit the description of a psychopath – except he valued the relationships he shared with a select few too much to be incapable of empathy.

He was complicated, and for some reason, he genuinely liked me, which was how I got away with what I often did when dealing with him.

"I don't need your shit," I replied. "Tell me what you want. I've got some looting to do."

"For such a talented man, you have such low ambitions."

"Bye, Cleon." I hung up but didn't put the phone on the coffee table.

In his circles, he was supposed to be diplomatic, indirect and politically correct, to the point no one was supposed to know what his true positions on anything were. I usually had to remind him once or twice not to play those games with me. I already knew what he was. Likewise, he understood the depths of me.

The phone rang again.

"Yeah," I said, answering it.

"This again." A flicker of annoyance was in Cleon's tone.

"We're past the foreplay stage, Cleon."

He released a slow sigh. "Half my personal security detail was in Florida in training this weekend. An opportunity presented itself I must take advantage of, and what remains of my personal detail is not likely to last until dawn. The city is a warzone. I'm not even certain who is attacking my convoy."

It was then I heard the sound of a gun report, followed by several answering shots and the accompanying shouting of men.

"If you are in the city and available, I would appreciate your support," Cleon said, ignoring the sounds.

I started to laugh. "You're in the middle of it, aren't you?" I asked.

"I am," the unflappable politician confirmed. "I may be in the need of an expedient extraction. Can you bring your team?"

"They're stuck overseas. But I'm here."

"It might take more than you this time."

"Text me your location. I'll see you in thirty." I hung up and tucked my phone in my pocket before strapping on my most light-weight protective vest. It was followed by various sheaths, ammo storage pouches, and weapons carriers. I had mastered the combina-tion of mobility and firepower after several missions overseas in hostile, third world countries. I paid an exorbitant amount of money for the bulletproof vest that weighed a mere two pounds and was an eighth of an inch thick. Everything else was custom made for my body, fitted in a way to ensure I could reload a handgun in seconds and also kick someone in the head as needed.

When I was ready, I checked the location Cleon had provided and then began calculating how to reach him fast. I wouldn't drive a car in this insanity if my life depended on it, but a motorcycle would be agile enough to maneuver through the chaos and carry me across the western part of the city towards his location, somewhere around Silver Spring, just inside the Beltway, at the border of Maryland and DC.

Leaving my apartment, I trotted down the stairs to the garage under the building and unchained my ride from the post I parked it next to. I walked it up the ramp leading to the street and paused. In the distance, first responder sirens screamed while the monotone blare of the foul weather warning system echoed off the cement buildings in my neighborhood. Otherwise, it was eerily still. No one on my street was out, though the lights in every building were on.

I slung my leg over the seat of my ride and didn't bother with a helmet. The police had better things to do than enforce the helmet law tonight.

My bike roared to life, and I took off. The side streets were quiet, vacant, and I began to wonder where Cleon's war zone was. It wasn't until I cut through downtown DC that I began to see the looters struggling to carry stolen goods down the streets. The police cordoned off the memorials and governmental buildings but hadn't yet barricaded the shopping and business districts – or the banks, which was where I would have been headed if Cleon hadn't called.

I skirted police barricades and walked my bike through crowds of people on the verge of killing each other to get to the money in banks and ATMs. DC was a political city where someone was always protesting something. I passed two large rallies, one whose speakers were condemning the gods and another whose leaders urged the world to have faith during the end of days.

On several blocks, the police and people were clashing, and the acrid scent of tear gas was strong enough for my eyes to water a hundred yards away. I tore down side streets when the main routes became too violent or crowded, stair stepping my way north. The closer I got to Silver Spring, the more I began to see the war zone Cleon had described. It began with a woman sobbing over the lifeless body of a man in the middle of the street.

I followed the trail of bodies riddled with bullet wounds until I heard the active sounds of gunfire ahead.

Rather than plough into it, I hid my bike among the bushes of a small park and darted into the nearest apartment building, taking the stairs two at a time as I went to the roof. When I reached the top, I trotted to the nearest corner to scout what obstacles were in my path.

It looked like a tsunami was poised at the northwestern side of the city. Instead of water, the wave about to hit the city was made up of people and vehicles. They jammed the roads, neighborhoods, and every inch of space between them in order to seek refuge inside of Zeus' protected city. The military had set up barricades and armored vehicles, the police riot gear, and they were both struggling either to slow or stop the surge of refugees pouring into a city already on the brink of collapse.

In addition, flashes of light from the muzzles of weapons and the report of rifles, as well as the occasional boom from a bigger gun - possibly from one of the armored vehicles - originated from a point just north of where Cleon claimed to be. Floodlights blazed along the edges of DC. The Beltway, and every other road leading into the city, was a parking lot.

To the north, in Maryland, the skies were clear as far as I could see, but to the west, over Virginia, from the direction the people came, fire rained down from the heavens to burn everything it touched to the ground. Everything within the Beltway was safe. I judged the firestorms in Virginia to be maybe thirty miles away, outside the Metro DC area.

Adrenaline surged through me, and I stood, mesmerized and grinning, as I watched the world outside of the DC area end. How Cleon could find any opportunity in this disaster, I had no idea. But the man was smart enough to capitalize on any chance he found to better his position, especially now that his primary complication – the Supreme Magistrate – was dead. Something here had caught his attention for him to travel from the relative safety of his home in northern Maryland to the city.

My phone rang, and I answered it. I was about to snap at him and tell him I was almost there when a scared, young voice spoke first.

"Mommy won't wake up."

The words, or perhaps the voice, yanked me out of my near-giddy state. Turning away from the chaos, I fought the sudden tension of my body. My chest tightened, and my free hand clenched in a fist. My primal side had already figured out what took me a full ten seconds to register.

"Sh...she said ... if I got in trouble to call ... this number," the child on the other end of the call was starting to cry.

"Tommy?" I whispered.

"Y...yes. Can you ... help us?"

Everything.

Just.

Stopped.

The voice belonged to my son, a six year old boy I had never met or spoken to before this night, a child I had willingly given up so he wouldn't be infected by the sickness that ran in my family full of lunatics.

I stood, frozen, barely able to breathe, as I began to understand the larger picture of what the apocalypse meant for me. Cleon would have known this at once, but I usually only saw what was in front of me. New York, the first city hit by the gods, was where my ex and my son lived. I should have realized their danger the second I heard the city had gone up in flames.

"Where are you?" I asked after a long silence, where I was trying to figure out how the hell I was going to make it up the eastern seaboard to New York without being fried by the gods.

"I don't know." Tommy started crying harder.

"Hold one. Don't hang up," I told him.

I lowered the phone from my ear and swiped through the screens until I came to a phone locator app. I had no shame; I wasn't embarrassed to admit I put a hidden tracking application on the phone of my ex, Theodocia, when I sent it to her. My merc jobs did more than fund my weapons and armor purchases; they also provided a financial cushion for my son in the form of a trust my ex had access to. As a High Priestess, she was supposed to give up luxuries and live on a small stipend that wouldn't buy her a daily coffee in New York. In addition to the trust, I sent her money monthly so she could take care of our son, and once a year, a new phone, because I knew she would never buy one for herself.

"You still there?" I called to Tommy.

"Y... yes."

I waited for the app to show me where Tommy was. To my surprise, he was less than a mile from Cleon.

"You're in DC?" I asked, puzzled. I pressed the phone to my ear and strode across the rooftop towards the stairs.

"I don't know." Tommy's next sentence was so garbled from tears, I had no idea what he said.

"Tommy," I interrupted. "I need you to take a deep breath and calm down. I can't help you if you can't talk to me. Do you understand?"

I heard him panting in response as he tried to obey.

"Are you in DC?" I asked again.

"We were going to DC and our helicopter crashed," he replied.

"Who's with you?"

"Mommy." His voice grew tight again. "Phoibe."

The name meant nothing to me. "Are you hurt?" I asked.

"No."

I was imagining Tommy the only survivor in some sort of horrific accident. "Are you safe? Are there people around you or anyone with a gun?"

"No. We're ... underground."

I leapt down the last three steps and slammed the door to the apartment building open before trotting across the street. "I don't understand. I thought you crashed," I said.

"We did. We went through the ground."

I couldn't imagine what that meant, but I had his location. "Listen carefully. I want you to sit down by your mother and wait for me. Okay?"

"Are you coming?"

"I am. Right now."

"Okay."

"If anyone comes and they have a gun or scare you, you hide. Got it?"

"Y...yes."

"See you in a few, kid." I hung up, wired, and sent a quick text to Cleon telling him where to meet me.

This time, when I took off, I was filled with a sick sense of urgency, one that left my stomach churning and robbed me of all my former exhilaration about the chaos ahead of me.

I hadn't wanted a kid. Theodocia and I broke up when she refused to have an abortion and took a job in New York. She abandoned me, chose a kid over a life with me. I'd never forgiven her for it and never would, more so because she knew why I refused to have children. Mental illness, drug and alcohol addiction, propensity toward violence ... all of these ran in my family. Ran in *me*. My kid had no chance, unless a High Priestess and the best person I had ever met in my life could save him like she almost did me. I wanted it to be true that her goodness would be able to drive out the half of Tommy that came from me, but I wasn't hopeful. The men in my family were drawn to violence and died young.

Reminding myself this could have been anyone's kid, I wasn't able to rebuff the sick sinking of my stomach or why this – *he* – mattered when I had never met him before, and I didn't want him in the first place.

I rode until I reached a barricaded area swarming with refugees, the military, SISA – religious police – and the regular city police. If anyone were in charge, I couldn't identify who. I maneuvered away from this mess only to wind up in a second one, this one a full fledged battle between two well-armed factions: one hidden in buildings and the second a combination of SISA and military. The SISA-military alliance was brittle without the chaos around us. I doubted they'd be on the same page for long, and their turf war was likely to turn nasty once it did turn, more so since their commanders in chief were killed in New York.

I went around this battle, or tried to. The fight between the unseen forces and the city's protectors extended north, towards the Beltway. It ran for a mile. When it became clear I'd have to enter the fray to reach Tommy, I pulled off the quiet road I was on, parked my bike and straightened my weapons. Any restraint I would have considered in not killing government officials vanished at the thought of Tommy being stuck in the crossfire. SISA, military, or other – anyone who crossed my path was going to be dealt with the same quick way.

Cleon had texted to say he was close – and my destination was where he intended to go in the first place. I didn't care what he was up to or even if he made it to my location.

Armed and ready to face every kind of threat, I struck off at a jog towards the battle. I chose a quiet area to enter the contested street and slinked through the shadows, close to buildings, in the direction where the phone had been located. The closer I got, the more concerned I became. What had Tommy meant by *underground*? According to the map, he was south of the junction of the Beltway and Colesville Road, a major vein leading from Maryland into northern DC. The road was above ground at every point.

A firefight erupted in front of me between two factions stationed across the street from one another. Both were hidden in multi-story business buildings, and I waited for the exchange to end. More weapons began firing, and I slid back the way I had come to circle the building.

Chink. Cement from the wall beside my torso exploded into dust. My gaze snapped upward in the direction of the rooftop across the street. Someone had thought to place a sniper there, one who seemed to think I was his enemy.

Backpedaling, I dived for cover behind a car. Two more bullets pierced through the car and slammed into the cement of the building nearby. I scrambled up and darted for the alley, picking up speed as I bolted down its long, dark length. Irritated, I bolted to the next street over, where no battles were raging, and ran parallel, determined to reach Tommy's position the fastest way possible.

I stopped once to gauge how close I was and checked the phone before tucking it away and breaking perpendicular towards the contested street. The fighting here was worse, and I cautiously moved down another dark alley, unwilling to alert those in the buildings across the street to my presence. When I neared the end of the alley, I saw what Tommy meant. Part of Colesville Road had collapsed beneath a massive sinkhole, too dark and deep for me to see into. Debris from the crash littered the area around the hole, and I studied my best route of approach, uncertain how anyone survived when the chopper's engine was in pieces. The amount of force and speed required to shatter an engine meant it had plummeted to the ground from a high elevation or at full speed or both.

I counted fourteen active shooters, most with semi-automatic assault rifles, one sniper, and two with machine guns, on the other side of the street, capable of taking me down before I reached the hole. If there were additional men present, they were lying low.

Bodies littered the ground, all of them armed, all of them close to the hole. It hit me then that maybe those fighting were also trying to get to, or protect, whoever or whatever had fallen into the hole. If I had time, I could determine if one of these factions was protecting the hole and negotiate with them.

But I couldn't think of anything except reaching Tommy before someone else did.

Easing back, I listened to the sounds of gunshots and mentally reviewed where the various shooters were located. Of everything I was prepared to handle, rappelling was not one of them, which left me with one alternative: jumping.

I grabbed two shrapnel hand grenades and a smoke grenade from the strap across my chest and balanced on my feet. A lull in the fire-fight indicated at least one side was reloading. Pulling the pin on the smoke grenade, I launched forward and flung it to the edge of the hole.

I pulled a second pin and flung the grenade into the bottom floor of the building nearest me, then threw the third across the street onto the main floor. Before either went off, I was firing with my handgun, hoping to confuse my opponents long enough for me to make it to the hole. The smoke grenade went off before the sniper found me. His bullet grazed my torso and threw me off balance. I wobbled and then threw myself straight toward the hole, dropping into it just as a second bullet whizzed by my temple.

I didn't fall far and executed a perfect roll when I did hit the ground, bounding to my feet with weapons drawn and senses straining. A blue glow came from one direction, and I started towards it. Glass crunched beneath my boots, and I carefully stepped over chunks of metal and what remained of the helicopter. I expected to be in the sewers running beneath the street, but the area I was in was much larger, an underground chamber fifty feet wide with at least two tunnels leading into the darkness. It was too long for me to tell how far it extended beneath the streets.

The glow came from forty feet away, from behind a mass of either debris or partition six feet high and several feet wide. I crept towards it, listening for any sounds indicating the battle aboveground had found its way here.

I halted at the sudden, subtle scrape of metal against leather from behind me. Holding my breath, I heard the crunch of glass across the dark space to my right. If reading people was my sixth sense, my seventh was an otherworldly knack for survival. Killing was a highly effective tool to someone like me, one requiring unerring precision, solid instincts, foresight, resolve and lack of inhibition. Within the course of seconds, I was able to determine a dangerous foe from a harmless bystander, the distance and size of an attacker, how well he or she was armed, and the amount of force it would require to subdue or kill my target.

The dark required me to listen more diligently to my instincts, but I soon pinpointed the threat closing in around me as well as the danger ahead. I slid a knife silently from its sheath, double checked the locations of the men around me, and acted.

I threw the knife into the throat of the attacker across the expanse from me then whirled and dropped to one knee, firing my handgun at the man behind me. Both dropped where they stood before either could react. But firing my weapon caused a secondary problem. It alerted those ahead of me that someone was coming for them.

I was on my feet a second after I heard a cry from the direction of the glow. I circled the obstacle blocking me from seeing what was going on and immediately threw myself down to avoid someone's kick. Three men, all armed. I let my instincts guide me and tore through two of them, putting a bullet in the head of one, the neck of another and smashing the third in the knee. When he dropped, I snatched his head, twisted and snapped his neck.

Releasing him, I looked around for any other attacker, my senses trained on my surroundings. When certain it was safe, I straightened.

A boy with Dosy's dark skin and my bright green eyes was staring up at me from several feet away. He was crouched beside a wall, holding his phone, which was set to a blue flashlight. I had seen pictures of him before, whenever Dosy would send them, but he had never appeared like this: with dirt on his features, bloody clothing and an expression of fear on his face.

A strange feeling slid though me, accompanied by a memory from my childhood. Raised by drug addicts on a farm, I learned to fear adults when I was Tommy's age and how to kill a few years later, after my father used me to bait his fighting dogs. I had no good memories of my childhood, and my first few years were nothing but a blur of confusion, fear and honing instincts that somehow kept me alive until I was old enough to fight back.

Tommy was staring at me the way I used to stare at the adults who beat and tortured me. I had given him up for the sole reason that I feared becoming what my parents had been and transmitting our mental illness to him.

Seeing the scared look on his face, I realized, on some small level, I was not like my parents and never would be. I couldn't witness my son's fear and continue to hurt him or ignore whatever was scaring him. Everything I'd ever done with regards to Tommy had been to protect him from people like me, to prevent him from understanding or fearing the world as he did now. I wanted him to have a chance at a good life. In this, I was aware of how my influence might taint him, unlike my parents, who hadn't cared about the boy they didn't want.

I sucked in a deep breath and reigned in the indescribable, sudden fury coursing through my veins. Was I angry with my parents? Or with myself, for failing to protect Tommy from the night-mares of the real world?

Replacing my weapons where they belonged, I crossed to Tommy.

He cowered away, against the wall, his eyes wide.

"Hi, Tommy," I said and slowed my approach. I knelt in front of him. "You called me, remember?"

He gave a half-hearted nod. His hands were shaking.

"Are you hurt?" I asked again, eyeing the fresh blood on his shirt.

He shook his head.

"Where's your mother?"

He pointed towards the darkness, and I made out the mouth of a dark hallway nearby.

"Show me."

Tommy stood. He was trembling, but he didn't move as if he were in pain. After seeing what remained of the helicopter, I didn't know how it was possible for him to have survived.

I stood and followed him. Oblivious to the danger tracking us, he made more noise walking ten feet than I did my entire journey to find him. My senses indicated no one else was present, but I wasn't about to draw anyone's attention needlessly, either. I picked up Tommy and shifted him to one hip while I walked with disciplined silence towards the hallway.

I didn't have to ask him where we were going; another glowing phone lit up a room ahead, its light spilling into the hallway.

"I told you to stay by your mother, didn't I?" I asked him, irritated he had unknowingly placed himself in danger.

"I was waiting for you."

I glanced at him in the dark. "Next time, do what I tell you."

"But what if you got lost?"

"I'm a lot older than you, an adult, which means I won't get lost."

"But mommy gets lost, and she's old, too."

So she hasn't changed. I snorted. Theodocia was one of those book smart types who was often on some other intellectual planet and never fully integrated to the real world.

I walked into the small room, taking in the bodies stretched out on the floor. Theodocia, a teen girl, a pilot with his headset in place, and another man, armed and wearing an earpiece, were all unconscious and neatly lined up beside one another.

"How did they get here from the crash site?" I asked Tommy. Setting him down, I crossed to Theodocia first. She hadn't aged in seven years, and I checked her pulse. She was alive. Mild relief trickled through me, and I gently scoured her body for any injuries. She sustained minor scrapes and bruises but no other damage.

Tommy wasn't answering.

Twisting from my position crouching between Theodocia and the girl, I saw him standing in front of the doorway, clutching the phone.

"You're safe, Tommy," I told him.

"Are you sure?"

"Yes. I can handle anything that comes near us."

He didn't move. Sensing his distress, I pulled my smallest knife free and rose, crossing to him. I knew nothing about comforting kids and wasn't interested in coddling anyone, even my own son.

"Take this," I said.

He looked up at me then down at the knife.

"It's up to you and me to protect these people, including your mommy," I said gruffly. "Your job is to stand guard over there. This knife is magic. It protects you and anyone you're close to, so stay close to your mom. Understand?"

Tommy nodded and studied the knife. "It can kill people."

"Yeah. So be careful. Don't drop it."

Tommy obediently went to stand close to his mother.

I checked the pilot next. He, too, was alive, with no sign of major injury and out cold. How had any of these people survived?

"How did they get in here?" I asked Tommy, puzzled by the way the four were lined up. None of them awoke when I jostled them to check for serious injuries, which led me to believe they'd been unresponsive for some time.

"It's complicated."

"You're six. What do you know about *complicated*?" I looked up, amused.

Tommy was gazing at his mother, worried.

"She's okay, Tommy," I said.

He was quiet for a moment, watching me, and then spoke hesitantly. "Are you my daddy?"

Kneeling beside the teen girl, I felt for her pulse. My kid seemed smarter than I thought a six year old should be. Then again, his mother was brilliant, and I knew nothing about kids.

"Yeah," I answered.

"Thanatos said you would come."

"Thanatos?" I bristled. "That your mommy's boyfriend or something?"

Tommy giggled but didn't answer.

Agitated by the whole situation, I checked the remaining unconscious man and then stood back. I had two options: searching the dark halls for a way out and risking someone finding Tommy before I could return for him, or staying here until daylight, when finding a route to escape would be easier. I didn't care about anyone else here, except for Tommy's mom, who I didn't want to leave behind but would if the choice was between saving Tommy's life and putting him in danger.

One of the four unconscious survivors groaned, and Tommy darted to the side of the teen girl. "Phoibe!" he exclaimed. He scrambled on hands and knees towards a wall and then grabbed the handles of a gym bag. Dragging it back, he reached the blonde girl just as she sat up. "Look, Phoibe!" Tommy pulled something from the bag.

I stared at the golden crown laden with jewels.

"I saved it!" Tommy said.

The girl didn't respond. Her eyes were glazed, and she appeared disoriented.

Tommy placed the crown beside her and then wrapped his arms around her. Phoibe grunted but instinctively tugged him into her lap.

My eyes remained on the treasure worth enough to support me for ten lifetimes.

The creak of leather boots yanked my focus outside the room.

"Tommy! Turn off your flashlight!" I ordered him quietly. I snatched the phone left beside Theodocia and tapped the light app alerting others to our presence.

Tommy obeyed, and I crept into the dark hallway, senses trained on the noise coming from the main chamber. I stopped where the corridor met the large room.

Five men, possibly six. Drawing my weapons, I went still, listening. Whoever it was, they were well trained, their movements nothing louder than whispers almost too soft for me to locate who was where.

The sound of Tommy's sneakers slapping cement as he ran after me was jarring compared to the relative quiet of those sneaking up on us. Whirling, I grabbed him and hurried back to the room where his mother was, depositing him on the ground.

"Stay here!" I snapped.

"But –"

"Shut up, kid. Don't move from this spot!"

Before he could argue, I returned to the hallway.

My attackers were waiting, tipped off by Tommy. Before I reached the end of the corridor, I was ducking a punch. I launched into action. Close quarter fighting was my forte. Before I had been forced to sell my services as a mercenary, I had been accepted into the Gladiator Guild, an elite organization for skilled single combat fighters where violence was cheered on by millions of viewers watching on television.

With a knife in one hand and handgun in another, I tore through four of the men, leaving none of them alive to threaten Tommy, before I crept into the main chamber. Another four or five were waiting for me. I snatched the first, preparing to drive a knife through his eye into his brain, when someone spoke.

"Niko!"

I paused.

"Gods, man, are you trying to finish off the rest of my detail?" Cleon snapped in indignation.

I slowly released my grip on the man I'd pinned between my body and the wall. Easing away, I checked with my senses to ensure no one else was ready to attack or headed towards the corridor where Tommy was.

"You couldn't announce yourself?" I snapped in return.

"I texted you."

I rolled my eyes and sheathed my weapons.

"We don't have much time. Do you know how to get out of here?" Cleon asked, approaching me.

"Not a clue."

He barked orders for two of the remaining members of his security team to find an exit before addressing me again. "I find it interesting you knew to come here, the destination I was trying to reach."

"And?" I challenged.

"Did you find any survivors?" By the note in his voice, Cleon didn't expect anyone to have lived through the crash.

"Why do you care about a helicopter crashing?" I asked warily.

"When the gods made you, they replaced your brain with muscle," he said in rare anger. "I was tracking the Queen of Greece's escape from New York when I heard through secure channels that the military shot her down. The only reason I am here is to determine if she survived."

The pieces fell into place. Theodocia was the High Priestess of

Artemis entrusted with the duty of raising and guiding the Queen of Greece. I had only been thinking of Tommy from the first time I heard his voice.

"She's alive," I said.

Cleon's silence was one of surprise.

"C'mon." I led him back towards the small room with the survivors. Turning on the flashlight of the cell phone, I shone it towards the five. Tommy was back in the lap of the girl I assumed to be the Queen of Greece.

Cleon stepped into the room, his eyes widening. "How is this possible?" he asked.

I shifted weight between my feet, uncertain why I tensed when he entered. My gaze was on Tommy. I didn't care at all about the girl, and I shouldn't have cared about Tommy.

"Daddy, who is that?" Tommy asked.

Gods dammit, kid, I thought.

"Daddy?" Cleon's focus shifted to me then back to the unconscious men and woman. "Of course. You knew to come because your ex called you. You never mentioned she was in the service of the Queen."

Cleon had been using Tommy and Theodocia against me for several years. Whenever I was reluctant to take a job he sent me, he threatened to cut off my ex and son financially. Tommy's trust was maintained by Cleon's financial management team, and he dumped all my earnings from the contracts he hired me for into it. Cleon had always known about the existence of Theodocia and Tommy, but something about the three of them being in the same room together rubbed me the wrong way.

The teen girl looked up at us. Her eyes were sky blue, her slender frame borderline frail. She nudged Tommy from her lap and climbed to her feet, wobbled, and then straightened fully.

"Phoibe would like to thank you for finding us," Tommy said.

My brow furrowed.

Cleon bowed his head and offered a warm smile. "It is my pleasure, Your Majesty," he purred. "May I ask what happened?"

Tommy looked up at the Queen, waiting. After a moment, he spoke. "We were shot down by the military. Thanatos saved us."

"Who is Thanatos?" I asked, eyeing the unconscious man who appeared to be part of their security detail.

Tommy giggled again.

"The God of Death, Niko," Cleon said with a look of disapproval.

"Phoibe asked him to spare us, and he did," Tommy added.

I knew the name of a handful of gods but not this one. "Why would a god help you, if they're fire balling the rest of the world?" I asked the Queen.

Her gaze slid to me, but it was Tommy who answered.

"We don't know."

"You are very fortunate to be alive," Cleon said, impressed. "But we aren't out of the danger zone yet. We face a difficult time escaping, I fear. The city has descended into chaos, and I believe everyone in a position of influence is searching for you, Your Majesty."

"Phoibe says if you can help us, she will be in your debt," Tommy said.

I almost laughed. The girl had walked straight into Cleon's trap. The politician was feigning warmth and gratitude as he responded, but I didn't have to guess what was going through his mind. He had secured the favor of the most powerful woman on the planet, the only surviving member of the Sacred Triumvirate. His foolish trek into the war zone that was DC was going to pay off, assuming he survived.

I took up a position at the door, close enough to Cleon to stop him if he made any sudden moves towards my son.

"My most trusted man is on the job," Cleon said with a look at me. "You must be Tommy," he said to my son. He started forward, and I snatched his arm.

"Don't," I warned.

Unfazed, Cleon stayed where he was.

"Phoibe is worried about Theodocia," Tommy said. "Is my

mommy okay?"

Both Queen and boy were huddled next to the High Priestess.

"She's alive and breathing fine. Whatever happened knocked you all out," I replied.

The two exchanged a worried look, and I sensed I had somehow missed the meaning behind the question.

"She will be well, Tommy, I promise," Cleon said. "My men are looking for an escape route. Once they find it, we'll be headed to safety."

"Which is where?" I asked quietly.

"The central compound in DC housing the Supreme Triumvirate. Her majesty has a palace there, and no doubt, security."

I didn't understand the extent of Cleon's game – but I could definitely understand taking the vulnerable Queen to the one place in DC where she might escape the riots and chaos. With any luck, I'd have the opportunity to extricate Tommy from Cleon's clutches before then.

"Sir," one of Cleon's men called, moving down the hallway towards us. He smelled of blood and sweat and was panting. "We found an exit. Our enemies figured out we're down here. We need to move now!"

Before he was finished, I was at Theodocia's side. I lifted her and shifted her over my shoulder. Phoibe appeared scared, and Tommy slid his hand into hers as they stood.

"How many men do you have left, including me?" I asked Cleon and joined him at the doorway.

"Three."

I shook my head. "Can you handle a gun?"

"I sport shoot."

"Those are rifles, not hand cannons." I handed him one of my spares. "Close enough. Same principles. Now, let's go."

"Phoibe says we have to help the pilot and her bodyguard," Tommy said.

"Can the woman speak for herself?" I snapped.

"She's mute, Niko. Your son appears to have a gift to be able to hear her," Cleon replied. "You two, grab the pilot and bodyguard." He ordered the remaining members of his personal security team.

"They'll slow us down," I objected. "They can't fight if they're carrying people."

"If Her Majesty wants them saved," Cleon said, "then we will save them."

"Phoibe says thank you," Tommy said.

I strode out of the room, annoyed with Cleon's attempted heroics when I knew he didn't care about anyone but himself. "Tommy! Stay right behind me."

He hurried to follow, tugging the young queen with him. With both my mobility and line of sight severely compromised, I had to stay sharper than before. One of my arms was wrapped around Theodocia's legs, and I held a knife in the other hand.

The member of Cleon's guard who had scouted the exit moved ahead of me, burdened by the weight of the pilot and carrying no weapons whatsoever. He moved quickly through the main chamber, in the opposite direction of the hole. I trailed him through a narrow tunnel that sloped upwards before opening up into a second chamber of indeterminable size. Aware of Tommy clinging to my belt, I kept my senses trained on what lay ahead of us.

We raced through another hallway before the bodyguard ahead of me stopped beside a ladder leading up to a manhole cover. We were all breathing hard from the pace and weight of those we carried.

I set Theodocia down carefully at the base of the wall and scaled the ladder fast. The manhole cover gave easily, leading me to believe we weren't the first people to use it. In fact, the entire underground lacked the smell of sewers or mold or even dust and dirt I would have expected. Whatever the chambers and hallways were used for, they were maintained by someone.

Without time to consider the purpose behind it, I used my shoulder to push the heavy cover up and over until I was able to slide my fingers through the open space to force it the rest of the way open.

From nearby, weapons were being discharged. The skirmishing between both sides sounded close.

"Stay here," I called down to those below before leaping out of the hole. I scouted the side of the street leading into an abandoned neighborhood to determine the best route for escape. The gunfire and shouting came from the other direction, though I heard the signs of a battle in the neighborhood past this one as well.

The place was a mess. If ever I wouldn't roll my eyes at Cleon using his helicopter, it was now, when such a thing was probably impossible. If the military had shot down the chopper belonging to the Queen of Greece, they wouldn't hesitate to blow Cleon's out of the sky.

When satisfied we had a somewhat safe route away from the main battle, I returned to the manhole cover and slid down the ladder.

"Go straight across the street and hide behind the house on the left," I directed them. "Do not stop under any circumstances."

No one spoke. If they chose to disobey, it wasn't my problem, so long as Tommy and Dosy made it out alive. I picked up the body of the unconscious High Priestess. Cleon went first, followed by one of his guards carrying the pilot, the Queen, the second guard, and finally, Tommy. Balancing Theodocia, I climbed the ladder after my son.

He waited for me again, and we both darted across the street into the boarded up neighborhood.

"How far is the compound?" I asked Cleon.

"Far," he said. "Too far to walk."

"If you hadn't noticed, we don't have any other choice."

"You're creative with situations like this. I'm certain you —"

"Niko," one of the guards called. He had set down the Queen's bodyguard and was standing at the corner of the abandoned house we hid behind. He waved me over.

I lowered Theodocia to the ground and trotted to him, peering around the corner.

"Someone has been tracking us all night," he reported. He was one of Cleon's longtime security members who I had met during one of my numerous visits to Cleon's home over the years. I wracked my brain for his name.

Dimitris. I had never worked with him, but I knew his reputation as a good guy, not too ambitious, who never disobeyed an order.

Two black vans had rolled up after we left the sewers, and no less than a dozen men piled out of the cars, gathered around a central person holding a tablet.

"When did you notice them first?" I asked.

"Not long after we left the manor up north."

"Isn't it protocol for you all to check for bugs?"

"We did. Except for the boss's phone, since he won't let anyone touch it."

"Any chance it's something else?"

"No."

Ducking back around the side of the house, I strode to Cleon and snatched the phone out of his hands.

"They're tracking you through this," I snapped. I threw the phone as far as I could. "Any idea why?"

Cleon glanced at the Queen and Tommy, who were watching. He shifted closer to me, so they couldn't hear him.

"You know very well I have a long list of enemies. I haven't been able to deal with all of them," he replied. "I also doubt I'm the only one who heard about the Queen's accident. There might be more than one player with similar ambitions to mine."

"Two vans full of armed men just showed up," I replied.

"I'm sure you can handle it."

I clenched my jaw. If I didn't believe Tommy's life to be in immediate danger, I'd let Cleon wallow in the mess he created. As it was, I had sufficient motivation to do what he wanted – even if I wasn't happy about it. "I'll take care of this mess and then you're on your own. It's not like a trust fund will be worth anything now that the banking institutions of the world are being destroyed."

Cleon frowned, as aware as I was he wasn't going to make it far, if someone wanted him dead.

For once, I had the upper hand with him. Once the danger passed, I could take Tommy and leave – and there was nothing Cleon could do about it this time.

"Niko!" Dimitris called once more. "Thirteen."

"What d'ya know? My lucky number," I said wryly and drew my weapons. It had nothing to do with saving Cleon's ass and everything to do with giving me the best chance possible at escaping with Tommy and possibly Theodocia, assuming she didn't weigh me down too much to fight. We needed a clean break, though, to give us a shot at putting some distance between us and anyone pursuing Cleon or the Queen.

I joined Dimitris at the corner of the house. We observed the newcomers in silence. They were well armed and wearing body armor, which meant mainly head shots or, if I had time and space, aiming for the vulnerable areas in their armor.

"Dimitris, keep the others safe," I said quietly.

He looked at me quizzically.

"This ain't gonna be pretty. If something bad happens, protect the kid."

"Um, we stand a better chance fighting in tandem than you alone," he said.

"You've never seen me fight. You'll get in my way."

When he appeared ready to object again, I rested my hands on his shoulders.

"I'm not a team player, Dimitris," I said deliberately. "You heard about the Athens episode, where no one was left standing, attacker or ally?"

He nodded. "I heard it was a massacre."

"That was me. I don't play well with others."

He shifted away from me.

I smiled. "Stay here. Protect the kid or I'll make sure you regret it for however long I let you live." Satisfied he was sufficiently warned, I left him standing at the corner of the house and darted to the adjacent home.

With frequent looks to ensure the small force wasn't positioning itself to attack Cleon's exposed group, I raced three houses down, far enough away to draw the fire of the men and hopefully avoid the kind of collateral damage that would place Tommy in greater danger.

Sliding the rifle off my back, I settled on the ground, concealed beneath a hedge in need of trimming, and took aim. I squeezed off a round.

"Twelve," I murmured and then lined up the next shot. "Eleven. Ten. Nine."

Number Eight fired on my position before I could put a bullet in his temple. I dropped the weapon in place then ducked back around the side of the house and snatched my sidearm. One of the attackers was belting out orders. Gunfire splintered the face of the home, and I dropped to my stomach, waiting for the automatic fire to cease. It stopped about sixty seconds later, and I remained completely still and silent. At some point, someone would be forced to check my position and determine if the threat had been neutralized.

I waited for the poor fool they sent first. When he crept around the side of the house, I slammed a knife into the side of his neck and covered his mouth with my other hand to keep him from crying out. Lowering him to the ground, I waited for the next attacker.

And so it went. In the course of ten minutes, I managed to kill every single one of them. A few got in punches, and one grazed my arm with a blade. Otherwise, the battle was one sided as I did what I did best: unleashed indiscriminate violence upon everyone in my path.

When it was over, I snatched the keys to the vans from the two drivers and double tapped a couple of the attackers who had taken body shots. Wiping the blood of others from my features, I collected the weapons I'd left in the bodies of the dead, or on the ground, before returning to the group waiting for me.

"All clear," I said. My pace slowed as I approached. Dimitris was down, holding his stomach, while the other guard was dead.

To his credit, Cleon was huddled with the Queen and Tommy, his arms around them protectively as he looked from me to Theodocia. My ex was awake – and holding the knife I'd given Tommy. It dripped with blood, and three bodies lay at her feet.

I definitely wasn't expecting that. Sweet Dosy hadn't had it in her to swat a fly when we were together. How did she manage to kill three armed, trained men with a tiny knife?

She shuddered and dropped to her knees and then passed out, slumping to the ground.

"Mommy!" Tommy ran to her and knelt. He murmured something to her I couldn't hear. Phoibe went with him, shaken but on her feet.

"Did she do that?" I asked Cleon.

"Slightly less brutal than your approach but not by much. I've never seen anything like you two," Cleon answered uneasily. "She fought like she was possessed."

"Maybe that was the infamous maternal instinct." Curious, I was nonetheless done with putting myself and my son in danger and shrugged off Dosy's strange display. Now was not the time to deal with it. I tossed Cleon the keys to one of the vans. The other set I kept for my escape.

"Tommy." I waved my kid over. "We're getting out of here."

"Niko, wait," Cleon said.

I ignored him, not in the mood for his shit. I bent down to pick up Theodocia. Her breathing was rougher and she was bloodied. I'd worry about her potential wounds later. My goal was to leave before someone else tracked Cleon's phone and showed up with more firepower.

Cleon trailed me. "This is the new world order. Those in power are gone. The whole world is up for the taking, and I plan on being the one who takes it," he said. "But first, I need you to get us to the compound in central DC."

"Or I can be on the north side of Maryland by the time you make it there."

"And where would you go? The protected zone isn't that large, Niko."

"It wouldn't matter," I replied. "When this fire stops, I can go wherever I want."

"You assume the gods wrath will not take on a different form once their initial attack is over. This isn't a warning, Niko. They are determined to punish humanity for reasons I can't comprehend."

"I don't care."

"You should. Can you face a god?"

I hefted Theodocia. "If I have to."

"You're a fool to believe so and to put your son at risk if you try," he said firmly.

"Thanatos says we won't survive outside the safe zone," Tommy said in a scared voice.

"Don't tell me you talk to gods, too!" I snapped with more heat than I intended. "I heard enough of that shit from your mother."

Tommy gasped. "You said a no-no word," he whispered, stricken.

The Queen of Greece nudged him. Tommy looked up at her.

"Phoibe wants you to stay with us," he said.

I straightened and glared at the tiny royal. She didn't back down, as small as she was.

"I agree," Cleon seconded. "We need to stick together."

"I can protect my own son. I don't need you," I replied. "Tommy, come on!" I started walking away.

"For this moment, yes. But what happens next?" Cleon called.

"Daddy, stay with us!" Tommy cried.

The panic in his tone sent coldness streaking through me. I turned and saw him hugging Phoibe. I didn't care about Cleon or the Queen, but it was Tommy's refusal to follow me that stopped me in my tracks.

Sensing my dangerous mood, Cleon approached and paused a short distance from me. "You're too selfish to care if I tell you we have a duty to save the Bloodline, the only person who might be able to talk some sense into the gods," he started. "Humanity will survive in some form, and the new world order is going to need her alive. I plan on being at the top when the world rights itself. You stand to gain a lot, if you are at my side."

"Pretty big ambitions for someone who won't survive 'til morning on his own," I pointed out.

"You're right. I won't. Not without you," he agreed. "What if tonight we renegotiate our business relationship to make it more advantageous to both of us? What if I could protect your son indefinitely in exchange for you taking us all to safety?"

I didn't know why this question sank in so much deeper than anything else. I didn't want to be in charge of the kid's welfare. At the same time, I was determined to ensure he survived. How did these two warring ideas exist simultaneously in my mind? How did I want to protect Tommy while also shying away from the responsibility of ensuring he didn't end up like me?

The kid was turning out to be much more similar to his mother than I liked. Aside from the ability to talk to deities, both of them were capable of scrambling my brain and making me question myself.

"Big picture, Niko," Cleon pressed. "When we do make it to the compound, which we will, what do you think happens?"

"I don't care."

"You should. The highest level political positions in the world are up for grabs. Not only this, but the Queen of Greece is in my hands," he said loudly enough for only me to hear. "The sole surviving member of the Sacred Triumvirate. Think about it. In a week, with her good favor, I can have control of the military."

"For what purpose? There won't be anyone to command!" I said.

"Perhaps. Or maybe, come dawn, this will be over, and we can rebuild. The truth is no one knows what's going to happen tomorrow. In a week. A month. A year. Are you willing to put your son's life at risk outside of DC?" Cleon asked. "Or take a chance everything I've worked for is about to pay off, and you'll be on the ground floor of what I'm creating, with Tommy safe at the center."

In a different circumstance, where my son wasn't directly involved, I would have walked away. "You never do anything without a reason."

"I always reward loyalty, don't I? And smash those who betray me." A dangerous glint passed through Cleon's gaze. "What happens to Tommy if you aren't here to protect him?"

I tensed, sensing the subtle threat. Much of what Cleon said made sense. I was leery of leaving the safe zone guarded by Zeus and equally aware of what happened if I earned the wrath of Cleon. I had never had a reason to doubt myself before now, never had another life depending on my decision. What if I made the wrong choice, and Tommy suffered?

This twisting emotion inside me was another reason I didn't want the responsibility of a kid in the first place. With Dosy unconscious, I alone had to decide how to protect our son from gods and men like Cleon or worse – men like me, who would rise out of the ashes of the apocalypse because of their ability to survive, at any cost.

"With the old world order gone, there will be no one to scrutinize either of us. I can make you an official member of my security team. You won't be forced into the shadows anymore, and you'll never have to grovel to criminals for some dangerous, bottom feeder merc contract in some third world country," Cleon continued. "You want to be my official security advisor? The job is yours. Stable enough for you to keep your son with you, and you can assign as many of my men as you want to his protection."

Cleon was asking me to think about tomorrow when I never thought past dinner. My gaze settled on Tommy, who was standing a few feet away, waiting for us to finish our adult conversation. The Queen of Greece had one of her arms wrapped around him, and the boy clung to her. It was clear they were close, two kids stuck in an impossible situation, vulnerable to whatever the gods threw at them. I alone would determine which of the people before me survived the night.

Tommy's life was a given. It was less Cleon's pretty words that convinced me and more my fear of how the unknown might hurt my son. I had seen Cleon in action. I understood how deep his ambition ran. There was nothing he would not do to become the person he envisioned himself. If anything was left standing in the morning, Cleon would find a way to claw his way to the top. But was Tommy better off in the reality Cleon hoped to create or with me, away from DC?

The moment I recalled the firestorms I had seen outside of the DC Metro area, I knew the answer. I had a choice between two evils.

I glanced at the Queen. She was a pawn – but a powerful one. Even I understood why Cleon had risked his own life to come to DC. I began to see how Cleon might be in a position to offer what he promised.

Before I could respond, I was distracted by Theodocia tensing. I shifted one arm to prevent her from falling as she began to struggle.

"It's okay, Dosy," I said with a grunt. I set her down.

With reflexes nearly as fast as mine, she snatched the handgun out of my belt and pushed me back, pointing the weapon at my chest.

"Whoa," I said, not expecting her to react this way. True, we hadn't parted on the greatest of terms, but ...

... something about her was off. I studied her eyes. Her dark skin was crimson around the edges of her face, and her gaze was hard and glassy. She appeared fevered. If she recognized me, she didn't show it.

"Mommy!" Tommy cried and hurried towards her.

Theodocia turned towards our son, cocking the hammer back on the pistol as she did.

Something was definitely wrong.

I snatched her wrist and disarmed her. My second surprise of the night: Dosy fought back. Her attempts at punching and maneuvering my body weight to her advantage were calculated and fast. She was pretty good. Not as good as me, but definitely better than most.

It took a minute to completely subdue her. With one arm wrapped around her neck, I hauled her against me.

"What's wrong with her?" I asked the royal.

Tommy glanced up at her as well, as if waiting for an answer. None came.

Theodocia's body relaxed in my grip. Her breathing became erratic, and she clawed at my forearm.

"Niko?" she asked, sounding baffled. "What the hell are you doing?"

The sudden change in her left me uneasy. "I could ask you the same thing."

"You stay away from Tommy!"

"The kid's cute. I kind of like him," I baited her.

"Let me go!"

I did so warily, not lowering my guard until she twisted out of my grip and faced me. The anger on her beautiful face was normal, and fire blazed in her eyes. I had always considered her to be the prettiest woman I had ever known, with a face that matched the beauty of her heart. She hadn't changed since we last saw one another. Whether she was smiling or furious, her direct look always lit my blood on fire.

"You shouldn't be here," she snapped.

"Our son called me. I saved his ass and yours."

Dosy's anger faltered, and she glanced around, as if not certain where she was or why. Her eyes went to the Queen, and I guessed the girl was talking to her.

Dosy shook her head. "No," she answered.

"You must be Theodocia," Cleon said, approaching. "I'm Niko's ... employer. I believe I have you to thank for bringing us together. He fell into my arms after you left town."

"Left town," she repeated, one eyebrow going up. "Is that what he said? That I left him?"

Glancing at me, Cleon didn't try to use any fancy charm at this question.

"Well you did," I said, unafraid of the woman who tore my heart in two.

"You left me," she retorted. "After telling me to abort my child."

"*Our* child." I gave a half smile, genuinely happy to see her again, even if she hated me.

"He's not yours."

"I pay for him. He's definitely mine," I snapped. Any second guessing I'd been doing about my place in Tommy's life melted away. If she didn't want me to see him, I'd definitely be there.

"Shall we table this discussion for later?" Cleon broke in before she could respond. "We need to flee at the moment."

Theodocia glared at me a moment longer then turned away and went to the two kids. She threw her arms around both Tommy and Phoibe, who hugged her in return.

I watched, unable to take my eyes off Dosy or my son.

"Now would be a good time to leave, if you've decided to accept my offer," Cleon prodded me again.

"Help Dimitris up," I said. I reluctantly turned my attention to our surroundings. "I'll check the van." I started towards the vans in front of the house.

Dosy, Tommy and the Queen hurried after me, while Cleon wrapped an arm around Dimitris' shoulders and supported his trek to the van. I hopped into the back of the van. Cleon's enemies had left body armor and weapons, a laptop I threw out the back door and two cell phones I also tossed, in case someone had them tagged.

The others gathered around the back of the vehicle, waiting for direction.

"Put this on," I told the Queen and handed her a heavy, bullet-proof vest. Nothing in the van was small or light enough for Tommy, though. After passing out armor to everyone else, I stripped off my weapons and then tugged off my lighter body armor. I draped it over Tommy's head and belted it in place. I handed Cleon and the Queen weapons, ignored Dosy's expectant look then cleaned off Tommy's knife before returning it to him. A quick examination of the van revealed it had been professionally modified to withstand minor combat. The walls and windows were lined with bulletproof material, the gas tank reinforced, and the underside covered to prevent damage to the transmission and drive train from explosives.

"Your enemies are well funded," I said to Cleon. "Any idea which one sent a small army and mini-tanks after you?"

"Why don't we discuss the challenges of your new position at a later time?" he countered politely.

I said nothing. I wasn't convinced trusting him was the best idea, but I did want Tommy safe on some government compound where the teen girl could order anyone who came near him shot on sight. Whether or not Cleon would follow through on his promise, I sensed Tommy was safe with the Queen.

I climbed into the driver's seat and placed three weapons within reach on the passenger seat. The others climbed in back, with the Queen helping bandage Dimitris. Cleon gave me the general location of where we were headed. On a good day with light traffic, it would take forty minutes to cross DC. I didn't know how long the journey would be this night but was pleased to have a full tank of gas.

When the back door closed, I shifted into gear, about to start driving, when Dosy climbed into the passenger seat beside me. I eyed her then shifted the weapons closer to me, in case she had another weird episode.

She stared straight ahead, ignoring me, and I began to drive.

My gut told me to head west and then south. I stuck to side roads and went out of my way to avoid any area I thought might be filled with looters, first responders or military personnel.

"Tommy seems smart," I remarked.

"What's that supposed to mean?" Dosy snapped.

"That he got those genes from you."

She glanced at me.

"For the record, you did leave me," I added under my breath.

"Only because you were about to walk out on me. In my book, you left me!" she replied.

"We'll have to agree to disagree."

"Can this night get any worse?"

"It's definitely not how I planned to spend it," I agreed. "What happened back there? You weren't you."

"What?"

I gave her a look. I knew when someone was hedging.

"It's complicated," she said more quietly.

"Second time I've heard that tonight."

She said nothing.

"You almost pointed a loaded gun at our son after you murdered three men, or do you not remember that?" I pressed.

"I would never do either of those things!"

"Ask the Queen or Cleon. They saw you."

I felt her eyes on me briefly before she twisted to view someone in the back of the van. When she straightened once more, she was silent, frowning.

"You've got potential. You need a good combat trainer," I said. "I can teach you to fight better."

"I don't want you in my life! In *our* lives!"

"Too late for that," I said. "If the world is done, and we're both going to have to defend our son, I want to know you can do it as well as I can. You already know no one can get by me. You're the weak link here, Dosy."

She wrung her hands together in her lap.

I had no idea what she was thinking.

I drove in silence for thirty minutes. I was moving us closer to our destination a little at a time, doing my best to keep us off the radar of anyone and everyone.

"I don't want that," Dosy said through gritted teeth.

"Don't want what?" I asked.

"I'm not talking to you."

I glanced in the rearview mirror at the Queen, who was gazing intently at Dosy.

"Phoibe's right. I'll be okay, Mommy," Tommy chimed in. "Daddy's here."

Theodocia gripped her temples. "We'll talk about it later."

"What's wrong?" I asked.

"None of your business."

"How can you not remember killing three men?"

Dosy sighed. "Just drive, Niko."

Whatever it was, she was serious about shutting me out. I wasn't as upset as I thought I would be. After all, it had been seven years since we last saw one another. If not for Tommy, we never would've seen each other again.

I began to notice SISA roadblocks the closer we drove to the compound Cleon spoke of. I avoided several. However, it soon became clear the compound had layers of security extending outward in every direction, blocking any attempts at entering illicitly. We'd have to bypass the outer layer somehow.

Drawing to a stop in front of a set of barricades, I evaluated the ten men on guard, displaying SISA riot gear. Behind them, a block away, was an armored vehicle blockade with some serious firepower and beyond that, a metal gate topped with barbed wire and probably sporting some serious security deterrents I wasn't able to see from here.

"Cleon," I said. "This is an official blockade. I suggest, before I smash through it, you do what you do best and see if you can't get us in another way."

"I'll handle this," he said and opened the back door of the van.

I put the vehicle in park then leaned down to grab weapons, just in case Cleon's political sweet talking didn't pan out. He approached the SISAns with his hands up and began to talk. Several minutes later, one of them radioed back to someone else. Cleon remained where he was, and my eyes stayed glued to the situation.

A full ten minutes later, two armored cars drove through the second layer of blockades to us. Two men dressed in purple exited the lead car.

"Oh, thank the gods," Dosy said when she saw them. "It's the Queen's royal guard."

Cleon led them to the van and opened the back doors.

The two men bowed deeply to the teen girl. "We thought you dead, Your Majesty!" one exclaimed. "Praise the gods!"

"Screw the gods," I muttered under my breath.

Dosy slapped my arm before she got out of the van and circled it to act as the intermediary between the mute Queen and her guards.

Within seconds, everyone was hurried out of the van and toward the awaiting cars. I hung back, eyeballing the SISA guards who lifted their weapons when they saw how well armed I was.

"Hey, Niko, can I have the keys to the van?"

Dosy's question drew my attention from the nervous SISAns. "Why?"

"Does it matter?"

"If you don't want to tell me, yeah."

She sighed. "I have to go somewhere."

"In this mess?" I asked.

"It's important."

We stared at one another.

"I don't know if I'm coming back," she said in a hushed tone.

"Want company?" I asked casually. "I'm pretty good at surviving shit storms."

She almost smiled for the first time tonight. "No. If I don't make it back, promise me you'll watch over Tommy. And the Queen. We've never met the DC arm of the royal guard. I don't trust anyone here yet."

But you trust me to protect our son. "Done," I said. I handed her the keys without another word. I couldn't begin to imagine where she was going, but I found myself looking forward to spending time with the boy I never wanted.

Dosy pocketed the keys and strode away from us, back through the barricades, and to the waiting van.

I watched her for a moment before facing the car my son was in. I slid into the backseat beside him.

"Phoibe says we're safe now so not to worry," Tommy told me matter-of-factly.

I glanced at the Silent Queen on Tommy's other side. I didn't trust her any more than I did Cleon, although, she appeared to be fond of Tommy. If Cleon's plan failed, then maybe the strength of the relationship between the Queen and Tommy would offer my son some protection from what was going on outside of DC.

Tommy slid one of his hands into mine. The knife I'd given him protruded from the pocket of his jeans.

"What's this mean, Daddy?" He touched the tattoo of a winged foot displayed on my neck. It was the mark of Hermes, the patron god of mercenaries.

"It means people hire me to do jobs they don't want to do," I replied.

"Like dusting the house?" he asked. "Mommy hates that."

"Something like that, kid," I said, the corner of my mouth lifting in a smile.

One of the guards closed the car door, extinguishing the light.

"Will Mommy be okay?" Tommy whispered.

"Yeah," I lied. I had no idea what she was doing or whether she was coming back. I didn't think Tommy needed to hear the truth after his rough night.

We were whisked away from the barricades and towards the compound, everyone except Theodocia, who, for some reason, had somewhere else to be.

My hand closed around Tommy's, and I couldn't help thinking again about where I'd been at his age. There was a time when it was smarter to keep my distance from him; that time had burnt to the ground with the rest of the world. Cleon was right. We were on the cusp of an existence very unlike the lives we used to live where we had to learn to survive both the wrath of gods and the ruthlessness of men. I didn't belong in Tommy's life when the world was safe, peaceful and secure.

But in this world, I was the right kind of dysfunction to keep Tommy alive. I'd do whatever it took to protect him, even if it meant working for a man like Cleon.

SHADOW TITAN

THE GOOD NEWS: I was alive. The bad: I was in enough pain, I wished the fall from the helicopter had killed me.

Something was wrong, and it wasn't just the fact I was lying in the middle of a forest in Maryland with a broken leg and bruised body. Usually, when I put all my energy into it, I healed at an otherworldly rate. When I hit the ground, I'd been in much worse condition, and I'd managed to heal the worst of it – drawing off my Titan power – until suddenly, my body stopped repairing itself.

The forest was tranquil and dark, and I lay still, watching the stars slowly track across the sky, until the eastern horizon began to lighten. The moon lingered, though, as if to watch me in my torment. Not that I blamed it. I was certain it had some reason to resent me. Most people and deities seemed to.

Smiling at the errant thought, I shivered and grimaced at the pain even this small motion caused me. I healed from the inside out, which meant my organs and bones were fine. It was my skin and the muscle beneath it that hadn't had a chance to recover before my power stopped flowing. And my right leg, which had to have been close to shattered, if it didn't heal with the remainder of my bones.

As I lay in agony, I dwelt on how and why my power had disappeared. My father had the ability to restrain it, since he was full Titan and I only half. However, this didn't feel the same as when he dammed it. I was able to sense my power but not reach it when he sought to punish me. This time, I couldn't feel the tingling energy of my power at all.

"Adonis, where are you?" I whispered to my closest friend. I'd been staring at the heavens, partially because it hurt to move but also because I hoped to glimpse him flying by, searching for me, in his grotesque form, which he transformed into at night. He'd come for me, in part because we were friends. But mostly, it was because I was his god and master. He was honor bound to help me.

Assuming he could find me. In hindsight, I probably should have contacted him before leaving New York. I had gone to the coronation alone, leaving Adonis at home in the condo we shared in DC.

"No one's coming, Lantos," I told myself as dawn overtook the sky. With a grunt, I managed to sit and gazed down at my leg. I'd seen a television show once where someone injured in the forest had used sticks and rope to brace his leg. "Rope," I said aloud, my words heavy with sarcasm. "Why didn't I think to carry some, just in case?"

With a sigh, I rolled onto my left side and began to maneuver myself up to standing. Hot pain throbbed through my right leg if I shifted it as much as an inch. Finally, after a great deal of discomfort and cursing, I was on my feet ... or *foot*, as it were.

Lifting my head, I looked around. The forest stretched in every direction, as far as I could see. There were no breaks or structures or any other sign of humanity, only the cheerful chirping of birds and the stir of animals, as if they had no idea the rest of the world was likely destroyed by now.

I hopped. The jarring sensation sent bursts of pain through me worse than if I tried walking on my leg. Frustrated, I looked around until I found a stick large enough to use as a cane and very carefully bent on my good leg to retrieve it.

Walking was horrible, but I forced myself to do it. Choosing a direction, I began to hobble toward what I hoped was civilization or a road or something. I didn't go far at all before the muscles burning in my good leg caused me to rest.

Come on! I thought, anger bubbling forth from deep inside me as I thought of how I'd ended up here. I'd gone with mostly noble intentions to the coronation of Queen Phoibe, only to be thrown out of a helicopter by her High Priestess after assuring their safety. I'd hoped to dovetail my endeavor into something more beneficial to me. How often did one have the undivided attention of royalty? How often was one owed a life debt by a queen?

The wealth and power I could've asked for ... But I didn't have the chance, and now, I was probably going to die in this damn forest.

The reality of my situation hit me then with such force, the constant stream of thoughts in my head fell silent.

I'd gone soft over the past few years. I was raised on the streets after being abandoned by my mother, a human who hadn't wanted to deal with society scorning her for raising a demigod child. When old enough, I earned money as a street corner magician and used my Titan power to wow strangers for money. At one point, until my mid-teens, I'd been a survivor, someone who had lived through cold winters under the bridge and survived stretches where I was too sick or injured by thugs to beg for food and money. My wits, charm, and my power had made me successful, even before I found Adonis to do my dirty work.

I was the son of a Titan. A forest wasn't going to best me.

"You're alive, Titan." The disembodied whisper was strained and faint, originating from the air itself.

"Oh, so you haven't abandoned me," I murmured. "I didn't think I'd be able to hear you without my power."

"I'm using my power, what's left of it," she replied. "You did as I asked. I'm grateful."

I debated how to answer. The Oracle of Delphi had spoken to me out of the blue three days ago. She was powerful, if she could talk to me without being present. One of the perks of being the son of the

Titan of the Unseen – I lived in shadows and secrets. But she'd *seen* me somehow when gods and goddesses could not. She'd then tracked me down. I hadn't expected to hear from her again after doing as she bade me and warning the Queen about the impending danger.

I wasn't going to perish in the woods, but did I dare trust her intentions were good? I knew better than to trust anyone with supernatural power; they were generally arrogant and manipulative, same as I was.

"You can show your gratitude by driving out here to pick me up," I replied wryly.

"That's not possible," the Oracle said. "But I can alert someone to help you. They cannot be a human or a god. If you know a priest or priestess, or another demigod, I can speak to them."

"For anyone else, that might be a problem," I said with a pained laugh. "Adonis, my companion, is neither god nor human. He's not a priest or demigod, either. I'm not sure how to classify him, except he's half monster."

"Where can I find him?"

"Can't you locate him like you did me? Suddenly and in such a terrifying manner, I didn't sleep for two nights?"

"You are an odd man, Titan," she said.

Was she amused or irritated? I couldn't tell, except there was a note in her voice I hadn't heard before.

"It took me quite some time to discover you," she continued. "If you want him here soon, you'll tell me where to start looking."

I rolled my eyes then wondered briefly if she were able to witness the act. "He's at our apartment in downtown Chevy Chase."

Silence.

I waited a few breaths.

"Do you need more information? Or will that suffice?" I asked, unable to sense her in any form.

"That was enough. He's on his way to you." She paused, and this time, when she spoke again, I recognized the suspicion in her tone. "What did you do to him? His mind is dark."

"It's not your concern," I replied. "So you can see me when no other goddess can and peer into the minds of strangers at will. What else can you do?"

"There are few limits to my abilities."

"Meaning what? You're more powerful than a goddess?"

"My power is derived from this world, which gives me the home advantage."

Along with my curiosity about her power, I'd been trying to figure *her* out. At times sarcastic and other times compassionate, she was very much human and yet distinctly not. "Thank you for alerting my friend. Shall I assume you're contacting me for another reason, other than rescuing me?" I began walking aimlessly again.

"I have a second request of you."

I said nothing, uneasy with the commands issued from a person I could neither see nor touch but who could find me anywhere, anytime. I shared a similar ability but had never been on the receiving end of it. Was this what it felt like to others when I crossed their paths?

"You will visit me," she said.

It wasn't what I expected. I was more relieved than I let on. "That doesn't sound so bad," I replied. "Unless you're located some-where outside of the safe zone."

"I'm at its heart, in DC, on the compound belonging to the Sacred Triumvirate and their government."

My thoughts went to Phoibe, and I couldn't help wanting to know if she'd made it there. Why did one woman's fate matter to me? Her life had always been important to me, and I never fully understood being compelled to her. "It'll take some of my power to sneak into such a place. I imagine it's guarded by an army right about now."

Energy fluttered through me. I recognized the flow of my power. There wasn't quite enough to heal and turn into a shadow and travel through the dark parts of the world, but the pain in my leg began to ease.

"How are you doing that?" I asked, unsettled by the idea she was controlling me. "That is you, isn't it?"

"I am the bridge between this world and that from which your power originates. I'm allowing you a piece of your magic so you can do as I request."

"I don't want to be owned by anyone."

"Funny, considering I chose not to do to you what you did to your toy Adonis. I have the ability."

"It was for his own good," I replied.

"And yours," she retorted. "Do as I ask, and I can give you what you have long sought."

"A ride home?" I quipped.

"The kind of power and influence that will win you a place at your father's side."

She's good, I thought. "So I get what I want if you get what you want."

"Exactly."

I understood this kind of deal too well. I was quiet for a moment, wishing Adonis were present to provide his insight. Despite having his memories and mind mostly wiped, he remained by far the greatest strategic thinker I had ever known, and he had an innate sense for people that rivaled any god's. He was smart and ruthless. We worked well as a team to increase our wealth and standing in the world. At least, we had, before everything began to fall apart last night.

"Why don't we discuss it when I come to visit?" I asked at last.

"Agreed."

Gazing around at the green forest, I ceased hobbling. "Which direction do I need to go?"

"I can't *see* you in real time," she replied, amused. "I'm an oracle. I *fore*saw you and then traced the visions backwards until I identified a point where I could find and approach you."

"You foresaw me. I want to think that's a good thing."

"It's not."

My breath caught. "Care to elaborate?" I prodded.

"You're a key part of a prophecy I've heard referred to as the double omega prophecy by gods and men alike."

"Omega, as in the end?"

"Yes."

"I take it if it's the double end, not many people survive."

"I can see no survivors in the original vision, which is why I interfered. Now, the world will end twice instead of once, but at least there will be survivors," she said, sorrow in her voice.

"That makes no sense to me," I replied. "How does the world end twice?"

"It ended once last night. What comes later will be much worse."

This time, when I shivered, it wasn't from the wind or the pain. It was a twisting of dread and fear. "You saw me in the end of days." Among other things, that meant the end of days would occur soon enough for me to live through them. "If there were other survivors, why did you choose to approach me?"

"Among other reasons, you happen to be the enemy of my enemy."

I opened my mouth to ask more when her previous statement clicked.

"You said *you* interfered?" I echoed. "By creating a safe zone or by destroying everything else?"

"That is not for you to know, shadow titan."

I wasn't easily scared, but she had succeeded in frightening me. "I'll definitely be dropping by to see you. I think we need to talk some things through," I said with what calmness I could muster.

My mind was racing with conjectures and possibilities, half of which involved trying to figure out if this was the kind of woman I wanted to be associated with. If she had the power to destroy most of the world, then I absolutely wanted to be in her good favor. But there was also something to be said for keeping one's distance from the kind of power likely to consume anyone in its path.

Eager to be out of the forest, I put pressure on my hurt leg and braced myself for more agony. Pain spun through me – but it wasn't as bad as it had been. My meager power was focused on healing my leg. Using the stick as a cane, I began hobbling with more conviction in the direction I'd chosen, hoping Adonis was able to sense me when he was near enough.

The Oracle fell silent, for which I was unusually grateful. A social person, I always chose company over solitude, but her tale of doom was not one I felt prepared to hear. My entire life, I'd been trying to survive a world hostile to demigods and win over my father. I was never compelled towards any greater cause, never considered I might be part of something so much larger than myself. My ambition had always been to help my father seek his revenge against the Olympic gods in what ways I could. The one time I fell off this course, to save the life of Adonis, I managed to piss my father off, which made it imperative now for me to find the right way of winning back his favor.

In truth, I didn't want to be part of anything as large as the end of the world, unless my position as one of the survivors was assured – and I received the respect of my father, as I've always wanted. Even then, I didn't want to have to abandon my sole purpose in life. I was in this life for me. I wasn't interested in helping anyone else.

Well, except for Adonis, who had been my friend and companion for several years, and maybe ... Phoibe. Something about the kid had always struck me like the beam of a flashlight in a dark room.

I walked with what speed I could bear through the early morning forest, headed in a direction I hoped would take me somewhere where Adonis could find me.

"Are you there?" I asked to distract my mind from the pain.

"For now." The Oracle sounded even weaker this time.

"What's wrong? Are you ill?" I asked. "You couldn't have possibly gotten hurt in the attacks, since you see the future."

"You'll see when you arrive."

"I survive the double end of the world, don't I?" I asked cautiously.

"Ask me again when we meet."

It wasn't exactly an encouraging response. My jaw clenched, as much from the misstep her answer caused, as from the shock of emotions I experienced thinking about how I might not only die soon, but she had the ability to tell me how I *would* die. Now this was true power, the ability to foresee events and use them against those she wanted to manipulate!

Did I want to know about my own death? Did anyone? Was it possible to prepare for such a revelation? Thinking about it made my mouth dry and my heart race. All I could think about was all the activities I hoped to do that I hadn't yet.

Talking to the Oracle was starting to unnerve me too much to want to continue. I shifted my focus on placing my feet, so I didn't extend my stint in the forest by making my physical condition worse.

Some thirty minutes later, I reached a narrow road in need of repairs cutting through the forest. I paused to rest my leg and glanced both ways before deciding to head towards the southeast. I didn't know where I was, but I assumed Adonis would be coming from the south, and I needed to return that direction anyway.

The asphalt was easier to navigate than the forest. I used my cane to brace my healing leg and listened for the sounds of a vehicle approaching. I had no way of knowing how long Adonis would take to reach me, or even if he'd find me in the middle of nowhere, but I kept on limping down the road.

The questions I'd entertained all night, as I lay helpless on the ground, began to circulate in my mind once more. What had happened to the rest of the world? Was there anything left outside of the safe zone? Had Phoibe made it to safety?

Most importantly, *why* had this happened? The Oracle had seen it coming. Was I the only person she warned? Had the gods gone completely mad and begun attacking those who worshipped them, or were the events of last night something different?

The newest question only confused me more: Who was the enemy of the Oracle? Was she talking of someone I currently considered an enemy or one I'd gain somewhere in the future only she could see?

It didn't seem possible she considered the very gods and goddesses she devoutly served to be her enemies. The Oracle of Delphi was the most revered of all humans, and she sat beside the Olympic deities in a place of honor. I couldn't imagine her having any motivation to frame them for annihilating most of humanity. If not them, then, who? I had no real enemies, except those of my father and his people.

At long last, when I felt like I'd been walking forever, I heard the sound of a car approaching. I shifted to the side of the road and waited, leaning on the cane and anxious to be out of the forest and back to the world, where all my questions would be put to rest.

A black van with tinted windows came into view around a curve. I watched it, puzzled as to what anyone was doing in such an isolated location. If it were Adonis, he would have driven our car, unless circumstances forced him to steal a van. Shifting to the side of the road, in case it wasn't Adonis, I grew wary when it slowed and then stopped.

The window rolled down to reveal a familiar face, and I laughed, startled.

"You need a ride?" Theodocia, the High Priestess of Artemis and foster mother to Phoibe – and also the very woman who had flung me out of a helicopter – asked with such reluctance, I laughed harder.

When I'd recovered, I shook my head. "You've thrown me out of one vehicle. I'll take my chances on my own."

She sighed and looked away. "It wasn't entirely me who did it."

I grinned, always entertained by how the Fates unfurled the future. Theodocia had dark circles beneath her eyes, and her hair was mussed. Her air was strangely charged, an energy I innately recognized, because it was similar to mine.

"Does Artemis or Thanatos have you on a leash?" I asked cautiously.

"I'm honestly not sure anymore." She slumped against the

steering wheel. "Artemis helped me find you but Thanatos ..." She shuddered.

Studying her, I glanced around and made a decision. "Get out. I'm driving," I said.

Her gaze went to my leg. "*Can* you drive?"

"I don't trust you not to throw me out, so if you want something from me, then I'm driving."

Theodocia placed the van in park and shifted over into the passenger seat. I climbed in, relieved to sit on something that wasn't the ground, and closed my door.

It took some jarring adjustment, but I figured out quickly how much pressure I could use with my hurt leg as I turned the van around. Feeling Theodocia's eyes on me, I ignored her, more concerned with getting away from the damn forest.

"Are you upset with me?" she asked finally, as we drove deliberately down the pothole filled road.

"You threw me out of a helicopter. What do you think?" I asked with a faint smile.

She was quiet.

"I survived," I informed her and then chuckled. "I'm actually not mad, now that you returned for me. I've been dealing with your temper for a few years. We're like an old married couple. I may have been angry while lying helplessly on the forest floor, but I'm over it."

"I have the urge to kill you again."

"Thanatos' gift will probably make you more homicidal than you've ever been." It took effort not to smile at her misery. "You're going to need to learn to control those urges and either avoid or master yourself in situations where his influence over you becomes powerful enough to take over."

"Because I'm his tool now."

"Exactly. Except, I think he's given you some autonomy to use his gift for your own purposes as well. I could be wrong, but I don't think the God of Death had a vendetta against me, which means you've been harboring a great deal of resentment towards me if you came to the conclusion I needed to be expelled from the helicopter."

"I have been resentful, but probably not for the reasons you think. I am grateful for your assistance since you helped me find Phoibe," she said. Theodocia gripped her head in her hands and squeezed. "Artemis' touch is so gentle. Thanatos feels like he's constantly smashing a bat against my brain."

"I might be able to ease the side effects of his gift," I said slowly. "But it'll cost you. I may not be angry about the helicopter incident, but I'm done helping you for free."

She said nothing.

"Did the Queen and your son make it to safety?" I asked. Despite the often rocky relationship I'd shared with Theodocia as I mentored her, I liked her. She was fiercely protective of Phoibe, intelligent and powerful in the way of a High Priestess who held the ardent favor of a goddess.

"They did, thanks," she replied. "They're at her secondary palace in DC."

"On the compound of the Sacred Triumvirate?"

"Yes."

I smiled. "Assuming you can get us onto the compound, I'll help you. Now, tell me everything you've seen and heard about what's happened."

Resting her head back against the seat and closing her eyes, Theodocia obeyed and filled me in on what they knew of the state of the world. She calmed as she spoke. I didn't know if Thanatos' influence over her was relenting, or if the exhaustion displayed in her features was taking a toll.

She had nothing remotely positive to impart about last night and the state of Washington DC. If not for the Oracle's assurances that the compound would remain secure, I would have been worried for Phoibe's sake. But it made sense the Oracle with the foreknowledge had arranged for more defenses around the compound. After all, she was located there as well.

When Theodocia finished, I was both relieved to know the entire world was not doomed and apprehensive about the timing of the second apocalyptic event of which the Oracle spoke. The need to meet with her was abruptly forefront in my thoughts, ahead of seeing Phoibe again, and ahead of pursuing my own agenda to cash in a favor from a queen.

"Do you have a cell?" I asked Theodocia.

"I don't but I saw one in the glove compartment. It belonged to the thugs who tried to murder us," she replied archly and opened the glove box. She pulled it out and handed it to me.

With my attention split between the holey road and the cell, I managed to dial Adonis' phone with only two mistypes. As if knowing it was me, despite the unknown number, he answered on the first ring.

"Hey," I greeted him with a smile. "I'm safe and headed towards the Sacred Triumvirate's central compound in DC. I need you to meet me there."

"Will do," he replied.

"Are you well? Any problems last night? I understand there's a great deal of unrest in the city."

"Nothing I couldn't handle."

From another man, I wouldn't wonder what that meant. But coming from Adonis, the calm statement could indicate anything from he sat at home bored all night to he set fire to the entire block and massacred several dozen people. Adonis was the kind of friend everyone needed, whose loyalty was assured and whose methods knew neither conscience nor limits.

"Glad to hear," I said, amused by my imagination.

"You are hurt?"

Adonis' ability to read people never failed to impress me.

"I am," I replied. "But I'm healing up. Took a bit of a tumble last night." I glanced at the High Priestess, who pursed her lips at me. "I should be fine by the time you arrive."

"Should I bring your clothes?"

I hesitated, uncertain what exactly our situation would be once we were on the compound. After a moment of internal debate, the opportunist in me made the call. "Yes. Bring yours as well, anything of value you don't want left behind, and Mrs. Nettles."

"Got it. I will head there now."

I hung up, satisfied. No matter what it took, who I had to sweet talk, or who I had to send Adonis after, we weren't leaving the one safe place in DC.

"Mrs. Nettles?" Theodocia lifted her eyebrows at me.

I smiled and then laughed. It wasn't possible to explain to outsiders about Mrs. Nettles, who was too special for anyone to understand, until they met her. But she was a part of our dysfunctional family. She preferred Adonis but often trailed me around the house as well. "She's our ... pet," I replied.

My focus shifted forward. We were drawing close to a main road – and it was packed with cars three deep across the two-lane road while families carrying everything they owned trudged through the ditches on foot. Everyone was headed south.

"This is nothing compared to the Beltway," Theodocia said. She reached over and grabbed the cell phone from the cup holder where I'd placed it after talking to Adonis. "I had a military escort to get this far."

I eased the van up to the main road and parked it, listening as she called someone and requested assistance. My eyes followed the long lines of refugees heading towards the only major city to survive part one of the apocalypse, and I couldn't help wondering how anything could be worse. Complete annihilation – where no one survived – would at least eliminate suffering. The Oracle's mention of the double omega prophecy puzzled me. How could two apocalyptic events be better than one?

Theodocia hung up. "They want us to go two miles back the way we just came. The military lost a high value individual earlier when their chopper was overwhelmed by desperate refugees."

"Think you can handle another ride in a helicopter without throwing me out?" I asked.

"We'll find out."

I turned the van around and did as instructed, stopping once more when we were two miles away from the road.

The audible thump of rotators soon reached us. Theodocia and I got out of the van, and waited. My curiosity as to how the helicopter was going to land, when there wasn't room enough for it, was soon answered.

Two soldiers in black rappelled down from the helicopter and strapped us quickly into harnesses. We were pulled up and whisked away, above the tops of trees, past a flood of refugees blocking roads, over barricades being erected just inside the Beltway encircling DC, and into the heart of the city.

The city may have been spared the worst, but, from above, it appeared as though it had been hit by a tornado. The brilliant lights of first responder vehicles were everywhere. Some parts of the city were jammed with people, others completely empty. The businesses and stores had all been decimated by looting and desperate people hoarding food and other essentials. Trails of glass, goods and bodies littered every major intersection throughout the center of the district.

DC wasn't much better off than the rest of the world. I wondered how the other two large cities in Maryland – Annapolis and Balti-more – had fared without the presence of military and SISA, let alone the smaller towns.

Sometime later, we landed in the middle of the compound, not far from a towering temple dedicated to Zeus whose pristine white walls reflected the sunlight. The helicopter left us and lifted off once we were clear, as if more people were in need of rescuing.

Theodocia and I looked around, neither of us familiar with the seat of power of the world. The massive central field in which we stood contained a large garden area, half a dozen temples, various sidewalks and bridges over small streams. It was hedged by stately buildings with pillars and glowing lights demarking the doorways.

"My friend is going to be at the gate soon," I said to Theodocia.

"I'll call it in. What's his name?" she asked.

I replied, half-listening as she gave instructions to whomever was on the other end of the call. My mind was on the Oracle. Where exactly was she? It would take me an eternity to search each building on the compound to find her!

"I fulfilled my end of the bargain," Theodocia said, facing me.

I met her gaze. "It's almost like you don't trust me," I murmured.

"We both know I don't."

"I never understood why. All I've ever done is drop everything I was doing to advise you when you call. We share the same central concern: Phoibe."

She looked away. "I know. But sometimes, Artemis reveals things to me I wish she wouldn't."

"About me?"

"About everything."

"I can't guess what she said about me to make you despise me."

"She said you'd betray us."

I fell quiet.

"That's why I resent you." Theodocia looked at me and drew a breath. "Because I've had no one else to turn to except for the person who will betray me. Because Phoibe adores you, even after all these years, and you'll betray her."

"Have you considered the idea maybe it's Artemis you shouldn't trust?" I returned, angry for the first time with her. "What right does she have to tell you something like this?"

"She thinks of nothing but helping Phoibe. She meant to warn me."

What bothered me the most wasn't the idea of betraying people, but that I had long ago fully accepted the idea I would probably hurt people I didn't want to on my journey to exact Titan revenge and earn the respect of my father. But I didn't want Phoibe to be one of those people. Until now, our paths weren't likely to cross. I was never supposed to see her again, never supposed to be involved in her life except to supply advice on occasion to her caretaker.

As big as this compound was, I had the sudden sense this new world was too small for me to avoid her completely forever.

"I can't see the future. To the best of my knowledge about deities, neither can Artemis," I replied pointedly. "If I'm meant to betray you, it won't be anytime soon. I, too, am concerned about Phoibe. I can't possibly ever see myself betraying her, even if, by some far stretch of the imagination, I manage to betray you."

"I don't care what you do to me. She's my Phoibe. If you betray her, you will answer to me. I will unleash whatever in Hades Thanatos did to me," Theodocia said firmly.

"I understand. I have no intention of betraying anyone, no matter what Artemis thinks. You know I would never do anything to hurt Phoibe. When I found out she was in danger, I left as fast as I could."

Theodocia's features softened. "I want to believe you," she said. "How did you know about her danger anyway?"

"We'll discuss it. I have to go talk to someone first, though," I said. "I give you my word I'll find you when it's over and fulfill my end of our deal."

Theodocia studied me briefly. "I can find your friend," she said reluctantly.

"I'd appreciate it." I forced a smile, unable to dismiss her claim as I wanted to. "Want to meet me back here in two hours?"

She nodded.

With confidence I didn't exactly have at the moment, I smiled and turned away, heading off in a random direction. Only when I was far enough away for Theodocia not to hear me did I whisper to the Oracle.

"Are you there?"

"I am," she replied. Her voice was stronger his time, as if our proximity made it easier for her to talk to me.

"I'm on the compound. Where am I going?"

She gave me instructions to an underground chamber that left me scratching my head. But I followed them and approached what appeared to be a small, heavily guarded shed complete with its own security system and steel doors. At that point, I had to use my power, which flowed more easily, as if the Oracle had freed more of it. I hid in the shade of a nearby tree and visually scouted my path to the building. In order not to be seen, I had to travel from shadow to shadow and stay in an unbroken line of darkness.

Once ready, I melted into the shade of the tree. Seconds later, I stood in the corner of the guardroom in the interior. I slid past the metal detector and full body scanner, clinging to the edges of the room and their shadows, before reaching the elevator. The interior was dim enough for me to remain a shadow. Red orbs in the ceilings left me thinking the lights were body heat sensors rather than true lights, another odd precaution I wasn't certain why it existed.

When the doors opened, I stepped into a room that felt like a sauna. I materialized, according to the Oracle's instructions. Sweat popped onto my forehead and the back of my neck. It smelled odd, of overpowering incense and sulfur. Most of the area was shrouded in darkness. At one with the shadows, I was able to see through the darkness and determine the size of the basement. There were three rooms in total, this main chamber and two smaller ones. No furniture existed here, no piping or air ducts leading to the outside world. It was completely isolated, a mini-dungeon.

"Why would you want to meet in such a place?" I asked.

"Because this is where I am."

I turned towards the voice and went to the far end of the room, searching the darkness with my eyes. I saw no one and paused a few feet from a railing lining a wall brightened by blue-white light.

"Is this some kind of trick?" I asked, puzzled.

"Look up."

I did so, and my whole world seemed to stop. My heart felt as if it tumbled to my feet, and my skin crawled with what was before me. Unable to look away, neither was I able to register what exactly my eyes were seeing. It ... *she* ... wasn't human. At least, not anymore.

"I need to tell you something no one else, save for the Oracles preceding me, has ever known," the Oracle of Delphi said. "And then, I need to tell you something even my predecessors did not know."

"You have my attention," I whispered in a combination of awe and horror.

"The prophecy of the double omega isn't the tale of the end of days. It's a person, an Oracle. The *last* Oracle, whose power will be far greater than that of the first Oracle, who opened the bridge between worlds that left us vulnerable to the gods," she began. "A door that can be opened can also be closed, cutting off those visitors to our world from their source of power and rendering the being who can open and close the door the most powerful person in our world. This source of power is where your magic comes from as well."

"You closed the door," I guessed.

"Temporarily. I can't hold it closed for long, and I can't hold it closed completely. But I can determine where the power slipping through goes. I was able to channel part of yours back to you."

"For what purpose is it closed at all?" I asked. "If you say vengeance, I will fully support you. This," I motioned to her dismembered body, "isn't my idea of an ideal job."

"You were not brought here to know this."

"Then tell me why I'm here."

"In every scenario and every variation of the future I have tested, the survival of our world comes down to the sacrifice of one life. My predecessors believed the destruction of Earth to be a foregone conclusion, once the double omega was born. I have had two decades to decipher the prophetic end of days, and I posit that it's not just the double omega who will determine the ultimate fate of Earth, but the life of another as well. The double omega will become corrupted, will turn on her own kind. It will take a second person to right her course."

I shifted my weight between my feet, not liking where this conversation was going. "Has the double omega been born?"

"She has."

"Why not stop this corruption before it happens?"

"In every scenario where I've tested this possibility, I've failed to stop the end of days."

"What do you mean by *test*?" I asked, frowning. "Have you gone forward and backward in time?"

"I am a human with a computer mind that knows no restrictions, the only quantum computer in the universe. Unlike my predecessors, I have the capability to run thousands of possibilities and probabilities in the time it takes you to blink," she replied. "I've been testing possibilities for twenty years in an effort to identify what my predecessors could not. In every scenario, in every probability, I fail to find a solution, except for one scenario. There's only one way for the end of days not to happen as prophesized by the first Oracle."

"I'm all ears," I said, on edge.

"Sit down. We'll talk."

My Titan energy was humming and my pulse racing. I did as she said and knelt on the cement floor, apprehensive about what she was about to reveal.

"It starts with the double omega, the last Oracle in a long line of Earth-bound goddesses whose powers far exceed those of the gods and goddesses, if the game of powers were played fairly."

"Hate the players, not the game," I joked weakly.

"The players perpetuate the game!" she snapped.

I rolled my eyes.

As she began speaking again, the rest of the world, along with everything I'd ever believed to be true about chance, life and power, began to fall away. I listened in stunned silence as she imparted knowledge to me the likes of which I didn't think was possible for any one person to know.

The longer I sat, the heavier the sense of doom at my core became. I listened. I learned. I broke down and cried at one point. But I didn't leave – not when the Oracle was giving me the keys to power and prophecy. I had always wanted to matter in my father's eyes. Finally, I had a way to do so. At least, I thought so, until she revealed the price of success, the one-way trip down a path I'd never choose for myself.

HOURS LATER, when I left the Oracle's chamber and stood in the middle of the mall at the center of the compound, I tilted my head back to gaze at the stars. Stuck in my thoughts, uncertain what my next step should be, I didn't register the circling creature overhead until it began to descend and filled my line of sight. Blinking out of the stupor I entered since shortly after the Oracle began speaking, I forced a smile at Adonis as the ugly, flying grotesque drew closer to the ground. I'd missed my meeting with Theodocia; after talking to Adonis, I'd have to find her and hope she wasn't angry enough to try to murder me again.

At this point, I might welcome death, I thought bitterly, unable to fully grasp all I'd learned from the Oracle.

Adonis landed a few feet from me and tilted his head. Over six feet tall, with a panther's lean body, a knobby bald head, fangs and lopsided features, he was terrifying to behold, except to me. To me, his frightening features were always welcome, especially now.

What is it? He asked, communicating telepathically as we did at night, when he was in his beast form. As always, he was sensitive to my mood, my energy, my expression.

"Imagine learning the world is going to end. Now imagine you can stop it but you're forbidden from telling anyone," I quipped.

Adonis folded his wings behind him. Their tips trailed on the ground behind him, and his tail snaked from side to side as he approached.

Can you tell a monster? He asked.

I laughed, always appreciative of the man-beast whose mind was quicker than lightning. "Alas, I cannot."

Does this have to do with the voice that sent me to find you?

"It does. Please don't ask me more. You know I hate to keep

secrets from you." Aside from the necessary ones, I added silently. Adonis would never know the secrets I stole from his mind or the parts of him I sealed off from the rest of him. If he did, he would never be my friend, let alone help me pursue my goals in life.

I respect your boundaries, as always.

"Mrs. Nettles isn't with you. Did you find a place for her?"

We were all provided rooms in the palace. I dare not show you in this form, but it is there. He pointed to some area behind me.

I didn't look. After all I'd heard, sleeping and dealing with people were off my to-do list for the immediate future.

Are you well? Adonis asked when I lapsed into stillness and silence again.

I shook my head in an attempt to jar loose the images stuck in my mind after the talk with the Oracle. "Physically, yes. Mentally, not really."

The gardens are beautiful. They may bring you peace.

I started to respond and then stopped, gazing at the creature whose mind I had erased in order to keep him with me. Should I have felt this pang of regret? I never regretted my actions with regards to Adonis before. But the world was different now than it had been this morning. I had learned more than I ever wanted to know, not only about what was to come, but about the fates and minds of those around me.

Including him.

"Walk with me," I said. "I could use the company of a friend tonight."

Adonis complied and fell into step beside me. We ambled towards the gardens. The scent of night blooming jasmine and roses reached us long before we made it to the stone pathway winding through the gardens. The laughter of fountains was soothing, as was the presence of the monster beside me.

Is there anything I can do to help? Adonis asked.

"No," I replied. "I've been thinking about something someone told me earlier today, that it's often better not to know some things."

You are fortunate to know too much. I have forgotten everything about myself, my life, my past.

"I have a feeling you'll remember one day," I said softly. For my sake, I hoped the inevitable day was far, far off.

We entered the gardens.

"I think we have an opportunity here," I said, running my fingertips over the tops of a bush. "A good one. It might require some deception over the short term. I've got to convince a lot of people I'm not who or what they think I am."

You excel at shadows and deception, Adonis observed.

One of the statues at the center of a fountain we were nearing caught my attention, and I stopped to gaze up at it. A young man in a loincloth carried a jar over his shoulder. The opening of the jar poured water into the warmly lit basin below. It wasn't his chiseled features that caught my attention, but the mask he wore over his eyes. Was I prepared to wear a mask? I had kept the secret of my Titan birth father my entire life, but the level of misdirection I'd need to harness over the next few years made hiding my taboo lineage appear to be the easiest thing I had ever done in my life.

I think everyone is too concerned about what they're calling the Holy Wars for them to pay attention to one man, Adonis added.

"Let's hope so. I need to move us into pretty prominent positions as discreetly as possible," I said. What my friend didn't realize was that I'd have to master deceiving *him*, too.

Wars make for excellent distractions.

"True. It might be possible to fuel the fire as well. Keep my opponents divided. I can't reveal everything, but I can tell you that the gods and goddesses are trapped on Earth for now, cut off from their sources of power. They're vulnerable in one way but still powerful in a different way."

If this is true, they will turn on each other easily. If you mean to distract them while you move into position where your Titan heritage may be suspect, it will require little effort on your part. Play off their fears and egos. If you mean to distract the humans, they, too, are already at each other's throats. Offer them a solution to their current woes. The world will fall at your feet.

I glanced at Adonis. I shouldn't have been surprised by his mind, but I was. Whenever I began to feel overwhelmed or discouraged, he knew exactly what to say to reinvigorate me. In his distant past, he had been a Greek prince and successful war commander at the head of vast armies. He knew a thing or two about waging war. It was me who hadn't really thought about our situation in this light. But he was right. We ... I ... was waging my own war, and the Oracle had just given me a powerful weapon with which I could accelerate my status significantly.

That is, if I were willing to do as she foresaw. At the moment, I was torn between serving my own interests and expanding my narrow view to include the fate of the entirety of humanity. It was a huge leap for me, one I didn't look forward to making.

Why *me*? Of all the questions remaining, this was the one that baffled me the most. I was selfish and the last person to be trusted by anyone, and the Oracle had not only revealed great secrets to me but had given me the most selfless act of all.

"You're a good friend, Adonis. I don't know if I thank you enough for being my friend," I murmured.

It's an honor, Lantos.

It wasn't, but he had no way of knowing that after what I had done to his mind. "Have you hunted yet?"

No. I waited for you.

"I'll be fine. Go hunt. I need to fulfill a promise to the High Priestess you met earlier. Her mind is hurting her. I can silence it."

As you do mine when it becomes agitated with strange memories?

I glanced at him. The brilliant, loyal, ruthless monster who was my friend had no idea what I really did to him when errant memories emerged from the depths of the mind I kept purposely darkened. "Yes, the same," I lied. "I'm going to help her."

I will not be gone long. Adonis stepped away from me and unfurled his wings. *Mrs. Nettles is waiting for you.*

I smiled. "I'll give her a huge hug when I find my way to her. Hunt well, Adonis."

Do not weigh yourself down with such heavy thoughts, Lantos. You will never have to face what comes alone. I will always help you.

"I know. Thank you."

He leapt deftly into the air with physical strength that always left me envious. Adonis soared straight up towards the night sky, his wide wings beating steadily and powerfully as he ascended.

I did not doubt him. Ever. But I also knew that the future the Oracle revealed would one day deprive me of my only friend.

"Not tonight," I told myself. I'd worry about the future of my friendship another night.

Tonight, I had to decide between my destiny and the fate of the world. It was a much harder decision than it probably should have been, because I didn't particularly care about the rest of the world. Given the choice between what I needed to do to win over my Titan father and protecting my only friend, I was stuck.

In the end, I had a feeling I already knew what choice would win out. Perhaps this was the real reason I experienced regret looking at Adonis. Wiping his mind was merciful compared to what I was faced with doing down the road. Even if my future actions were for the greater good, even if they would end up serving my personal interests, I couldn't decide with ease to lose the faith and friendship of Adonis.

"I hope you'll understand one day," I whispered to the night sky. "If there were any other choice, I'd make it."

I sat on a bench in the gardens and closed my eyes, soothed by the fountains, singing crickets and rustling of leaves in the soft breeze while my mind fought to justify a decision I never dreamt I'd have to make.

PEOPLE'S CHAMPION

"... and this is the part where he won the gold in swimming and later that afternoon, in judo!" Alessandra boasted.

I paused to listen, concealed from view by the night and trees in the forest where I had lived with soon to be thirteen-year-old Lyssa, the female nymphs who kept her company, and the priests managing the orphanage where we all lived.

"Wow!" breathed one of the slender, elegant teens with her. "I heard he competed in seven separate events in one day and won gold in all of them."

"He did. He's called the People's Champion, because everyone loves him," Lyssa said proudly but in a whisper. "He's stronger than all the gods combined."

"That's not possible!"

"But it's true!"

I smiled despite my disapproval. Lyssa knew I didn't want her talking about my gold-medal past. She was too young, and sheltered, to understand why, but I couldn't think of my past without recalling everything I was ashamed of. Would she look at me with the same glow of admiration and love, if she knew what I did to her real parents?

The past was best left in the past.

Even knowing this, I hesitated to interrupt. No one had ever loved me the way she did, never believed in me. Since we hid in this forest seven years ago, I'd enjoyed a life I never thought possible, one of peace, family and happiness. Alessandra was my adopted daughter, and I her ugly protector.

One day, she'll learn the truth. The soft whisper in my mind tormented me from time to time.

"But not today," I replied quietly.

Today, I was her Herakles. The nymphs who had appeared from the forest to play with her when she was six had remained with her, sensing what the priests knew. Alessandra was important and one day, she was going to need all of us to protect her. They were part of my family, too, sisters to the special little girl the priests and I had to hide at all costs.

I purposely snapped a twig before moving forward into the light of the small campfire Lyssa had started. She quickly closed the browser on her cell phone, and the clips of my days as a champion disappeared from the screen. I pretended not to notice, and she hastily tucked the phone away.

Two of the other nymphs had accompanied us this night to camp in the woods. Usually, five or six of the thirty girls came. Recently, however, they'd discovered the campground next to our forest and worse, the boys who often visited it with their parents. All of my past heroics paled in comparison to the appeal of teenage boys.

The nymphs giggled, and I sat down across from them. Lyssa's bright blue eyes found me. She was smiling.

"What did the priests teach you this week?" I asked gruffly, already aware of her slow progress in class. The priests blamed me for her lack of interest in school, and I humored them the best I could. I was no scholar. I didn't see the use in most of what they taught. The potential threats to Alessandra wouldn't be defeated by her ability to speak Greek, or how many deities she could accurately name in under sixty seconds, or how well she recited the credo of the priests who plotted to rid the world of gods.

None of that mattered. But I had to pretend it did, for the sake of what normalcy a secret orphanage run by rebel priests, and filled with magical creatures, could provide.

Lyssa sighed and rolled her eyes. "Nothing."

I raised an eyebrow.

The nymphs giggled and glanced at one another.

"Shut. Up!" Lyssa snapped at them, features flaring red.

"What?" I asked.

"We started health class this semester, and Lyssa is the only girl in class who hasn't ... you know," one of the nymphs said cheerfully.

Alessandra groaned.

My brow furrowed. "Hasn't what?" I asked.

"You know," the other nymph said impatiently. "Started."

"Shut up, Hectate!" Lyssa snapped.

"Started *what*?" I asked, confused.

"Her ... period." Hectate whispered the last word almost too quietly to hear.

Oh, Gods. Lyssa and the nymphs were starting to transform from children into young women. I wasn't ready for that change. Not yet. Maybe not ever. My first instinct was to back away and disappear. Discussing a woman's monthly cycle was as far from my comfort zone as anything could be.

"Some people are *slow*," the other nymph, Leandra, taunted.

"You can never have kids if you don't have one," Hectate said matter-of-factly. "You're going to be a lonely, old maid, and no boy will ever kiss you!"

No, I was not at all ready for this stage of raising a daughter.

Too stunned to speak let alone react, I saw the look in Lyssa's eyes before she launched up and tackled the blonde girl but was too surprised to stop her. Leandra screamed. Alessandra drove the nymph to the ground and punched her before I caught her around her waist and hauled her back.

Leandra scrambled to her feet, glaring at the angry Lyssa. "You hit like a priest!" she shouted at Alessandra.

"Then come back and let me hit you again!" Alessandra wriggled in my grip.

"Enough," I said quietly. "Leandra, sit over there. Alessandra, there."

Alessandra pushed my grip off her and obeyed grudgingly. Leandra went to the other side of the campfire. Prying Alessandra off a nymph had become second nature. My sweet Lyssa had a temper and the combat arms training to cause harm, if she wasn't careful. The priests believed her aggression to be a stage. For the sake of others, I hoped so. For her sake, I hope she remembered how to punch better than she spoke Greek when she was out of this stage.

An awkward silence fell. Secretly relieved by the change of subject, I was trying hard to erase the image from my mind of my little girl kissing anyone ever, let alone growing up and wanting to leave the forest and me behind. The priests had tried to talk to me about what to expect, but I ignored them. In hindsight, I should have listened.

Leandra and Alessandra were glaring at one another. At times, I was concerned that Lyssa wasn't quite ... normal. At least, not compared to the nymphs, who were probably not remotely normal either. But I had no one else to compare her behavior to, and the differences between her and the nymphs were clear on most days. They excelled in school, rarely threw temper tantrums, and were generally less wild than my Alessandra. I didn't care if she was wild, but every day, I witnessed her struggle to fit in with the other girls. She, too, was aware of how different she was, and this hurt me on a level I wasn't able to escape or treat with medicine.

It was this concern that led me back to a topic I didn't feel remotely qualified to discuss.

"Is there a reason you haven't started ... uh, your ... female cycle?"

I asked, uncertain what else to say. "Are you eating well? Sleeping enough?"

"Herakles!" Alessandra groaned.

"I don't want your training to interfere with your development," I reasoned.

She covered her face with her hands, embarrassed.

Leandra giggled and then laughed.

"Don't you laugh at him!" Alessandra bolted to her feet.

I tugged her back down. She sat heavily, fuming.

"That's not how it works, Herakles," said Hectate. "When she's mature enough, she'll start."

"That's right. You're just a silly little girl, and we're women now," Leandra added.

"Like I want to bleed to death every month!" Alessandra retorted. "At least I won't end up pregnant if I kiss a boy!"

"Like any boy would kiss you!"

I was starting to sweat just listening to them. "No kissing, no boys," I growled, unable to help it. "And no one is getting pregnant. Understand?"

The words came out much harsher than I intended. Even Lyssa gazed up at me in surprise.

"Yes, Herakles," the three girls chorused.

I preferred breaking up fights to discussions of boys, kissing, pregnancy ... Gods, I wasn't going to survive Lyssa going through puberty or the knowledge she would one day want to be on her own, alone to face the world. I understood too well how dark and disgusting the world was, how twisted and deceitful people could be. I wanted to save her from those things.

Aware it wasn't fair or possible, I likewise couldn't help thinking I wanted her to stay a child forever. I glanced at her. Her cheeks remained red from embarrassment. I didn't want to press the issue and decided to talk to the priests about her development. I was not a traditional father figure, and her life was not normal. If some part of how I was raising her was interfering with her growing into a woman, even if I didn't really want her to, I needed to know.

Hectate gasped, drawing all of our attentions. She was gazing up at the night sky.

"Meteor shower!" she exclaimed and pointed.

I looked up, and my jaw went slack.

The streaks of light crossing the sky weren't meteorites or anything else natural. They were too low – barely higher than the tendrils of fog drifting inland from the Maryland coast – and consisted of orange fire rather than the cold burn of a meteorite.

The girls stood, excited, and started to file through the forest to a clearing nearby, where they could see what was happening better. My eyes lingered on the sky as I tried to sort out what exactly I was witnessing.

As I watched, more streaks filled the sky, until the night was lit up as bright as twilight. I stood, alarmed by the unnatural display.

The cell phone in my pocket vibrated. I pulled it free as I followed the path the girls had taken to the meadow.

We need you to return now with the girls. Quickly. The message originated from Father Cristopolos, who was the head of the priestly order managing the orphanage.

"Lyssa, Leandra, Hectate!" I bellowed. "We're going back to the orphanage."

"But, Herakles, we have to see the –" Alessandra objected.

"Now, Lyssa."

She knew better than to argue when I used that tone. Assured they would obey, I returned to the camp and put out the fire then swiftly picked up our camping supplies and loaded them into my rucksack. I handed Lyssa her pack when she appeared and then stood aside for her to lead us all back towards the center of the forest refuge.

They were excited, oohing and aahing at the night sky, while I grew more perplexed. Such a display wasn't manmade, and it was located too close to the little girl we were hiding from the world to be coincidence. Had the gods or politicians – both of which were feared by the priests – figured out where we were? Was this some kind of attack? If so, why were the fireballs crisscrossing the sky without striking our refuge?

Three hours later, we reached the manor house at the center of the forest unscathed. The other nymphs were gathered in the greens, most lying on their backs, as they watched the show overhead.

Lyssa went to join them, as did Leandra and Hectate, while I hurried inside to find Father Cristopolos.

"Herakles!" a voice called behind me. "Come quickly!"

I spun and struck off, following the smallest and youngest priest – Father Renoir – as he rushed through the corridors on the ground level of the manor house. He had hiked up his brown robes to help him move faster, and I kept pace with him, sensing his urgency in his pace and quick breathing.

He led me past the halls and conference rooms that had been turned into classrooms for the girls and into the instructors' break and administrative area at the end of the hallway.

I entered the break room, and Father Cristopolos closed the door behind me. The other priests were gathered in front of a television.

"It's everywhere," Father Cristopolos said in a tight voice. With a sturdy build and baldhead, he was the only one of the priests who ever took me up on the offer to teach them to fight.

"What's everywhere?" I asked.

"This firestorm. The Gods are setting fire to the world."

Although critical of the intentions of supernatural beings of any kind, even I had a hard time processing this statement. He joined the others in front of the television and I trailed more slowly.

Newscasters were panicked as they reported on the fireballs raining from the heavens, and the tickers at the bottom of the screen raced too quickly for me to catch much at all. My reading was rusty, but I managed to make out some words before returning my attention to the panicked woman on *the* screen.

... New York, LA, London, Paris ... fireballs in every major city ... the ticker had read.

My body became tense, and my pulse raced. I glanced upward, as if I could see the fireballs through the stone roof.

"Is Lyssa safe here?" I heard myself ask without being fully aware of anything beyond my shock.

No one answered.

I grabbed Father Cristopolos by the arm. "Is Alessandra safe here?" I demanded, ready to snatch her and run as far as I had to in order to protect her.

His eyes remained glued to the television, but he nodded. "These will protect us." He lifted the red cord he and the other priests wore at their waists. I didn't understand magic or the powers of the gods, but the perimeter of our forest refuge was lined by the ropes, which were said to turn our home into a blind spot. We were hidden from men and gods – everyone except for our Titan benefactor, Lelantos, and our Olympian benefactress, Artemis.

"Turn the channel!" Father Renoir urged.

Static was on the television. One of the priests flipped channels with a shaky hand, until he found another news station. This one lasted five minutes, the next two, and the third a full ten minutes before it, too, followed in the footsteps of the rest of them and disappeared.

Silence filled the break room. No one was willing to say what I was thinking, that we could end up the only people left on the planet. My hands trembled from emotions, and I stared at the blank television screen, willing someone else to pop up and tell us what was going on.

Of everyone, Father Cristopolos was the first to react.

"Renny, bring the girls in. Francois, cut the cable, internet and phone feeds to the girls' rooms. Until we know what to tell them, we're going to hide this," he said.

My first instinct had been the opposite, to warn the girls about what was going on. Father Cristopolos was shrewd and smart and had been elevated to the rank of leader long before I met the priests. He was also more aware of the dangers facing Alessandra. I trusted his instincts in his area.

The two priests hurried out of the break room, and Father Cristopolos returned his gaze to the blank television screen.

"Herakles, would you be willing to check our boundaries? Ensure none of them are hit by fire?"

"Of course," I said instantly.

"I plan on seeking out Artemis. I don't know if she'll be willing to talk to me after all this, but ..." He drifted off, and bewilderment expressing the same shock we were all experiencing crossed his features. "This can't be the end!"

"It is not what was foretold," one of the remaining priests agreed. "But I can't explain it either."

Their belief in a prophecy involving Alessandra was yet another of the differences we shared. I believed no one, not even a god, could overrule my free will, and I didn't give much credence to the existence of gods anyway. For the most part, the priests believed in the gods and free will, with the exception of Alessandra. They believed her fate to be something that had been determined ten thousand years ago.

Which had always run counter to my own beliefs. It was pure madness to believe everyone had free will – except for one person. Everything around me, and everyone in my life, had one purpose: to protect Lyssa. I shared this priority, even if I didn't always understand or agree with the reasoning behind why the priests did what they did.

"I'll go now," I said when no one else spoke. "I need to grab some supplies from my shed."

"Cell reception will be coming down soon, if it hasn't been knocked out by the fireballs," Father Cristopolos said. "I know you plan for everything. Do you have backup communications? Something analog or line of sight?"

I had never asked, but I often suspected Father Cristopolos had been in the military at one point. His easy command and pragmatism elevated him above the other priests, who were often too scholarly for me to relate to at all. "I do," I said. "I'll bring you a radio."

Without waiting for his response, I hurried out of the break room. The girls lived in rooms on the second through fourth stories of the manor house, while the priests and I shared the two guest cottages tucked behind the house. I had taken over one of the maintenance sheds as well to store gear and emergency supplies.

Exiting the orphanage, I heard the girls complaining to Father Renny how much they didn't want to go to bed yet. Unlike usual, I didn't stop to help. The idea we could be on fire soon if I didn't check the ropes around the boundaries possessed me with the kind of fear a father felt knowing his family was in danger. With jerky movements, I snatched everything I thought I'd need from the storage shed and slung a pack with weapons, water and more of the red ropes onto my back.

I ran a radio into the break room quickly before racing into the forest.

In all my feats at the Olympics, I had never felt the need to move as fast as I did now. I tore through underbrush, vaulted over logs close to my height, scaled the dirt walls of ravines, and sloshed through streams as I headed to the nearest point of the perimeter. By the time I was a few meters out, I was panting and dripping with sweat – and I'd broken my own record of the fastest time I'd run through the forest by nearly half.

The scene before me held me mesmerized. I didn't need a flashlight to find the rope perimeter. On my side, all was quiet and dark. On the other side, brilliant white light had created a wall that prevented me from seeing anything beyond it.

I stood, awed and fearful of the display, and finally believing the priests that their red ropes actually did something I could explain only as magic.

Rather than feel relieved to know the fireballs couldn't reach us, new urgency sent adrenaline spiking through me, as I realized what would happen if any of the ropes along the perimeter were damaged or missing. The girls knew better than to mess with them, and I checked them routinely every week. Sometimes, during a rainy spring like this one, heavy downpours would push them out of place or animals drawn by the color would try to take the bright cords to their dens or nests.

I moved along the edges of the woods making up our home. The wall of light remained just outside the boundaries. I drew as close to it as I dared. Expecting the brilliant white light to be hot, I was surprised not to feel heat radiating off it. When I was close enough, I could almost see what lay on the other side of the light, as if I were peering through an opaque curtain. Morbid curiosity about what was happening outside our protected home made me want to step through the wall, but my primary priority was ensuring we all survived.

Setting aside my intrigue, I spent the next twelve hours racing along the perimeter. The western, northern and eastern boundaries were all secure, all hedged by brilliant white light.

But at the southern boundary ... no wall of light, and no fireballs, as far as I could see. I ventured past the rope perimeter, past a small lake and into the campground adjacent to our land, and paused, listening. Fireballs didn't streak across the night sky here either. The orphanage's grounds were protected by the priests' magic, though I couldn't explain why no fire fell south of our home. The newscasters claimed the fireballs were everywhere in the world, so how did none touch the quiet forest before me?

Unable to explain it, I shivered and stepped back inside the boundaries.

I radioed in my latest observations, lingered, and then turned away.

I returned to my starting point, at the western boundary. Only then did I wriggle out of the rucksack and drop to my knees, thoroughly exhausted from the pace I'd forced myself to endure.

The wall of light remained despite the light of dawn overtaking the skies above. The sun rose, and the fire continued to fall. Fatigued, I pulled out my canteens and downed the contents one of them before I ate half a dozen energy bars.

"Herakles?" Father Cristopolos called over the radio I'd slid into my cargo pocket. "Are you well?"

I pulled the radio free and sat with my back to a tree truck, eyes on the wall of white surrounding the forest. "Here," I said into the receiver. "Perimeter is intact."

I expected him to make a remark about the magic of the ropes that I'd openly criticized for years. The priests had steadily refused my insistence we emplace a legitimate security system. I understood why now.

"We may have another problem," Father Cristopolos said instead.

I tensed, alert and ready to run back to protect the girls.

"Artemis contacted us and said we're in a safe zone that extends down through southern Maryland. She also said she won't be able to contact us again for some time," the priest said.

"Is that such a bad thing, since her kind did this?" I responded.

There was a long pause before Father Cristopolos spoke again. "I can't see her doing this," he said quietly. "There must be another explanation."

I rolled my eyes. "Is that the problem or is there another one?"

"Our boundaries stop supernatural discovery and creatures from entering. They don't stop animals. We've had five cougars and a bear cross through the greens this morning."

I hadn't paid any attention to the wildlife during my mad run around the perimeter. Suddenly, I wished I'd taken notice of any unusual activity among the wild animals inhabiting our forest. It made perfect sense for animals to flee the fiery territory towards us. They had the instincts to guide them to safety.

"Four-legged refugees," I said. "Are the girls okay?"

"We're keeping them inside today," Father Cristopolos replied. "Our generators are down. Our weapons of choice are faith in the

Old Ways and civil unrest. No one is volunteering to face bears to reset the generators manually."

I snorted, amused at how he chose to describe their intent of over-throwing the gods one day. Men as devoted as they were to their cause would do whatever it took to see their purpose through. No part of me doubted the priests would use the weapons they scorned, if their cause were threatened. "I'll go now," I said. "Keep everyone inside until I clear the area. Lock the doors."

"Understood."

Tucking the radio away, I stood. For the first time since arriving to the forest refuge, I didn't feel safe, despite the magic boundaries repelling the gods' wrath. I pulled out two hunting knives from my pack and placed one at my waist and the other at my thigh.

After downing another canteen of water, I adjusted my pack on my back and set off at another hard run. I reached the manor and stopped inside the greens – the vast lawns surrounding the mansion – to look for animal paw prints. Sure enough, I spotted the evidence of the visitors Father Cristopolos had spotted and quite a few more. An entire herd of deer had moved through the greens, along with a dozen predatory animals as well as squirrels and rabbits.

Twisting to squint in the direction they'd gone, I realized all of them were headed south.

They sense the safe zone, I thought to myself. If that were the case, then we weren't likely to see any of the dangerous animals hanging out around the manor, a threat to the girls. But, the migration might also take a while. I respected wildlife more than I did the gods, and I understood animals better than humans. They operated out of instinct. Rarely did that instinct tell them to attack humans if they weren't being threatened.

I stood, pensive, and gazed towards the south for a moment. The wildlife right now was feeling threatened, which made them danger-ous. A curfew would be in order for the girls until the forest creatures settled, which could take a week or more, depending on how long the fireballs fell. Fortunately, the animals appeared to be taking a direct route and following a set path past the manor house. As long as everyone in the orphanage knew to avoid this path, they would hopefully be safe.

I finished circling the greens to ensure my initial theory was correct and found a second, well-trodden path along the eastern side, opposite the first. The animals were making an effort to avoid people, which was a good sign.

When satisfied with what I'd learned, I radioed the information to Father Cristopolos and then continued on my mission of returning power to the orphanage. The hidden generators and underground power station were located on the southeast corner and the lake where we drew our drinking water on the southwest.

I kept my distance from the path the wildlife followed while walking in the same general direction towards the southeast corner of our property. Originally, when we arrived, the orphanage had been connected to the public grid. In an effort to remain hidden from everyone, the priests created an off-grid electrical system relying on a combination of sunlight, water, and backup generators for those rough days in winter when neither light nor water was enough. We pumped our own water and brought in a private waste management company to tend the septic system as needed. We bought our food from a local farmer and maintained a two-year supply of food and fresh water for emergencies. We were completely self-sufficient.

A mama bear and two cubs loped down the path towards the south, their fur singed by fire. I relaxed after they'd passed me. Birds seemed content to remain in their trees and sing, but the chatter of chipmunks and other small animals was missing.

I spotted the southeastern corner of the property long before I reached it. The wall of light remained on the eastern boundary. As I watched, five deer darted through the curtain of light and raced towards the south. Aware I wouldn't see the animals until they ran me over, I quickened my jog to a run and did my best to stay alert for the sounds of anything approaching the other side of the wall of light.

I stopped at the tree marked by one of the red ropes. It stood over the entrance to the underground facility, and I bent to grab the metal doors and fling them open.

Except ... the doors were already open to reveal the dark space beneath them. It was unlikely that animals had done this. In the seven years I'd been in the forest, no animal had yet to disturb the entrance or the generator room. The hum and sounds the underground facility usually made was enough to drive off most wildlife.

Frowning, I paused and then drew one of my knives. Had one of the priests made it down there despite my instructions to remain inside?

"Thiebald?" I called out to the priest most likely to rebel as I started down the stairs. "Are you here?"

No answer. The generator room was utterly quiet, an indication none of the systems were working at all. The manor house probably didn't have water either, if the pump wasn't thumping.

My feet settled on the concrete flooring, and I stretched for the flashlight kept on the wall beside the light switch for emergency situations like this one. Light in one hand and knife in the other, I started forward into the cool cellar. My senses picked up on nothing out of the ordinary, and I shifted to the main control station. Several lights glowed on the panel's face.

The priests had taped picture instructions on the wall above the panel when they realized how poor my reading skills were. I lifted the flashlight to the wall and quickly reviewed the illustrations for resetting the power. Logging into the computer, I clicked the buttons to start a reset of the system then left to manually adjust the individual generators and water pump. Working down the line of bulky equipment, I was soon immersed in quick inspections of the equipment before deliberately initiating the reset sequence for each one.

I took a side step towards the final generator – and froze. My foot didn't land on the solid ground but on something that felt distinctly like I was stepping on a *person*.

Snatching my knife, I yanked my leg back and shone the flashlight down on the ground.

The crumpled form of a man was on the cement, partially tucked behind the final generator, as if he sought to hide. With clothing that was burnt in several places, he lay with his back to me. I'd stepped on his arm.

"Hey," I said in a low voice. "Get up!" I nudged him with my foot.

He didn't move.

Wary, I knelt and leaned forward far enough to snatch his other arm and pull him onto his back. Recoiling, I gazed from his open, empty eyes, to the severe burns down the side of his face, deep enough to expose the milky white of his skeleton beneath. Only when I was this close could I pick up the scent of charred flesh and hair, otherwise hidden by the smells of oil and machinery around me.

I released my breath and tucked my knife away. Until this moment, I hadn't considered the idea that the gods' wrath might drive more than animals into our domain. I stood and searched the rest of the generator room before returning to the dead man. Hefting him onto my shoulder, I exited the cellar and took him above ground, walking twenty meters before setting him down. I pulled my radio out.

"Father Cristopolos," I said and glanced around, looking for more refugees of the human category.

"Yes?" he answered.

"You're keeping everyone inside, aren't you?"

"Of course. How are things looking?"

"Did you check on Alessandra to make sure she's in her room?" I asked, suspecting if anyone decided to break out, it was her.

"The doors are locked from the inside. No one has left."

"Do me the favor of sending Renny or someone up to her room," I said.

"Very well. What's this about, Herakles?"

My eyes settled on the dead man. "There might be people in our forest as well as wildlife trying to escape the fires."

Father Cristopolos murmured a curse. I heard him order someone to check on Lyssa before he spoke to me again. "How many people have you seen?" he asked.

"Just one. He's dead," I said.

"Good. You did what you had to."

"He was dead when I found him," I clarified, not expecting the peace-loving priest who doted over the girls as if they were his own to react so nonchalantly to the death of anyone.

"If we have any favor with the gods remaining, they will prevent more people from trespassing. Our secrets must remain secret."

I frowned. "And if I run across more people?" I asked. "What do you want me to do?"

"I trust your judgment. You above all know how important it is that we protect Alessandra."

Surprised he assumed I'd murdered someone, I didn't know how to respond to this vague statement. It almost sounded as if he expected me to kill anyone whose path I crossed! He knew of my background. Perhaps he assumed I was still that man. I didn't doubt my ability to kill, if Alessandra were in danger, but the idea Father Cristopolos assumed I'd do it no matter what the circumstances left me feeling ... uncomfortable.

"All right," I said finally. "I've got to get back to the generators. Should be up in twenty minutes."

"Lyssa's in her room," he reported.

Thank the gods. "You might want to have someone stay with her. If she gets curious, she'll find a way out."

"Will do."

Tucking the radio in my cargo pocket, I returned to the underground room.

I searched it again, not wanting any more unpleasant surprises, before I finished bringing all the generators and pump online.

Half an hour later, I left the generator room. We had no need for locks; no one had crossed into our isolated territory uninvited in all the time I'd been here. I covered the metal doors with leaves and brush to prevent anyone else from breaking in then returned to the body.

I stood over the corpse, uncertain how to handle it. I didn't have time to dig a proper grave, and burying him too shallow would only invite the predators crossing through our forest to remain. And eventually, the girls would probably find the body, if the predators didn't drag it out of the ground first.

My gaze flickered to the wall of light then to the fireballs overhead. I picked up the man and walked to the wall. When I was this close, I could see shapes through it. Heart pounding, I stepped closer and closer, until my toes hit the brilliant wall. Leaning forward enough for my face to pass through it, I gasped at what I saw on the other side.

How anyone or anything survived this, I couldn't imagine. The world outside of our boundaries was fiery, barren, with all the trees for miles on fire or completely disintegrated. As I watched, another fireball landed several meters from the boundary in an explosion of dirt and fire. I stepped back instinctively, horrified by what was happening to the world.

Did the priests understand why this was happening? Did it have anything to do with Alessandra? The fact we were protected by the mass destruction by at least one god left me feeling embarrassed to have questioned the motives, and power, of our benefactors on multiple occasions.

I was not a man of deep thought. I couldn't explain what I saw or why it happened, but I saw an opportunity to rid the forest of the corpse slung over my shoulder.

With a deep breath, I stepped through the protective curtain of light and into the scorching, barren zone outside the boundaries. Smaller fireballs rained down around me. I darted to the nearest fire and carefully threw the body into its center. Not about to be struck down, I raced back to the protection of the forest beyond the wall of light, visible from both sides of the boundary.

When I was safe again, I wiped the blood of the dead man on my pants and retrieved my backpack. Tired yet wired, I began to wonder how many more people would find seek refuge on our land. Rather than return to the orphanage, I struck off once more to check the perimeter.

Not long after depositing the corpse outside the boundaries, I ran across two more people hunkered just inside the wall of light, at the base of a tree. The young couple in their late teens both displayed the burnt clothing, skin and hair I expected. Dark circles shadowed wide eyes, and they were staring at the light barrier they'd just crossed through.

I lingered in the brush, studying them. They were a few years older than Alessandra with similar eyes and noses, indicating they could be brother and sister. Scared refugees posed no threat to my Lyssa, even if I didn't like the idea of strangers passing through our forest. These kids were harmless.

"Thanatos has claimed us, Natalie," the teen boy said.

I chuckled. "Unfortunately, that is not the case," I said and stepped out from the brush. "Can you both walk?"

They leapt to their feet at the sound of my voice. The boy clutched one arm to his chest while the back of the girl's body appeared as if a fireball had scraped her from head to foot.

"There's a campground directly south," I said and pointed. "You'll be safe there."

After a surprised pause, the girl spoke. "Which way is south?"

I twisted to visually locate the trail created by fleeing wildlife. "Follow that path. Beware of bears and wild cats. They're all headed in the same direction."

The two were studying me uncertainly, as if not yet convinced they were still alive. After a moment, I took pity on them and tugged protein bars and a canteen of water from my rucksack. I tossed them to the girl, whose limbs all appeared to be in working order.

"You need to go now," I said. "There's nothing for you here. Understand?"

The two exchanged a look and then nodded. I stepped out of their way, and they began walking, dazed and fatigued.

"Stay on the path," I called after them.

The boy glanced over his shoulder at me.

I remained where I was, confirming they found the path south, before I began walking again. Debating whether or not to tell Father Cristopolos about the trespassers, I decided not to after our strange exchange earlier. I wasn't an indiscriminate killer. Well, not any more. When I was under Cleon's control, I had been brainwashed to follow his commands alone. Most of those memories were dream-like blurs that didn't seem real, even though I knew they had to be.

Shaking off my past, I continued my inspection of the perimeter.

I walked for an hour before running into anyone else.

Three men and two women, as dazed as the siblings, surrounded a sixth person lying unconscious on the ground. His burnt body appeared beyond salvaging to my untrained eyes, and the other members of his party were in rough shape with burns and bruising.

I glanced around. They were splitting the distance between the eastern and western paths created by animals moving south. I didn't trust anyone to wander these woods alone, not with the secret orphanage at the center.

A soft gasp from behind me startled me, and I whirled.

Alessandra stood in the forest, wearing her backpack and an expression of concern.

"Lyssa!" I hissed, cursing the priests under my breath for not being able to keep up with the wild girl before me.

"What happened to them?" she asked and pointed.

"Go home. Now!" I replied.

"Hello?" one of the wounded women called. She wandered through the brush separating us from them. "Is someone else there?"

I released a sigh. "Don't move," I told Alessandra. I strode forward to intercept the trespasser.

"There's a safe zone to the south," I said, emerging from the forest. "I can show you the path to take."

She looked up at me, dazed. Two of the others turned to face me.

None of them spoke. They had the lifeless gazes of living mannequins.

"Follow me, okay?" I prodded, pitying them, and started towards the western trail, away from where I'd left Alessandra.

"Can't leave him," one of the women whispered and motioned to the unconscious man. Two others bent to heft the downed man and made it four steps when I realized how long it would take us to walk a kilometer, if they moved this slowly. Anxious to continue checking the rest of the perimeter, and guiding survivors away from Alessandra, I moved forward and picked up the man effortlessly then began walking.

"Do you want me to help?" Lyssa asked, melting from the forest with stealth I'd taught her.

It was a very rare day when I was angry with her. One look at her compassionate expression, though, and I recalled she had no idea why she was being raised in secrecy or why refugees were streaming through our forest. Reacting the way I wanted to would only draw attention to the wrong things, to Alessandra, and invite questions from her I wasn't ready to answer. If I sent her home alone, she was likely to run into more refugees or animals. The wildlife, I trusted her to handle. But people ...

She was safer with me. These strangers couldn't possibly know who or what she was.

One of the trespassers dropped to her knees.

In the split second that followed, I made up my mind. "Do you have your emergency medical kit?" I asked Alessandra.

She nodded and darted forward, tugging off her backpack. I placed the man in my arms on the ground. Kneeling beside Alessandra, I ran her through our medical emergency checklist, this time with a living patient, and watched as she bandaged the wounded woman's arm and neck before offering her water and painkillers. While Lyssa may not have done well in school, she followed the procedures I taught her without hesitation, even stitching a gaping wound in the woman's shoulder on her own.

Proud, yet concerned about her interaction with the strangers, I didn't praise her as I normally would. Instead, when she had finished, I stood.

"We need to leave," I said as much to her as the others. "There's a campground to the south and a few towns nearby. You will find better medical care there."

Alessandra obediently replaced her emergency medical kit and stood, pulling her backpack on. I picked up the unconscious man, certain he would be dead before they reached a hospital, and started to the west again.

"Stay by my side, Alessandra," I said with a glance over my shoulder. She was looking with unabashed curiosity at the people, and I knew questions were soon to follow. "There was a fire to the north."

She appeared to accept the explanation and moved to my side, navigating the forest with ease.

The refugees limped and supported one another as they followed. I kept my senses alert for wildlife and other survivors while trying to calculate how many people I was going to find this day. It didn't seem possible that anyone had survived and yet, I'd met eight people already. I would need to return Alessandra to the orphanage, and give the priests stricter instructions on how to safeguard my wily Lyssa, before I tracked down any more survivors.

We reached the western path, and I helped the two ablest bodied among the refugees to support the unconscious man. Stepping aside, I couldn't help the flicker of anxiousness that floated through me when I realized how close this path would take them to the manor house. Not one of them seemed too aware of anything at the moment. With any luck, they'd pass through the forest quietly and miss the orphanage. If what Father Cristopolos said was true about a safe zone, then there were several towns and cities between here and Washington DC where refugees could find food and shelter.

"Is that why the animals are all running through our forest?" Alessandra asked me.

"What?"

"The fire."

"Yes," I replied. "It's engulfed the entire forest outside our home."

"Wow," she breathed. "It's a good thing we helped those people."

"Yeah." I switched directions towards the orphanage. My muscles were aching and my mind tired. I wanted to take a break and quick nap, but if I weren't here to reroute the refugees, who else could do it?

"I should've sent the other ones to the campground, too," she added.

I stopped. "What other ones?"

"I found three others and told them where the orphanage was," she replied cheerfully.

"When was this?" I faced her, struggling not to display my dismay.

"Ten minutes before I found you." Alessandra gazed up at me with a smile. "Aren't you glad you taught me to navigate the forest? They would've been lost otherwise."

At the moment, I was wishing I'd taken the priests' warning about her being too wild more seriously.

"Some of these people could be looters or worse," I told her firmly. "You're going back to the orphanage and staying there."

She made a face. "Can't I help you round them up?"

"No."

Disappointed, Alessandra sighed and began walking towards the orphanage.

I dreaded what I'd find when we arrived. After the conversation with Father Cristopolos earlier, I was unsettled. I didn't know what he would do when strangers showed up on his doorstep. We were on new territory.

As we walked, my slow mind began to unravel what exactly left me uncomfortable.

I never wanted to be under someone else's control as I had been under Cleon's. But it was more than this bothering me.

Just as I didn't want Alessandra to grow up, I wasn't ready to give up the peace I'd experienced for the first time in my life over the past seven years. Part of me knew it was inevitable, or a man like me wouldn't have been chosen to protect her. But I had hoped to wait until she was old enough to understand her importance and place in the world before our lives changed.

"You have blood on your hands." Lyssa's voice broke into my unpleasant thoughts. She had stopped a short distance away and was reaching into her pack for a rag.

At one point, my hands had been accustomed to being bloody. They were rarely clean. I didn't object as she wiped my hands free of the stranger's blood before carefully folding the rag so it wouldn't make a mess out of the contents of her backpack. She tucked it away, turned, and began walking again, this time humming.

No, I wasn't ready for any of this to change. The world, my peace, her bloom into womanhood.

We reached the greens around the orphanage. My sharp eyes scoured the lawns and house for any sign of the strangers Alessandra had sent this way without spotting anyone.

When we neared the door, it was flung open by Father Renoir, the youngest and the girls' favorite, who resembled a bug with his thick glasses. He was frowning and planted his hands on his hips.

"Alessandra," he chided gently.

She rolled her eyes and breezed by him. "I know."

"Kitchens! You've earned another week cleaning up after the cook!"

Alessandra groaned. She tugged off her backpack and tossed it on a chair in the hallway before heading towards the kitchens.

"I told you. You need to keep a better eye on her," I said to him, folding my arms across my chest.

"I'll admit she's smarter than she leads us to believe," Father

Renoir said. "But I plan on watching her personally and keeping her too busy to leave the house again."

I nodded in approval, not fully convinced any of them could keep track of her unless they were tied to her. I had trained her how to move with discipline and agility. If they turned their backs, she was gone.

I started to say as much, when Father Cristopolos spoke behind me. "I know you're tired, Herakles, but there is something else I must ask of you."

Hearing the hushed note in his tone, I turned to face him. The priest's robes were muddied around their hem, and he slid a hand flecked with blood deeper into the sleeves of the robe as I looked at him.

"You're well?" I asked.

"I am. Renny, tend to your flock. Herakles, accompany me, please."

Father Renoir nodded and closed the door. Father Cristopolos walked around the manor house, towards the cottages where we all lived, and then beyond to the maintenance sheds. The lock on my supply depot was broken, and the door open.

Unease stirred within me again. Father Cristopolos was thus far not acting the way I had grown used to him acting. I lingered in the doorway of the shed while he dug around in one of the many boxes.

When he turned, he held a gun.

"Careful," I said and grasped it.

"Before I came here, I was in the militant priesthood of Ares, Herakles. I know how to handle weapons," he replied calmly.

Uncertain what to say, I watched him load guns expertly. He handed me two. "Bears?" I asked.

The moment he met my gaze, I knew the truth.

"Three strangers at least saw Lyssa," he said. "And everyone who passes through our forest sees the boundary of light. Did you not stop to think that those in SISA and the government looking for her wouldn't be able to identify the work of gods when they saw evidence of it in reports from refugees? And when they did, wouldn't they wonder what's here?"

"I didn't think of that," I replied quietly. My concern had been the orphanage and the hidden knowledge of what Alessandra was, not about what the refugees would tell others about the magical wall of light.

"She is safe and protected only as long as no one knows she's here. We could cover up what she is, if someone knocked on our front door, be we can't pretend the boundaries didn't somehow spare us the gods' wrath. Anyone who witnesses our magic will speculate why this patch of forest is protected by magic." He held up the red rope tied around his waist in emphasis.

"And this is your solution?" I asked, hefting one of the weapons. "I murder every refugee who walks through the barrier?"

"Your history leads me to believe you have the ability."

"But not the desire! Why not send them south?"

"And what? Pray for protection from loose lips?" he countered. "The gods may have forsaken us. Even Artemis has abandoned us for the time being. Either we handle this, or we risk someone reporting what they saw. Do you want that?"

"I'm not what I was," I growled. "I do not kill indiscriminately."

"Then I will." Father Cristopolos met my gaze. "I will always err on the side of caution when it comes to the girl whose life will determine the fate of humanity." He snatched a bag of ammo and draped it over his shoulder. "No one will find her, or destroy her, because we failed in our duty to protect her. I made this promise the day we found you. If a river of blood must flow to keep her safe, I am prepared."

"There has to be another way!"

"You are her protector for a reason, Herakles. You were chosen by the gods. Have you forgotten your duty?" he countered. "Have you forgotten the world that exists beyond our forest? And what it will do to her, if you fail to protect her? You did unspeakable things in your past, but you are what you are for a reason, and that reason is *her*."

He left.

I remained in the shed. The weight of the weapons in my hands was nowhere near as heavy as the dread settling at the base of my stomach. Father Cristopolos had never confronted me about my past. At times, I convinced myself no one else knew what I'd really done. Did I also convince myself to forget or deny the hazy memories of violence and blood? Or the world where a man like me was able to do such things without penalty?

And when Lyssa found out what I did to her parents? Or that they were two among the hundreds I murdered? There was no denying my actions. Would I look back at this moment and point out how I had stopped being that person after I killed her mother and father in cold blood? Was that really going to make a difference to her?

Did I not one day have to atone for everything, even if I hadn't been in the right mind at the time? The people I had wounded could not be un-hurt, and the lives I'd taken could not be returned.

I had carved up my face, so that every day, when I confronted myself in the mirror, I was reminded of what I really was. And yet, every time Alessandra looked at me, I forgot that ugly part of me and dared to hope we could stay here forever, my little girl and me.

The happy vision in my mind faded, as additional truth began to penetrate the fantasy I'd created after seven years of peace.

A monster like me was never meant to have a real family or to live a happy life. Did I really believe I could be the father of the girl whose parents I murdered? This delusion was destined to end, if not when she discovered what I had done, then in a situation like this one.

What I felt, what I *wanted* in this life, would never matter. I was damned when Cleon found me and transformed me from a boy into a monster. The only good to come of my existence: Alessandra, not because she was an Earth-bound goddess I was sworn to protect, but because she loved me, and I owed her everything for the only moments of peace I would ever experience in my life.

Somehow, I had gotten lost in the tranquil life here and forgotten my purpose. Alessandra was special, and I was sworn to protect her. She was not my daughter, and I would never be her father, no matter how much I wanted that to be true. I was her guardian, which meant, if Father Cristopolos believed her to be in danger, I was responsible for eliminating each and every threat.

The sense of urgency I experienced earlier returned. Alessandra was in danger from a nontraditional threat, and I had gotten too contented and lazy to realize it.

I drew a deep breath and left the shed. Jogging after the shorter man, I caught up to him just as he reached the tree line.

"Go back," I told him. "Keep everyone inside until I radio in. If you have to tie Alessandra to a chair, do it."

Father Cristopolos studied me. "You will take care of this?"

"I will. All of it. I am only sorry I caused you to doubt me," I replied stiffly.

"I never doubted you, Herakles. I know this is not easy for you."

I took his weapons and the ammo bag. "It doesn't matter what I feel. This is what I'm here to do."

"We all make sacrifices. The priests, for the sake of humanity. You, for Alessandra," he observed.

I was quiet, positioning the weapons and ammo around my body.

"She'll still love you, Herakles. No matter what you do," the priest's voice was warm. "She'll understand why, when she's old enough."

No part of me believed him, but I nodded once before striding away, into the forest. Spotting footprints, I knelt to gauge the direction the group of four was traveling. Today, instead of hunting for game, I was hunting humans.

No one could ever understand, I thought as I walked.

Less than a kilometer from the orphanage, I spotted fresh blood. Soon after, the refugees came into view. The four were headed south and moving slowly. One was being supported by two others, which made them easy targets. With any luck, the other refugees who passed through our forest were gathering in the campground, where I could pick them off, one by one, or in small groups, if I used the shrapnel grenades Father Cristopolos had placed in the satchel.

I lifted the rifle to my shoulder, mentally calculating distance and potential wind resistance.

"For Alessandra," I whispered.

I dropped all four refugees with single shots to their heads and then lowered my weapon. With any luck, she would never find out everything I'd ever done. My actions were my burden alone to bear, my guilt the price of keeping her alive and hidden.

Alessandra was born to save lives, and I was created to destroy them. At least there was a purpose behind what I did. Redemption was lost on me, but perhaps, it took someone like me to protect the goddess destined to save the world.

I had always hoped to stand beside her as she became the woman and savior our world needed. But maybe, I was right where I needed to be: standing between my Alessandra and the rest of the monsters.

Leaving the bodies, I loped through the forest, south, towards the campground, until I picked up the footprints of another group and began tracking them. I'd eliminate the threats then come back for the bodies later, once I was certain our refuge was safe.

I didn't care if the gods ever forgave me, but I hoped one day, Alessandra would.

ALSO BY LIZZY FORD

Young Adult Fiction

Non-Series Title

The Door (teen sci-fi)

Between (paranormal) (2019)

Esme (teen paranormal)

Halloween

Thanksgiving

Christmas

Lost Vegas Series – young adult post-apocalyptic

Aveline

Tiana

Arthur

Black Wolf

Lost Vegas Series Omnibus

Spell Realm Series – young adult romantic fantasy

Water Spell

Dragon Spell (2019)

Moon Spell (2019)

Sword Spell (2020)

Omega Series – teen dystopia with Greek Gods

Omega

Theta

Alpha (2019)

Omega Beginnings Miniseries – individual episodes

Alessandra

Mismatch

Phoibe

Lantos

Theodosia

Niko

Cleon

Herakles

Omega Beginnings Miniseries Omnibus

Theta Beginnings Miniseries

Silent Queen

Mercenary

Shadow Titan

People's Champion

Theta Beginnings Miniseries Omnibus

Anshan Saga – new adult science fiction romance

Kiera's Moon

Kiera's Sun

Witchlings – young adult paranormal

Dark Summer

Autumn Storm

Winter Fire

Spring Rain

Broken Beauty Novellas – new adult dramatic fiction

Broken Beauty

Broken World

Broken Chains

Foretold Trilogy – young adult fantasy

Elle's Journey

Shadow Rising (2019)

Journey West (2019)

Voodoo Nights - young adult paranormal

Cursed

Erotic Romance

Non-Series Titles

Star Kissed (erotic sci-fi)

A Night Worth Dying For (short story, contemporary erotic thriller)

Trial Series – erotic paranormal romance

Trial by Moon

Trial by Thrall

Trial by Blood

Trial by Heart

Trial Series Omnibus

Heart of Fire – sexy dragon shifter

Charred Heart

Charred Tears

Charred Hope

Incubatti Duet – Buffy meets 50 Shades

Zoey Rogue

Zoey Avenger

Writing as SE Reign, erotica writer

101 Nights Box Set (featuring all seven serials)

————————

Adult Sweet Romance

(no graphic sex scenes)

Non-Series Titles – 2014 - 2018

White Tree Sound

Black Moon Draw (fantasy romance)

Highlander Enchanted (historical romance)

Last Resort (2019)

History Interrupted – Time Travel Romantic Adventures

West

East

North

South (2019)

Super Villainess Chronicles – twisted superhero romance

It's Not Easy Being Evil

It's Not Easy Being Good

Starwalkers Serials (with Julia Crane) – new adult science fiction serial

Severed

Trapped

Exiled

Revealed

Escaped

Ascended

Starwalkers – Omnibus

Sons of War – contemporary military romance

Semper Mine

Soldier Mine

SEAL Mine

Rhyn Trilogy – new adult paranormal with demons

Katie's Hellion

Katie's Hope

Rhyn's Redemption

Rhyn Eternal – Death finds love

Gabriel's Hope

Deidre's Death

Darkyn's Mate

The Underworld

Twisted Fate

Twisted Karma

Sammy's Demon

Untitled (2019)

War of Gods – paranormal with gods, guardians and exceptional humans

Damian's Oracle

Damian's Assassin

Damian's Immortal

The Grey God

Damian Eternal

Xander's Chance

The Black God

Hidden Evil – paranormal with angels and four horsemen

Hear No

See No

Speak No

Unnamed Series

Unnatural (TBD)

Short Stories

Santa's Ninja Elves: Natasha

Santa's Ninja Elves: Hunter

Snow Whisperers (retired)

Non-Series Titles – 2011 - 2013

A Demon's Desire (paranormal romance)

The Warlord's Secret (fantasy romance)

Maddy's Oasis (contemporary romance)

Rebel Heart (sci-fi romance)

ABOUT THE AUTHOR

I breathe stories. I dream them. If it were possible, I'd eat them, too. (I'm pretty sure they'd taste like cotton candy.) I can't escape them - they're everywhere! Which is why I write! I was born to bring the crazy worlds and people in my mind to life, and I love sharing them with as many people as I can.

I'm also the bestselling, award winning, internationally acclaimed author of over sixty titles and counting. I write speculative fiction in multiple subgenres of romance and fantasy, contemporary fiction, books for both teens and adults, and just about anything else I feel like writing. If I can imagine it, I can write it!

I live in the desert of southern Arizona with a pack of spoiled dogs.

Connect with Lizzy

Website: LizzyFord.com
Facebook: www.Facebook.com/LizzyFordBooks
Twitter @LizzyFord2010
Instagram: @LizzyFordAuthor